WOMAN
OF THE
PRAIRIE

BY BARBARA OAKS
AUTHOR OF "THE BANNISTERS"

Barbara Oaks

WOMAN OF THE PRAIRIE
By
Barbara Oaks
4312 E. 26th St. #36
Sioux Falls, South Dakota
57103
Second Printing 1990
First Printing 1989
South Dakota's Centennial Year
All Rights Reserved.

Library of Congress
Catalogue No. 88-61831

ISBN No. 0-9618582-1-4

C·O·N·T·E·N·T·S

Prudy

Prologue

We are the sum total of our lives. Yet, one wonders why some lives turn out so differently from others, given the same circumstances.

This is the story of Prudy, a hard-working woman of the prairie, whose life was not as blessed as others, yet without whose life those she left behind would not have been.

There are many unmarked graves on the wide open spaces of Dakota. One wonders how many lie there, turned to dust, long forgotten, some interred with dignity and grace, others who were not. Some of the dead are best forgotten, or at the very least remembered for the untimely ends to which they came as the result of lives misspent. Most will be remembered for the courage their lives exhibited and for their noble accomplishments.

The writer does not presume to know the answers. However, one can be grateful for the benefits of the present which were made possible by the deeds of those who went before us in the not too distant past.

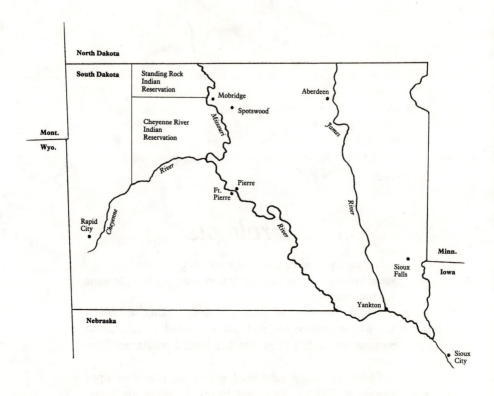

CHAPTER ONE

The Garden

The woman patted the earth with the flat of the shovel, smoothed the area, and stepped back. She heaved a deep sigh, cupped her hands on the handle and scrutinized her handiwork.

The setting sun cast her shadow over the plot of ground, giving her slight figure a looming omnipresence. She felt as tall as her exaggerated shadow. She was tired, but jubilant; she gave another deep sigh and smiled in satisfaction. Her completed task lay in a depression half way between the house and a clearing where a few straggled trees stood and a pile of rocks had been stacked. It was an old rundown farm with tattered buildings that hadn't seen paint in so long one would be hard pressed to say the barn had once been bright red. The house was a two-story and stood stark against the brilliant sky. A porch ran along the front of it where a dirt road led to the highway. A narrower porch lined the back where a rocking chair with a wicker bottom stood beside an assortment of containers. Various tools leaned against the side of the house. The doors of a root cellar lay open on the dusty ground. A short distance from the back porch was a stone well with a wooden bucket hanging from it. A nearby water trough was occasionally filled when the wind blew hard enough to turn a rusty windmill. A few yards from the windmill was the barn which was slowly caving in on itself. A shabby lean-to was home to a few chickens. An outhouse with a sagging door completed the back yard.

She'd best get busy and finish. She picked up the handles of an ancient wheelbarrow and pushed it to the edge of the clearing, lifted rocks of various sizes into it and trudged wearily back to the mound of dirt. Carefully, but not too carefully, she placed the rocks in an irregular pattern around the narrow patch. One more trip ought to do it. It was cooling off in the country, but perspiration dotted her brow and ran in dirty rivulets down her grimy arms from all the digging. Her breathing came in heavy pants, but she didn't stop until it was done. Finally she sat down on a weathered tree stump, wiping her forehead with a frayed bandana, filling her lungs with the fresh air that crept over the prairie in the approaching evening. The pleasant sound of a meadow lark drifted into the quiet. Bessie mooed uncomfortably from the leaning barn. She had forgotten about her. She'd have to be milked soon. The meadow lark called again and the sun sank deeper into the horizon. The flat land with its scattered trees would remain at dusk for a long time before the last remnants of the red sun would fade from the west. Nevertheless, she must continue.

7

She groaned as she rose. Her muscles ached, but she had to put the plants out that night so the morning sun would bring them to life. They were ready and had been ready for several weeks, all lined up on the back porch in cans and broken crockery.

"When're a gonna plant these damn shoots, Prudy?" Lester said more than once when his rocking chair would slide into them and a stream of invective accompanying a stream of brown tobacco juice would issue from his mouth.

"Pretty soon now," she would always reply. "Got to make sure I don't plant 'em too soon. It could still turn cold and I worked on them plants too long to risk having 'em freeze on me."

Lester would continue to grumble and spit and knock some of them over, not always accidentally, but he accepted her explanation. After all, a garden was woman's work and a flower garden was purely woman's work. Sheer tomfoolishness to his mind. What does she need a flower garden for anyway? Just more for that fool woman to tend to and she frittered her lazy life away already. What in tarnation did she do all day? She rose and pushed the wheelbarrow to the porch, loaded some plants into it and trundled it back to the fresh dirt. Not so far to go this time. She had nursed those plants all winter, grown from seed she had started in the house. Lester had roundly cursed when she spent her pennies from her egg money for a few flower seeds. She had just not been able to resist the bright packets that crinkled so enticingly. Old Sam, the peddler, had been out on his irregular rounds of the country folks and he knew her weak spot, a bit of color to brighten her drab existence. She didn't usually buy anything from Sam if Lester was around because he made such a fuss and could make it real embarrassing. But if Lester was out in the fields or gone to town she would get her egg money, which she kept carefully hidden, and buy a few seeds for the vegetable garden or some buttons or ribbon to fix up her homemade dresses — for Sunday services she said, but Lester would always notice any frills, as he called them, on her one Sunday dress and, although he never went to church, he would speak scornfully about the highfalutin' airs the women put on when they went.

"We just want to look nice in The Lord's House, Lester. Ain't nothing' wrong with that."

She soon decided that what he didn't know wouldn't hurt him and she had told him the seeds were some that Lettie had given her, didn't he remember? Lester's German background would not let him admit that he might have forgotten anything, and he never replied to that, just grumbled to himself as he rocked on the porch. So she raised her seeds and they were ready to transplant. Not that she had much time to tend to them with Lester harping at her all the time and with making do in their outmoded way of life, but she had watered them, poured coffee grounds on them, kept them in the big bay window to catch the steady prairie sun, and was rewarded with sprouts that grew into sturdy zinnias, petunias and marigolds. She even had a red geranium that she had coaxed through the winter. Lettie had actually given that one to her. It had survived and budded out and now it would be the very center

8

of the plot. It took three trips with the wheelbarrow. She carefully removed each plant from its shabby container and tenderly transferred it to the freshly turned earth lined with the mismatched rocks. When she had each one properly interred in place she tossed the empty containers in the wheelbarrow and pushed it back to the porch. She'd take care of them in the morning.

She walked to the well and pumped a bucket of water. She carried it back with difficulty, the twine rope cutting into her dirty, bruised hands, and set it down. She was very tired now and her breath came in gasps, but she continued with her task, using a dented tin dipper to gently water each plant. Satisfied at last, she stepped back and critically surveyed her work. It looked pretty good, by golly. They shouldn't droop too much in the cool night air, and the warm morning sun would perk them up real nice. She grinned and filled a dipper with well water for herself. She took a long draught to slake her thirst which she had ignored during her toil. Then she sipped slowly, savoring the cool water, the gathering dusk, and her garden. Suddenly she threw her head back and laughed, at first just a giggle, then deep in her throat as if she had just heard a very funny joke, then a convulsive guffaw that rumbled from her abdomen. She flung the remaining water from the bucket, whirling it around her in delight, and walked back to the well, swinging the bucket in one hand, the tin dipper in the other. She tossed the dipper into the bucket with a flourish and walked with a light step to the barn, still laughing, as Bessie mooed her irritation.

Later, seated in an old iron washtub, scrubbing the sweat and dirt from her worn body, she relaxed, her work done. The dismal kitchen was lit by a single kerosene lamp, but she didn't need much light. No one to see her anyway, not that her body ever got any man very excited, she thought wryly, except —. Besides, she needed the solitude and the intimacy that the shadowy room provided. The harsh realities of her existence were softened when she couldn't see them.

The kitchen was small compared to the rest of the house, which was the architecture of the time it was built, something the women often complained about to the amusement of their men.

"Hell, you've got a good cookstove, a cupboard with dishes in it, a sink with a pump, and table and chairs; what more do you want?"

What more indeed? More room to move around would help. With three or four women in the kitchen at mealtime when there was company there was hardly room to move. And canning season was torture with the cramped quarters and the steam from the cooker making the humidity even worse. The large dining room helped. There was room in there and the bay window on the south gave lots of light. The living room, or front room as it was called, was ample enough. Upstairs were the bedrooms, three in all, each with its own chamber pot. The outhouse had two holes, which turned out to have been a good idea, but Lester was fond of saying who needs company there? especially when Lettie got on his nerves. Lettie Dannenbring was her best friend in the world who lived two miles down the road and who often stopped to visit when she had occasion to drive to the highway to go to town for groceries. Lettie had it better than she did and looked it. Lettie often berated Prudy for accepting the life Lester provided for her.

"Look at you. You should have it easier. You're worn out. Lester has money and he should spend some of it on you. He could fix up this place, paint it, install indoor plumbing, get a generator for electricity. Even a septic tank is simple. Heavens to Betsy, Prudy, this is 1929 after all!"

Prudy would reply, "You know how Lester is. And he's not so bad when he's sober."

Prudy remembered a lot of things as the water lapped at her body. She squirmed on the corrugated bottom of the washtub. Even with an old towel folded in the bottom her thin buttocks felt every washboard curve. If she didn't know already she could even make out the letters encircled in the center of the tub: Sears, Roebuck, 1902. She remembered when the tub had first been placed in the kitchen with such pride, all shiny and new, but that was years ago when things were better. Now the tub was rimmed with embedded scum from many bars of Fels Naptha soap. It didn't look new anymore, but the scum softened the rough interior a bit.

Her breathing was easier now and she settled her body into a semblance of comfort while the bubbles spluttered into a thin film of dissolved gray soap. There was no urgency about sponging off and getting out and thinking about putting supper on the table. She was alone tonight, or in different circumstances, in donning her homemade muslin nightgown and padding reluctantly off to bed. She didn't even have chores to think about.

Bessie was contentedly chewing her cud now that she had been milked and set for the night. Rambler, the old nag Lester kept for reasons only he knew, had long since disappeared. Good thing the Model T still ran. It shared the barn with Bessie, who occasionally stared at it for long minutes, wondering. The few chickens that were left were roosting in the lean-to, their heads tucked under their wings. And that damned, accursed dog —. But she had Bunting, her cat. She had named her Bunting because she was such a cuddly ball of yellow fur, once she had gained some weight. She found her at the edge of the clearing one day where hunger had driven her, thin as a rail. Lester hadn't liked Bunting either, mainly because Prudy did and Bunting belonged to her and never took to Lester. But she kept out of his way and paid for her keep in reducing the mice population in the barn. She even kept that stupid dog at bay. She turned her head and the lamplight caught the steady shine of two red dots in the corner. Funny how light turned a cat's eyes red.

"Nice cat," she said.

The red was briefly shaded as the eyes blinked in acknowledgement. I wonder what that rascal is thinking watching me take a bath. She just stares at me and leaves me alone unless she's hungry. Then she can get real friendly. And she could walk so softly around the house you would not always realize the cat was there until you became aware of her steady stare.

She dismissed her strange thoughts. Deep thinking was foreign to her and it made her uneasy. Some questions a body can't answer. It had been a long time since she had entertained any kind of real thought, having been so constrained in her life with Lester. It was best to stick to what a body knows and to stay out of trouble. And what Prudence Deters knew at that moment was an immense sense of relief. Too bad Lester couldn't appreciate that.

The water was cooling down so she finished her bath, rinsed off the best she could from the hard well water, stood up and wiped her thin wiry body with an old gray towel. She slipped on a worn nightgown and brushed the dust from her hair. When she could catch some rain water she'd tend to it. Her hair had once been a thick, lustrous dark brown, but now it was an iron gray. She tugged and pulled the washtub across the torn linoleum to the door of the kitchen onto the porch,

where she carefully dumped it, and watched as the scummy water followed the ruts in the yard to the lowest point, her rock-rimmed garden. It would be all soaked in by morning. It was May and the spring was turning out real nice.

She decided to turn in even though it wasn't quite dark. She was really done in. She had worked hard and was too tired to be hungry. The bath, not a regular ritual, had soothed her and she was relaxed and sleepy. She took the lamp and trudged up the bare steps to the second floor and turned into the largest room, the room she and Lester shared for as long as she could remember. Her five children had been born there on that very bed. Only four had lived; her little Mary had died when only a few days old. It had been a particularly difficult birth, one which left her barren, but she still felt a pang when she thought about it, something she tried not to do. Her little girl, her only daughter, had died without having any life at all. The pastor had come and christened her before she died and they had taken her away and buried her in the Spotswood Cemetery, a small tract of land just outside of town. Prudy had been too weak and sick to go and wept all day while Lester cursed her for being so puny.

"You could go if you wanted to," was his comment.

Lester had to go to the cemetery by himself and it angered him. He was out of place with church folk, and the pastor made him feel like he had taken his little girl's life himself with his stony stares and his preaching about forgiveness and all. When he came home he started in drinking and she was glad when he fell asleep on the couch in the front room, even though she had to clean up the mess he made when she ventured downstairs the next day to see what had happened to him.

The ancient iron bed creaked as she climbed in. The old springs had held up pretty good all those years, but they were a mite noisy, with every movement sounding loud enough to wake anyone within earshot. In later years she could not really respond to Lester's lusty love-making because of those noisy springs, afraid the boys would hear. Maybe she'd get a new bed one of these days, one with a soft mattress and a fluffy comforter like her sister had. Patience, her younger sister, lived in Minnesota all her married life in the lap of luxury, to Prudy's way of thinking. Her husband, Lars, had built a home in New Ulm with an enclosed porch, which circled the house, running water with two bathrooms, a big kitchen, plus a dining room, living room, parlor and four bedrooms. She couldn't imagine why she needed four bedrooms when she had only one child, a frail, skinny girl named Millicent. Prudy and Lester had raised their boys with much less than that. But that was a long time ago and they did their growing up when the home place was in better condition.

I don't want to think about anything anymore.

She fell asleep with a light breeze wafting through the open window, fanning the threadbare curtains. The repetitive call of a night bird sang to an unknown. Did another bird of the night return the cry, or was it the same bird calling over and over, hoping for an answer? She didn't care. It lulled her to sleep.

12

CHAPTER TWO

The Beginning

Prudence and Patience were the only children of Patrick and Molly Malone, who came from the state of Virginia in 1875. Patrick was a tall, dark, good-looking idealistic young man who enlisted in the Confederate Army when he was seventeen, lying about his age. His three years in the South's struggle matured him in a hurry and his idealism gave way to despair. At twenty he was older than his years, but he emerged from the war relatively unscathed, with only a badly mended broken arm to show for it. It was his left arm and it gave him little trouble unless he was very tired or it rained, when it felt like it was broken all over again. Nevertheless, he knew he was lucky.

His idealism returned slowly. He turned his anger at the outcome of the war to hard work in setting his parents' tobacco farm into what it once had been. His parents had not survived the ravages of war and the farm was ruined; the workers were long gone to seek their fortunes and get a piece of the pie. He and his younger brother, Seth, who had remained at home with his parents and had hung on to the farm, were left to do the work alone, and their enthusiasm soon faded when the enormity of their task became apparent. Prices were up due to the scarcity of goods; times were booming, but only the strong would survive. And Patrick and Seth were not as strong as they used to be, malnourished and weak, falling into untidy beds every night exhausted and frustrated, alone in the world with no one to tend to them, little food, and dwindling hope.

Then Patrick met Molly Lynch, the prettiest thing he had seen since before he left for war. She was a tiny woman, dainty, with golden curls which framed her heart-shaped face and blue eyes shaded by long lashes, a southern belle in every sense of the word. She was eighteen and lived with her parents on the plantation where her family had lived for sixty-five years. It had been miraculously saved from the destruction of General Sheridan's devastation in Virginia toward the end of the Civil War. Still, it had lost much of its past grandeur. Part of the large house had been shut off due to lack of help, with the family using only the downstairs rooms until renovation could be accomplished, and that happened slowly, depending upon money, which was scarce. They, too, had no one to plant and harvest the tobacco crop, or cotton, for that matter, although the cotton crops didn't do well enough to bother, tobacco being the big money maker, with some farmers turning to planting corn. The Lynches relied on their considerable savings, spent frugally to exist. Times were hard for some and booming for others, with role reversals often the result.

Molly brightened Patrick's outlook, giving a boost to his flagging idealism. She returned his admiration and soon he was coming in from the fields a bit earlier and cleaning up to call on Molly Lynch. He even took to attending the Catholic Church to which generations of Lynches had always belonged, just to sit with her and hold her hand. He paid little attention to the ritual that was so familiar to Molly, being content to just be with her. The Lynches thought it odd that anyone with an Irish brogue and the name Malone was not a practicing Catholic, but Patrick explained that, although his Irish father had been a Catholic when he immigrated to America shortly before the 1850s, he had not been a regular churchgoer, and after his marriage to his mother who had been born and bred in England and brought up in the Presbyterian faith, he just didn't attend any church. Patrick had strayed from religion, but as long as they didn't object he would attend church with Molly. The Lynches were happy to agree, since they felt it was only a matter of time before he would be converted to the true faith. So, Patrick and Molly enjoyed the closeness of sitting together with their hands clasped together as the priest intoned the Mass, while they felt a vicarious pleasure in an intimacy provided by this time that the conventions of the era prohibited.

It was 1868 and the lives of many were at a crossroad. Patrick's and Seth's lives were among them. It became apparent that to work the worn, war ravaged land by themselves was useless. They could not afford to hire help and no darky would return to do it. Patrick had asked for Molly's hand in marriage and her father had, in no uncertain terms, told him that as much as he liked him his future was bleak. He could not let his daughter enter into a union with less than what she had always been accustomed to. There were those who were suffering, to be sure, and compromises must be made, but as long as he could shelter his daughter, he would do so. She was young and she was safe and secure with her parents. In the future, if Patrick could earn a satisfactory living to support his only child he would gladly give his blessing. He was sure Patrick understood. But Patrick was humiliated and angry. Molly had waited anxiously in the parlor to learn the decision which she was confident would be favorable, and had fled and taken to her bed when she learned otherwise.

So Patrick and Seth put the farm up for sale, but continued to work it simply because there was nothing else they could do. Patrick and Molly were permitted to continue to court, and for five long years they kept company under the Lynch's strict supervision. Eventually, Patrick took a job at a feed store in town, but Seth stayed on the farm, which he decided to keep, since he married a country girl and a family was on the way.

Patrick's love for Molly remained constant, but he wanted her passionately; he wanted a home and a family, too, and Molly epitomized the ideal woman to make that dream come true. In 1873 they made plans to marry. Times were improving. Even Mr. Lynch agreed. Mrs. Lynch had long ago tried to soften her husband's rigid stance on the nuptials. Plans proceeded smoothly, but hopes were dashed once more with the Panic of 1873, a panic which sent the finances of the newly united

14

country into a tailspin.

It was during the administration of President Ulysses S. Grant, who had been elected overwhelmingly after the Civil War. Congress passed an Act ending the coinage of silver, which meant that bank notes and greenbacks were the only currency in circulation. On September 18, 1873, the banking house of Jay Cooke failed, with disastrous results. Panic ensued and spread from financial instutions to the entire industrial structure of the country. The boom was definitely over. Factories and banks shut their doors. Ultimately even the banks in Europe tried to withdraw their funds from their investments in America.

Patrick's wages were cut to alleviate the expenses of the feed store. Some employees quit rather than take a cut and moved north, leaving Patrick with added duties because no one was hired to take their places. But the love between Patrick and Molly endured and grew stronger. Their lives were entwined as though they were really married although, in fact, they had not consummated their love. It was not until 1875, two years later, that they were married in early April. It was a grand affair, held in the Catholic Church, with a ceremony that rivaled any since before the war. Mr. and Mrs. Lynch were proud hosts to the elaborate wedding and reception. Seth had been married in the Presbyterian Church several years before in a modest ceremony. He and Columbine, his wife, still eked out an existence on the farm and were doing well. They and their three healthy children were the only representatives of Patrick's family left. They sat in the front row, beaming, but somewhat unsettled by the ritual that was foreign to them. They participated as much as they could, bobbing up and down uncertainly, until they gave up and sat quietly and just watched as Patrick and Molly were married.

Then the newlyweds stunned them all with their announcement that they would be leaving immediately for the west, to Dakota Territory where there was limitless opportunity. No more tedious drudgery at a job Patrick hated. He was a farmer and needed to be outdoors. Molly was in full agreement; they should move away and begin a brand new life of their own. They had waited so long. They had kept this news from everyone because of the opposition they were sure to encounter. Molly had grown up protected and cherished and her parents were getting on in years and not likely to take kindly to her going off into an unsettled region, into a place full of unseen dangers, not the least of which were wild Indians. They had read the reports. It was painful for Molly to deceive them, but her life was with Patrick now.

They had made plans and were to meet up with a wagon train at Cumberland Gap, a natural pass to the west through the Appalachian Mountains at the meeting point of Virginia, Kentucky and Tennessee. They were leaving in the morning following their wedding night, to be spent at the best suite in the hotel. Their provisions had been packed and loaded into a wagon in the livery stable and covered with a tarp, with no one the wiser. All they had to do was to hitch up a team of horses and be on their way in the morning. Everything was purchased with the dowry money, a fact which did not set well with the Lynches, who had thought the money would be used to furnish a house not far from them.

15

They were taking advantage of the Homestead Act passed on May 20, 1862, during the Civil War. The Act granted public land to settlers free or at a low price, on the condition that they live on it and make it productive. Settlers must be twenty-one years old or the head of a family, an American citizen, or having declared an intent to become one. Each settler could own up to 160 acres, and it belonged to him after he lived on it for five years. Patrick met all requirements. He was then twenty-nine and Molly was twenty-five. They had waited for each other longer than most, sure in their minds about what they wanted to do with their lives together.

They set out, trying not to see the tears of Mrs. Lynch and the scowl which disguised a deep sorrow of Mr. Lynch, and the worried looks of Seth and his family, while Molly tried not to cry. The crack of the whip over the team of horses propelled the couple ahead into the unknown, leaving behind their pasts and the people who loved them.

★

Their love and the intimacy while alone on an exciting trek into their future sustained them on a very difficult journey. They traveled west through hundreds of miles of beautiful scenery to the Appalachians. They met the wagon train at Cumberland Gap on the way to the Ohio River. The Ohio River, a long branch of the Mississippi River, flowed southwest through several states before it joined with the Mississippi. It separated Ohio, Indiana and Illinois from West Virginia and Kentucky, meeting the Mississippi at Cairo, Illinois. Over the many weeks of their journey they had been joined by others along the way until there were dozens of wagons of all kinds in the train, sometimes a mile or two in length, pushing toward an exciting, but unknown future.

Upon reaching the Ohio River wagons and travelers, with their livestock, transferred to barges to continue over the water to the Mississippi, then on up the Mississippi to St. Louis to continue overland. No matter what the mode of travel it was tediously slow. Some fell ill. Some died. Cholera took a toll, especially of the children. Some simply gave up and stopped along the way.

But Patrick and Molly continued, content to be with one another and on their own, full of optimism that the future would be good. Their love and cheerfulness inspired the others, who called their marriage made in heaven. And they learned, their innocence giving way to renewed idealism from their hardy experiences. They soon learned to weatherproof their wagon, erecting a makeshift covering that doubled as a shelter. After getting across the Mississippi they took the wagon train master's good advice and got themselves a covered wagon, called a prairie schooner because of its resemblance to a ship of the sea, but covered with canvas instead of sails. This required the addition of two more horses. Some of the larger wagons had six horses, but it was an expense few could afford. Patrick guarded their money closely, doling it out carefully, knowing it must last until they reached their destination, the free open prairies of the Dakotas. Once outfitted properly, they proceeded at a faster pace and more comfortably, with additional space and better shelter. Molly sent letters home whenever she could, giving her parents glowing accounts of their trip, omitting what would worry them. She wanted them to remember their departure as a joyous event. Neither she nor the Lynches could bear to think they might not ever see each other again.

Nevertheless, the rain soaked them and their provisions and they were often miserable and uncomfortable. Swollen streams had to be crossed with frightened and fidgety horses. Provisions were sometimes swept away. The trails west of the Mississippi were full of ruts and dusty. But finally the vast plains began to show themselves. The land grew flatter, there were few trees, just huge expanses of grass covered ground and an endless expanse of sky. And Molly did not feel well with all the jostling. A doctor by the name of Gideon Walsh had accompanied the wagon train all the way from the South, traveling by horse with only a saddle bag and a black medical case. He had a mysterious air about him and kept to himself unless someone needed his services. He maintained he was on his way to the new frontier to establish a medical practice among those who would surely need a doctor in their midst. He examined Molly and smiled, telling her what she already knew, that she was in a family way. Patrick's elation was tempered with some apprehension, since this was an event he had not planned on right away. A baby would surely complicate matters.

Molly's figure grew, as did the weeks and months of travel westward. The endless plains never seemed to promise a destination. The area had been called the Great American Desert, and all who crossed it considered it aptly named. But their goal was getting closer. They had been instructed to leave soon enough in the spring to meet at the Gap and from there to continue to Dakota Territory in time to erect shelters before cold weather set in. Since cold weather in Virginia was somewhere around the forty degree mark, when stoves were lit and heavy clothing was doned, the cool nights of September were a surprise. They left the campfires burning for warmth and to keep the wild animals away, the yelps and howls of which sent shivers through the already chilled settlers. They huddled together wrapped in every blanket they had brought.

Molly was getting near her term. She had not told her parents that she was with child at the time of her wedding. Their engagement had been so long that when they had set the date they just couldn't wait any longer to consummate their love. Their coupling had been an ecstatic experience which only deepened their desire. She had also not told Patrick because she was fearful that he would not start out on the trip, and she wanted freedom from her oppressive, but loving parents and to begin the long awaited life with Patrick. So her secret was not revealed until her condition became obvious. They must find a homestead by October. She wanted her baby to be born in a house, not in a prairie schooner.

17

Dakota Territory was a large tract of land encompassing what became the states of North and South Dakota. The port of entry from the east was the town of Yankton on the Missouri River in the southeastern tip of the territory. Several wagonloads of travelers decided they had gone far enough and stopped there. The rest followed the Missouri River which turned north and which divided the future state of South Dakota in two. Some dropped off at Pierre, which would eventually be the capitol. It was called "Peer," a pronunciation which persisted, though it was obviously a French name. The name was derived from Pierre Chouteau, Jr., a fur trader.

Patrick and Molly continued north, following the river until Molly could go no further. Those left in the train decided to remain with them, having forged close friendships on the trail and deciding that what lay ahead would be only more of the same, lonely emptiness. They were all weary and so they stopped. They settled near what would be the border between North and South Dakota. They named their settlement Spotswood because it was merely a spot in the broad landscape with a few trees.

As soon as they could the men set out to claim their individual homesteads. To claim them they had to record them at the nearest land office which was under the Federal Bureau of Land Management, in the Department of the Interior. There was a land office in the town of Mobridge, a few miles away. Ground had to be broken to prove their intent to stay and improve the land. At so late in the season the ground breaking was more ceremonial than actual, but they made an occasion of each one, getting together to share a meal and to solemnize the event, solidifying the comraderie they had formed during their recent tedious journey.

Shelters had to be erected fast, because the northern climate was far different from what they were accustomed to. Time did not allow for a proper house, nor was there adequate lumber to build one, so huts were built from the plentiful sod until something more substantial could be erected. The sod huts were reinforced with lumber from the covered wagons, utilizing the canvas for the windows. The "soddies," as they were called, turned out to be very practical dwellings, warm in winter and cool in summer. The strong buffalo grass made the sod tough and durable. Fuel came from "cow chips" and buffalo droppings which were plentiful.

Patrick fretted about the stark contrast in homes which Molly could not ignore, but she shushed him and reminded him that they were all going through the same thing. They would be all right. They would make it and not to worry.

The shelters were better than the open wagons, but before the winter was over that year the women would be eager to leave them and to move into a real house. They would grow tired of earth floors and weary of the clumps of dirt that would fall from above and of the strange sounds of the hooves of beasts wandering overhead. They were grateful for shelter from the wolves and coyotes, whose cries on a silent night would strike terror into their hearts. The spring rains leaked inside and some of the soddies simply collapsed. Some were built so well they lasted for several years. Much depended on the nature of the builders. By spring the women's hopes were pinned on a house with glass windows and a garden. The men were anxious to leave the confines of the soddies to put in a crop and to erect a sturdy house. Most of their hopes were fulfilled. Future droughts, insects, blizzards, and sheer loneliness were events they were blissfully unaware of.

Patrick's and Molly's feelings were no different from the rest. But their thoughts were filled with other things during that fall and early winter in 1875. On October 12th Molly gave birth to a healthy baby girl with a lusty voice. She named her Prudence.

CHAPTER THREE

The Early Years

By the time Patience Malone came along five years later on May 6, 1880, Patrick had erected a large two-story house where she was born. This was done at great cost to himself in the pain his left arm was giving him. It was getting harder to ignore it, to concentrate on the positive accomplishments over the past five years and the attainment of his goal for independent self-sufficiency. His 160 acres were productive with corn, wheat and oats, with some acres given over to the grazing of a few head of cattle. It was not a large spread, but he was attaining success steadily, each addition a part of his plan, and he had his eye on bordering land when a farmer gave up or moved on. Molly had her garden full of vegetables which kept her overworked and tired, along with her household duties and the care of the children, but she took pride in the produce carefully stored in the root cellar. They were all in comparative good health and fit, but Dr. Walsh told Patrick and Molly that they needed more rest, that they should take better care of themselves. Patrick should not use his bad arm at all, but he could not obey that sensible advice. There was so much to do, satisfying work that yielded fine results, and he had a family to support. His dream was coming true. He could not slow down or stop. He would just have to bear the constant pain. Molly would massage his arm every night and soothe him to sleep until the pain woke him too early before his body had rejuvenated itself. But he was, on the whole, happy and content with his life, and he had more to show for it than some.

The house was not the usual run of dwellings hastily thrown up in the early years. It was erected with care, solidly built, with a front porch on the west and a back porch on the east. The back overlooked a fine, sturdy red barn and there was the beginning of some livestock to fill it, including the four horses which had pulled their wagon to the plains. The horses tilled the land and pulled the wagons at harvest time. The small herd of cattle, added a few at a time, was increasing. They provided meat and milk, plus some breeding stock to sell, and one day he would see a goodly store of cured meat hanging in the root cellar alongside Molly's increasing store of foodstuffs. His family would not go hungry. Chickens, the newest addition, were housed in a small building near the barn. An artesian well had been dug which gave forth cool, sweet water, and a windmill was being raised to provide energy to pump water into a trough for the animals. A large stump of a fallen tree also stood in the back yard where a big elm had been chopped down to provide room for the farm buildings. It was a huge tree and a shame to cut it down, but it stood alone, apart from the others which were at the edge of the clearing on the south, right smack in the middle of the area Patrick wanted to build upon. So down it came and the wood was used to build the house. The stump remained and was used to chop wood on.

Patrick and Molly had weathered frontier life well, considering the many hardships. They retained their handsome looks, but Molly longed for the soft white skin that had been hers at the beginning of their adventure and for the golden curls that had framed her sweet face. Her hair was still lovely, but it had turned a shimmering pale yellow from the sun and she kept it in a neat bun at the nape of her neck. A broad-brimmed bonnet shielded her face from the relentless sun, but she still turned a delicious golden brown every summer, which made her all the more beautiful in Patrick's eyes.

He had grown rugged and lean. His features were chiseled into an open, honest face that people liked and trusted. A beard, which he had grown to save time in his full day and to protect his face from the elements, enhanced his handsome features, and a graying at the temples gave him a distinguished look.

Patrick and Molly were still very much in love, but there would be no more children. Patience had been born with great difficulty, after Molly had already had three miscarriages. Dr. Walsh clucked at her every year, telling her how foolish she was to persist in getting herself in a family way far too often. But Patience had come into the world healthy, although not very strong, and the family was complete.

Spotswood had become a township with a block-long street lined with a hardware store, a grocery, a haberdashery, a general store, a barbershop, a livery stable, a post-office with adjoining bank, and Dr. Gideon Walsh's office above it, plus two saloons. A church stood at one end of the street and at the other a one-room building which functioned as a school for the growing community.

The township was small, not large enough to be called a real town. A township comprised a unit of land six miles square, containing thirty-six mile-square sections. Some townships grew into actual towns on the map of Dakota Territory. Others eventually disappeared, deserted by its inhabitants and blown away by the prairie winds. Some settlers preferred life in town and soon there were clusters of houses dotting the landscape. Others preferred life on the farm and would remain there all their lives.

Much of the land was still unturned, not being developed as quickly as had been hoped for. Word had reached the east of the austere life the pioneers had found. And there were Indians. Most were on reservations, but their presence was felt. The Standing Rock Reservation was near Mobridge and people were accustomed to seeing the natives. They were called savages by the eastern press and in some ways they were right. Once on the reservations they were considered to be "tamed." Nevertheless, it made good copy for eastern readers to hear of the wild Indians. Indians could be tolerated and they could be gotten along with if you knew how, especially if there was only one to deal with. But if a group of them arrived at the doorstep it was often cause for concern. If they wanted food people soon learned not to argue, to just give them what they wanted, rather than risk any consequences.

However, this usually guaranteed their return. And the unease generated by the uprising of the Santee Indians in Minnesota spread to Dakota Territory, keeping people away. The Sioux Indians of Dakota were a fierce, warlike tribe and it was not a good idea to get them stirred up.

Even so, European immigrants settled in Minnesota and Dakota Territory, glad for the wide open spaces and freedom after living in cramped quarters and enduring the oppression of falling empires. The teeming cities they gravitated to in the east spewed them out and the vast American West absorbed them. The promised land beckoned to them. News of a gold strike in the Black hills in 1876 further west enticed others. For those who settled in Spotswood it held no fascination. They had found what they wanted. They had formed a bond and kinship on their long hard journey and they stayed put together. The land was productive. Life was not easy, but hard work was rewarding; it made them strong. Their community grew.

Prudence and Patience were as different as night and day. Prudence was small like her mother, but she had her father's dark coloring. She had an abundance of energy, was playful and full of fun and the light of their lives until Patience came along five years later. Her younger sister was blond like her mother, but she grew tall like her father and was as winsome as her still beautiful mother. Looking at the two of them it was hard to realize that they were sisters.

Prudence's enthusiasm for life was dampened upon the birth of her sister. At the age of five she had more energy than most children her age and, since Patience had come into the world with much less vitality, Prudence was often shushed and admonished to curb her noisy ways because her baby sister needed her sleep or too often cried from being disturbed by her exuberant older sister.

"But, Mama, I want to play with her," wailed Prudence.

"She's not old enough yet, Prudy. She needs to rest. Go out and play."

So Prudy would fling herself from the house. She soon found plenty of playmates, more boys than girls. Boys accepted her as one of them and took for granted her daring ways and roughhousing. But she grew irritable from being constantly curbed in her natural behavior when Patience was around and from all the attention being focused on her often ailing sister.

As the years passed their differences intensified. Patience grew tall, slim and beautiful with graces which were not easily come by in Prudence, who remained slightly built, never to be stately, willowy or sylph-like, traits which her mother epitomized and so prized and which her father adored in both of them. Prudence was loved but in a different way. She was their first born conceived in love. She knew they loved her but she felt removed from the flow of life in the neat, ordered house which had a smooth, direct course for all but her. So Prudence decided to be different if that is how she was perceived. In fact, she merely decided to be herself. She accentuated her difference and became known as a tomboy, a designation abhorred by Patience, but which Prudence encouraged, if for no other reason than to get her share of the attention she so craved. Since the arrival of Patience she had definitely been shoved into second place.

22

The girls were companionable most of the time and loved each other as sisters, but Prudence resented the ease with which her lovely sister sailed through life chiefly because of her frail beauty. She actually was a good student and did well in school with intelligence, but Prudence was also blessed. The difference was that Prudence had to work so much harder to get the same grade on her paper.

"Prudy, you must apply yourself," her father said to her when she brought a paper home from school. She proudly presented it to her father as he chopped wood in the back yard. The arithmetic paper had a mark of "B" which she had thought would bring a word of praise. But instead, her beloved father told her she must apply herself.

"But, Papa, 'B' is a good grade."

"You can do better. Patience got an 'A' on her arithmetic paper." He paused and stuck the ax in the old tree stump.

"Patience is in second grade and I'm in the seventh. It's not the same thing. Besides, she's prettier than I am and teachers like her better than me." She began to whine in her frustration.

"Don't whine. I'll expect a better paper next time," he said, absentmindedly rubbing his left arm.

Prudence continued to flaunt her tomboyishness as her resentment at the injustice grew. She was more daring than she needed to be and it got her into trouble, once stranding her in a tree at the edge of the clearing where she had climbed on a dare issued by the boys. When she couldn't get down the boys scampered, laughing at her predicament and ignoring her cries for help. Patience usually watched the shenanigans at a distance, being too timid to get close to anything remotely dangerous, and more than once she ran squealing to the house to report on some outlandish prank of her older sister's.

Molly's proper upbringing of her daughters inlcuded instilling in them the values she had been taught. She taught them by word and example, proper conduct, social graces, manners, the way to dress and faith in God and the Holy Catholic Church. Patrick did not object even though he was not a churchgoing man. He attended Mass with Molly whenever an itinerant priest passed through, ususally from the Standing Rock Reservation, which was under the authority of the Catholic Church, but he did it to make Molly happy. He would do anything to make her happy because it made him happy. Patience was a good and willing student. Prudence was indifferent and raised awkward questions which shocked Patience who accepted her Mother's word as Gospel, but both girls learned the ritual. Patrick insisted on the girls' sharing in the daily chores, but the sharing was not an equal division because of Patience's weak resistance to illness. She was often sick with fevers and colds from which she recovered, but far too slowly to Prudence's way of thinking.

"You're doing that on purpose," Prudence said accusingly.

"I'm not," Patience replied as she lay on her bed with swollen eyes and a red nose. "I'm sick. I don't know why I get sick so much, but I can't help it. I'm sorry, Prudy, really I am, but I don't do it on purpose. Do you think I like being like this and looking like this?" And she fell back on her pillows, tears flowing — from her cold or her distress — it was hard to tell. So Prudence did her chores for her.

But they grew and learned and blossomed through the years and soon Molly was talking about her girls getting married and having a home of their own, close by of course. Prudence would be first, being the oldest, although this was said with some hesitation, because there were no immediate prospects. However, Patience always had more than enough admirers and one in particular, Lars Hanson, was very serious in his intentions. They wanted to marry and waited in vain for a suitor for Prudence. Lars was a well-to-do merchant who had made his fortune in the fur trade. He wanted to return to Minnesota where his parents had settled years before. They had left him some land and he was eager to take Patience to the verdant land that was Minnesota, a land of trees and lakes and beauty. It was a fine setting for his intended bride to be surrounded with the good things in life which he could provide, a better setting where she belonged. Patrick and Molly found him eminently suitable. It was 1897 and Lars was anxious to claim his legacy.

Patience was impatient and disgusted. "Oh, Mama! Why do I have to wait for Prudy to marry first? What difference does it make if I get married before she does?"

"Because that is the way it is properly done, dear. You know that," she said calmly.

"But Mama, this isn't the old South. These are modern times."

Molly couldn't help but smile. "You are but seventeen, very young. Goodness, I waited years for your father. You must be patient. I was patient a very long time before you blessed our lives and then you almost didn't pull through, nor did I. That's where you got your name. You are our last child. We hate to let you go."

She had heard it all before and the story was wearing thin. "But, Mama —"

"Hush," Molly said patiently. "You have your whole life before you. There is no hurry."

Patience bit her lip. A lot she knew. How could her mother know how it felt to love someone so much you could hardly stand it? Her mother was old. The age of forty-seven seemed incredibly ancient to her. She stalked off in a sulk, not daring to show her feelings.

In the end, Patrick and Molly gave in and Patience and Lars were married in the community church by a Catholic priest from Mobridge. They could have been married in the Catholic Church in Mobridge, but they wanted to make it convenient for their guests, most of whom had been with them through all the hardships of many years. Most of them did not share the true faith, which Molly forgave, because she needed her friends and neighbors to be with them at the blessed sacrament of marriage, and the support they would give at the change in their lives.

There were no kneeling benches in the interdenominational church, so pillows were provided, painstakingly sewn on the sewing machine which had served them well. Many pioneers brought sewing machines west with them, considering them to be a definite necessity. Sewing was one of the many talents of Molly Malone. After months of preparation and when Patience had just turned eighteen in May, 1898, she and Lars were married in as elaborate a ceremony as could be managed.

24

Molly was determined that, as long as this event must take place, it would be done properly with full Catholic pomp and ritual.

The folks in Spotswood were familiar with Molly's religious preference, but ignorant of Catholic dogma, and were eager to accept the invitation from their good friends, the Malones. Curiosity was also a factor and they were not disappointed in the fine show that was presented. Like her parents before her, Molly stood beside her beloved husband, proudly hosting the nuptial day, meticulous in every detail. Patience was resplendent in a white gown, her blond beauty set off by a cloud of veil. Guests were impressed with the long train of embroidered satin as she stood beside Lars, who was proudly tall and erect, handsome in his blond good looks alongside his bride's, and presenting a self-assured appearance in his nicely fitted suit with a long coat. Prudence was the maid of honor and a close friend of Patience's was the other attendant. Lars chose two of his business friends to stand up for him. They stood before the priest in his somber black robe, a picture of solemn propriety. It was the talk of the town for weeks. The departure by buggy to catch the train east to Minnesota was far different from that of her parents on their wedding day.

Molly cried remembering. The sudden sense of loneliness in losing Patience meant another part of herself was being given up to the wilderness. She felt very alone, even among loved ones and friends. Molly's parents had long ago died of old age in Virginia, leaving their estate to their only child. By the time Molly received her inheritance it amounted to very little, but it had been deposited in the bank in Spotswood, drawing a modest amount of interest until it was to be used for her daughters' weddings. Most of it had been spent on Patience. Molly had grieved over the loss of her parents, berating herself for not having seen them again. It was not until she saw what her enduring sorrow was doing to Patrick that she pulled herself together. But now that Patience had gone, the long submerged feelings of loss engulfed her. Her former comfortable existence with her doting parents seemed like a dream. Youth, beauty and eagerness had been tempered by her harsh life, with a daily endurance made tolerable by the goal of her daughters' happiness in a good marriage. Now the main reason for that was also gone. Patience had represented what Molly had held onto for so long — a culture that was doomed to fade away, a quality of life impossible to maintain on the prairie, but which Molly had strived so hard to hang onto and to perpetuate. She embodied Molly's past, a reminder of a lost glory, and she was gone.

"Don't cry, Mama," said Prudence, patting her mother's arm. She realized, more than Molly knew, what was going through her mind.

Molly looked at her elder daughter, appearing oddly out of place in her wedding finery, the frilly pastel gown and gloves and wide brimmed hat accentuating the contrast to her beautiful sister. The tears increased and Molly took her in her arms, comforting them both.

Prudence grew increasingly restless. She had thought that once Patience was happily married and living in Minnesota she would begin a new life, too, that she would have her share of gentlemen callers. It was not to be. There were plenty of men around in the wide open sky-filled prairie, but they had accepted her as a tomboy, as one of them for so many years that they couldn't think of her in any other way. She was not taken seriously, even though she was a nice enough looking, dark haired woman of twenty-two who dressed in a more decorous fashion and minded her manners. One by one the men courted and married other, more comely women in the area.

And then, in 1899, she met Lester Deters.

Lester Deters was a big, strapping man, built like a German warlord. He came to Spotswood as an itinerant worker at harvest time. He was one of many workers who traveled the harvest circuit in the fall, staying at a farm for as long as it took to get the crops in, traveling north throughout the season, earning enough to see them through the winter when they returned to wherever they originated.

A crew was at the Malone place and Prudy was helping Molly serve the noon meal. She had always done more than her share of the work, because Patience had always hated harvest time due to the rough men and of the upset in her routine, plus having to work so hard in the kitchen, chores she despised and to which she easily succumbed with her customary fatigue. Room and board were part of the wages and the men slept in the barn in the loft, where it was comfortable and private. Most of the men were polite and had a certain amount of manners, coming from some sort of background.

They drove the teams in from the fields at noon, after five hours of hard work. Hay racks hauled unharvested grain to threshing machines which separated the grain from the straw. The grain was then stored in sacks. They baled hay; they picked corn. By noon they had worked up a hearty appetite. They washed at the trough by the windmill and lined up to accept their plates of food, nourishing fare of meat, potatoes, home grown vegetables, fresh bread with churned butter, and usually a thick slab of pie, plus generous mugs of coffee. They were always ravenous, ate quickly, and rested before they returned to the fields to continue until sundown when they returned for supper and an early bedtime.

Time was important. It was imperative that they get the crops in while the sun shone and before a storm, which could come up fast on the prairie. Hail, a cruel trick of nature, could fall from innocent looking clouds and wipe out months of hard work, which meant no income. The men worked hard and fast, moving on to farm after farm, putting money away for the long winter ahead. In the heat of the afternoon it was the custom to take the men a cool drink for a break in the long day. Prudy had that job while Molly laid down to rest with the shades drawn. Her day was tiring and she wasn't as young as she used to be. Patrick supervised the crew since his left arm was becoming quite useless and the pain constant. He also looked to the animals and repair of the machinery.

Prudence couldn't help but notice Lester Deters. He was a big man. He carried himself with an air of confidence, bordering on arrogance. He was handsome and assertive with a smile that melted the hearts of any woman he looked at. His sandy hair was combed straight back and was streaked almost yellow by the sun, making his intense brown eyes stand out, eyes that teased, yet flattered. The first time Prudence arrived with the lemonade, a drink which satisfied the thirst and nourished the body, she was quite taken by the charisma of this giant man. She was embarrassed and pleased when Lester swooped her up into the air like a child and said in his strong voice so all could hear, "Well, look what we have here. If you aren't the purtiest gal I've seen in a long time. Ja."

"Put me down. Who do you think you are?"

He just laughed and set her on the ground beside the lemonade.

"Lester Deters, that's who, the best danged worker on this crew. What's your name, little lady?"

"Never mind. Just bring those jugs back when you come in," she flung at him. She strode away, but felt his eyes on her all the way back to the house.

At supper she tried to avoid him and his merry eyes, but she was drawn to his gaze irresistibly. He made her feel unladylike and it made her squirm, yet she could not deny what she felt. And Lester knew it. That Saturday noon he asked her to go to the dance in Spotswood with him after supper. By Saturday the hands were tired, but not too tired for some jollity. They looked forward to some entertainment, which varied from place to place, but there was always somewhere to go to have a drink, to dance, and to have a good time after a hard week's work.

"I'll see what my folks say," was her reply, hoping to put him off and for lack of a better answer.

"You have to ask, Ja? You are not old enough already to decide for yourself?"

She didn't like to be made to feel so defensive but, since his demeanor demanded an answer, she rose to his dare, to the taunt in his dark eyes.

"Of course I can decide for myself, and yes, I will go to the dance with you. But you have to get cleaned up." She said this with just as much fervor as he had given, not to be put down.

"Ja, sure. I will clean up. You'll see. You won't even recognize this handsome face it will be so clean, and the rest of me as well." He laughed at her discomfort.

Prudence mentioned her date to her mother as they were doing up the stacks of dirty dishes, trying to be as nonchalant as she could and endeavoring not to blush. Molly turned to her with a surprised smile.

"Is he the big, strong German who works so hard?"

"Yes, Mama."

"Well, I think that's nice. He seems pleasant enough with nice manners and he presents a good appearance. But, isn't he a little older than you?"

"I don't know."

"Well, you go and enjoy yourself, Prudy." She patted her arm.

The condescending attitude rankled a bit, but on Saturday night Prudy got dressed in one of her good dresses, one of many she had accumulated in her twenty-three years, but which she seldom wore. The blue gingham was a good color for her. The sash cinched in her already small waistline. Her thick hair was held back with a matching blue bow, and her cheeks glowed pink with the warmth of the fall evening and her excitement. She was ready when she heard the clump of Lester's boots on the back porch. There was also the sound of muted laughter of the men as they rode off into town. She was glad she could not make out what they were shouting to Lester.

She opened the door and caught her breath at the transformation of her gentleman caller. His good looks had been scrubbed and his sunburned face shone with cleanliness. The stubble had been shaved from his angular face. He was clothed in clean trousers and shirt with a string tie, and a neat suit jacket that was obviously saved for dress-up occasions was draped over his arm. He held a bouquet of wild flowers in his massive hands. His broad smile left her weak.

"For you, Miss Prudence Malone."

She accepted the flowers and replied, "Thank you. I'm ready."

CHAPTER FOUR

I Take Thee, Lester

What a night it was, how romantic. Prudence Malone and Lester Deters were the center of attention at the dance that night. The dance spilled over outside to the dirt street because of the number of celebrants and to Prudy's relief, because she had promised her parents to stay out of the saloons, although at the time she didn't know quite how she would manage that. It was noisy and dusty, but riotous fun. It was not uncommon on any Saturday night to fill the streets of town with boisterous, often drunken dancers. The piano was moved onto the wood sidewalk in front and everyone joined in the festivities.

Lester was a good dancer, light on his feet despite his size, and he was a courtly date. He danced with the other girls, but not until he had handed Prudy to a cowhand with stern instructions to mind his manners and to treat the little lady right. Prudy had a glorious time. Never had she felt more appreciated, more cared for. Lester made her feel special. He watched over her, he flattered her and fetched her a cool sarsaparilla when she grew warm from the activity. He enjoyed his beer and Prudy might have, too, if offered one, but she was glad she didn't have to make that decision because spirits had never passed her lips. Liquor had never been allowed in the house and the girls had been strictly taught concerning its evils and the temptations it brought.

The night was warm, but with a cool breeze. There was a full moon and Prudy was feeling good. She was at last one with other women, accepted, experiencing womanly feelings with increasing self-confidence. When it grew late and some of the men were getting rowdy and foul-mouthed she told Lester she had best be getting home. Although he was obviously having a good time he didn't argue with her, and they got in his wagon and left the clamor of the wild Saturday night in Spotswood.

They rode in silence for awhile. The noisy sounds of the night which had transformed the usually quiet town grew faint behind them. The dark road ahead was illumined by the bright moon in a starlit sky as the horses clip-clopped leisurely home.

"Come here, girl," said Lester as he drew her close to him.

She did not resist. She relaxed against him, pleasantly tired. "I had a real nice time, Lester."

"Ja, so did I, little one. You dance good."

She giggled, not answering, because the dancing was like nothing she had ever seen, not the way she and Patience had been taught, with definite measured steps.

It had been more like frenetic leaping about with hoots and yells, beating time to the piano, which was played with dexterity by a young man with thinning hair and lots of vigorous talent.

She just said, "It was fun."

When they pulled into the farmyard the house was dark, with only a single lamp burning in the kitchen to light her way. She knew her parents were asleep at such a late hour. Lester helped her down from the wagon and took her to the back porch. He placed his big hands on her slight shoulders and looked down into her eyes, shining brightly in the shadows.

"Good night, Miss Prudence Malone. Thank you for your company. I will see to the horses."

"Good night, Lester. Sleep well. You'll probably have the loft to yourself for awhile."

"Ja, but it will be good for the quiet. I will think of you as I go to sleep."

Swiftly he pulled her to him in his firm grasp and kissed her full on the mouth. He released her as suddenly, turned quickly and left the porch, leading the horses to the barn silhouetted in the darkness. She struggled to collect her swirling emotions, then went into the house to bed.

During the next few days Molly was pleased and surprised to see the change in her eldest daughter. Previously sullen and uncommunicative, she now hummed as she went about her work, uncomplaining, totally unlike herself.

The noon meal was over and they had completed the mountains of dishes and pans and were seated in the cooler front room, out of the hot kitchen, with a glass of lemonade. Molly looked quizzically at Prudy and asked, "Prudy dear, it's good to see you so happy. Is there a reason I should know about?" Her eyes teased.

Prudy flushed a deeper pink than warranted by the heat which wafted from the kitchen. She didn't answer right away. She and her mother had never been confidantes and she found it awkward to talk to her about any intimate subject. Patience and their mother had been closer and shared confidences and secrets that had not included Prudy, not for any reason, just that it came so naturally. Prudy did not feel natural with her mother. But she was bursting to tell her news, so she took a sip of the cool, refreshing drink and, with her brown eyes lowered to the glass, said, "Mama, I think I'm in love."

Molly looked startled and not so amused this time.

"But Prudy, dear — "

"I know, Mama, it's so sudden, but I have been waiting for a very long time for someone, and I'm almost twenty-four, not a child. Patience has been married for a whole year now and she was in love at a much younger age — she wasn't even seventeen."

"But Prudy —"

"Mama, why is it so different? You are acting like I've done something wrong. Well, I haven't!"

"Listen to me, dear. I am not passing judgement. I am only wondering. Please tell me about this young man."

She calmed down. Her defensive attitude had developed over years of rejection, from being shoved into the background. Now that she knew her worth she viewed any question of her feelings as a criticism. She looked at her mother in a new light. She was talking to her as an equal, another first. Molly was still a beautiful woman, her figure erect and womanly. Her face had fine lines that only gave it character. She wore her forty-nine years well and, despite the years of hardship, her kindness and compassion were embodied in her person. Prudy's love for her mother and her own released feelings for a man who returned them gave her an awareness that years of covering her hurt had ignored. She had her mother's attention and concern and she opened up to her. She smiled shyly and spoke.

"It's Lester, Mama, Lester Deters. He took me to the dance in town last week. I know that it was only a few days ago but I am so — so overwhelmed by him. He is so gallant, a gentleman. He brings me things — hair ribbons, flowers. I know they're just wild flowers, but they are pretty and he gives them to me with such a flourish. I don't feel like an old wallflower, an old maid anymore. Do you know what I mean?"

Molly looked into her glass. The realization of the intensity of her daughter's emotions really struck home. Had she been so occupied with her own deep love and contentment and with her preoccupation with Patience that she had not seen what was happening to Prudy? It couldn't be. She loved them both the same. Or did she?

"I'll try to understand, dear. Please go on. Tell me about this Lester Deters."

Prudy beamed with pleasure. "He isn't really a young man, as you said, Mama. He's thirty-four."

Molly gave her full attention at that information. "That means he's more than ten years older than you."

"I know, Mama, but it doesn't make any difference. He's not an old man, by any means, and he is such fun to be with. He treats me like a real woman, not like one of the boys as the other fellows do. I've grown up and Lester treats me that way. He's had such an adventurous life and is so interesting to talk to and listen to. And he's traveled all over the country, doing mostly harvest work, but he can do most anything. He makes me laugh and feel good about myself. No one has ever made me feel the way he makes me feel."

She paused, embarrassed at her unaccustomed animation. She had not talked to anyone about such things. Molly merely smiled at her, pleased to see her so radiant in her happiness. But was this man for her? What was his background?

"Prudy, what do you really know about this man? Now don't get all upset. I just want to know about him and I want your future to be secure, as does your father. Parents raise their children with that in mind."

"I know. I'm sorry, Mama. I didn't mean to be snippy."

"It is natural to have emotions such as you are feeling when a handsome man pays attention to you, very natural. I just don't want you to jump into a situation that might not be good for you or might not be what it seems to be. Marriage is

31

forever, you know." She looked pointedly at her.

"Lester is a good man. He has never gotten out of line."

"You have not known him long enough for him to get out of line."

A good point, she persisted. "I know what I feel, Mama, and I love him. I really want him."

"Prudy, do you know what a man expects from a woman he is thinking of taking for his wife?" She looked into her eyes frankly with a thinly veiled inference. "Do you know what a man considers a husband's rights to be in a marriage?"

"Yes, Mama," she murmured. While she was not ignorant of the sexual aspect of marriage and familiar with the breeding of the farm animals, she did not know as much as she tried to convey.

"And do you know that the church forbids denying one's husband for any reason, and that babies are conceived?"

"Yes, Mama." Prudy thought for a moment, then dared to say, "But, if as the church says babies are conceived only through a desire for them why are there so many children in some families? Most of them are so poor. Can they really want so many babies?"

Another of Prudy's awkward questions. Molly thought of Patrick's passion, then of the Clanahans with their ten children and Mr. Clanahan barely able to make a living from his 160 acres. Clarice Clanahan was the same age as Molly and looked years older. How could she answer Prudy's question when she couldn't come to a satisfactory answer herself? She said, "I don't know Prudy. God's will is sometimes hard to understand."

"Well, I would never refuse Lester — if we were married," she added hastily.

"Marriage teaches much and there are always compromises to be made. Are you prepared to make them?"

"Oh yes, Mama," she replied eagerly.

"I suggest that you think this over carefully. If Lester's livelihood depends on the harvest that means a life of constantly moving around. Don't you want to settle down and have your own home?"

"I just want to be with him, wherever he goes."

Molly sighed. Young love did not think clearly.

"Has Lester indicated his intentions to you?"

"No, not yet, but he will. I just know it." She perched on the edge of the chair earnestly.

"Please give it some serious thought. I know you are of an age where you know your own mind, but your father and I want you to be happy and secure. The choice of a life-long mate is very important. What about Lester's family? Where does he come from?"

Prudy answered hesitantly. "He said he is an orphan. He has been on the move since he was sixteen. But he has always worked very hard," she continued more confidently. Her shared confidences made her bold and she asked, "You and Papa are happy, aren't you, even after all these years?"

"Oh yes, dear. Your father is a wonderful man."

32

"What do you think he'll say?"

"Would you like me to talk to him?"

"Would you please? I don't know how he would look on having a roving farm hand for a son-in-law, especially since Lars has such a good job."

The two women were lost in their own thoughts as they rested in the quiet room. The drapes were drawn against the sun that beat through the partially open west windows and a warm breeze stirred the lace curtains.

That night, as they lay in bed, Molly massaged Patrick's pain-ridden arm as she said, "Prudy has a beau."

"Mmph," came his muffled response from the pillow.

"Really, Patrick, you could show a bit of interest. Prudy is really in love."

He turned over and looked at her. She had captured his attention. He rubbed his left arm absently and asked, "Who is this man?"

"Lester Deters."

"Lester? The big German?"

"Yes, that's the one. They seem to have taken to one another. Prudy is quite smitten."

"In such a short time?"

"Yes, Patrick, in such a short time. How long did it take you to fall in love with me?"

He grinned and pulled her down to him. "I'm still in love with you, you beautiful doll."

He ignored his arm and gathered her to him and began to kiss her. She pulled away reluctantly.

"Patrick, please, we must talk about this. I think they want to marry and we must be prepared to accept the fact."

"But this Lester travels the harvest circuit."

"I know, but Prudy isn't getting any younger, and I'd hate to think she missed her chance just because we didn't take her seriously, to say nothing of how she would regard our refusal."

He released her. "You're right, of course." He sat up. "Well, Lester Deters is not exactly the sort of man I had hoped for to marry our Prudy. But there is nothing wrong with good, hard work and he can work circles around anyone I've ever seen. He'll have his own spread some day."

"Then she would have your consent?"

"If it comes to that, yes. Now come here."

Molly laughed as she went into his arms for his passionate love making. If only Prudy will be so fortunate she thought, babies or not.

★

The harvest crew finished at the Malones and moved on to the neighboring farms, but Lester and Prudy kept company for a month. They went to every Saturday

33

dance, becoming a popular, familiar couple at the weekly festivities, and he spent Sundays at the Malones sitting on the back porch until it was too dark to see the big barn. He always kissed her discretely good night before he strode off to his horse to return to where the rest of the crew was quartered to endure their friendly jibes.

"Ja, you're all just jealous, that's the truth of it," he'd say.

One Sunday after church and the noon meal during the free time when the hands could relax, go to town, or just sleep, they rode their horses along the road to Spotswood that went beyond to the town of Mobridge, letting the horses have their heads, taking their time, enjoying the warm autumn afternoon, with the edge off the heat. The cooler air was a relief from the constant, hot winds of summer or the breathless humid air.

Sometimes the tolerable weather preceded a storm that destroyed crops and buildings. Tornadoes were an early summer threat and hail was a dreaded occurence. Now that those threats were behind the farmers they enjoyed the respite from the battle of wits with the elements to get the crops in and to be ready for the winter which was harsh, cold and interminably long. Lester and Prudy were passed in both directions by others on horseback or in buggies, still in their Sunday clothes, out for a ride or a visit. They tipped their hats to one another in comraderie. Lester and Prudy rode in silence much of the way, relishing the closeness they shared. They were on a stretch of road just past Spotswood. Tall fields of corn lined the dusty road.

"That looks about ready," remarked Lester.

"Is that your next stop?" asked Prudy.

"Ja, soon, but we can still see each other." He glanced at her with longing.

Prudence Malone had blossomed with love that summer. Her petite frame was nicely shaped. Her dark brown hair hung loose in natural thick waves to her small, shoulders. Her bonnet shaded her dark eyes, but her cheeks were flushed from his look. She was tanned from long days in the sun and she looked to Lester like a ripe plum, ready to pluck.

"You'd make a fine wife, Prudence Malone."

She looked up in delight, her lips parted. What a fine, big man he was, so strong and self-assured. His sandy hair and face freckled from work in the outdoors gave him a boyish look. His sleeves were rolled up past his elbows, displaying arms bronzed by the elements, with beads of perspiration standing up on bleached golden hairs. His steady, intense gaze unnerved her, yet stirred her past control.

"Let's get down and walk a little," he suggested softly.

They dismounted and he led the horses to the side of the road and hitched them to a fence post.

"Come on, let's see how tall the corn is."

"But we could get lost in there," she protested.

"I won't lose you. Come on."

He pulled her into the tall corn with a firm grasp. The corn was taller than he

34

was and it completely dwarfed her. It was like a jungle. He laughed his hearty laugh and picked her up, as was his custom, and held her to the top of a corn tassel that tickled her nose.

"Lester, put me down!"

He continued his deep laugh and put her down, then pressed her to the ground, enveloping her in his arms, kissing her thoroughly on her lips, her eyes, her neck. She couldn't move from his grip, but she found she didn't want to, and she responded to him with a passion she had not known she possessed. His eagerness brought out an equal response in her and she clung to him as he caressed her and pulled at her clothing.

"Lester, no."

But she didn't really mean no as he undid her blouse and pulled up her skirt. When he tugged off his trousers she reached up and eagerly submitted to him. Later, as they lay in each other's arms, they looked to the clear blue sky above the waving corn tassels, the only witnesses to their passion. Fluffy white clouds hung lazily in the air. A meadow lark sang somewhere in the distance and it was peacefully quiet. Prudy had given as much as Lester had given and she gloried in her womanhood. She had at last come into her own with this man. She looked at him, lying with his eyes closed, loving him. He turned to her and his look of total possession completely engulfed her.

"Prudence Malone, I love you. Ja, you will be wife."

The news of the engagement of Patrick and Molly Malone's eldest daughter did not create the stir that surrounded that of Patience and Lars, but Prudy didn't care. She was happier than she had ever been. "We'll have an early spring wedding," declared Molly.

"But Mama, do we have to wait that long?"

She had not extended her confidence to her mother concerning her indiscretion in the corn field and of those that followed. She did not want to reveal to anyone the intimacy which she and Lester shared. The harvest season was coming to a close and Lester's departure was imminent. There was another reason for her impatience. Prudy suspected she was in a family way and wanted to be married at once. It was October and it would be too late to be married in the spring. She couldn't bear to hurt her parents that way. The disgrace would be worse for them than for her. What was to be done?

"Couldn't I be married on October 12th, Mama, on my birthday? I'll be twenty-four then. I'm getting older by the minute!" She stamped her foot in frustration.

"I will tell you what I told Patience. Be patient. You are young; twenty-four is not middle age, you know. There is plenty of time. I was older than you by the time I married. Now what colors would you like, dear? Perhaps a pale green with your coloring."

She was worried, and Lester would not be put off once they had made love. "Ja, Prudy, you are mine now. You cannot say no to me, can you?" And he would laugh mockingly as she willingly went to him. She didn't know how to tell him that he would be a father in the spring. She told him of her mother's plans for another big Catholic wedding and that was the first time she saw him angry, and it frightened her. His face grew livid and he stiffened.

"Nein! No, no! Never a wedding in a Catholic church!"

"But why not? What difference does it make?"

"I don't believe in the Catholic church, all that mumbo jumbo and worshipping idols. And no priest is going to tell Lester Deters what he can and can't do. No. I forbid it."

Forbid it? Her heart gave a jump. She admired Lester's strength and firm nature, but forbid was a strong word and the wildness in his dark eyes alarmed her. She tried not to cry.

"I must tell you something, Lester. Please don't be so angry. I — I am with child." Seeing the look on his face, she hurried on, "We have to do something. What can we do?"

The stunned look turned triumphant. His anger drained away. He picked her up and held her above his head, laughing with glee.

"You are to be a mother. You will give me a child. That is good, Ja!"

He kissed her soundly and she was awash with jubilance. Her confidence returned and there was hope that somehow they would find a way out of their predicament without hurting anyone.

"We will go away and get married, on our way to Canada. That is what we will do, Ja."

"You mean elope?"

"Sure. We don't need any fancy wedding."

It would be a solution; she didn't want a big wedding either. Her mother did and it was customary and proper, the thing to do. They just couldn't wait much longer and she couldn't bear to tell her parents about the baby.

"All right. Let's do it. We'll elope! Oh, Lester, I knew you'd know what to do." And she flung her arms around his neck.

Her fear subsided and she was suddenly excited and full of daring. Lester was in control and she was a part of him now. She was safe. The harvesters were winding up their work in the area and would be moving north to North Dakota and on into Canada in a few days. Many things had to be done, preparations to be made and done in secret. Lester's packing was second nature and he carried his worldly belongings with him in his wagon. Prudy had choices to make deciding which items of clothing from her ample closet to take, personal items that she had had as long as she could remember. It wasn't easy to sort out the important from the trivial or sentimental. They must travel lightly.

She had never been further away than Mobridge and the Standing Rock Indian Reservation, so it was a challenging adventure getting ready for the rest of her life. She had a trunk that had been her parents. They had given it to her after Patience had left as a sort of hope chest to which were added various linens and silver and a fancy dish or two, gifts from many Christmases and birthdays. She piled various items of clothing and shoes on top of the contents of the trunk.

The night before the crew was to leave in late October Lester crept up the stairs and carried the heavy trunk down and silently through the house to the buggy out by the barn. Prudy was ready, dressed warmly against the frosty night. They had a long ride ahead of them. They would reach Mobridge before midnight and would be married by a Justice of the Peace who had been instructed by Lester to expect them. The marriage license was obtained one day when the Malones and Lester had driven into Mobridge for supplies before winter set in. Lester had been asked to go along since he and Prudy were engaged and also to help Patrick, whose arm was of no use to him. So they were all set.

Prudy climbed into the seat of the wagon beside Lester and paused, looking at the silent, dark house where her unsuspecting parents lay asleep. She had tried to be as sweet to them as she could be that evening, to say goodbye in a way that satisfied her but so they would suspect nothing. Nevertheless, she felt a pang of guilt.

"Come, Prudy. Time to go. After we're married you can send a letter to them and tell them where we are. You belong to me now."

He was right. In spite of it, tears welled up in her eyes. She seldom cried, but this was like nothing she had ever known. She was leaving her home, her loving parents, her entire life up till then. It was hard to do, but she would have a new life with Lester and they would be happy. She would explain everything later, and they would understand.

They moved quietly down the road, through the sleeping town of Spotswood, and on to Mobridge, where they were married by an unshaven Justice of the Peace, who complained about the late hour, with a frowsy wife who played a hymn on an out-of-tune piano and also witnessed the ceremony. But Prudy didn't care. She clung to Lester and happily said, "I do." Lester unhesitatingly said, "I do," and they were man and wife.

The next morning Patrick came down to breakfast to find Molly weeping. She handed him a note:

"Mama and Papa, Lester and I have eloped. Please don't be angry. We just couldn't wait. Please be happy for me. I'll write soon. I love you both, Prudence."

Patrick and Molly drank their coffee without speaking, occupied with thoughts that combined surprise, anger, hurt, a little guilt, and also gratitude in Prudy's happiness. One's children had a need to strike out on their own and both of theirs were gone.

At last Molly spoke, "It's come full circle. How strange life is. I always thought Patience's life paralleled mine, but it is Prudy who is following in my footsteps." She started to cry once more. "But oh, Patrick, is she really ready? Is she really prepared? Why do I feel so apprehensive?"

He took her in his arms and they clung together. Suddenly they felt very old.

CHAPTER FIVE

The Homecoming

Prudy was deliriously happy with Lester. She had never known such love, the sense of freedom in belonging to him. She did not miss the ordered life she had left. Lester was in control and she was happy to leave all decisions to him, unaware of the contraditcion in her thinking, exchanging parental control for that of her husband's.

Lester was proud to introduce his woman to the hands they met in their travels that fall of 1899, on up into North Dakota, following the mighty Missouri River, then straight north into Saskatchewan, Canada, to acres of rolling wheat fields waiting for the threshers. While Lester worked the fields Prudy worked as a domestic, work she was well familiar with. Her pregnancy gave her a glow and an energy that enabled her to keep up the hectic pace of the life that was Lester's.

"Ja, I will be a father in the spring," he would proudly declare. Prudy would avert her eyes and blush, pleased at the attention and feeling very well.

The weather was turning cold, but the harvest went on as fast as before, because it was just as imperative to get the wheat in before freezing rain, followed by heavy snow, made it impossible.

And then November was almost gone and the work was done. Lester was strangely downcast, almost as though there was nothing to look forward to. It was time to return south.

"We'd best be heading for the states, Prudy. I don't like the smell of the wind. A winter in Canada is no picnic."

It was true. The spacious land had a thin, flat look now that the wheat, which a few days previously had waved in the wind like a golden sea, was cut; and the wind had a strange, sighing quality that held the promise of drastic change. Even the sun was struggling to make its presence known. Prudy ventured a question that had been on her mind the past few days.

"Just where will our home be for the winter? You've never really said." An understatement; Lester rarely informed her of his plans.

"In Oklahoma, I think, someplace close to a settlement."

She looked up at him, her dark eyes pleading. "Couldn't we stop in Spotswood for a few days? I'd dearly love to see Mama and Papa. Why, we could even stay the winter. They wouldn't mind, there's plenty of room and they'd be glad for the company. Maybe — "

Lester was glaring at her. "You and that baby are mine. You'll stay with me wherever I go. And we're going to Oklahoma. I'll provide for you. I've done right by you so far, Ja?"

"Of course. It's just that I'd like to see them, tell them about the baby, that's all. I'm not homesick, really I'm not. And it will be months before we see them again otherwise. Please —"

He said nothing, just stared into space, making his decision. Then he looked at her, so appealing and small and pregnant.

"We can stop for a day or two, no more than that. We've got to get to Oklahoma while the weather holds."

"Oh, Lester, thank you. Thank you!" She jumped into his arms and hung around his neck, while he grinned.

The next morning very early they set out on the long trip south in the wagon, bundled up warmly against the cold and the brisk wind that stung their faces. And so it was that the urgent telegram from Dr. Gideon Walsh missed them; and unknown to Prudy, the letter she had written to her parents remained in Lester's pocket.

They pulled into the yard of her parents' farm the second week in December with spitting snow swirling around them. To Prudy it seemed she had been gone a lifetime, when in reality it was almost two months. Eagerly she climbed down from the wagon and ran to the back porch. A lamp was lit in the kitchen in the gathering winter's dusk. She burst into the kitchen and happily exclaimed, "Mama, we're here! Mama, where are you?"

She heard a faint "oh" from the front room and the wail of a baby from one of the upstairs bedrooms. She removed her heavy coat and paused. "Mama? Papa?" She hurried through the dining room with the bay window on the south which was already frost-covered in the corners, and into the front room where she stopped stock-still. Molly was struggling to raise herself from the overstuffed sofa which was covered with rumpled bed covers and being restrained by Patience. The look of pleased surprise on her mother's face could not hide the ravages of sickness.

"Mama! What's wrong with you? Patience, what are you doing here?"

"Prudy, my child," her mother said in a shaky voice, "how good to see you. We didn't know where you were. Why didn't you let me know you were coming? I would have made preparations."

"But, Mama, I did. Didn't you get my letter?"

"No, there was no letter."

She sat beside her mother, with Patience standing beside her, and put her arms around her, holding Molly closely. Her mother was thinner and frail and inexplicably sad. She returned her daughter's embrace weakly, then gently pushed her away and said warmly, "Prudy, you are going to have a baby. How wonderful. Millicent will have a playmate."

Millicent was the daughter of Patience and Lars, a sickly baby born the previous June. It must have been her cry she had precipitated when she entered the house so noisily. She looked at her younger sister in admiration. She looked elegant clad in a blue wool dress and warm high button shoes. Her silky blond hair was coiffed in

39

the lastest style, piled high on her aristocratic head. They smiled, pleased to see each other. Patience reached out her hands to Prudy and said, "You look lovely. Pregnancy agrees with you tremendously."

Indeed, she was right. Prudy's slight form was blossoming with her baby. Her thick dark hair was caught in combs away from her pink cheeks. Happiness shone in her face and her dark eyes sparkled. But the light was dimming by what she had found upon her return home.

"Our baby will be born in the spring. We're excited about it, especially Lester. You should hear him brag. Where's Papa?"

Patience bent her head and Molly's eyes filled with tears. "You mean you came, but you don't know?"

"Know what? What are you talking about? Patience, what's wrong?"

Molly's hands covered her face and she was convulsed with sobs and a fit of coughing. Alarmed, they laid her back against the pillows. She had dissolved into uncontrollable crying. Prudy looked from one to the other in dismay. Finally, Patience said in a low voice, "Papa is dead."

"Papa, dead?" Prudy's voice was a whisper, as if to say the words louder would make them a reality.

Lester had come into the room to warm himself by the wood burning stove at the north end of the room and had heard the news, which laid over all of them like a heavy blanket. Prudy wanted to run to him for comfort, but did not because Lester's stony expression held her back and because her mother needed her. She rose and pulled an afghan over her and tried to calm her. Patience was trying not to lose control. Lars had followed Lester and walked slowly into the room to stand beside his wife. He nodded to Prudy and drew Patience into his arms and held her tightly to him as she wept.

The room was growing dark and chilly. Prudy went to Lester, needing the warmth of his touch. He stood before the stove, expressionless. She leaned against him, expecting his strong arms to surround her, to comfort her, to make it all better. But he just said, "I suppose this means we have to stay longer than I expected."

He didn't look at her shocked expression. "Lester, Mama needs us. Papa is dead and she is very sick. We can't decide anything until we know more about what has happened."

Frustrated and hurt by his lack of feeling, she left him and sat on one of the overstuffed chairs. Patience came to her. Lars lit the lamps and said, "Dr. Walsh will be here soon. He comes every day."

The stomping of feet on the back porch and a brief knock announced the good doctor, who didn't wait to be admitted but wiped his feet on the rag rug by the door and came into the front room. He strode over to Prudy.

"I'm really glad the telegram reached you. It took some doing, but I finally tracked you down."

"But it didn't reach me. We're on our way south and just now stopped off to see Mama and Papa and we found — this. Mama didn't get my letter telling of our coming either. I don't understand."

Lester sprawled in the easy chair and said nothing, staring out the west window at the gathering darkness and the pellets of snow, pondering the turn of events that had upset his plans. Dr. Walsh walked to the sofa and looked tenderly down at Molly Malone. Her thin face was flushed and her breathing uneven. He sighed deeply in resignation. It was up to him to repeat the sad news to Prudy. He returned to her and sat in the chair beside her. The doctor was of an undetermined age. The folks of Spotswood knew and respected him as one of their own, despite his reticence in disclosing any facts about himself. There had been many rumors over the years, from an indiscretion with a female patient to some sort of malpractice, but nothing was ever proven. Most dismissed the rumors as being of no consequence, considering his actions to speak for him. He had endured hardships with them, nursed them through influenza, pneumonia, cholera and offered compassion when early death claimed some of them. They trusted him. But he was getting on in years and he was tired. His straight black hair was thinning and streaked with gray. He wore spectacles in his declining years and his hands with their long, slender fingers were showing the effects of the labor of his years, gnarled and not quite as steady as they had once been. But he was not incompetent and his patients swore by him. He looked at the young women seated before him, whom he had brought into the world, and said, "Prudy, I have explained this to Patience and Lars and I feel I should be the one to tell you and Lester here what happened. Your father was a good man, a hard worker, a man beloved by all who knew him, not the least of whom was me, which is why this has been so hard for me to bear."

A lump was forming in Prudy's throat. She looked at the doctor curiously. Dr. Walsh averted his eyes, looked down at his clasped hands, and said, "Your father died of blood poisoning."

"What?" She looked at him in disbelief. This statement also caught Lester's attention.

"Yes, I'm afraid so. It was his arm. You know how it pained him. He just didn't take care of himself and he let it go too long. He wouldn't listen to me."

"You sure make a lot of excuses, Doc," grumbled Lester.

Dr. Walsh ignored the remark. "He got infection from a cut and I just couldn't control it." He hesitated, hating to repeat his failure. "I had to cut off his arm, Prudy."

Patience stifled a small cry. Prudy screamed, "No!"

"I had to do it. The arm was badly infected with septicemia. It was spreading all through his body. It was killing him."

"You cut off his arm and it did kill him!" she shouted.

Dr. Walsh hung his head in despair. Molly moved fitfully in her fever. Prudy ran to her. "Oh, Mama, what have I done? What have we all done to you to leave you and Papa all alone?"

Lester shifted in the easy chair. "How were we to know, woman?"

Dr. Walsh swung around angrily, but held his tongue. He said to Prudy, "She'll be all right for awhile. But I must tell you what I told the others."

Her heart sank as she listened.

"Your mother is very sick. She has not been well for several weeks, perhaps months, but never let on to anybody about how she was feeling. She got through the last harvest season in extreme exhaustion, which further weakened her condition."

Prudy was filled with guilt. How could she not have seen it? Was she so in love that she was blind to her mother's suffering? Had she been that selfish?

Dr. Walsh continued. "Patrick's death was too much for her, too much of a shock. We all know how devoted they were. She just went to pieces and has not reconciled herself to his passing. Her grief has been overwhelming in her weakened state. And with both of you girls gone she just gave up, with nothing to live for."

"Doctor, what's wrong with her?" asked Prudy.

"I'm afraid she has tuberculosis."

"Oh no. No!" Prudy's shoulders slumped. Her despair was so deep that tears would not come. The hopelessness of the situation weighed heavily. "But how could she have gotten consumption? She has always been healthy and keeps an immaculate house."

"I'm not sure, but the Standing Rock Reservation is rampant with the disease. It is practically impossible to instill proper sanitary practices there and the government and the church can't come up with the help or the money that is needed to help; and even at that the Indians want to do things their way. They rely on their medicine men, not trusting the white man's ways. In fact, they figure it's the white man's fault, and they could be right about that. But if a cow has the tubercle bacillus it can be transmitted through the milk. And Patrick had recently bought a cow for his herd from the reservation. Molly drank the milk to help her get her health back. Ironic, isn't it? I've done some checking and, so far, Molly seems to be the only victim, so it is likely the cow was the culprit. I say was, because it has since been destroyed."

The silence was broken by a heavy cough from deep down inside Molly's chest. Dr. Walsh went to her and held her in a sitting position, patting her back until she produced a sticky phlegm from her congested lungs. The back of her nightgown was soaked with perspiration. Exhausted from her effort she lay back on the pillows panting softly, her breath coming in wheezes. Prudy stood in shock at the sight. Patience buried her head in Lars's shoulder.

"Doctor, what can we do? How long will she be like this?"

"Tuberclosis is an insidious disease that requires meticulous care."

"Patience and I will take care of her."

Lester spoke up, "Look, Doc, we've got to be on our way in a couple of days. You'll just have to find someone else to be nursemaid."

"I'm afraid it isn't that simple. Molly will require at least six months of bed rest, maybe more if she has a relapse."

"Six months! That is foolish, Ja."

Dr. Walsh had difficulty in not shouting at the arrogant man, but only said, "I

42

did not invent the disease, Mr. Deters. There is no cure, only containment. Bed rest, nutritious food and absolute cleanliness are essential." He looked at Prudy.

"You are with child. The winter is soon upon us. What better place could you find to spend it and at the same time take care of your mother?"

She nodded, tears finally spilling down her cheeks.

"Oh no, we're heading for Oklahoma, Ja!"

Dr. Walsh said, "You've both had a long, hard trip and have come home to much less than you expected. Get a good night's sleep and in the morning things will look better. Talk it over and make your decision then. I'll be back tomorrow. In the meantime, keep your mother warm, help her to cough, keep the bedding clean — no need to tell you she cannot go up those stairs to her bedroom. We've put the chamber pot down here. And I don't want all the neighbors dropping in tiring her out and maybe catching the germ themselves. Understood?"

They nodded in agreement, all except Lester. He did not get up. Dr. Walsh proceeded to the back door with Prudy accompanying him.

"Be careful, Prudy. Tuberculosis is contagious. You must protect yourself and your unborn baby. Patience will stay with you, I'm sure. Make sure everything is very clean. Wash your hands often."

"I will, Doctor. Thanks. Dr. Walsh, please forgive my outburst. I was so outraged at my father's leaving us — I didn't mean what I said."

He patted her shoulder. "Never mind that. Take care of yourself." He paused on the back porch and looked up into the black sky over which oddly shaped clouds were scudding swiftly, periodically blotting out the dim moon with their erratic passage. The flat landscape had an eerie look.

"Better have Lester bed down that team. Looks like a storm's coming." He walked quickly to his horse, holding onto his hat against the wind.

That night the first blizzard of the winter came up, lasting for three days, and depositing several feet of snow for miles all around, burying some farms up past their windows. There was no way they could even consider leaving the homestead. Prudy was secretly glad because in her heart she knew she could not have left her mother, and she dreaded a confrontation with Lester. The blizzard solved that problem. It would be only for the winter, maybe until the spring and the baby was born. Lester would get used to it.

It was a hard winter with north winds that whipped the snow into huge white drifts banked against buildings and fences. Lester kept a path open to the barn and strung a rope from the porch to the barn to grasp for security when the snow flew into opaque curtains of biting flakes. More than one farmer was found frozen to death a few yards from his house or barn when he got lost in a storm and could not see to get his bearings.

During their time together Prudy and Patience renewed their friendship with awakened feelings of kinship. Millicent was a fretful baby and a fitful sleeper, but she had two motherly figures to tend to her needs, neither of whom complained. They took joy in watching the tiny baby grow and in having a new life to

43

contemplate as another life was ebbing. During those times it was not uncommon for a guest from a distance to stay for some time, so it was not unusual for Patience and her child to remain with her mother indefinitely. But after Christmas Lars had to return to New Ulm, so he took the Milwaukee train east, which now made a regular stop in Spotswood on its way to and from Mobridge. He had to take care of his mercantile business after an extended time away. He worried about his family, but knew that in the event of any emergency there were plenty of good folks who would be happy to help.

Molly was grateful for the presence of her daughters and, although she grew progressively weaker, she maintained her slim hold on a life that had taken on meaning with them there. She depended on Lester to lift her to a chair while the bedding was changed or when they gave her a bath, and his assistance was needed to place her on the chamber pot. His charm that evidenced itself during these tasks and the respect he showed Molly was a change that was welcomed by the girls, but it was not clear whether it was genuine or only a veneer for his true feelings. His sullen acceptance of their situation otherwise did not lessen the intimacy and closeness that Prudy and Patience shared during the trying time of Molly's illness. Molly's frail body would be wracked with paroxysms of coughing, and they would sit her up and pat her back until she brought up the thick phlegm that strangled her breathing, only now it was bloody. When Dr. Walsh could make it out to the farm he would talk gently to her, listen to her raspy breathing with his stethoscope and smile kindly at her, but in the kitchen with Prudy and Patience he would only shake his head in sorrow.

In the middle of January, 1900, they welcomed a thaw. The sun shone brightly, the mounds of snow diminished, balmy breezes from the south boosted the spirits of winter weary people, and a false spring settled in for ten days. Molly rallied and took pleasure in sitting in the dining room close to the bay window on the south, basking in the warmth, drinking a cup of tea laced with cream and sugar. One sunny day she sat there, her frail body resting against the feather pillows, her thin legs wrapped in a quilt, contentedly enjoying her tea. She smiled as she gazed at the house plants that had survived the cold and were perky in the warm area. She looked through the big window which was streaked with the soil of winter.

"It will soon be spring, Prudy. Won't it be nice to be in the garden again? The children will enjoy being outdoors. And Patience, we must wash this window."

Prudy almost said, "Mama, it's only January," but instead agreed. "Yes, Mama. What will you plant this year? It should be a good year for tomatoes with all the moisture in the ground. Don't you think so? Or will it be mostly flowers? Mama?"

The sound of the teacup as it fell to the floor spun them around. Molly lay back against the pillows, her lovely eyes closed in death, the lines of pain in her face eased, her pain-wracked body at peace.

Molly Malone was buried in the Spotswood Cemetery beside Patrick with most of the community in attendance, in shock at having lost two of their most revered citizens. The sisters clung together at the grave in their grief. Only Lester did not attend the funeral which was officiated by a Catholic priest from Mobridge. He remained adamant in his refusal to ever set foot inside a Catholic church. So Prudy made his excuses to her friends, friends from childhood, and to the elders in attendance who came to say goodbye to lifelong friends with whom they had braved a new frontier.

Patience was of tremendous help, not only in comforting Prudy, but in the social graces necessary at such an event. She wrote a long letter to their Uncle Seth, Patrick's brother, relating the sad events of the past months, along with the current news of the lives of herself and Prudy. Prudy was grateful for her presence. She needed family now, a family greatly diminished, and Lester couldn't seem to satisfy that need. It would be different when they had their own family, their own baby who would hold them together.

The deaths of their parents so close together was a trauma from which they would not soon recover, but it drew the sisters into a close bond. They at least had each other. They were blessed to not know the circumstances that would eventually fling them apart. A new century was beginning and winter returned to the desolate prairie.

CHAPTER SIX

The First Born

Amid promises to write often, the sister parted. Patience and Millicent took the train to New Ulm while the January thaw held. Patience had been away from Lars too long and there was nothing to keep her in Spotswood, yet she felt guilty about leaving Prudy in her condition with Lester, whom she did not like. It was a mutual dislike, thinly concealed. Patience considered Lester to be coarse and potentially violent. Lester looked on Patience as a useless female without strength who put on fancy airs. Fortunately, little time was spent in the other's company. Patience spent her time with Prudy and Millicent.

The sisters shared confidences and learned much about each other in their long talks, dispelling past years of rivalry. Despite the five year age difference they were now equal, and they vowed to never lose what they had discovered. This bond, together with the loss of their beloved parents, made the parting even harder.

It had been decided that Prudy and Lester would remain on the farm, at least until the baby was born. Even Lester could see the wisdom in that. Besides, he had become used to the comfortable house, and the thought of falling into possession of a place of his own instead of having to work for years to get one was worth considering. It was agreeable all around that they should have the homestead, an agreement reached before the arrival of a Mr. Swenson made their agreement binding. They had been surprised by a visit from Mr. Karl Swenson, a local attorney, who arrived the day after Molly's funeral. He informed them that a few months earlier, shortly after Prudy had left, Patrick had paid a call on Mr. Swenson and arranged to transfer his property to Lester and Prudence Deters and had signed a deed to that effect, with the provision that Molly Malone retain a life estate and be allowed to live on the homestead until her death.

Of course, with events happening so fast, all provisions had been met, and the property was transferred to Lester and Prudy. This news made Lester better-natured about his lot. He took pride in being a man of porperty and lost no time in informing anyone he met that he was now the owner of the prosperous Malone place; he, Lester Deters, who had once been a farm hand there, now owned the property. He never mentioned Prudy's interest in it and she didn't either, not wanting to spoil his new enthusiasm and energy, content to be Mrs. Lester Deters and lucky to have a readymade home, and a familiar one at that.

Her spirits lifted and throughout her pregnancy she continued to feel very well. The sorrow at the unexpected loss of her parents was always with her, but her gratitude at her good fortune helped in healing the hurt because of the love it conveyed from them. As for Patience, she was settled in New Ulm and would never have to worry about her future. If the truth be known, she was glad the farm could be disposed of so easily without the necessity of a sale and all the incumbent problems of complicating finances.

The harsh winter continued unabated until the end of March, when a final burst of snow and ice made its mark on the northern plains. There were some deaths from the cold, as it was not uncommon to freeze to death in the sparsely settled area. And tuberculosis took its toll, adding five more victims to the Spotswood Cemetery. When April arrived it was greeted with relief, but then came flooding from the tons of melting snow into overflowing streams, making lakes of empty fields, too muddy to plant. The warmth and sunshine of May was cause for thanks that most had made it through the difficult winter.

It was an evening at the end of May, 1900, on the 30th.

"Lester, we need more wood."

Prudy was past her term and moved heavily about the house. It was a warm evening, but the kitchen range required wood and the bin was empty.

"I just fetched you some wood the other day," was his irritated reply from the front room where he was seated in the easy chair which he had claimed as his own ever since the cold night in December when they had arrived at the farm. He had come in from the fields and was waiting for his supper.

"Lester, if you want your supper I need some wood." She spoke a little sharper than she intended, but her discomfort often made her cross. Why wouldn't the baby come?

Grumbling, Lester banged the screen door of the kitchen, stepped off the porch and stomped to the old tree stump that held the marks of innumerable blows from the ancient ax that was embedded in it. He easily lifted the tool and in no time had an armload of wood. Still grumbling, he carried it into the kitchen and dumped it noisily into the bin.

"Now, Lester, don't get all riled up. I'd do it myself if I could, you know that. It won't be long now." She held her abdomen.

He looked at her swollen belly and began to chuckle.

"You look like a little toad, Ja," he teased.

She laughed with him glad to have avoided an argument. Lester pulled her to him, tried to lift her into the air, but she protested. He squeezed her tightly to him.

"Lester, please, that hurts."

"I didn't hurt you. I'll be mighty glad when that boy gets here. I want my woman back. It's been a long time, Prudy. How do you expect me to wait so long?"

She blushed. "Dr. Walsh said —"

"That phony. He has no business telling a husband what he can and can't do. Come here. I want you. A man has his right."

He grabbed her, tugging at her ill-fitting garments. She cried out in alarm at his fierceness and pulled away.

"No, behave yourself."

47

She tried to push him away as he became increasingly insistent, even violent in his animal desire, his merry laugh gone. She was clumsy and could not keep away from him.

"No, Lester, please."

"Don't say no to me, woman." Angrily he struck her and she fell, hitting a kitchen chair and scraping her back. She was stunned and then realized she was sitting in a puddle and knew her bag of waters had broken. She began to cry, looking up at him in surprise and fear. He reached down and helped her up.

"Prudy, Prudy, I'm sorry. I don't know what came over me. Are you all right?"

She clung to him, shaking, bewildered. Deep inside she felt a pang of movement unlike the kicking she had been experiencing for the last few months.

"I just banged my back a bit. I'll be all right, I think. Oh!"

The pang came again, a sort of tearing and it was lower down this time.

"What is it? What did I do? I'm sorry, I'm sorry." Lester was contrite.

She collapsed on a chair, holding her arms around herself. "Just let me catch my breath for a minute," she said. Another jolt doubled her over, frightening Lester into action. "I'll get the doc," and he was gone before she could answer.

The stabs of pain subsided for a few mintues, but she knew it was her time. She shouldn't remain in the kitchen. The instructions that Dr. Walsh had given her in case she was alone when labor began were clear in her mind. She took several deep breaths and pulled herself up from the chair. She lit the lamp on the table because it would be dark when they got back. Then she carefully made her way to the hallway that connected the downstairs rooms to the stairs and slowly ascended the steps to the bedroom, the one that had belonged to her parents. She and Lester had the room now; it was large with a big four poster bed at the opposite wall. She clung to one of the bedposts to steady herself after the climb as another pain coursed through her body.

She had lain awake many nights, unable to sleep from her discomfort, going over in her mind what she should do, and dreading it as well as looking forward to what would be the deliverance of her burden. She was alone a great deal and that frightened her, too. But now she knew what she must do; it was clear n her mind, made all the more so by the sharpened awareness of what was happening to her. She removed her misshapen clothing and the wide shoes from her swollen feet and put on her nightgown, a tent-shaped garment which she had fashioned to accomodate her girth. She stripped the bed of its covers and folded each piece neatly and laid it on the chest at the foot of the bed. Then she covered the bed with an old, but clean, cotton blanket. She moved slowly, breathing deeply, but performed the tasks with calmness, between pains that were coming closer together. Clean rags of assorted sizes were folded beside the wash basin and water pitcher on the stand beside the bed, all in readiness. She had forgotten to fill the pitcher after washing that morning. Someone else would just have to do that, because she simply could not go down the stairs to the kitchen pump. Finally, she laid down on the bed, fatigued, and was doubled over with pain as the baby made its relentless journey to life.

48

She was gripping the bed frantically. Where could Lester and the doctor be? What was taking them so long? It was growing dark. She couldn't stand much more of this, not all alone. She tried to remember what Patience had told her when she was home. Oh yes, try to breathe normally. Easier said than done. How could skinny, complaining Patience have endured an experience like this? Small wonder she had confided there would be no more children, that the doctor had forbidden it. That, too, was easier said than done. If Lars was anything like Lester, it would be nigh to impossible. The pains were very close together now. She was drenched in perspiration and could not get into a position that would help her distress. She desperately wanted the baby, but there must be a better way. She was jerked to her back by a movement that took command of her body. She grabbed the headboard and pushed down hard. A cry escaped her lips. Damn Lester. Tears rolled down her cheeks. Damn the pain. She bit her lip to keep from screaming. Damn God for what he was putting her through. Her blaspheme did not give her time to feel guilty. She let out a scream as the baby surged through the narrow birth canal. She could scarcely get her breath as the pains combined into one hideous assault on her small body. One last hard push and she knew the baby was out. She was bleeding profusely onto the bed. She heard her baby cry and lay limp and exhausted when she heard Dr. Walsh's welcome voice.

"I see we are somewhat late. You'd better wait outside Lester."

She sobbed in relief, "Thank goodness you've come. I was so scared. Is the baby all right?"

The good doctor was busily tending to the baby which he laid on top of Prudy's abdomen. "You have a fine, healthy boy — a big boy." He tied the umbilical cord and cut it, wiped the child clean with the rags he found beside the basin, then smiled while Prudy groaned as he gently pressed his hands down on her and she said, "Oh no, no more," and the afterbirth emerged.

"No, Prudy, it's all over. You did just fine, but you are too small to have such a big baby."

He placed the baby in her arms. She looked down at a red faced, robust child with his eyes tightly closed, his mouth working. Dr. Walsh had made a hurried trip to fetch some water in the pitcher and sponged Prudy off after he had packed her tightly to contain the bleeding.

"Lie still for awhile to keep from bleeding too much. You will be fine. You have a tear down there, but it will heal if you don't move around too much. Just rest."

She could feel the soreness and would have no cause to disobey him. Otherwise, she was feeling much better; her burden was now nestled safe in her arms. She smiled in awe at her child and then at Dr. Walsh who, satisfied with how everything had turned out, disposed of the soiled linens in an old pillowcase and said, "I think Lester can come in now."

He let him in and Lester approached the bed eagerly.

"We have a baby boy, Lester," she said shyly.

"I knew it would be a boy, a big one, big and strong, Ja," he said proudly.

She handed the baby to him and he cradled him gently in his arms. The softening in Lester's face melted Prudy's anxiety about the preceding hours and she looked at him in love and forgiveness. Lester made no mention of it.

Dr. Walsh spoke up, "I believe my work is done here. Actually, you did all the work, Prudy. I'll bring Mrs. Johnson over tomorrow morning. She assists me and helps new mothers; that is, if that's all right with you. You will need some help." He looked at Lester.

"How much is it going to cost me?"

The doctor sighed. "It is customary to pay 50¢ a day for the two weeks she should stay with you and the baby."

"I suppose she expects room and board besides."

"Yes. Her help is invaluable. Remember, your wife has had a pretty tough time delivering this baby all by herself." He thought for a moment. "Usually, first babies take their time coming into the world. I don't understand why this one came so fast. How long were you having pains before Lester came for me?"

"Not long —"

Lester laughed nervously. "Maybe such a big boy couldn't wait."

The doctor took in Lester's squelched bravado and Prudy's lowered eyes. Something had happened, but he did not pursue it. He took the baby from Lester and returned him to his mother and said, "You must rest now. This child will be wanting to be fed in a few hours. I believe you know what to do."

Prudy turned crimson and Lester rocked on his heels, his thumbs thrust through his suspenders. "If she doesn't, I'll show her," he joked.

The doctor didn't find this amusing. He looked at Prudy. "Now you have to take it easy for two weeks. Get your strength back. Mrs. Johnson will tend to you and the baby and will fix the meals and do the washing as well. You are getting a bargain." He looked pointedly at Lester, who continued to grin. He said his goodbyes and when they heard his buggy leave the yard she said, "Lester —"

"Never you mind. You did a good job. You'll make a fine mother. I have my son and you will give me many more, Ja."

He went downstairs, taking the steps two at a time, and she heard the doors of the root cellar flung open and his whistling as he went into its dank interior. Her heart sank. That was where he kept his beer, beer he brewed himself from an old German recipe, he said. He had kegs of it down there. Prudy pined, I need him here with me, not down in the cellar getting drunk. And I'm hungry.

But she was not to get out of bed, could not in fact, and she was very tired. A crib had been placed close to the bed, the very crib she and Patience had used as infants, saved for just that purpose by her mother. She laid her baby carefully in the crib and looked with wonder at her child who slept so peacefully. She sighed in satisfaction and drifted off to sleep.

It seemed like only a few minutes later that she heard a knock at the back door. She roused from a comfortable slumber to find the sun shining into the room, birds were singing, and it was morning. She stretched luxuriously and smiled at the baby

50

in his crib. He was beginning to fuss. Lester could get the door. It must be the doctor with Mrs. Johnson.

"Lester," she called. The baby stirred. Where was he? Surely not still in the cellar. She ventured another, "Lester." Still no answer. The back door opened and Dr. Walsh's voice came up the stairs. "Good morning, Prudy. We're here. We're coming up."

The baby began to cry and the sound of his voice startled him into a more lusty howl. She turned to him, not quite sure what to do.

"Now, now, Mrs. Deters, let me do that. I have strict instructions from Dr. Walsh that you are not to stir yourself for a spell."

Prudy was pleased with what she saw. Mrs. Johnson was a large, heavyset middle-aged woman, with gray hair gathered in a bun on top of her head. She presented the appearance of being a capable, motherly, no-nonsense person who took charge. Her long brown dress was covered with a white apron, her sleeves were rolled up, and she wore serviceable shoes with laces tied in a double knot. She bustled about the room, inspecting the baby, clucking at what a fine boy he was as she prepared to bathe and change him.

"I'll be back in a jiffy with some warm water," she announced.

Dr. Walsh tended to Prudy, discarding the tightly packed bandages. He inspected her carefully from her distended breasts down to her slightly puffy abdomen to her toes, murmuring approval, until he saw her scraped back. Without a word he applied a soothing ointment and silently swore at Lester Deters.

"Fine, just fine. Today you had better see if the boy will take a nipple. He will want nourishment."

"I can hear that," she replied. The baby was clearly demanding attention.

"Mrs. Johnson can take over from here. Let her help you until you are stronger. I'll stop in now and then to see how everything is going. By the way, where is your husband?"

She hesitated, "I — I'm not sure. But he'll be coming in for his breakfast, I'm sure."

"I see. Prudy, he is to leave you alone for six weeks, remember."

"Yes, doctor," she said in some embarrassment.

Mrs. Johnson returned with warm water in a large teakettle, humming as she busied herself. The doctor spoke to her, "Take care of these two. I'll leave them in your good hands."

"Don't you worry. We'll get along just fine. There is coffee on the stove if you'd like some before you go."

The doctor smiled at them, pleased with his good fortune in finding such a perfect caretaker, and left the room.

"Now let's see to you first, Mrs. Deters, so you'll be all spic and span for your baby," and she stripped the bed of its coverings and Prudy of her soiled gown. Expertly she washed her, muttered to herself at the sight of Prudy's back, helped her to the chamber pot while she changed the bed clothes, and returned her refreshed to a clean bed. Prudy relaxed and watched as Mrs. Johnson talked soothingly to the baby as she gently wiped his wriggling body with the warm cloth. She was fascinated at how the child responded to her touch. It looked so easy. Mrs. Johnson dressed him deftly in clean clothes and gave him to Prudy, matter-of-factly explaining how to offer him a nipple and laughing as he demonstrated that he needed no coaching on what was expected of him. As he nursed, Mrs. Johnson dumped the dirty water into the chamber pot and carried it and the soiled laundry to the door where she said over her shoulder, "I'm sure you are a mite hungry, Mrs. Deters. I'll take care of this and rustle up some breakfast."

Prudy was in her glory in being so thoroughly pampered. Might as well enjoy it, because in two weeks she would be on her own and she knew nothing about taking care of a baby. Mrs. Johnson returned with a tray and propped her up against the pillows, placing the breakfast on her lap with a flourish.

"It looks wonderful. I am hungry."

Mrs. Johnson moved about the room, setting it in order, checking on the baby who was asleep, content and satisfied, while Prudy polished off every bit of her eggs and toast and coffee. When Mrs. Johnson left with the empty tray and Prudy had settled back against the pillows, relaxed and happy, Lester appeared at the door.

"Lester, where have you been?"

"Cel'bratin', toasting my son. I'm here for somethin' to eat. Where's my breakfas', P'udy?"

He weaved into the room and she could smell the beer.

"You're drunk," she accused.

"Not drunk, just had a couple cups of beer. I've a' right. I'm a father now. It's proud I am to have my son at last, Ja."

"He's our son, Lester. Ours. And we must decide upon a name. What do you think of Patrick Charles?"

"Nein. He'll be called John Lester Deters, after me, Ja."

"But can't we talk about it?"

"All decided. He's called John Lester."

He staggered and sat heavily on the bed, leering at her through bloodshot eyes. "And soon I'll take you again, wife."

"Dr. Walsh said — not for six weeks."

"Six weeks! Foolish. See about that. Man has his right."

She was grateful for Mrs. Johnson's appearance. "You must be the mister," she said. "Breakfast is on the table."

" 'Bout time," he mumbled as he stumbled from the room.

Mrs. Johnson looked after him in disgust and flung a "Humph!" at him as he passed her, then looked at Prudy with pity and shook her head. She had seen it all too often. She was sure to earn her pay in this house.

CHAPTER SEVEN

The Boys

John Lester was the first of four boys born to Lester and Prudence Deters. At even intervals, about two years apart, three more boys added to Lester's pride. Alan Manfred came along in 1902. Chester Patrick was born in 1904 — Prudy prevailed in adding her father's name. In 1906 Fred Samuel made his appearance. Each pregnancy was as hard as the preceding one and birth was sudden, as was the first born's, leading Dr. Walsh to caution Prudy once again.

"But, doctor, you know how Lester is. He won't be put off."

"For your own good, Prudy, you must refuse him. Look at you. You're thin as a rail, run-down and overworked. Who will take care of these boys if you take sick?"

It was true. Prudy lived in a state of exhaustion with four small boys underfoot, meals to fix, preserves to be put up, and heaps of washing to do. She was hard pressed to keep the house in order, the house she was brought up in that her mother had kept in spotless condition. Lester didn't seem to mind as long as his meals were on the table and his boys were seated there. Prudy often ate after the others had finished, picking at what was left. She managed to stay on her feet and was confident that when the boys were older it would get easier and she wouldn't have to keep such a sharp eye on them.

She tried to talk to Lester about Dr. Walsh's warning, but he tossed it off as foolishness. A man had his right. Besides, she liked it now, didn't she? "Admit it. You cannot refuse me," he would taunt. She never replied to his teasing because if he knew how she really felt it would anger him. She was too tired to really enjoy her wifely duties; she just submitted to him. When she got pregnant and gave birth, Mrs. Johnson appeared and took charge, and Prudy enjoyed her two weeks of rest and comparative happiness in being able to enjoy her children without too much responsibility.

Mrs. Johnson felt it her duty to admonish Prudy, too. Catholic or not, she had expressed her opinions on the subject of too many children to the Clanahans, all ten children of the elder Clanahans that Molly discussed with Prudy years before, all of whom were propagating with abandon and filling the pews of the newly formed Catholic Church in Spotswood. She had years of experience and an accumulation of knowledge which she was impelled to impart to those who needed it; otherwise her conscience would give her pain.

"Keep him at your breast for two years. That's the best way to keep from getting pregnant."

Prudy didn't see what that had to do with it. Besides, she had too much to do and, after a year, a bottle would suffice. Lester was no help.

"Ja, we have four strong boys," he would boast. "Good stock, and we will have more. A man needs sons to carry on his name."

Prudy kept her mouth shut and made the best of the situation. Lester was a lusty lover and she had to caution him to be quieter as the years passed, because she never could be sure when one of the youngsters might wander into their bedroom for some reason, and she couldn't answer any awkward questions. She certainly didn't want Lester to answer any, because his explanations could be crude.

Depending on when the new child was born, he would toast his new heir either in the root cellar or ride Rambler to town and stay at one of the saloons until it closed. More than once he had been found in the barn lying in the hay where he had fallen from the horse in a stupor. It wasn't long before he needed no excuse to get drunk.

"You drink too much."

"Shut up. I can drink as much as I want to."

"What will the boys think if they see you like this? They're too little to understand."

"They'll have to learn how to hold their beer some day."

"Do you call this holding your beer? Just look at yourself — you're sick. John is hardly more than eight years old. He needs a better example from his father than how to drink beer."

They had walked from the barn to the water trough and Lester was washing after a fashion. He had immersed his aching head in the cool water and was shaking it out of his eyes. She moved back to avoid the spray and from his stink.

"Hurry up and clean yourself before breakfast."

"Who do you think you're orderin' around, woman?" he snapped, and grabbed her arm as she turned to go into the house.

"Lester, you're hurting me. Why don't you sober up and behave?"

Those Deters Boys!!

She had grown used to his verbal abuse and increasing use of profanity and occasionally talked back to him and, so far, he had not really hurt her, so she was not expecting the hard slap that sent her reeling, falling in the dirt and nearly striking her head against the old tree stump. She was dazed. He strode past her into the house, not looking at her.

"Get up and get me my breakfast."

She was angry and tired of being treated like a hired hand, especially when the children were present, and she was growing fearful of his temper. It was worse when he drank, which was a daily occurence, after he came in from the fields. He would not listen to her. He considered anything she or any woman had to say was of no consequence and usually was cause for derision. What did a woman know? He had lashed out at her with insults whether she spoke or not, causing disconcerting situations when they had company or were the guests of neighbors. She would make excuses for him to the women, saying, "Oh Lester's not so bad when he's sober. He's a good man, really."

The men saw little out of line in his behavior, considering him to be a rousing, all-around good fellow, a good provider for his family, and a man who could hold his beer.

Prudy got up and brushed herself off, only a bit shaken. A raised red mark smarted on her left cheek. What did she do to provoke him like that?

"Are you coming, woman?"

She took a deep breath and went into the house. Lester was seated at the head of the table with two boys on each side of him, all looking at her in expectation. She turned her head from the boys so they would not see the bruise.

"We're hungry, Mama," said John.

What a pleasant picture they made, her boys, scrubbed and combed. She smiled and said to them, "The oatmeal is ready and the toast will take just a minute," and she placed four slices of bread into a square wire container and placed it in the oven.

Lester did not object when she buttered the toast and spread it with thick, homemade apple butter she had canned herself and gave the toast to the children. He was a doting father, although his discipline was hard, not hesitating to use a switch on their bottoms when he felt they needed it, which to Prudy's mind was, on the whole, unecessary. The coarse oatmeal had been bubbling on the back of the black iron cook stove ever since she had risen more than an hour before and was a hearty, nourishing accompaniment to the wholesome slices of toasted homemade bread, and they ate with the gusto that growing boys display when they are hungry. Lester also ate with enjoyment and his disposition improved with something in his stomach and in being surrounded by his family, the proof of his excellent manhood. Then he rose, took his ragged hat from a hook by the door and, without a word, left for the fields. It was June and there was lots of work to do. Then in no time at all it would be harvest time again and she would be even busier with precious little help to ease the added burden. Lester agreed to a hired girl at that time; otherwise, she would not be able to manage, but he complained about how much it was costing him.

She ate her breakfast alone with only Fred, the youngest, in his high chair, picking his toast into tiny pieces, for company.

Fred was two years old and Prudy was not pregnant. She was puzzled, but pleased. On her trips to see Dr. Walsh in connection with an ailment or injury one of the boys sustained she had laughingly commented on her new conditon. He only remarked, "It's a good thing, because you are too run-down to have anymore children. I don't think you could get pregnant, Prudy, or if you did, you would lose the baby. Your body just can't tolerate another one."

As she drank her coffee and talked to Fred, she thought it wouldn't displease her to not have anymore children. Four were enough; in fact, the four boys were a handful. And if she had a little girl she wasn't sure how Lester would react. In his unpredictable way, he might regard a girl as an insult to his manliness. Men were strange that way. She sighed. She was content with her boys, stair steps in her productive years. They all had brown eyes and varying shades of brown hair; otherwise, their differences were markedly evident.

John was eight that year of 1908. He was a big boy, built like his father, tall and strong, and he took delight in mimicking him. He adored Lester and often went to the fields with him, strutting along beside him, his hands in his pockets, listening intently while his father told him all about farming, that he had worked that farm before he had married his mother, that it all would be his some day, his and his brothers. But he was the oldest and he would be in charge. John loved it. He would boss his younger brothers and they obeyed him, not seeming to mind. He led them in play and sometimes the play erupted into a rough and tumble rowdy fight that was determined by who could yell the loudest and get in the most punches.

"They're just playing. Boys will be boys. Let them fight it out. They have to learn," scoffed Lester, whenever Prudy objected to the rough play.

Alan was six. He would be tall as well, but he was built differently, more like the Lynches, Prudy's mothers' side of the family. He had a softer look about him and more often than not wore a half smile on his heart shaped face. He was the peacemaker and offered an alternative to the scuffling and shouting, disliking violence. He was a perceptive child and his father's mean streak didn't escape him causing him to worry about his mother. John may have been the leader, but Alan watched little Fred with more care and compassion.

Chester was four and an appealing, chubby child. He looked up to his older brothers and would not be left out, as Fred was left out until he was older and could keep up with them. Chester didn't have to stay behind with his mother as Fred did, and though he was the smallest of the three oldest, he ran and played with them until he dropped. Sometimes he curled up in the hay in the barn and went to sleep, not wanting to run home to mama and be taunted for being such a baby. He was a roughneck and had no fear, causing Prudy much alarm because of his reckless climbing on farm machinery and getting too near the livestock, not realizing that one of the cattle or horses could take a backward step and squash him. Lester took

56

pride in his daring. Prudy had to rely on the older boys to watch him; otherwise, she was constantly running after him.

Fred, the two year old, was an eventempered little boy. He was smaller than the others had been at two, but he was healthy and gave her little trouble. He smiled at her, oatmeal crusting his face and bits of toast littering the floor. If he was the last one that was all right. He was the easiest one. She picked him up from his high chair and decided it was time to change his diaper. That was another chore she would be glad to be done with. Prudy was thirty-three and Lester was forty-three. Why, they were middle-aged. Where had the time gone?

She changed Fred and set about cleaning up the kitchen before she began the washing, while Fred sat happily on the floor banging pots and pans, when she heard a howling that caused her heart to stop. It sounded like Chester. John and Alan raced across the yard and into the kitchen, out of breath.

"Mama!" Alan shouted. "Chester's hurt."

"What happened? Where is he?" Her contentment vanished.

"In the barn. He fell from the loft," said John. "I told him to stay back from the opening but he wouldn't listen to me. I was watching him, Mama, honest I was; he just fell through."

He hollared his explanation as she picked up her skirt and raced to the barn. There on the straw-covered floor, lay Chester. His eyes were closed, his chest labored in his breathing. She knelt beside him.

"Chester, it's Mama. Wake up, Chester. Come on now. Don't you play games with me."

She put his head in her lap, talking soothingly to him, and checking his body for broken bones or signs of injury. He had a large lump on the back of his head that stuck out like a walnut, but otherwise nothing was hurt. He made a funny little sound.

"Chester, wake up now."

He stirred and opened his eyes. He squirmed and said, "It hurts."

The boys were standing back looking scared and hoping not to be blamed for their brother's accident and hoping he wasn't going to die. Prudy gathered him in her arms and said, "John, run ahead and open the door. Alan, fetch a pail of water from the well."

They did as they were told and Prudy carried Chester into the front room where she laid him down on the sofa. Alan was manfully struggling with the overfull pail of water, sloshing much of it onto the floor in a wet path trailing behind him, and John had the foresight to bring a washrag. Prudy wrung water from the rag and wiped Chester's face, stroking the damp hair away from his face and then holding the cool rag against the knob on his head.

"Chester, are you all right? Does it feel like anything is broken?"

"I'm awright, Mama. My head hurts though."

Fred had toddled into the room and was dropping spoons into the water. He dipped his hands into the pail and made ripples, then looked at Chester with big eyes and patted him with his wet hands. This made them all laugh, except that Chester stopped because it hurt. Prudy sponged him off once more and held the rag to his head, then issued orders that he had to stay inside for awhile, that the lump on his head was going down and that he'd be all right.

When Lester came in for dinner at noon he was surprised to find them all in the front room gathered around Chester who was still on the sofa with a damp rag on his head.

"What the hell happened here?" he demanded.

"I fell out of the loft," answered Chester with a boast in his voice.

"You fell? When did this happen?"

"This morning just after breakfast," answered Prudy.

"Is he hurt bad? What happened to his head?"

"He's all right, Lester, just shaken up. He got the breath knocked out of him and has a bump on his head, but nothing's broken. He's been lying here all morning and is much better." She ventured a nervous laugh but noticed that Lester's glower was deepening.

"He fell all the way through from the loft by himself," said John, as though it had been a feat of accomplishment.

"And we came to get Mama and we all took care of him," Alan said proudly.

"Oh you did, did you? You boys are old enough to watch out for your younger brothers. You should have stopped Chester."

"Now, Lester, it was just an accident. Chester is fine and the boys were a great help to me. You should be proud of them."

He whirled on her. "And you! Where were you that this should happen?"

"I was cleaning up in the kitchen and tending to Fred. Really, you're making a mountain out of a molehill."

"These boys are your responsibility. What kind of mother are you not watching them. You're getting lazy, that's why, Ja."

And with that he shook her by the shoulders until she felt her head would fly from her neck. When he stopped he raised a fist as if to strike her. She was dizzy and lost her balance, falling into a chair, thereby missing the swing of his doubled up fist.

"Mama!" cried Alan, running to her side.

John stared at his father, not knowing what to think, what to do. He backed away and stood beside Chester, cowering on the sofa, frightened by their father's display of anger. Fred began to cry. Lester hovered over the chair, glaring at her.

"All this is your fault, woman. Now get up and put my dinner on the table. You're lucky I don't thrash you good first."

They ate their dinner in silence. Fred was cranky from the tension he felt and couldn't understand, and threw his food on the floor, which made his father even more cross. John stayed behind when he returned to the fields. Alan kept Chester company. Fred took a nap and it was a quiet afternoon, and Prudy pondered her second assault that day.

CHAPTER EIGHT

Lettie

Prudy had decided. She had to talk to someone smarter than she was, so shortly after that awful day she took advantage of a visit from her good friend, Letitia Dannenbring, called Lettie for short, and confided in her.

Prudy thanked her lucky stars for Lettie. They had become fast friends the summer after the harsh winter when the Deters had come home to stay. Lettie and her husband, Meyer, lived two miles north on a farm that Meyer Dannenbring had bought for taxes just after Prudy had eloped with Lester and before Patrick Malone could buy it and add it to his growing acres of land to leave as a legacy for his girls. Prudy and Lettie met at a quilting bee that fall eight years ago. It was a social event when neighbors gathered to make quilts during the long winters, with each neighbor taking her turn to host the event. Quilt making was painstaking work, made easier and more tolerable by the combined efforts of several agreeable women who gathered at a house with a large enough dining room to accomodate a large frame upon which was tacked securely in place a piece of material covered with another piece upon which a design had been traced. In between the two pieces of material was cotton batting to give the quilt substance. The penciled-in design was covered with colored bits of cloth, delicately sewn into place to form an overall pattern. Some of the ladies took pride in their skill at the feather stitch which bordered the individual pieces of cloth in bright thread. Popular patterns of the time were the Friendship, Sunburst, and Wedding Ring which incorporated intertwined circles of multi-colored cloth. Another popular pattern requiring less attention to detail was the crazy quilt, where various shaped bright pieces of cloth were sewn together with no regard for design or color. They were colorful and warm because the pattern covered the entire top of the quilt. Work progressed inward, so the quilt was worked as far as the women's arms could reach and then turned under and held in place by clamps.

Lettie had hosted the first quilting bee Prudy had taken part in. She was familiar with them, because her mother had had bees, but Prudy had never been adept with needle and thread. But she wanted to go and she promised Lester to be back in no time. The women brought their children who played together, usually very well, until they grew tired and fell asleep on top of the winter wraps on a bed. At the time of their meeting, John was the only child Prudy had, so there was no problem. When it came Prudy's turn to host a quilting bee one winter she was glad she didn't have to go out with three children and carrying a fourth. She loved the amiable companionship of the neighbor women. Winters were long and lonesome and

Lester was possessive to the point of excluding her contact with them. He gave in on the quilting bees not wanting to appear unsociable. Sometimes the men attended, as well, and each woman brought something to eat, with everyone enjoying a satisfying lunch and conviviality when the ladies had sewn as much as they could in the lamplight.

Lettie and Meyer had three children, two girls and a boy, and they were considerably better off than the Deters, being of thrifty Dutch extraction. Everyone said a body could eat off Lettie's floors they were so clean. Depsite their frugality, they lived well, due to proper money management, Meyer was fond of saying. They had come from Ohio to live on the plains and to invest their money in real estate and livestock and they were successful at it. They decided to live on one of their properties, two miles from the Deters place, and had fixed it up as modern as the times dictated, with larger plans for the future.

A close friendship sprang up between Lettie and Prudy, despite their obvious cultural differences. Lettie saw in Prudy a woman of unaffected taste, a genuineness and honesty with others with no pretense of being anyone but who she was. She also saw right through Lester Deters. "He is a cruel man," she would say to Meyer, who didn't see him that way at all, but he deferred to his wife in most matters of judgement concerning other people. After all, he realized he wouldn't be enjoying their present prosperity if it weren't for Lettie. She had a good business head on her shoulders and she had been right in urging him to leave the cities in the east and coming west to make the most of his future.

The Dannenbrings had a Model T which was a symbol of their wealth. They were admired for having been able to afford the latest in transportation, but cursed, too, when the noisy vehicle stirred up the dust on the road and frightened their horses. Lettie shocked the women by learning how to operate the vehicle, but this did not bother her, since she had always been a forward looking, progressive woman. She could see no difference in driving the Model T than in driving the team on the wagon before they got the vehicle. "People look at progress in different ways, especially when it is a woman making the progress," she told Prudy. Prudy was happy to be her friend and basked in her friend's accomplishments, glad to know a woman who embodied all that Prudy could only dream about.

So she felt comfortable in being very frank with Lettie, and one sunny afternoon in June as they sat in the living room, sipping lemonade, she screwed up her courage to talk to her. Lettie was a solid, well built woman, somewhat taller than Prudy. Her hair was almost red and usually uncontrollable unless firmly anchored with combs and hairpins. She had a square face and clear blue eyes with a steady gaze, a handsome woman. Prudy felt safe with Lettie. After she had told her story, trying to cover the brutal parts which did not fool Lettie in the slightest, Lettie said,

"What you have told me does not come as a surprise, Prudy. I have seen how Lester treats you, and I've seen your bruises, too, no matter how you try to hide them. Why do you put up with it?"

Prudy sighed. "I love him and, besides, he's a good man, he really is, especially when he's sober."

"What kind of rationalization is that?" Lettie countered, her blue eyes flashing. "Why don't you just leave for awhile. Take the children and go visit your sister in Minnesota?"

"Oh Lester would never permit that."

"But you permit him to abuse you," she stated matter-of-factly.

Prudy had no immediate answer. She couldn't look Lettie in the eyes anymore. She said lamely, "He needs me here. He depends on me."

"Lettie snorted. "It would do him good to fend for himself for a few days. He'd appreciate you when you got back, you can be sure of that."

"He does scare me sometimes. I just wouldn't dare cross him."

"I can't help you, Prudy, because you don't seem to hear me. I think you should listen to someone in authority, someone who knows about these things, someone who knows people. I'm thinking of Pastor Kaufman."

"I couldn't talk to him. He knows me."

"Who better to be in a position to help, or to at least have some advice or words of comfort. I have to go into town Thursday. I'll stop by for you and we'll both go to see him."

Over Prudy's misgivings Lettie made plans and Thursday rolled around all too soon. Prudy dressed in one of her better frocks, one left over from her youth that she had seldom worn and which still fit; in fact, it was almost too loose on her thin frame. She put on a hat with a small brim and a pair of gloves and felt like she was preparing to go to a funeral. The boys were in the care of Mrs. Johnson, the entrepeneur, who still made her living assisting Dr. Walsh in birthing babies, and in tending to children when parents could not take them to any given event. Lettie's children were in her care, too, all at the Deters farm. Prudy's egg money paid for her services and there was an unspoken agreement that the women would not speak of Mrs. Johnson's engagement that afternoon.

She had not told Lester of her plans out of fear of what he might do and because it would probably shame him, something she had learned never to do. She would be back in plenty of time to fix supper. Mrs. Johnson was her usual capable self, telling her not to worry, that she would watch over these darling children. Both women trusted her and knew the children loved her and would mind.

In spite of all the preparations Prudy was apprehensive and feeling like a conspirator. She climbed into the Model T with less enthusiasm than when she joined Lettie and Meyer for Sunday services, but she waved gaily to the children and tried to appear happy to be going to town, something they accepted as what she did with Lettie on occasion. They drove off in a cloud of dust as Mrs. Johnson covered her head with her apron and chickens scattered in all directions, clucking alarm.

There were two churches in Spotswood in 1908, one which was the first one established there, an interdenominational protestant church, and one Catholic, which had been there only about ten years. Prudy had given up attending Mass in

Mobridge long ago, because Lester wouldn't take her and she had no way to go alone, and because the church held no inspiration or solace for her anymore. So, at Lettie's suggestion, she went with the Dannenbrings to the First Community Church, not without some objection from Lester, who finally agreed, providing she get home in time to fix his dinner. The weekly sojourn was uplifting, not necessarily because of the sermons, although the uncomplicated service of worship suited her, but because of the companionship of Lettie and her family, and in getting away from the burdens of her life even for a little while. She grew to look forward to her weekly release. Lester was left with the boys, but he didn't mind being in charge, once he got used to the routine.

Prudy sometimes worried about what he might be teaching them without her being there to soften his coarseness, but she said a prayer while she was at church and hoped it mattered.

The distance to Spotswood was not far and travel in the Model T was faster than by horse, and they were soon at the parsonage next to the First Community Church, a white clapboard building with a belfry and a cross on top, making it one of the tallest structures on the flat landscape. A few trees shaded the front yard. Lettie parked in what shade she could find and the two women walked to the door of the parsonage.

Prudy kept a few paces behind Lettie. "I'm so nervous. What on earth will I say to him?"

"Just tell him what's troubling you and ask him what you should do. Ministers are supposed to do these things. Their job is more than just taking up a collection. Now come on," she said decisively.

Their knock was answered by Mrs. Kaufman who still wore her apron, having just finished the dishes from the noon meal. She patted her hair, a bit damp from the warm June day, and asked them in. They were led to a sitting room and Mrs. Kaufman went to fetch her husband when she discovered it was not a social call. When Pastor Kaufman entered the room his presence did nothing to alleviate Prudy's anxiety. He was a big man, appearing bigger in the small room than when he spoke in the pulpit. She knew she should have known from her Sundays in church listening to his strong Dutch accent that she would be likely to get little actual comfort from this man. She had made a mistake in coming to him on such a personal matter, but it was too late to leave.

"Hello, ladies. What a pleasant surprise on such a warm day."

He had put on his suit coat and, even though the drapes gave a feeling of coolness in the room, it was a heavy coolness with no breeze to fan the air. His steel gray eyes were shaded by bushy brows that were beginning to gray. His generous head of hair was also gray at the temple and sideburns. His look was piercing and unsettling.

Would you care for a lemonade?"

She just wanted to run, but she shook her head and was glad to have Lettie say, "Pastor Kaufman, my friend Prudence Deters here has need of some advice on a matter of some delicacy. I feel I should wait in the other room."

Prudy opened her mouth to beg her to stay, but she rose and gave Prudy's arm a squeeze and left. Pastor Kaufman eased his big frame into a chair across the room and looked at his slight visitor with interest and curiosity. He remembered her as being rather new in the congregation and that her husband remained at home with the children on Sunday. He would get out to the Deters place soon and persuade the man to accompany his wife to church and bring the children to Sunday School.

"Well now, Mrs. Deters, how may I be of help? A church bazaar perhaps? A social to raise money for the Ladies Aid? I am always glad to lend my presence to these affairs."

Oh dear, how could she ever explain? She plunged ahead and said, "I haven't come for anything quite so grand, Pastor. You see —"

"Oh yes, Mrs. Dannenbring said it was a delicate matter. Are you troubled about something?"

"Yes, that's it, troubled. It's Lester, my husband."

"Oh yes, he doesn't come to church with you, does he? Well, I'll be happy to come out and talk with him."

He beamed at her, pleased with himself in having solved her problem. He was surprised to find out he hadn't.

"No, that isn't it. You see, Lester wouldn't set foot inside a church no matter what you said to him. But the thing is — Lester has a very bad temper, and sometimes he —"

"He uses foul language, he swears?"

"Well yes, he does that, but it's worse than that."

"Come now, Mrs. Deters, swearing is ugly, but it isn't a mortal sin."

"I'm afraid I'm not making myself clear, Pastor Kaufman. You see, Lester gets rather violent, and he drinks."

"I see. Perhaps I should still have a talk with him."

"Oh no, please don't. He'd hate that. And it would be unpleasant. Besides, he doesn't know I'm here and if he ever found out, he'd — well, he'd hit me."

"Surely you exaggerate, Mrs. Deters," he said smiling at her condescendingly.

This was impossible. How could she continue? He didn't understand at all. But, she would try to make him understand.

"No, I am not exaggerating. Lester hit me and has even knocked me down lots of times. I don't know why. I have tried to be a good wife. But I don't know what to do anymore." She sat in the chair, rigid, her back very straight. She was not going to cry.

"Have you thought about what it is that makes him hit you? What do you do to upset him so that he strikes out?"

Prudy looked at him dully. She wanted to go home. Pastor Kaufman cleared his throat and went on.

"Perhaps if you prayed about it, God will give you an answer. Come, let us kneel right now and we will pray together for repentance and forgiveness."

Stunned, she obediently knelt and bowed her head and heard only a steady droning of meaningless platitudes issuing from his mouth. Tears of frustration were released and lay on her cheeks in shame, which the good pastor took to mean that she had truly repented and that his task was done.

They rose and he clasped her clammy hands and said, "Surely God has granted you forgiveness. Go home now and be a good wife. Everything will be all right. God be with you."

She left the room swiftly and hardly looked at Lettie who hurried along behind her, while Mrs. Kaufman closed the door quietly behind them, puzzled at the behavior of their visitors.

"Prudy, what's the matter? What did he say?"

As she sobbed out her story in the car, Lettie got angrier and angrier. She started the ignition and left a cloud of dust in the ruts the tires made as she left the parsonage. By the time they got back to the farm Prudy had collected herself and Lettie had calmed down. Lettie was going to come in for a cup of coffee to discuss what had happened, but they were denied that comfort, because when they drove into the front yard they were surprised to find Lester there, standing with his hands on his hips, waiting for them. Lettie didn't get down, just called her children in to the car, and reluctantly left Prudy facing a furious Lester. Mrs. Johnson was gone.

"Where have you been with that woman all dolled up?"

"We just drove into Spotswood for a little while," she answered unevenly, still upset by what had happened.

"What for?" he demanded.

"We stopped to see Pastor Kaufman."

"You never asked me. Why didn't you tell me what you had up your sleeve?"

"Lettie and I just drove into Spotswood, that's all. I didn't spend any money."

"You left the boys all alone."

"Mrs. Johnson was here, you saw that. And I paid her from my egg money."

"You are to take care of our boys, not Mrs. Johnson. That is your job." He stared at her obvious distress. "What is it you're keeping from me? I have a right to know, Ja."

"Nothing, Lester, nothing at all."

"You've been crying. What the hell do you have to cry about?"

"I'm a little upset, that's all. The pastor wasn't much help."

"I coulda told you that. And what do you mean, help?" He was gripping her arm tightly. She couldn't look at him. She stammered, "I hoped he could help me to deal with you —"

His grip grew tighter, his face was dark, "What the hell are you talking about — deal with me?"

She cried out and tried to pull away from him and said, "Help me to be a better wife and not get you so mad all the time."

"You told that preacher things about us, about our business? You had no cause to do that." The fury in his face frightened her. The boys stood close together on the porch.

He kept a firm grip on her and pulled her up the front porch and into the front room where he roared his rage at her. He flung her to the sofa. His fist went back and he bashed it into her face again and again. When he had finished he spat at her and shouted to the boys who huddled in the doorway of the dining room, eyes wide in terror. Fred was screaming frantically. They scurried out of the way as their father swept toward them. Their happy afternoon was ruined and, once again, had been turned into a horrifying experience. Lester went to town. Prudy served a cold supper.

Prudy didn't attend church that Sunday. Her face was too puffy and discolored for her to leave the premises. When the Dannebrings drove up to fetch her they could see what had happened, despite Prudy's futile efforts to disguise Lester's handiwork and her refusal to leave the porch to come to the car to explain. Lettie promised to come by to see her the next day.

The following Sunday Prudy went to church with them as usual. She didn't really know why, perhaps just to get away, maybe for the consoling words from the Bible that Pastor Kaufman read, maybe for a favorite hymn. She loved "God Will Take Care of You." She needed the atmosphere of the church, the safety it promised. She wore her hat with a dark veil which she kept close over her face to hide the remnants of her healing. Then the service ended and the congregation was leaving. She tried to avoid Pastor Kaufman as he stood at the door greeting the parishioners. She didn't want to shake his hand and have to look into his smiling face. But he saw her and was about to greet her warmly, but did not. He was mortified to observe what the veil could not completely conceal and to realize his awful error in judgement.

The Crawford Sisters

CHAPTER NINE

The Crawford Sisters

Cecelia and Penelope Crawford were sisters who had traveled with their parents to Dakota Territory with Patrick and Molly Malone thirty-three years before in 1875. Their parents died very soon thereafter and the sisters lived modestly in a small house in Spotswood. They were spinsters in their late sixties that year of 1908. They knew everybody and everything about them and were the bane of anyone who tried to keep a secret. They were inseparable; where there was one, there was also the other.

Cecelia was the eldest by a few years and had assumed her rightful role as decision maker long before the turn of the century. Penelope was glad to not have the responsiblity of making up her mind about troublesome details, so the two of them got along admirably to the point of nearly knowing what the other was thinking. Their clothing was dated and they were in no hurry to catch up with the times, fashion-wise. As those who could afford such luxuries displayed the changes in style — most of which were acquired from boxes of castoff clothing from better fixed relatives from the east — the sisters kept to sedate, dated attire, including bonnets neatly tied under their chins, regarding the shorter, less cumbersome skirts and looser clothing for ease of movement as improper and sometimes even scandalous. They wore gloves whenever they left the house and carried drawstring purses which contained a few coins, a comb and a handstitched handkerchief. They occupied the same pew in the First Community Church every Sunday and on holidays; were active members of the Ladies Aid, more often than not to the chagrin of the other ladies; did charity work with modesty augmented with a certain amount of superiority, deeming such deeds a matter of Christian duty; and had a strict schedule which governed their lives and gave them a profound feeling of security. Their lives had purpose.

Cecelia was taller than Penelope and carried herself with a regal air, never forgetting her background nor letting anyone else forget it, but which most had in fact forgotten, if they could remember in the first place. She kept her colorless hair in a tight bun at the back of her neck held in place with the jeweled combs of her mother, which was always aimed above the heads of the other people in the community. Her pale blue eyes did not overlook a detail and her thin mouth was set in resgination at mankind's imminent decline despite her valiant efforts to lead along the correct path. Her arrival often struck terror on whomever she chose to come calling. She loved her sister, Penelope, and was glad they were still together despite their advancing years in the harsh land of the Dakotas, and because Cecilia simply needed someone pliant enough to tolerate her bossing and Penelope was perfect for that purpose.

Penelope was smaller boned and fair of face, favoring youthful ringlets to frame her hazel eyes and a flowered hat to set it off and to cover the thin lines from uncomplimentary light, looking every inch the aged belle. Her cupid's bow mouth was usually pursed in a serious expression as she carried out Cecelia's orders. She could not function without Cecelia, simply could not cope all alone. Her wardrobe was more feminine than Cecelia's, but she had to admit that Cecelia had excellent taste in clothes, in what would wear well and stand the test of time.

They kept their small house clean and tidy and had a small garden in the back to provide them with necessities; the surplus was canned and preserved and stored in a tiny basement on wooden shelves. "Waste not, want not," was Cecelia's stern reminder. She did the cleaning to make sure that every corner was bereft of dust, and she did the washing because it was hard work and she was bigger and stronger than her sister. Penelope had ironed and cooked and baked, chores which Cecelia didn't have an aptitude for and which Penelope enjoyed doing, puttering and humming as she worked.

They didn't seem to mind the lack of male companionship in their meager lives. Both had had a beau years ago, but they never married, not understanding that the customs of the south with long courtships and tedious manners were out of place on the wide open prairie where feelings ran high and life was faster paced. Any men interested soon lost interest in the rigid lives of the sisters. During their long evenings in the lamplight they would sew or embroider or read until their eyes got tired, interspersing the quiet with reminiscenses about their younger days, or with timely gossip which kept them attuned to reality. Sometimes only the tick of the mantle clock broke the stillness, with each sister lost in thought.

Since the Crawford sisters had established their roots with a long history in the small community of Spotswood they were a familiar part of every event, every church benefit, school play or recitation, every holiday observance. They were accepted as a part of the lives of the people who lived there. The sisters did not exactly intrude, but they were always there and they made their presence felt. They would not be excluded nor would the good folks consider barring them from any affair. Everyone knew the sisters were lonely and enjoyed being where there was activity. It was the substance of their social life. Sometimes they were merely endured, as at funerals, whether they were friends of the deceased or not. At every funeral the Crawford sisters sat in their pew dressed in their best black finery with veils covering their grieving faces. At the lunch afterwards they were first in line to fill their plates, not having to bother with supper that night. If they heard comments about this practice they elected to overlook them. After all, they knew proper etiquette. Their place was with the bereaved, with those who needed their comfort. Their charity belonged to the community of Spotswood.

So, when Prudy heard a knock at the front door that warm day in August she knew it was not an ordinary visitor, since most people used the back door. Company always came to the front door. She smoothed her rumpled dress, tried to cover the hole in her stocking, checked the laces on her worn shoes and hoped her hair wasn't too wilted, then took a deep breath and wondered if she had any cookies left to serve with coffee. When she opened the door there stood Cecelia and Penelope Crawford dressed in their fancy, outdated clothes with drawstring purses in their gloved hands in the heat of the afternoon sun beating on the front porch. Prudy didn't know whether to laugh or utter a groan, but manners prevailed and she greeted them cordially and ushered them into the front room. The boys were out somewhere playing and Fred was sleeping, thank goodness. Maybe the sisters wouldn't stay long.

Cecelia spoke, "Good afternoon, Mrs. Deters. We hope it is not inconvenient for us to call."

Penelope said nothing but smiled sweetly, her ringlets bobbing.

Prudy said, "No, of course not, please come in." She motioned them to be seated and asked, "Will you have some coffee? I have some on the stove."

"Yes, thank you," said Cecelia with a proprietary air.

Prudy excused herself and hurried to the hot kitchen. The coffee pot was always at the back of the stove, with water added to the grounds now and then during the day, until it turned a dark, murky black, but also turned a delicious, savory flavor to most of the taste buds of the people on the prairie. The heat at the back of the stove reflected the remnants of the fire that had cooked the noon meal, and the coffee was still hot. She searched the cookie can and found three sugar cookies the boys had not absconded with, put them on her best dish and poured coffee into three of the good cups, the ones that still had handles and saucers. She climbed up on a chair to reach the top shelf of the cupboard where serving dishes that were seldom used were kept and got down a silver tray that had been her mother's. It was tarnished, but she laid a clean linen napkin on it, placed the cups of coffee, some cream and sugar and the cookies, along with demitasse spoons that were stored on the top shelf with the tray, and carried it with as much grace was she could muster into the front room where her guests were engaged in quiet conversation, although a bit animated, which ceased as she entered.

"I hope the coffee isn't too strong, but there is fresh cream and some sugar if it is," Prudy said.

"Thank you, Mrs. Deters. I'm sure it will be quite satisfactory," replied Cecilia.

Penelope smiled and bobbed.

Prudy glanced around the room and noted with relief that she had had the good sense to tidy up some that day with everyone out of her way. She had planned to take a nap herself, but there was company to tend to and, besides, she could use a cup of coffee.

"Aren't you having a cookie, Mrs. Deters?" inquired Penelope in a lilting voice.

"No, I don't believe I will. It hasn't been long since we had dinner, but please help yourself."

She hoped they wouldn't want more cookies, because there weren't anymore, but she couldn't say that. Thank goodness the ladies were of an era when good manners dictated no such inquiries. She relaxed a little, but she was curious as to why they had come to call. Their visit to the Deters house was a first. She wasn't sure if she should regard it as an honor which had been postponed until now. They sipped their coffee, made small talk, and when the cookies had been devoured — Penelope had been convinced to take the last one — Cecelia cleared her throat, folded the napkin on her lap, and looked directly at Prudy through her spectacles.

"Thank you, Mrs. Deters, that was very pleasant. Tell me, where are your children? You have boys, do you not?"

"Yes, we have four boys, Miss Crawford. The oldest three are out playing somewhere and my youngest is upstairs taking a nap. I enjoy these less hectic afternoons."

"I'm sure you do."

"It will soon be harvest time again, and then there will be a lot for me to do with little time in the afternoons."

What did they want? She didn't know what to say next. Cecelia Crawford, it turned out, had plenty to say.

"Mrs. Deters, we come on a matter of some unpleasantness. My sister, Penelope, and I find it necessary to bring to your attention the rash actions of your boys."

"Oh dear. What have they done?" Prudy's heart sank.

"It is difficult to put the problem into words, having been brought up in a more cultural environment, you see, but this unpleasantness has continued past our tolerance for it. So-called boyish pranks have turned into — an unpleasantness."

"I'm certainly sorry if our boys have caused you any trouble, Miss Crawford. You must tell me what they have done."

Penelope bowed her head and twiddled her thumbs. Her face had turned pink. At a look from Cecelia she straightened and tried to smile.

Cecelia continued, "You see, Mrs. Deters, Penelope and I have an ordered life and that order has been threatened by the actions of your boys, especially the biggest one."

"That's John," Prudy said.

"John. The other two are undoubtedly his brothers then."

"The three of them are always together, yes."

"Well, Mrs. Deters, I must insist that you make them stop bothering us."

"I will, Miss Crawford, I surely will, but what is it they do?"

Even Cecelia found it awkward to proceed. She stiffened her back, looked sternly through her wire-rimmed spectacles beneath her brimmed hat which was set squarely in the middle of her head, and said, "Mrs. Deters, those boys lie in wait for Penelope and me every morning and sometimes at night when we are obliged to perform our physical duties."

"I don't understand."

"On our way from the house and back we are taunted by your boys, and it is humiliating to say the least.''

"On your way from the house — and back?" Prudy just didn't see what they were getting at.

Cecelia saw she wasn't making herself clear. Penelope's face was growing pinker by the minute.

"On our way from the house to — the small house."

"The outhouse?" Prudy exclaimed and turned red herself trying to contain her unexpected mirth.

"A primitive word but, yes, that is when your boys shout their remarks to us."

Prudy took a deep breath that shook from held in laughter and said, "My dear Miss Crawford, I apologize for my sons. I didn't know. They will be dealt with, and you can be sure it won't happen again. I am so sorry about this."

Their task completed, the sisters rose, expressed their thanks for a lovely afternoon, and left by the front door to get into their surrey, another possession that had seen better days.

Prudy closed the door against the western sun and started to giggle. She clasped her hands over her mouth to keep from waking Fred, because if she really let go she would have him wailing in no time. The outhouse! Good Lord, she could just picture it. But, of course, it wasn't right. They shouldn't do such naughty things; they could not permit it. She would speak to Lester when he came in for supper.

Lester had no reservations about expressing his emotions and roared with laughter as he slapped the supper table, making the boys laugh with him. Fred banged the table with his spoon, not wanting to be left out. Even Prudy had to grin, but she knew that the boys must be reprimanded.

"Now, Lester, that's enough. It is sort of funny, but it's not right." She looked at each boy in turn. "You all know it's wrong to do such a thing. And you must stop. You are not to tease the Crawford sisters ever again. That's too far away to be from home anyway. Isn't that so, Lester?"

"I suppose so, but boys will be boys," he said with an impish look.

She looked at him sternly, risking contradicting him, but he backed down and spoke to John.

"Was this your idea?"

"Yeah," John said proudly, with a sheepish grin.

"Well now, I know that must have been a heck of a lot of fun, but you're big enough to know that everybody uses the outhouse, even those old biddies, Ja."

"Lester!"

"Well, ain't it a fact?" he replied. Then to the boys, he asked "Just what was it you said to them ladies?" He had a queer look on his face.

Chester spoke up eagerly, "We just hollared, 'Do you hafta go real bad?' when they went in and 'Do ya feel all better now?' when they came out, mostly, that's all."

"Just don't do it no more, hear?"

The boys agreed to stay away from the Crawford sisters. Prudy yearned for school to begin again, which wouldn't be until September after the harvest. Lester didn't see what all the fuss was about, but he was in a genial mood with a good crop that year, and maybe Prudy was right in teaching the boys some manners, more than he had.

That night he made love to Prudy as was his right, one that he exercised almost nightly, and declared his love for her, saying he would not be so hard on her in the future, and then he laughed so that the bed springs jiggled alarmingly.

"If that ain't the hog's jowls about them Crawford sisters." And with a guffaw. "I wonder if they have a one-hole or two."

They were interrupted by Alan, who stood uncertainly in the doorway and asked, "I guess they didn't find the garter snake yet, huh?"

CHAPTER TEN

Mary Elizabeth

Prudy lifted the ax and brought it down with a resounding thump on the Hubbard squash which she had positioned on the old tree stump. It split neatly in two. Prudy was uncomfortable and cross. She was in her fifth month and in no mood for company. Still, there was a pang of guilt. She should be happy that Patience and her family would be spending Thanksgiving with them, but she had absolutely no place to put them up and she felt bad about that, because it was only fitting and proper that a host should provide a comfortable place for guests. But the house was full to bursting with her own family. She hadn't seen her sister for years, not since their mother had died, and she really wanted to see her and Lars and Millicent, who must be eleven by now. Nevertheless, she fretted that her beautiful sister should see her in such a state with four rowdy boys and Lester with his unpredictable temperament, and she knew there was no love lost between her and Lester. Knowing both men, Prudy knew they would discuss business, although the mercantile business and the business of farming, which no one regarded as a business, were far removed from the other. Lester's bravado would carry him through any discussion of how best to make a dollar, and he had indeed done surprisingly well in that regard, having become a savvy farmer and a good provider, but frugal to the point of stinginess, as Lettie often told her. Lester was rough around the edges, as opposed to Lars' polished ways, but the end result was the same, being successful at what they did for a living. So, perhaps everyone would get along and the holiday would go well. Wisely, Lars had decided to take a room for sleeping in Spotswood at the boarding house. That way there would be no crowding and the days could be devoted to visiting; besides, Lars could easily afford the cost, a cost Lester would never consider. Their company would be there for only a week because of the uncertain weather in November and, also, Patience wanted to be home in plenty of time to prepare for the Christmas season. The Hansons of New Ulm, Minnesota, were prominent residents and had many social obligations.

Thanksgiving dinner necessitated pie. The Deters' garden which Prudy tended daily had yielded more than enough produce that year to see them through the winter easily, and the root cellar was filled with Ball canning jars full of tomatoes, beets, dill pickles, green beans, corn, and peas. Those provisions, along with a store of potatoes and carrots and mounds of squash, which had literally taken over the garden, filled the cellar, together with smoked meat which gave the cellar a pungent aroma that clearly satisfied Lester and proved to all what a fine, successful farmer he was. He gave Prudy no credit for the long hours spent in the garden all summer, the tedious hours of canning in the fall, and the annual butchering, sandwiched in between the harvest. Prudy was grateful for their store of food and the independence it signified, but she would have appreciated a word of praise. She tried so hard to please Lester and was disappointed when in the pleasing there came no approval. Lettie would comfort her, telling her that the women understood and they knew how hard Prudy worked. Prudy acknowledged that it would have to suffice.

Lester kept his barrels of home brewed beer in the root cellar and often after one of Prudy's company meals he would take the men down to sample it. It was a secret recipe from the old country, he would say. Prudy didn't approve, because it was Sunday, the day for company, and most of their guests had come to dinner from church. In addition, Lester didn't know when to quit. His one drink meant a minimum of three or four, and usually his guests kept up with him, and soon there was a noisy session of drinking in the root cellar for a couple of hours. Prudy's dilemma was solved by the wives, who began to refuse invitations to the Deters for Sunday dinner. Company dinners were now few and far between, and Prudy was relieved in a way, except now she was isolated, because there were no invitations to the Deters. Invitations were reciprocated and, even though they were issued by Prudy and refused, the refusals automatically meant none would be forthcoming to the Deters family.

Prudy sighed in frustration and continued the task of dividing the large squash. Hubbard squashes were big, heavy, knobby green vegetables that yielded a large quantity of golden pulp. But to get to the delicious insides was a test of one's strength. A knife just wouldn't do the job. It could not penetrate the hard rind, so Prudy had become adept at using the trusty ax that had rested in the tree stump since her father had used it. She even chopped wood when she had to. For a petite woman the secret was in the momentum of the swing. Although Prudy was strong and wiry, she was small, and results depended on the follow through, so the ax did its work with a well placed, perfectly timed whack. She divided the halves with another hefty blow and stopped, realizing she was too tired to divide the squash further. She decided to bake the four large pieces instead of boiling several small ones. Baking would not require extracting the pulp from the hard rind beforehand. Her energy just wasn't up to par. She leaned on the ax handle and held her aching back.

The pregnancy was unexpected and this one was different. She had felt unwell for five months, was sick in bed too often, and her disposition had been strained to the limit. Lester was elated at the prospect of another child, a boy of course. Didn't he always give her boys? He even tolerated her crankiness sometimes, joshing her out of her snits, lifting her in the air like he used to while she voiced her objection. But she tried not to annoy him because of his unpredictable ways, how he could be loving and charming one minute, especially in front of others, and the next minute become a beast who lashed out at her, sometimes with his fists. In the first years he was always contrite and begged her forgiveness, but in the decade of their marriage, that attitude had vanished and their roles had reversed, with Prudy asking Lester's forgiveness for getting him all riled up. Then she would stay away from others until the purple marks faded. Lester was a jealous man and would not overlook even Prudy's friendly smile at a man from a neighboring farm, considering it a violation of their wedding vows.

"You shame me, woman. Stop your flirtatious ways, or I'll have to teach you, Ja."

The boys knew what their father was capable of and obeyed him without question. John aped his father's ways, but stopped short of sassing his mother. He was a big nine year old and the pride of his father. Alan was older than his seven years and worried about his mother, trying his best to ease her distress. Chester, the five year old, was too busy keeping up with his brothers and using up every ounce of energy daily to realize that the state of affairs with his parents was not normal. Fred's world was the family and he accepted whatever occurred as being the usual run of things. They were a comfort to Prudy; tucking them in safely at night gave her the courage to go on. Things were sure to get better soon.

She gathered the pieces of squash in her apron and carried the heavy portions into the house. She decided to bake them at once. Then the tender, golden insides could easily be removed and used for several pies, more savory than pumpkin. She scooped out what seeds she could, cleaned the pieces and put them into the oven which had been heating while she worked with the ax. Panting from the exertion of the morning, she sat in one of the wobbly wooden kitchen chairs and looked out the sunny window. She had risen early, as usual, and with her work done she enjoyed another cup of coffee. It didn't taste as good these days, and she was more hungry all the time than anything else, so she poured herself a glass of foamy milk provided by the few cows they still had, and chewed on a piece of cold toast left on Fred's plate. It was a pleasant day for November, sunny and warm, with no sign of the approaching winter. It reminded her of another sunny day the previous June. She was filled with a glow just thinking of it. She didn't dare think of it unless she was alone, lest her thoughts show on her face, because her thoughts were of a secret she had told no one, not even Lettie.

In June, 1909, she had just hung out the wash which was blowing and drying in a light breeze. Lester had informed her that he had to go into Mobridge for some supplies — parts for the threshing machine, twine, machine oil, and such — and that he was taking all of the boys as a special treat. Fred was then three and old enough to tag along and was thrilled to be included. He had always made a terrible fuss when he couldn't go where his older brothers went. It was an unexpected respite for Prudy, a treat for her as well, and she sent her men off merrily with the boys' excited voices fading in the distance. They were going by team and buggy, which meant they would be gone for most of the day. She didn't even have to pack a lunch; Lester said they would get something to eat in Mobridge, a decided luxury. He was in one of his rare good moods. Prudy had learned to make the most of it when she had some time to herself, with no one to account to. He seldom left her alone for very long, so to have the entire day gave her such a lift that she had trouble to not sound too delighted. She simply cautioned the boys to mind their manners and to behave themselves and tried to believe them when they assured her they would be very good.

All that time to herself. What should she do, or not do? The possibilities were so numerous she couldn't decide. In the end she finished the washing still in the tubs on the back porch, emptied the dirty water and dragged a tub into the kitchen. She heated water in a copper boiler on the cook stove for a bath. There would be time for a leisurely soak without interruption or fear of a small boy coming into the kitchen for a drink of water. As the water heated she undid her long dark hair and brushed and combed it until her scalp tingled and her hair glistened. Then she pinned it to the top of her head and stepped into the tub of warm water and leaned back for a few minutes with her eyes closed. The wash tubs were a gift from Lester a few years before. He made sure folks knew how generous he was to buy her two new cast iron wash tubs from Sears, Roebuck & Co. Such a suitable, versatile addition to their property was a feather in his cap. They could be used for doing the washing and, with two tubs, the boys could take their weekly baths two at a time. He had beamed with pride and she smiled, remembering. For her part, she was grateful to have a more modern convenience, as her chores grew harder with each passing year. Four growing boys meant a lot of extra work, not less.

She soaped herself and rinsed off and stepped from the tub, refreshed and glowing with cleanliness and serenity. On that dazzling June day she was very daring, donning only a clean chemise for comfort; who was to see her? She left off her cumbersome shoes and went outside to check the washing. She squiggled the soft dirt of the yard between her toes beneath the clotheslines as the clean clothes billowed in the breeze. The washing could hang for awhile. She stood beside the fresh smelling wash as the wind swirled her chemise around her slim body, surveying the flat land with the sun causing every detail to stand out in bright relief. A feeling of contentment swept over her. She decided to take a walk.

She felt as ripe as the growing, budding grain. There was a meadow to the northeast that was never planted because of the irregular roll of the land and of rocks, which some mysterious force had dumped there eons before. There had been rocks around the house, too, in the beginning, but they had been collected at the edge of the clearing on the south by her father. The meadow held a fascination for Prudy, because of the break in the monotonous bleakness in the land, but it was an irritant to Lester, who regarded the meadow as useless land, unproductive and an insult to his endeavor to reap every inch of soil. To Prudy it was a bit of beauty in the unforgiving land. It had remained untouched and contained tall prairie grass where sturdy roots grasped the earth firmly, roots which were longer than the shoots above them. Wild roses grew there, delicate pink roses with spiny stems and scratchy leaves, taken for granted as wild prairie flowers and of little value outside of providing a welcome splash of color. The meadow was Prudy's refuge when she had time to be there, and this is where she walked, soaking up the sun, reveling in her loosed bonds, able to be herself if she could, in fact, remember just who she was. The gentle breeze blew her long hair away from her face and her chemise clung to her body. She walked briskly, savoring the fresh, sunny air. The quiet contained the song of a meadow lark like a firefly in a glass jar. She was an embryo in a cocoon, enjoying the solitary time that was special to her and uniquely her own. The world was shut out. The buzz of an unseen insect contentedly going about its business gave an underlying cadence to the existence that was hers. Elated, she began to run, abandoning herself to a freedom that only she understood. She whirled in ecstatic circles, her chemise brushing the tall grass; she flung out her arms and hummed a tune with no melody; round and round she twirled as the balmy breeze caressed her, until she collapsed in a giddy heap in the waving grass. Her arms were outflung, her hair was in a fan about her happy, flushed face, once again youthful with the daily care erased, at least for a little while. She closed her eyes as her breathing slowed and was drifting off to sleep when she sensed a presence.

She opened her eyes and looked upon the most beautiful man she had ever seen. She blinked to make sure he was not an apparition. He was perfectly formed with broad shoulders on a tall frame, long legs in trousers with the legs rolled up past his ankles. He was barefoot. His shirt was faded with cut-off sleeves and he was bronzed from the sun up to his hair which gleamed golden in the brilliant light. Very blue eyes looked at her in admiration over high cheek bones. His generous mouth was smiling and he stood with his legs spread, his hands on his slim hips. A knapsack lay on the ground beside him. She sat up hastily.

"Don't be alarmed, Mam," the golden man said. "My name is Eric Johansen. I'm passing through these parts looking for a job. I was on my way to that farm over there — must be yours — when I saw you. What a vision you were, running and dancing. I was captivated just watching you. May I inquire as to your name?"

The realization came to Prudy that she was sitting in her chemise with a man she had never seen before. Her hands fluttered to her bosom and she stammered, "Prudence Deters, Mrs. Lester Deters. And yes, that is our farm. I was just —"

Eric smiled broadly as if to say that he knew what she was doing. He walked the short distance to her and sat beside her. Prudy started to get up, thoroughly flustered.

"Please don't leave, Mrs. Deters. It's very nice here, don't you think? What a perfect day to be alive. Reminds me of home."

Prudy's look led him to explain. "I come from Sweden. I'm a good farm worker with much experience. Do you need a hand?" His deep blue eyes penetrated her soul.

"No. No, I'm afraid not. My husband manages just fine until harvest time."

He continued. "Ahh. Well then, I'll just have to keep moving." But he made no move to leave. Prudy could find no words. Eric went on. "I am in your America at the insistence of my family who felt I needed some exposure to life, to rough it a bit. They feel I am a lazy one, with no purpose."

"You have a command of the language, Mr. Johansen."

He laughed. "I've had enough schooling; I should speak it well. I spent as many years in college as my family would tolerate, then they sent me to an uncle's farm in Sweden where I received my experience. You are sure you cannot use my services?"

"I'm sure."

"You look very fetching, Mrs. Deters. What a fortunate man your husband is." He moved closer and she felt his warm, sweet breath. "You inspire the poetry that your famous writers are known for. Do you like poetry, Mrs. Deters?"

"Please, Mr. Johansen, you must leave me. My husband will be home soon."

"I don't think so. You would not be dancing in the meadow in your underclothes if he was." He smiled softly at her.

Prudy blushed and tried to get up, but he took her by the shoulders and kissed her. His kiss was tender and he held her gently. When he released her she was trembling. Why wasn't she afraid? She tried to sound angry.

"Mr. Johansen, you had no right to do that. You must —"

He enveloped her in his arms and pressed her to the fragrant ground and kissed her again and again. She grew limp. What was happening to her? Who was this man? What was he doing and why was she permitting it? He drew her chemise from her and traced her body with his smooth fingers. She quivered and could not move. He removed his shirt and pants and lay beside her in the waving grass. Fluffy clouds drifted lazily overhead in the blue sky. The meadow lark warbled its melody. The insect's buzzing grew to a crescendo of passion in Prudy's ears, and she went to him. There were no words of everlasting love, just a mutual acceptance of the natural progression to the union of their bodies in the euphoric setting. Eric loved her softly, gently and thoroughly and she was completely pliant in her surrender. She ceased to wonder why.

They slept and when she awoke he and his knapsack were gone. Had it all been a dream? Surely this could not have happened. Such things just didn't happen, only in fairytales. But she knew that it had. She slipped on her chemise and got up. Something fell to the ground. She picked up a photograph the size of a post card. The likeness of Eric Johansen standing in an expansive yard with a fancy house in the background, surrounded by beautiful landscaping, smiled at her. He held the reins of a horse. She turned it over and read, scrawled in a careless script: "Your Ralph Waldo Emerson said it all with these sweet lines, my dear Prudence: 'Give all to love; Obey thy heart . . . Nothing refuse.' Forever, Eric."

She clasped it to her, shaded her eyes and looked around her in every direction. There was no trace of her phantom lover.

The position of the sun indicated that it was past noon. She hurried back to the house. How odd that she should feel so radiant, like hugging herself. Lester had never made her feel like that, even when Prudy first loved him. Lester was a vigorous lover and a frequent one. But Eric had made her feel very different. Maybe it was because she was a part of the union, of their loving, not merely the object. That was probably the most profound thought Prudy ever had, but it pleased her on that heavenly day. It was a pleasure that she would have to make last for the rest of her life. She was guiltily happy and she would keep her secret. Strangely, she didn't feel obliged to berate herself for such an indiscretion, such a blatant breach of her marriage vows. Lester would never know. No one would ever know. Maybe Eric would come back in the fall for the harvest. Could she manage that? She had no idea where he was heading. Maybe she would see him again sometime. But she knew she would not.

When Lester and the boys returned from Mobridge Prudy had the washing in off the line, folded and put away and a fine supper on the table. She was humming "In the Sweet Bye and Bye" when they walked in the door.

"Well, now, that's what a man likes to find when he comes home, Ja," boomed Lester, while the boys crowded around telling her of all the wondrous things they had done in Mobridge. Prudy just smiled and fed them their supper.

A few days later Lettie paid her a visit and remarked about a nice looking Swede who has stopped and inquired about work. They were sorry they couldn't help him out, but it was too early in the season. Had Prudy seen him?

She answered, not looking at Lettie, "It must have been the day we were all away from the house." It wasn't a lie, but not exactly the truth.

That was five months ago and Prudy's condition was showing. The glorious feeling that one day in June had left with her was never to be recaptured. It wasn't long after her romantic encounter in the meadow that she knew she was with child again. She was sure it wasn't Lester's; somehow she just knew it wasn't. She was nervous about that fact. What if the baby looked so different from the others with their brown hair and brown eyes that it was obvious to everyone that Lester had been betrayed? What if it was a girl? What would Lester do? How could she possibly explain? The worrisome thoughts compounded the pain and her troublesome pregnancy. And now Patience and her family were coming.

They all met the train in Mobridge when they arrived and the happy greetings made Prudy forget her apprehensions for a time. Lars rented a surrey and they proceeded to Spotswood and got them settled at the boarding house before they drove to the farm. Prudy decided to forget her worries and enjoy the visit.

It helped to have Patience around. Prudy admired her younger sister, so beautiful like their mother, only tall like their father. Her perfectly coiffed hair and well made clothes made heads turn. Millicent was a carbon copy, frail and very prim, dressed in flouncy dresses and petticoats. Her blond hair was curled in precise ringlets which hung down around her pretty head. She was fastidious and was careful to step carefully in the farmyard, not wishing to dirty her daintily shod feet. The boys were in awe of such a delicate creature and didn't know quite what to do with her. Millicent was just as much in awe of her rugged country cousins, not having been around boys much. The boys had a fast course in proper decorum around young ladies and Millicent had her fine edges roughed up a bit.

Millicent always entered the house through the front door, as that was what they did in New Ulm. On the day before Thanksgiving she came in quietly and slid into a chair, clutching her soiled coat to her, her bonnet askew on her mussed curls.

Prudy and Patience were in the front room going through some picture albums.

"What is it, dear?" inquired Patience.

Millicent merely hung her head, looking miserable.

"Take off your coat if you're going to stay inside."

Millicent said nothing and remained seated. The women looked at her, puzzled.

"Is something wrong?" asked Prudy.

Still no answer from the child. They put down the albums and Patience went to her daughter. She removed her bonnet and cupped her face in her hand. Tears rolled down the small face.

"Why, Milly, what's wrong? What is it? And what is that awful smell?" She unbuttoned her rumpled coat and stepped back in disgust. "Oh."

Millicent burst into tears. "It was those boys, Mother. I didn't do it. Honestly, I didn't."

Prudy got up to see what the fuss was all about and she, too, recoiled at the odor. The front of Millicent's frilly frock and her expensive coat were covered with what looked like a splash of brown something. The odor left no doubt as to what the stain was. Prudy turned and strode to the back door.

"Boys, come in here this instant," she shouted.

Four shamefaced boys made their appearances at the back door, shuffling their feet and looking at the rag rug. They seldom had to face their mother's wrath, but they were experiencing it now. Patience and Millicent stood in the doorway to the kitchen, Millicent's face rosy from shame and the cold. Patience was waiting for an explanation, as was Prudy, who didn't think it was the least bit funny.

"John, tell me what happened. How did Millicent get that manure on the front of her?"

John tried to bluff it out as his father would, but he was only a little boy, despite his size, and words wouldn't come. It was Alan who spoke.

"We were just showing her the barn and all the cows and horses and chickens. She wasn't watching where she was going, bein' so particular about where she was steppin', and old Bessie stepped back and — she just got too close. She got sorta dirty, I guess."

Millicent's voice rose to a shriek of rage and she stamped her feet. "You are nasty, dirty boys and I don't want to play with you anymore." Patience hustled her off to the sink.

Prudy said sternly, "Take off your wraps and go on up to your rooms until I tell you to come down. No roughhousing now. Scoot!"

They scooted, grateful to have gotten off so easily. Patience removed Millicent's clothes, discarded the soiled dress which the child declared she would never, ever wear again, and washed her down from head to foot until they couldn't smell anything but the strong soap. Patience promised she would salvage the wool coat, but Millicent wasn't convinced until her mother let her cover herself with some of her lavender scent, just to make sure the smell was all gone. They didn't relate the incident to Lester, although Prudy was sure that Lars got the whole story. Supper passed without mishap, and Lester commented on the good conduct of his boys at the table with a young lady present.

The Thanksgiving feast was a success. There was no turkey, but plenty of fried chicken, mashed potatoes, corn and peas, with tangy cucumber pickles, home baked bread, thick whipped cream on the fragrant golden squash pie. The children were friends again, with Millicent holding the upper hand, and the dining room was filled with good spirits and laughter. Prudy's discomfort and worry lessened and she was thankful that everything went so smoothly and that there were enough pieces left of their mother's china for the grown-ups to make the table look nice.

But the company and extra work tired her. She welcomed the relief that Patience's presence provided by way of getting her off her feet. They had long talks and rememberings of their childhod. But Patience was concerned. She could see her sister's distress.

"Prudy, are you sure you're all right? You look so tired. And now another baby on the way. Really, how can you possibly care for another child?"

She sighed and replied, "You know what Lester says, 'There's always room for one more.' I'm fine, really." This was said half-heartedly. "I'm just older, that's all, and the four boys do take a lot out of me."

"What do you need? What can I get you and the baby?"

"Oh nothing, Patience. You know how Lester is, so proud and all. He doesn't take kindly to anybody giving me things."

"That's too bad, because I've brought you a present, and he doesn't need to know. What he doesn't know won't hurt him."

Prudy brightened. She got few presents. Patience handed her a shiny box tied with blue ribbon. "Go on, open it," she urged with a pleased smile.

Prudy pulled the pretty ribbon and lifted the cover of the box. Inside were personal items, dainty things any woman would love, a pearl handled brush with comb to match; a file with a fancy handle for her ragged nails; a buffer to make them shine; ribbons for her thick hair; a lace handkerchief; and an elegant bottle filled with soothing lotion for her skin. Prudy gasped in pleasure.

"Oh Patience, thank you! How wonderful of you to give me such beautiful things. I love them."

She gave her a hug and kissed Patience's cheek. Her face was aglow with delight at the gift just for her and her needs, lovely feminine things that were not easily come by on the prairie and, although the gifts in the shiny box were out of place in their humble surroundings and would be sparingly used, they were just what Prudy needed to lift her spirits. When she was alone she placed the box in her drawer in the antique dresser underneath her worn clothing, but not before she tucked Eric's photograph beneath the lace handkerchief where it would be safe from all eyes but her own.

Patience was also concerned about the condition of the family home. She was not blind to the changes in the home that had once been hers. She saw the gradual decline, the rundown condition of the house and out-buildings. They all needed repair and a coat of paint. The curtains were tawdry and should be replaced. Furniture was tattered and the sturdy pieces left by their parents had long ago been treated badly. Her heart went out to her sister. How hard her life was, and Patience could not make it easier. She despaired of the future; how could Prudy manage with another baby coming? What should be viewed as a welcome blessed event would surely only plunge the family into further decline and perhaps bitterness. What could be done? She was glad her gift had brought Prudy such joy. Her Christmas box would contain more practical items.

All too soon it was time for the Hansons to return to New Ulm. The visit had been mutually agreeable, with Lester on his good behavior. Patience urged them to return the visit. They had plenty of room and would love to have them come. The sisters' parting was harder than their first one and they promised to write regularly.

In March, 1910, during a bitter cold spell heralding the end of winter on the prairie, Prudy's time came and she gave birth to a baby girl. Dr. Walsh was worried about his patient and had stayed the night, wanting to be there when Prudy needed him, not daring to take a chance on the weather. Lester wasn't happy with the arrangement, but Dr. Walsh ignored him the best he could, which wasn't easy, because Lester harped about the intrusion into his life, and that such things always cost him money, and he worked hard for what little he had. Dr. Walsh knew that he had enough to see to his family and he also knew that Lester kept his money somewhere on the premises, not trusting banks, despite advice to the contrary and to Prudy's entreaties to put his money in the bank in Spotswood where it would be safe and earn a little interest. Not even she knew where he kept his stash and she didn't know how much he had hidden away, just that there was money elsewhere in a secret hiding place and that when she had to ask for some it was available, even though grudgingly handed over.

Prudy's labor was longer than the others and more painful, with her strength sapped beyond endurance. When the baby was finally born early in the morning her tiny wail foretold the lack of strength to survive and, despite valiant efforts of the good doctor and the skillful care of Mrs. Johnson, the baby died in Prudy's arms, living barely three days. Prudy was devastated and guilty. Surely this was God's punishment for her sin and His wrath took her love child from her. In her fever, with only Dr. Walsh privy to what her hot brain caused her to speak, she said "Eric, — our baby —." Dr. Walsh didn't mention it to her nor would he repeat it, understanding well kept secrets more than anyone could know. Pastor Kaufman came to the house and christened the baby Mary Elizabeth a few hours before she died. Prudy collapsed and was prostrate in bed for days afterward.

Lester's pompous behavior was dampened considerably with the news that his baby turned out to be a girl, and a sickly one at that. He yelled at the doctor as if it were all his fault. He berated Prudy for not giving him another boy, and when the baby died he shouted at her that it served her right. The worst insult to his ego came when Prudy was too sick to attend the funeral and it was expected that he take care of the arrangements.

"If you weren't so puny you'd go and do it yourself," he accused, shaking his fist at her. Prudy buried her face in the pillow.

But, for appearances sake, he appeared at the First Community Church in Spotswood with his four boys at his side looking scared and bewildered. Pastor Kaufman delivered a short sermon on the brief life that God had sent to the Deters family. Surely, this innocent child was in a special place in Heaven, and the family could take comfort in that.

The whole business only made Lester angry and when he could leave the cemetery, he dropped the boys at home with their ailing mother, started drinking in the root cellar until he realized it wasn't the same as when he toasted the births of his boys. Finally, he went to town to get drunk.

CHAPTER ELEVEN

The Years of Change

The states of North Dakota and South Dakota were formed from what was left of the original Dakota Territory, which originally encompassed those future states, plus Montana and parts of Wyoming and Idaho. In 1889 the two states became individual entities and it would be years before some of the towns within their borders would become cities, and those cities would enter the 20th century.

Living was hard with most of that living taken up with the struggle to survive in a harsh land. For some the want of a better life and moving upward to a goal was never realized. There would be no time or energy to concern oneself with progress or to keep up with the times, only to hang on and try not to slip into a mere life of existence. Spotswood was somewhat larger than it had been when it was founded in 1875, but it would not become any bigger or even noteworthy. Most maps never included it. Eventually, it would simply disappear without a trace, with no evidence of the inhabitants' years of strenuous endurance. Survival became the only goal of the prairie people, and it often became a contest between the people and the forces of nature. Nature was more often the victor and there was no compassion in the victory. Bumper crops were wiped out by hail that pounded the grain into the ground in minutes. Insects devoured tender plantings. Prairie fires were started by lightning from summer storms that rolled noisily across the sky and laid waste to the land, destroying everything and anyone caught in their paths. They came with precious little warning, just a deep rumble that made one pause from its strangeness. By the time the haze of smoke was seen it was often too late and, with a wind fanning the flames, acres were blackened in a flash. A prairie fire could not be outrun; as powerful as that instinct was, it was best to get to the highest point at once, preferably unplanted land or at a point where there was a patch of dirt or gravel. It took calm courage to remain still in such a spot while a thunderous, raging fire burned around, but to do otherwise was to die. Settlers soon learned to set back fires where possible to contain the flames. The knowledge of the tremendous forces of nature either humbled or destroyed the people of the prairie.

The Deters farm had so far escaped such catastrophes. Perhaps Mother Nature had something else in mind, because the home place had not been improved nor, for that matter, even maintained. The slow, inexorable decline, evident to the folks in the community, was more cruel than having to start anew with improved facilities and modern, painted buildings. According to Lester, the cost was too dear and they could do without any fancy trappings. What they had was plenty good enough. Lettie kept reminding Prudy that she was a fool to put up with his stinginess, that he had plenty of money to afford improvements, and it should be used. Otherwise, it would cost him more in the long run. Prudy knew she was right and she looked with envy at her friend's well kept, profitable farm two miles down the road and knew that it stood as proof that Lester was wrong. But she didn't dare approach Lester about it again, knowing what an angry response she would get. Lester perceived the finances of the farm to be his business and he put his money away in a safe place, a place that only he knew about. He doled out a few coins to Prudy for the few personal items she needed, usually grumbling as he counted the money into her palm, not seeing the need for pins, new material to sew, flower seeds, and such. But he couldn't touch her egg money. Everyone knew that chickens were a woman's business. Prudy tried to keep up the inside of the house the best she could, but there was not much she could do about the frayed furniture except recover it, which took too much expensive material, or patch it, and she didn't like the looks of that. She ended up using an old blanket as a throw to cover the worn spots. She got no cooperation from the boys who had no concept of why tidiness was a virtue. John put it bluntly, "That's woman's work." She knew where he got that.

John was the oldest, was also the biggest and the image of his father. He emulated him in every way right down to the way he walked. Prudy worried, though, because he also talked like him and his younger brothers copied him, because they knew that what John did was just fine with their father, so the profanities issuing from their young mouths was a source of distress. Lester pooh-poohed her fears. "Boys will be boys. John is becoming a man. He'll talk like a man and drink his beer like a man."

"But the others ape him and they're too young for such words."

"Hell, woman, what're you gettin' all het up about? Boys do things like that. My boys are normal and there's nothing to worry about, nein."

Eventually Lester did worry, but not because of the use of bad language or the future drinking prowess of his heirs. In 1915 when John was fifteen his interest in girls peaked along with his sexual appetite, much to Lester's amusement, until John turned his affections to Colleen, one of the many Clanahans. He came upon them accidentally in the haymow one afternoon and his rage was so intense that he struck out at his son, sending him sailing into the hay. Colleen flew down the ladder and out of the barn. She knew enough about menfolk to know that she would be the object of Lester Deters' ire next.

"Damn you, boy, what're you doin' foolin' around with one of them Clanahans. They ain't nothin' but priest lovers."

"But, Dad —" John protested.

"Don't you know how them folks operate? They have instructions from the priest, who got 'em from the Pope himself, to get converts, get 'em any way they can. And the females know only one way."

"Aw, Dad, that ain't so."

Lester jerked him up and his fingers dug into John's flesh.

"Oh ain't it now? They're supposed to go forth and multiply like they claim the Bible says. Well they sure do that. And I don't want you doin' any of that

Prudy

multiplyin', you hear me, boy?"

He was shaking him and John squirmed in his tight grasp.

"Sure, Dad, but Colleen's not like that."

"Oh, so she's not like that? Just what was she doin' rollin' around in the hay then, answer me that? Fixin' on a shotgun wedding and a convert, that's what, Ja."

"No, you're wrong."

"I ain't never wrong. You stay away from that hussy. Stay away from the whole tribe. The Clanahans are no good."

It was the first rift between them and it hurt the pride of both of them. Lester's was damaged to think that his son would lower himself to the likes of a Clanahan. John's pride in his manhood had been ridiculed in front of a girl. From that time on Lester's lenient attitude toward his favorite son waned and he kept a tight rein on him.

86

Lester's pride was dealt another blow when, in 1918, John became of age and he joined the Army and was promptly sent overseas to fight the Hun. The United States had entered World War I on April 6, 1917, and young men were eager to enter the fray, to be a part of the war to end all wars. This act of defiance was too much for his father, who felt he had been betrayed. To be fighting against his heritage was not right. The Deters were Germans and a proud, hard working people. Lester knew nothing of the politics involved, just that the war was thousands of miles away and of no consequence to him until now and he could not understand why John was compelled to leave his family and fight the Germans. His frustration was compounded by the attitude of those who knew the Deters family, whose contact with them had cooled from friendship and recognition of Lester's management of a successful farm to suspicion because of his background and also of his accent. Lester didn't like this change and tried to bluff his way through the difficulty, but only his arrogance came through. So he took to concentrating on dropping his accent and his frequent "jas." That feat lessened the outward expression of skepticism, but nothing was the way it had been.

He took his frustration out on Prudy. His temper was seldom held in check, even without provocation. He frightened the boys, because he made no effort to hide his annoyance with their mother, and he regarded them as being old enough to know how a man handled his wife. Alan, then sixteen, would burst into tears at his father's violence, which only made Lester lash out at him as well. Chester and Fred would run to their bedroom when the fighting began. Alan remained to help his mother and would bury his face in her lap when his father's tirade ended and he rode off to town. Prudy was grateful for Alan's soothing presence and she would stroke his soft brown hair and tell him not to cry, that she was all right. She'd just have to be more careful and not rile him, that's all.

After John went off to war Prudy coaxed Lester into letting her go to visit Patience in New Ulm in June, 1918.

"Come with us. We could all have a vacation together."

Lester would not. He had work to do. Lord knew he had plenty of work to do with John gone off to war and being short a hand. He really didn't want to go to New Ulm, but made sure Prudy knew that it was because of her leaving him that he could not leave himself. It was, after all, her fault that John had left. She had sent him away to bring Lester down, to bring shame on the Deters name. When she assured him that she had not, he grabbed her thick, dark hair, pulled her head back and hissed in her face, "You shut up. You are to blame. You came between me and my son. And don't think you can run away from me, your husband. Where do you think you could go — to that hoity-toity sister of yours? Do you think she'd take you in? Not if I can help it. If you're not on that train a week from Thursday I'll be after you."

"Lester, please, you're hurting me." Her head was at a painful angle and she couldn't straighten up.

"Don't you hurt Mama," said Alan in as strong a voice as he could muster.

"Are you gonna cry if I do? Some man I've got in you. The best one goes off to war and I'm left with a pantywaist."

With that he released Prudy and she stumbled backward onto the sofa.

Prudy took the train from Mobridge east to Minnesota. Alan, Chester and Fred went with her and they could hardly contain their excitment. She kissed Lester goodbye and told him they would be gone only a few days, ten at the most, and they would be back a week from Thursday. The time apart would be good for both of them. He just turned, got into the buggy and slapped the horse's rear savagely with the whip.

Prudy had not seen Patience for more than eight years, circumstances being what they were. She never traveled, being so tied down and because of the cost, which Lester had not let her forget as he bought the tickets. In addition, he did not take kindly to her going off anywhere alone, even into town to get what few items of groceries they didn't grow in their own garden. Patience had not made another visit since Prudy had been expecting Mary Elizabeth.

She could not bear to see the farm in its poor condition, successful or not, or her sister in such miserable circumstances and all the turmoil in her life with four boisterous boys. And she had her own problems. She had never been a strong person and still fell ill now and then with colds and fevers. Millicent took after her in that regard and led a protected, sheltered life. She was subject to asthma as well and the dust and animal dander of the farm had sent her to bed after their return to New Ulm those years before.

Lars was protective of them. He loved his women dearly and took pride in keeping them comfortably established in the beautiful setting that was the home he had built for them. His life was good and it suited him. Lars was a kind man, an honest business man who owned the mercantile trade business in the area. He treated his clients fairly and was known as an honest man who never cheated them. The years had been good to him and he was still a handsome man with chiseled features, his blond hair turning a silver gray. He had an erect carriage and was a popular addition to the many social events that his position demanded.

He had not objected to the forthcoming visit when Patience had asked to invite Prudy and the boys. He was relieved that Lester would not be accompanying them. There was something about him that was unsettling to Lars, who was a civilized man who recognized the animal in Lester Deters. He looked forward to some masculine company and a more lively atmosphere that the boys were sure to provide for a change.

They were tired when they arrived in New Ulm but were revived by happy greetings from Patience and Lars. Millicent stood apart; she remembered the Deters boys as being less than desirable playmates. Besides, she was a young lady now and too old to play, being of the age of twenty, but looking younger because of her frailty. All they had in common was that they were cousins. The Hansons had arrived in a fairly new Pierce-Arrow automobile and the boys were thrilled into silence by the smooth ride to the house.

"There are so many trees," exclaimed Prudy as they drove through the streets.

"Yes, Minnesota has lots and lots of trees, and lakes and rivers. I love it here."

They drove along streets lined with tall trees with the tops of elms bent over the avenues like a covered bridge. Sunlight shone through the leaves dappling the cobblestones before them. Sturdy brick houses and stone buildings were predominant. Lars explained, "New Ulm is a mostly German settlement. They erect buildings to last forever. I think Lester might have appreciated seeing our town." Prudy exclaimed over each new sight or beautiful yard. Patience laughed softly, happy to see her so delighted.

Millicent remained aloof from the rough boys, her country cousins, who were obviously unused to the finer things in life, although she thought Alan had possibilities. He was better mannered, less coarse than the others. She caught his eye and he flushed. Alan considered Millicent a magnificent china doll, delicate and exquisite. Millicent saw in Alan a tall, slim, nice looking young man with a smooth face, brown eyes that seemed to pierce right to the heart of things, and a paler skin than his brothers with their ruddy complexions. He had a shy smile and an air of sensitivity that was appealing.

When they drew up in front of a large house on a shady street, Prudy gasped, "Oh, Patience, I had no idea."

The house was huge by Prudy's standards, quite unlike the home they had grown up in. It was a three-story brick house with a wide enclosed porch around most of it. Trees and shrubs surrounded the house providing gentle shade on an immaculate green lawn, sprinkled with flower beds.

"Holy cow," said Chester.

"Don't be vulgar, mind your manners now," reminded Prudy, as they stepped to the brick walk. "Each of you boys grab a valise. And wipe your feet before you go in."

They walked up a long walk, climbed wide steps to the porch and the door, which had an oval etched glass window above a fancy doorknob. Lars opened the heavy door and carried in the rest of the luggage to a spacious entryway. The inside of the house was cool. The rooms were large with high ceilings and tall windows covered with velvet drapes. Prudy looked around her in wonder. It was a side of her sister she had not thought about. The splendid environment presented a deeper perspective of her younger sister.

"Come, let's get you all settled first. Then we'll show you around," said Patience.

They climbed a carpeted flight of stairs to the second floor. "I do hope the boys don't mind sharing a room, but there should be plenty of space and there is a comfortable cot in here in addition to the bed."

"Holy cow," said Chester.

The room was much more ample than the one they shared on the farm with a double bed that had carved bedposts and a roomy cot beside it. They decided at once that the two youngest would share the bed and Alan would take the cot. After all, he was sixteen and too big to sleep with anybody. Patience showed them where they could put their things and left them happily hanging up their few belongings as she led Prudy down the hall. Lars followed with her bag.

"This is our bedroom. As you can see, it is the largest."

Prudy was envious. The room held a big bed with sturdy bedposts and a canopy, a wardrobe, a full-length mirror mounted on swivels, a chaise lounge, and a dresser that would have contained the clothing for her entire family. Millicent had been trailing behind, but she joined them now that the boys had been disposed of. She smiled with affection at her aunt. "You'll like my room, too, Aunt Prudence. It is on the south and there is always sunshine. I love the sunshine, don't you?"

"Yes, I purely do, Milly. It is a very nice room to be sure."

It was strictly feminine. The bed was covered with a frilly pink canopy, a chair covered with matching fabric, a dressing table with a ruffled skirt and a round mirror over it. A bookcase lined one wall with volumes of worn books. All had a well read look, no doubt used to pass the hours spent in bed. Millicent had always been frail like her mother. Prudy looked at her fondly. She was a sweet girl and she brought to mind the daughter Prudy almost had. She wondered what she would look like now. She wondered . . .

"And you will be in here, Prudy," said Patience. She led her to an adjoining room down the wide hall, and Lars put her suitcase on a covered chest at the end of the bed.

"I hope you'll be comfortable here," he said sincerely. "You could use some rest, I'm sure. We're glad to have you here. And don't worry about those boys of yours. I'm taking time off and have plenty of things planned for us to do. You and Patience can have a good visit."

"Thanks, Lars. Your house is so grand. We'll be fine."

She looked around the room and admired the sheer curtains covered with drapes bordered with tassels and tied back with matching green cord.

"Why don't you unpack, and we'll have some lunch. Freshen up and come down when you're ready," Patience suggested.

Prudy was unwinding and starting to relax. She tugged off her thin gloves which she had carefully mended for the trip and flung them and her unfashionable hat on the bed, then flung herself down upon it, looking at the ceiling. A long chandelier hung down with several glass shades. Electricity! Elegance! Surely she must be in paradise, and she would enjoy it, even if for only a little while.

They enjoyed lunch served on matching china by a hired girl in a dark, long-sleeved dress covered with a small apron and a starched hat on her carefully groomed hair. The boys were embarrassed and flustered to be waited on and struck dumb by a way of life they had not known existed. But they were ravenous and ate with gusto, having to be reminded to place the napkins in their laps and corrected now and then in proper table etiquette. Millicent sat straight and demure with a faint amused smile on her pretty face. Light from the tall windows slanted across the room and shone on her golden hair like a halo, a picture Alan was not to forget.

When they were finished the boys busily stacked all their dishes into one pile in front of them, not understanding the disapproving looks of the hired girl, who quickly removed them. Patience just smiled and overlooked it.

"Let us show you the rest of the house," she said as she rose.

The dining area was big enough to entertain any number of people and they often did, she said as they left and entered the living room, a room filled with settees, sofas, chairs and tables with flowers.

"The carpet can be rolled up for dancing," Lars explained, and quickly added, "I'm not a good dancer, but my wife insists that to dance is a part of entertaining, so I dance after a fashion."

The boys could not imagine any man, even their uncle Lars, as dancing at home in fancy clothes. Only in town at the saloons did any man they knew ever dance, but wisely they said nothing. Alan decided earlier in the day that he would cover his ignorance and learn by keeping his mouth closed.

A smaller room, the parlor, adjoined the living room for small get togethers and it was often used by the family because of its informality. A piano stood in one corner.

"Who plays the piano?" asked Fred as he went toward it.

"Don't touch," admonished his mother.

"Why not?"

"Because I said so. Maybe later we can listen to someone play."

"I've taken lessons ever since I was a child," said Millicent with an air of superiority.

She was easily talked into sitting down and gracing them with a tune and soon they were singing along to "Let Me Call You Sweetheart," "Till We Meet Again" and "There Are Smiles." Millicent waxed professional as she easily fingered the keys and led them in the words of all the latest tunes. Chester and Fred stood beside her watching intently as her skillful fingers flowed over the keys. Alan watched and listened, entranced, seated beside his mother. There was hearty applause all around when the concert ended, and the ice was broken.

They left the parlor, walked down a hall, through a well stocked kitchen with attached pantry, and were impressed to notice a bathroom next to it. There was a bathroom upstairs near the bedrooms, too, containing a cast iron tub, a toilet with a pull chain and a fancy porcelain sink. The third floor was largely unfinished, being mostly for storage. Lars was thinking of putting an office up there one day.

Lars was true to his word and took the boys someplace every day, whether fishing, to a motion picture show, or just for a ride in the Pierce Arrow. Lars enjoyed their hearty ways. Patience and Prudy had leisurely days, shopped the stores in town and enjoyed pleasant afternoons in the cool living room while the hired girl tended to their needs. What a treat it was for Prudy to be relieved of her motherly duties and to enjoy the company of her sister, while being waited on hand and foot. She felt guilty at first, but then threw caution to the wind and decided to enjoy it all while she could.

At the age of thirty-eight Patience was not quite so thin as in years past, but all the more lovely because of it. Her blond hair was still beautifully piled on top of her regal head and she carried herself with an air that inspired deference. Prudy thought of herself as a dowdy forty-three, but Patience insisted that she vastly underrated herself, that she had a good figure, a trifle too thin perhaps, and that her graying hair gave her an aristocratic look. Prudy giggled at that remark, never in the world believing that she looked aristocratic, but Patience worked magic with comb and brush and transformed Prudy's uninspired appearance into one that was entirely satisfactory and flattering. Even the boys said she looked pretty. She was eager to know what Lester thought. The lines in her face that were put there by the cruel past decade were smoothing out, she was rested, eating well without having to cook first, and becoming accustomed to a more refined way of life. She was captivated by the indoor plumbing, but had a hard time convincing the boys to take a bath almost every day and that the water was to be drained out before the next one got in the tub.

"But, Mama, at home we fill the wash tub once a week and take turns. We don't dump the water out till we're all of us clean," said Fred.

"Never you mind," she countered. "Your Aunt Patience would be mortified if we did that. Do as I say and be glad that you can each have a nice bath in clean water. And scrub yourselves good now, you hear?"

The days flew by. Prudy was amazed at how smoothly their lives went, without friction, without fear of upset, and she grew to like the feeling and to wonder why hers wasn't like that. She knew it was more than just the difference in social standing. Patience broached the subject one day.

"Prudy, are you all right? Are you content?"

"Of course," she answered too quickly.

"Forgive me for saying this, but how does Lester treat you? I've been concerned about you ever since we spent Thanksgiving with you years ago."

Prudy averted her gaze. "Lester is Lester."

"Prudy, dear, you must be honest with yourself. Tell me, does he — has Lester ever struck you?"

Prudy looked up, her eyes wide, wondering.

"No one has said anything," Patience continued, "they don't have to. I can read the signs."

"I get him riled up sometimes, that's all."

"Prudy, you don't rile anyone to the extent of being hit."

Prudy got up and walked to the window. Her sister's query was unanswerable and she didn't want to talk about it, not now when everything was going so well in her life. Patience was suddenly filled with remorse.

"I'm sorry, Prudy. Forgive me for bringing it up. We won't talk about it. Just be careful, and you must realize that Lester has to accept more blame for his behavior. He is at fault, not you."

Prudy turned, tears rolling down her cheeks, tears released from the dam that had for so many years contained any signs of her emotion, lest it goad Lester into violence. Patience gathered her into her arms as Prudy sobbed.

"There, there, dear, please forgive me. I spoke out of line."

Prudy sniffled and dried her eyes.

"It's all right. I'm fine. Just needed a good cry, I guess. I was so glad for your invitation. One reason was I hoped that my absence would be good for the whole family. Lester and I needed to get away from each other for a little bit, and I was so glad when he decided to stay in Spotswood, although I urged him to come along because I felt I should. This has been so wonderful for me and the boys. I can never thank you and Lars enough for what you've done."

The sisters smiled with love through moist eyes. The complete acceptance of the other was worth the time it took.

"We don't see much of each other, but each visit becomes more precious, doesn't it?" said Patience.

Millicent, too, was buoyed up by the presence of their company. Her comfortable, but humdrum, life of semi-invalidism was brightened by the boys' noisy ways and unexpected happenings when they were around. Millicent lived with her parents because of her health, merely biding her time until a suitable husband could be found for her. Several suitors were being considered, none of which excited Millicent very much, but she knew that her situation required careful consideration and left that decision to her parents. She confided in her mother one day before their guests departed for South Dakota.

"I think Alan is really nice, Mother."

"Yes, he seems to have grown up into a fine young man, compared to his brothers. Don't misunderstand, I love all of your cousins. It's just that Alan seems more sensitive than the others, not at all like John. He's much too —"

"Nasty, that's what he is," said Millicent with vehemence.

"Now, Milly, that was a long time ago."

"I don't mean just that awful cow in the barn. John was always flipping my skirt, trying to peek underneath."

"I didn't know about that," said Patience, frowning.

"He never really did anything, but he was so suggestive and — and nasty, that's all."

"I must admit that he is a lot like his father."

"Uncle Lester is sort of different, isn't he? He used to frighten me. I'm so glad he didn't come. Aunt Prudence is so nice."

"Yes, dear. You must always hold your aunt in high regard."

The time arrived far too soon for the guests to return home and Prudy wasn't at all sure she wanted to go. Patience urged them to stay a little longer. Ten days was hardly long enough to have a really good visit. And Lars and the boys were having a splendid time.

"Thank you, but Lester will be wondering what happened to us. We really have to go."

With happy, yet sad, goodbyes and hugs all around they got on the train to Mobridge and waved from the windows until they could no longer see the station in New Ulm. An extra bag had been packed with new clothes for all of them, including a shirt for Lester, over Prudy's strenuous objections. What would Lester think? He was so proud.

"I don't care what Lester thinks. Lars and I are giving you all a gift. Anyone can accept a gift in the spirit in which it is given. Lester can talk to Lars if he doesn't like it. Please let us do this. We mean nothing by it. It's just that we never see you and want to give you something."

So she agreed. They were quiet and thoughtful on the journey home. They had experienced a different kind of life and it was a good life, and it had been an education to have experienced it. She hoped Lester would understand. It struck her that she had given him scarcely a thought all the time they were gone. A sadness overcame her as she sat in the noisy, soot-filled train and looked out at the countryside that got steadily more flat and barren. Trees disappeared and they were on the prairie budding with crops maturing in the sun, with flat land covered with waving prairie grass that stirred in her a melancholy. Yet she was eager to return home where she belonged, to Spotswood and familiar things. The sisters had seen each other in her own environment and each was content with her own, although more understanding of the other; there was a mutual respect. She would be satisfied with that. As for anything else, it was just too late for her to be anyone else than what she was, Lester's wife and mother to their sons. She would try to do better and to keep Lester happy and content. A feeling of renewed energy and confidence surged through her and she looked forward to their return home.

She was surprised to see that nothing had changed. Lester was there to meet them with the buggy, but his face was dark with held-in anger. She ignored it and said cheerfully, "Lester! I'm happy to be home."

"Where the hell have you been, woman? You sure stayed at your fancy sister's long enough. What's the matter with your hair?"

He dismissed the excited voices of the boys as they tried to tell him at the same time all about the marvelous things they had seen and what they had done with their Uncle Lars.

"Get them suitcases, you boys, and get 'em on the buggy. Got to get on home so your Ma can get supper on the table."

She sighed. Their happy homecoming had been squelched. By the time they pulled into the farm yard they were exhausted and famished, and there was supper to fix. Prudy's heart sank as she entered the kitchen. She could see through to the front room that the house was a shambles. The kitchen was full of dirty dishes and spoiled food. It stank of stale beer. Her shoulder slumped with fatigue and her head was heavy. She was too tired and miserable to cry. Any hopes she had of circumstances changing were dashed.

Lester and the boys took the bags upstairs and she set about putting the kitchen to rights so she could see what there was to fix for a meal. She hauled out the slop pail from under the sink where a stench was issuing and gagged at the accumulation of garbage. She hurried with it to a distance behind the outhouse, where a deep covered hole held the slop, cans, boxes and other items of assorted rubbish and dumped it, then rinsed out the pail at the pump by the water trough and returned to the mess in the kitchen. She stacked the dirty dishes to one side to make room for any clean ones she could find, and swept an accumulation of dirt and scraps on the floor into a pile and was dumping them into the empty scuttle to dispose of later when they came downstairs.

"I guess I left things in sort of a mess," Lester said matter-of-factly. "When a man loses his help, things tend to pile up some."

Prudy said nothing. She found some smoked pork in the root cellar and a loaf of bread that was edible and brought up some jars of vegetables from the previous fall's canning. It would have to do until the morning, when she would have her work cut out for her.

"We'll need some fire wood by morning, Lester," she said.

"Got to find the ax first," he mumbled.

They ate the meager meal and the boys' enthusiasm faded in telling their father about their trip, as it was clear that he wasn't interested and regarded their recitations as proof that they put him in a bad light, comparing him like that with that dandy, their Uncle Lars.

"That's not what they mean, Lester. They just want to tell you what a nice time we all had."

They finished eating without comment. Then Lester said, "What's in that new suitcase you brought home?"

She chose her words carefully, having thought of what to say all the way home.

"Just a few things from Patience and Lars for the boys."

"I can provide for my boys."

"Of course you can and they know that; they just wanted to give them something. It's just a few new clothes. They have grown so and, besides, with school starting in a couple of months just think of all the money it will save in not having to buy new — or to buy material to sew them, for that matter."

She stopped, not wanting to overdo it. She used Lettie's sewing machine on occasion to sew shirts for all of them, but it was tedious work. However, it saved money because material was cheap, even though it might be short on quality.

Surprisingly, the logic made sense to Lester. If he could put more of his hard-earned cash away, for whatever reason or by virtue of anyone's deeds, he was just that much more ahead of the game. He pushed back from the table and they were relieved to have avoided an incident.

"Just leave all this, Prudy. You can clean it up tomorrow. You boys get on to bed. You too, Prudy."

Fatigue made it easy to obey him in spite of the fairly early hour. Lester took the lamp and led the way up the stairs. Alan missed having a bath in a nice tub in privacy, but Chester and Fred slid back easily into their familiar life and were soon sound asleep. Alan dreamed of Millicent. Prudy slept as soon as Lester would let her. A man had his right, and he had not exercised that right for a long time, according to his habits; that is, if you didn't count the woman in Spotswood over the saloon. But Prudy would never know about that if he could help it.

CHAPTER TWELVE

The Aftermath

When Prudy informed Alan that, no, cousins do not marry, and Lester had raised the roof when he had spoken to his father about the possibility, Alan was thrust into a depression that would not lift. No amount of entreaty on Prudy's part nor of swift punishment on Lester's part could change his feelings.

"He's just a boy yet. He'll get over it. Don't make so much of it," she said to Lester.

"I won't have such talk in this house. Such foolishness. See what happened when you left me to go visit that fancy sister of yours? This never would have happened if you'd stayed home."

"But, Lester, I did it for us, so that we could have a fresh start. I hoped things would be better."

"Well, you hoped wrong. Things got worse now, didn't they?"

She sighed and yearned for the harvest to keep the boys busy and then for school to start so Alan's mind would be occupied with studies, although at his age not many of the young men attended school. Chester and Fred thought it highly amusing to see Alan moping around, in love with a silly girl and a cousin, at that, and at every opportunity teased him unmercifully.

"Nyah, nyah, Alan. Willy-nilly over Milly," they would chant and laugh with glee to see him turn red with embarrassment and flee.

Prudy couldn't stop them and Lester thought it was only what he deserved, being so foolish. Alan's devastation was complete with the arrival of a letter to the family from Patience a few months later, together with an engraved invitation to the wedding of their daughter Millicent to a Mr. Howard Larson. She realized, the letter said, that they might not be able to attend, having recently made a trip to New Ulm, but wanted them to have the invitation anyway and to know how pleased they all were with the selection of such a suitable son-in-law. She closed with expressing again how much they had all enjoyed their visit.

Alan could not understand why no one could see what was happening to him. To be so blithely ignored by Millicent when they had shared so much and had so much in common was the cruelest blow of all. He made a decision. He would give his life to the church. He would become a Catholic priest. Catholicism was in his background and he was perceptive enough to know that his sensitive nature made him well suited for it. His life had to have some purpose. His purpose had been to make Millicent his wife and now that was impossible. He was stunned at the rage this news inspired in his father. Alan's gentle nature naively assumed a like response from others, especially in those he loved, and violence caused him much grief. Lester could not ever respond in a gentle manner; it wasn't manly. He raved and threatened, and finally hit Alan with his closed fist, raising an ugly welt on his cheek and making his nose bleed.

"What's the matter with you, boy? You shame me. Why can't you be a man like your big brother? At least he joined the Army to do a man's work, but not you. Oh no. You think you're goin' to be a goddam priest, a pope lover. What are you anyway, some kind of sissy?"

His father's words were worse than the pain of the blow. That night Alan packed his belongings, all his earthly possessions, in the bag that Patience had sent home with them. He needed it and he reasoned that it would only cause his mother pain to have it around. He fought the tears that came too easily to him, wiped them from his face in frustration and annoyance. Maybe his father was right and he was a sissy, a word that was a scourge to any man worth his salt. But he wasn't. He was just as much a man as any. He just felt differently about some things, that's all. A man didn't have to be mean and slovenly to be manly did he? He'd leave and not cause his family anymore anguish. He left swiftly and very quietly when they were all asleep, not indulging himself in a last look around at the home he was leaving, lest tears start again.

He walked into Spotswood, not noticing any tiredness, lost in his morose thoughts, alone on the road with the moon lighting his way. The only sound was the scuffling of his feet in the dirt and of the wheeling night bird sending out its call of inquiry. When he arrived in Spotswood in the early morning hours he slept in the livery stable until he was awakened by the blacksmith who wanted to know what he was doing there. He was not an unfriendly man and after he gave Alan a bite of breakfast, arranged a ride for him into Mobridge with a man who was driving there to transact some business. He was a prosperous business man, judging from the Dodge sedan he drove. The comfortable ride only reminded Alan of the drives in his Uncle Lars's Pierce-Arrow, and that made him think of Millicent all the more. He responded little to the man as he kept up an amiable chatter all the way into Mobridge. The man didn't seem to mind, being accustomed to talking in his line of work, which was in sales.

"Where can I drop you?" he asked upon their arrival.

Alan convinced him it didn't matter, despite the man's insistence of letting him off at wherever he was going, and thanked him courteously for the ride, which had been of much assistance to him. The man finally gave in and let him off just inside the city limits, puzzled at the attitude of his young passenger.

Although Alan had never been in the Catholic church or rectory on the trips to Mobridge during his younger years he knew how to find them. The church spire stood above the other structures in town and all he had to do was to keep it in sight and he would get there all right. He didn't know the local priest's name or anything about the Catholic religion, only what his mother had told him. He had largely dismissed the things his father said about it. As he walked through the long blocks of Mobridge he attracted curious glances. It wasn't every day that a young man carrying a brand new leather valise walked through town. Offers of assistance were made, but refused. He could manage just fine he would say. A quiet "thank you anyway" accompanied his refusals.

He finally stood before the imposing church and looked up at a long flight of steps, stained glass windows, a steeple with a bell, and a golden cross at the very top. It inspired reverence and a deep comfort, a comfort that he needed badly and one that was sorely missing in his young life. He climbed the steep steps, now feeling the ache in his right arm from the steady pull from the suitcase. He pulled open the heavy door and walked inside.

Alan's departure left a void in an already diminished family. He had left no note so they had no idea where he had gone or what had happened to him. It would be a long time before they knew the facts. Prudy grieved for her sons and the family that was falling apart before they were fully grown. She felt more helpless than ever. The disintegration worsened with Lester's reaction. Any upset sent him to town to get drunk. He claimed that he didn't care what had happened to Alan. He was only a sissy, what did it matter.

But Prudy knew that he did care, that he missed him and that now with the two oldest boys gone there was a big hole in the family unit. Lester no longer cared about his appearance and seldom shaved, more often than not exhibiting stubble where before there had been a clean shaven face. He used to take pride in his handsome features, but no longer. He wouldn't go to the barber shop and only occasionally did he permit Prudy to trim his hair, declaring that hair and a beard showed a man's virility. Prudy prayed that nothing bad happened to her son. Alan was an unsuspecting, believing young man, and she worried about his welfare in a world that was not so kind. If only they would hear from him.

Chester and Fred were drawn closer to one another and felt lost without their older brothers and confused about what was happening to all of them. Prudy tried to smooth things over, but they were unconvinced and were sure they would never see them again.

Late one afternoon in the week of Prudy's birthday in October, 1918, they were startled to hear a knock on the front door. Company or a stranger? Lester answered the knock. Prudy stood behind him with Chester and Fred on either side of her, curious as to their unexpected visitor. Mr. Jasper Wilson from the telegraph office in Spotswood stood on the porch. He wore his green-visored cap and his spectacles were perched on the end of his nose. His vest was open in the warm fall air, displaying his wide, striped suspenders which held up his baggy pants. His thin face was somber and he looked like he wished he were anywhere else than at the Deters' doorstep. He tipped his cap and said, "Telegram arrived for you, Mr. Deters."

He hesitated, uncertain, then said an abrupt, "Sorry," and swiftly left the porch to the dirt road where his old mare waited patiently, head downcast.

Lester and Prudy looked at each other with only a question on their faces, nothing more. Lester opened the slim envelope and Prudy read it aloud with him:

"The Department of the Army regrets to inform you of the death of Pvt. John Lester Deters on September 30, 1918. The Department extends its deepest sympathy."

Prudy uttered a soft "Oh no," and fainted, not hearing Lester's howl of outrage nor the boys' frightened cries.

On November 11, 1918, the war ended and John's body was sent home to Spotswood where he was buried in the family plot beside his baby sister, Mary Elizabeth. The worn stones of her parents were silent witness to the grief that engulfed the Deters family, who clung together and cried for all of them.

CHAPTER THIRTEEN

On the Just and the Unjust

He maketh his sun to rise on the evil and on the good, and sendeth the
rain on the just and on the unjust. — Matthew 5:45

There was no hope of restoring things to the way they were. Prudy's despair was so deep she could scarcely hold on to the hope that her remaining two sons held for her. They, too, moved in a sphere of confusion and bewilderment at the turn their lives had taken. They continued in school mainly to get away from home where gloom hung like a stormy sky. Prudy was left alone to deal with Lester who was totally unconsolable in the loss of his two eldest sons, one to death and one to the Catholic church, both unacceptable. His once ramrod straight figure began to droop, his purposeful stride slowed. He began a steady progression downward in speech and appearance. His face was seldom clean shaven. The scraggly stubble on his face grew into an unsightly beard and mustache, peppered with gray. He drank daily, whether in the cellar imbibing his home brewed beer or in town, where he could be found at the merest excuse, sometimes without Prudy's knowing he had left. The boys eventually ceased asking, "Where's Dad?" knowing the answer would be, "He went to town for awhile." He was quick to argue with anyone, with Prudy his convenient target. She knew she must keep her distance from him, to just go about her work and not say or do anything to rile him. His low boiling point kept her nervously servile. But no matter what she did it was never enough to calm him.

How she longed for his comfort in the losses they shared. How she yearned for him to take her in his arms, to soothe her, to tell her that everything would be all right, that together they could face whatever life threw at them. She hoped in vain, so she reasoned that she would let him know her feelings, that perhaps she could comfort him as well. She had turned to him, had reached out to him in bed while wracked with sobs, only to be pushed away and to have him turn his back. The hurt of his callousness was deeper than the anger she felt. She had never seen Lester cry. Any emotion was carefully hidden from any who might see his weakness, as he regarded it. She knew he was filled with fury at what life had done to him in taking two of his sons from him. He could show fury, that was manly, but tears were the province of women.

Oddly enough, the Crawford sisters proved to be of help. They were at John's funeral and the lunch afterwards, and she didn't begrudge them their ample

100

helpings. They even made a special visit to the house to offer what comfort they could while they enjoyed a cup of coffee in the front room. Prudy was surprised to find that they were indeed thoughtful and kind in spite of their eccentricities. They brought an apple pie and expressed their condolences in the thin afternoon winter's sunlight which entered the south windows. They smiled sympathetically and kept up a polite, pleasant conversation, allowing Prudy the luxury of not having to say much. They knew their duty and had come to offer solace. They did not mention the embarrassment of the many years previous when the boys had been into mischief, only that they recalled John as being a big, strapping boy, and what a pity it was that war took the best the country had in its youth. They did not bring up the subject of Alan's departure, though it was common knowledge in the community. They were sorry they had missed Mr. Deters, although secretly they were not and had shown considerable courage in coming to the house when he very well could have been there, grousing around in one of his dark moods that were becoming so familiar or, heaven forbid, even drunk. Prudy thanked them warmly in all sincerity for their courtesy and saw them out.

Patience sent a long letter of sympathy and a sum of money to help with burial expenses. Prudy opened the letter before Lester came in from the barn and tucked the cash into her apron. She could not face him in explaining. He assumed that John's burial was part of the duties of Pastor Kaufman and the funeral director. Hadn't his son given his life for his country? Even if he knew otherwise, Lester was not about to pay one red cent. She gave the money to Pastor Kaufman one Sunday after church to take care of the expenses incurred. Lettie and Meyer waited patiently for her in the car while she took care of her sad business.

Lettie had been a Godsend. She was there at once to comfort, to aid, to help out at the house, not backing down from Lester's obnoxious remarks. She was smart enough to not talk back to him, just stood as tall as she could and looked him straight in the eye, her own eyes flashing, staring him down. Lester could not handle a strong female and would not risk a confrontation and possibly looking foolish in the process, merely turning away with a grumble. Lettie was Prudy's confidante, but she knew that she was not told everything that went on in Prudy's life. Lettie always cheered her, gave her hope, and helped her over the rough spots which the traumas of the years had inflicted on her. Eventually, the Dannenbrings bought a new car, a Chevrolet, and sold their old Model T, which still ran perfectly, to the Deters. They would have given it to them, but knew that Lester was too proud for that, so upon the agreed price of $50 it became the property of Lester Deters. He learned to drive it in no time, preferring to gun the motor, which needed no priming, roaring it to life and taking off in a cloud of dust. The Dannenbrings intended the vehicle to be mostly for Prudy's benefit, to give her some mobility. They were concerned for her. Lettie gave her lessons when Lester was not around and relaxed in the knowledge that her friend had transportation in the event she needed it.

The year 1919 began with optimism, grateful people looking to the future after the devastating war. Prudy did her best to present a hopeful outlook for the boys' sakes. She would live the best she knew how for them. They were growing up. Chester was a husky fifteen year old, strong and a big help to his father. Fred was a nicely formed thirteen year old, glad to go along with what was happening, not liking to have to make decisions, happy to follow. But fate is not always kind, and good intentions are often defeated. In 1919 the land was rampant with flu, called Spanish Influenza, followed by pneumonia which killed thousands of people. The Deters were spared simply because their contacts were so few. One of the victims was Dr. Gideon Walsh who nursed the sick folks of Spotswood and the surrounding area until he dropped. He had grown old with the people he had known for decades and had dedicated his life to them. He had never married, lived alone in rooms adjoining his office above the bank, and was content to live out his life in modest surroundings.

His tired old body could not fight off the infection and he succumbed in February, leaving the community without a doctor. There was Mrs. Johnson, who herself was getting on in years, but was still hale and hearty and determined to keep all the folks well. She made a mighty effort to take care of the sick, and she took it upon herself to train two young women in what nursing skills she knew. As a result, there was a competent nursing staff in Spotswood, which fact was instrumental in obtaining a new doctor, a young man who had been an intern in a hospital in Minneapolis, a dedicated new doctor who was eager to savor the wild west and to care for its rugged inhabitants. His arrival in late March, 1919, was greeted with welcome and relief. They had never been without a doctor; Dr. Walsh had been taken for granted, having always been there. His death was a definite shock, bringing home the realization of their own mortality.

The new doctor's name was Lawrence Michaels and he was a striking contrast to the man he replaced. He was around thirty years old with a kind face, rather long and clean shaven, with twinkling blue eyes and an abundance of black wavy hair. He was an instant hit with the young ladies. He proved to be as competent as his spit and polish appearance led people to believe. His first task was to undertake a complete cleaning and rearranging of Dr. Walsh's office. The old doctor had been of inestimable benefit to the community, but he was untidy. Since he had no family or heirs that anyone had been able to ascertain over the years, especially since the good doctor was always so secretive about his past, it fell to Dr. Michaels to dispose of the contents of his office. Much of what he found he threw in the trash barrel, including some decrepit office furniture, having brought with him a few items of his own. But, he found something which he felt he should make public, and it created a stir, the likes of which the people of Spotswood had never experienced. His discovery was a yellowed newspaper clipping that had been jammed in the back of one of the heavy drawers in the antique roll-top desk, shoved between the drawer and the back of the desk, whether by chance or on purpose it was hard to tell.

The clipping was published on the front page of the Spotswood Journal, a weekly newspaper. An additional run was necessary due to the demand, including the

Mobridge News.

"April 4, 1919, Spotswood, South Dakota:

An historic find has been reported by Dr. Lawrence Michaels, the new doctor in Spotswood, who has taken over the practice of Dr. Gideon Walsh, late of the area. This reporter was informed of Dr. Michael's discovery and was privy to same and did peruse with his own eyes the object of discussion. An old newspaper account, brittle and yellow with age, was found in the desk of Dr. Walsh, and its contents should be of interest to the people of this community. The late Dr. Walsh served the area from 1875.

'April 20, 1865, Bowling Green, Virginia:

John Wilkes Booth, actor, was found dead in a barn in Bowling Green after being sought by authorities for the murder of President Lincoln on April 14, 1865. After reportedly firing a bullet into the back of the President's head as he sat in his box at Ford's Theater in Washington, D.C., watching the play, Our American Cousin, Booth leapt to the stage, injuring himself, but escaping. It was learned he had broken his leg in the daring leap, having caught his foot in the American Flag. He was subsequently tended to and his leg set by a Dr. Samuel Mudd, who was later arrested for the deed. Dr. Mudd's assistant, one Dr. Gideon Walsh, managed to elude authorities. His whereabouts are unknown.'

"We thank Dr. Michaels for generously sharing this bit of history with our readers. Dr. Walsh served the community with skill, compassion and devotion, and we are certain the residents, his patients, and our readers hold no ill will toward him. His actions speak for themselves."

Spotswood enjoyed the limelight for a few weeks after publication of the story and enlarged upon it and Dr. Walsh's talents. All of them had benefited from his skill and generosity and his willingness to accept a chicken or produce for his services. At least he didn't go hungry. Dr. Michaels benefited, too, and was lauded for what he did. His practice was brisk from the time of his arrival, despite a corresponding rise in the cost of his services, but his expertise soon lived up to his reputation.

Then came the ultimate blow to Prudy, the one that destroyed her. At the beginning of May when the throes of winter had dissolved in gentle spring rains and the warming sun brought forth new life, greenery and promise, she received a letter from Lars.

"My dear Prudy,

It is with deep sadness and a heart filled with sorrow that I write to tell you of the passing of your sister, Patience, my beloved wife. It was the Spanish Influenza that took her. She was only thirty-nine and not ever a truly healthy woman, and she just couldn't fight off the infection of the virulent virus that has infected our country. Through the tears of my grief arises an anger at God that he should take such a fine, gentle woman, one who had survived a tenuous life, one who unselfishly gave of herself to all who knew her. Yet I know we must have faith.

Millicent is beside herself. A bride, she should be giving her full attention to her new life with her husband, Howard, who is a fine young man. Yet, without her, I honestly don't know how I could cope with this blow to us, the loss of the center of our lives, the core of our family.

Due to the highly contagious nature of this flu, it was imperative that we inter our dear Patience as soon as possible. Therefore, I am sorry to have to notify you of these sad events after her burial. It is my entreaty that you understand and can forgive us, but we felt you could not arrive in time and we know you have certain difficulties in getting away. We regret we were forced to take this course of action. She is laid to rest in a beautiful tree filled area of the New Ulm Cemetery.

Patience's absence has left a void that will never be filled. I don't know how I can go on, but I must. Thank God for Millicent. Howard and I shall make sure she remains forever safe and sound. We are otherwise well.

Our thoughts are with you. Please convey our regards to your family.

With affection, Lars"

He had enclosed a framed photograph of Patience. The letter slipped from Prudy's hands and tears splashed on the gilt frame. She laid her head on her arms on the kitchen table and wept. Her years weighed heavily on her. How could she go on with the knowledge that her sister was no longer there? The two of them had forged a rapport that could never be broken. She could turn to Patience and look up to her as a person to be admired and emulated.

Why had God seen fit to take her beautiful, cultured sister, who was kind and good and never hurt anyone? She was all that Prudy had left of her family. She did not understand. Now Prudy was all that was left. She sobbed even more at the thought. What a creature to have left! What had she done to be spared? She had married a hard, cruel man whom no one liked and who was abusive to her and the boys; she had borne five children, one by another man; two of her boys were gone. Some day she would have only Lester. The prospect frightened her. Her future looked utterly hopeless, full of foreboding, and she could do nothing about it.

She sat up and wiped her eyes with her torn hanky, her body shaking from her crying. She looked at the photograph that Lars had enclosed through blurred vision. A lovely, smiling, blond Patience looked out at her in contentment. Her hair was piled on top of her regal head as was her custom, and she looked like a queen to Prudy. She clutched it tightly to her. She would write a long letter to Lars and Millicent to thank them for it and to try to console them the best she could. She was not good at words, but she would try. She straightened and heaved a sigh laden with the burden of coping with her miserable life. There were still Chester and Fred. There was still hope that their lives could be better. She must carry on for their sakes. When she told them of their aunt's death they cried, too. They had loved their Aunt Patience and didn't understand why she had to die. Lester was unsympathetic, but said little, just telling them to stop their sniveling. This time his attitude was the beginning of his sons' perception of the man who was their father.

Life continued. South Dakota experienced a boom in agriculture, the state's mainstay. The operation of the farm and the profits from wheat, corn and oats kept Lester going and his harvests were proof of what a good farmer he was. He tucked away in his secret place all the money he derived from his sales of grain and livestock.

The year dragged on monotonously for the Deters with no word from Alan, but there had been news of his being seen in the Mobridge area and on the Standing Rock Indian Reservation. He would be almost eighteen now, practically grown. Prudy missed him terribly, missed his sensitivity and thoughtfulness, and she hoped and prayed that he was all right. How she needed him at home where he could give them strength from his goodness. The boys missed him, too, but they had each other and were together most of the time, inseparable, as though their closeness would keep them safe. Prudy longed to drive to Mobridge to check on Alan, but didn't dare take the risk. She hoped in vain for a letter.

In December, 1919, Congress passed the women's suffrage amendment. Women had been permitted to vote in South Dakota the year before, but Prudy never gave it a thought. Even if she had she knew that Lester would never allow it. She was gratified to know that women had made that tremendous step in progress in a male dominated society that looked down on women, regarding them as chattel with few brains, just enough to bear children and keep house. With the vote, maybe women could change that. There were women in the area who took advantage of their hard-won battle, among them Lettie. She was one of the first women in the area to cast a ballot and she lost no time in letting Lester know about it and didn't back down at his snide remark that voting would do women no good, that it was a waste of their time, since they knew nothing anyway. Prudy enjoyed Lettie's more adventurous life vicariously and took pride in her friend.

The agricultural boom was short lived. The year 1920 brought an entirely different outlook. Wheat that sold for $2 a bushel in 1919 now brought only 90¢. Lester ranted and raved about such a state of affairs and was forced to dip into his stash of cash, making sure Prudy didn't know when he did, because she would spend it foolishly. The money was his and it was safe from thieves and bankers, terms he deemed to be synonymous. He threw up to Prudy his wisdom in keeping his money in a safe place and in being a frugal man when in 1922 the small bank in Spotswood failed and depositers lost every cent.

"See there, Prudy, what'd I tell ya? We've still got money, safe and sound."

But he took pains to not appear to have any more than his neighbors, lest they try to borrow from him. He hoarded his cash and, at last, had a valid excuse for not making improvements on the farm. He couldn't afford it. Then he had to sell some of his cattle to provide for his family and to buy the makings for his home brew, which to his mind was a necessity. The boys were of an age where they should be learning how to drink their beer like men.

"But they're too young," Prudy protested.

"No they're not. Drinkin' beer is part of growin' up."

She sighed and hoped that Chester and Fred would not like the taste of it. At least they had a very good example of what it did to their father.

They had a few cattle left and some milk cows, but Lester sold the horses. He declared he didn't need them. He'd buy a combine cheap. There were plenty of farmers who had called it quits and were selling their machinery. He kept an old nag named Rambler, as cantankerous as his master, whom Lester swore he'd really break one day. He'd ride the big black horse when he was full of beer and fury, whipping its hind quarters unmercifully to make him gallop faster over the prairie or on the gravel roads, whooping and hollaring so everyone could hear him vent his frustrations. Then Rambler threw him one dark Saturday night and stomped around the prostrate drunken man on the dirt road before he whinnied in triumph and took off over the flat land to disappear forever. Lester was at loose ends until he took under his wing a ragged hound, a lanky, shaggy-haired, long-eared mutt that followed him home one day. He called him "Dog" feeling that to be name enough. He treated him little better than he had his horse, except that he didn't use the whip, only goaded him into prolonged barking and yelping, sounds which Lester seemed to enjoy. He was the only one who did, and he received numerous complaints from neighbors when the slow-witted hound sat and howled all night long at nothing in particular while Lester snored and Prudy lay awake. By morning's light Dog was sound asleep. Lester paid no attention to the neighbors, content to have Dog follow him around close at his heels.

Lester seldom gave Prudy any money. She had her egg money and that was enough. He didn't touch her egg money. It would be a sissy thing for him to do; egg money was women's pittance. It didn't amount to much anyway. Besides, he didn't know where she kept it. Prudy put her egg money away faithfully, saving it for special things like Christmas. She would drop the coins into the pretty shiny box tied with the blue ribbon, which was frayed form repeated tyings and untyings, the box Patience had given her. Most of the original contents were still in it. Every time she opened it she took out the photograph of Eric and gazed at it lovingly, smiling at the remembrance of that golden day. Patience's photograph in its gilt frame was in the box, too. She treasured the box, her only bit of beauty in her drab world. No one knew about the box. She had never shown Lester and the boys would not appreciate it. It was hers and hers alone. It held all that was left of her material life. She owned nothing else.

In October, 1922, Prudy was forty-seven years old. Lester was fifty-seven. Her birthday went unnoticed, as usual. She had almost forgotten it herself. She was getting old. She certainly did not look aristocratic anymore. She smiled remembering how sincerely Patience had said she looked aristocratic and had fixed her hair so smartly and made her come alive and look attractive. Even the boys had commented and, except for Lester's cruel remark, she would have kept it up. Her thick dark hair was streaked with gray. Her brown eyes were sometimes stark in her white face, lined with fatigue and depression.

She had no incentive to keep up her appearance other than sprucing up before she spent an afternoon at Lettie's place or Lettie came over for an afternoon of coffee and chat. She looked forward to those visits and cleaned the house as best she could, took a bath and washed and combed her hair carefully. She would bake cookies or a cake to go with the coffee and the two women would enjoy the afternoon. Except for those times, Prudy had no self-respect or confidence. Without Lettie to bolster her sagging morale she was useless. She couldn't manage it alone. She was a completely defeated woman. Lester would never change. Her life would not be any different, just drudgery and hardship until she died. To ease her gnawing pain she shut out any emotion and merely existed, going about her duties automatically. She longed for an exchange of affection. Her life was becoming intolerably barren.

Then she found the cat. A bedraggled yellow cat sat at the edge of the clearing on the south. She spotted it from the dining room while watering her plants on the window sill one day. Poor thing, it must be cold huddled there she thought, and went to the door to call. But as soon as she raised her voice the cat bolted and ran. She was disappointed and sorry for the animal. It was getting colder and snow would soon cover the flat land. But the next day it reappeared and didn't run away until she started across the yard to the edge of the clearing. She called and looked for the cat, but was unsuccessful. She left an old cracked bowl with milk in it at the edge of the clearing and returned to the house. The next day she found the empty bowl. She filled it again and this time moved it from the clearing closer to the house. She also left a few table scraps. The next day they were gone. She repeated the routine until the bowl and the cat were under the clothesline every morning. The cat was looking better, but it was thin, its coat was matted and dirty, and its ears bore the signs of battle. One day Prudy went quietly out on the back porch, pretending not to notice the cat. She walked cautiously to the south edge of the porch and heard a throaty meow. She let out her breath and stepped from the porch.

"Nice cat. Here kitty."

It didn't move nor did it run off. She was almost beside it when the cat stood up, lifted a crooked tail, tilted its head and meowed again. Delighted, Prudy refrained from picking it up, fearing to spook the scrawny animal. She sat on her haunches and put out her hand that held a buttered scrap of toast. Timidly and cautiously the cat approached her, gently took the scrap from her and chewed it down. Then it sat and looked at her with another meow. Prudy scooped it up with a happy laugh. She carried it to the porch and carefully inspected the cat from head to tail. It was a female. That was nice. She fed her and watched with satisfaction as the animal ate ravenously, then sat in the sunshine and proceeded to clean itself. It was clear that she needed help in that endeavor and Prudy picked her up, stroked her gently and combed and cleansed as the cat relaxed and let her. Prudy noticed scabs and old wounds and determined there would be no more of that. Soon the cat was curled in Prudy's lap, purring contentedly. She felt like purring back. She named her Bunting.

CHAPTER FOURTEEN

Alan

With Bunting, Prudy had a living creature to talk to that did not talk back, one who never sat in judgement, who regarded her as the mistress of the house where the cat had staked a claim, who accepted her as she was and demanded the same in return, yet she remained aloof and independent and very selective in dispensing her affection. Never having had a pet, the experience was totally new and exciting, and the companionship gave her a decided lift. Bunting was not a noisy or intrusive cat, being content to lie in the sun or catch mice in the barn, or bother Dog, whom she despised.

Dog had a nasty habit of bringing home to Lester small animals, gophers, squirrels, rabbits and such, oftentimes still alive and struggling, and tearing them apart at his master's feet while Lester laughed. But Dog kept his distance from Bunting, recognizing a formidable adversary when he saw one, being all bark and no bite. At first he had obeyed his primitive instincts and barked loudly at the cat, then chased her to the clearing on the south and up one of the straggler trees that had survived. But once was all. At the next aggressive move on Dog's part Bunting had jumped a foot from being startled, the fur on her back and tail all bushed out like the back of a porcupine, and then surprise turned to fury and she jumped on Dog's back and rode the yelping animal around the barnyard, spitting her disgust, until he had learned his lesson. Bunting jumped off and climbed a post to the hay loft where she remained sitting on her paws, pupils wide with animosity and victory. From then on they kept their distance from each other. Dog circled wide around the cat, who didn't budge, just sitting still where she was with her ears back, never taking her glinting eyes off the wary dog. They put up with each other for years in this fashion, growing old with their masters.

Chester and Fred enjoyed the animals and took pleasure in watching them. They didn't urge Dog to attack Bunting as did their father, who couldn't understand why he wouldn't, and Lester soon tired of the game because Dog simply would not. The cat was safe and she knew it, looking with disdain upon him as he loped around her with his tail between his legs, his tongue drooling out of the side of his mouth as Bunting stared at him unblinking and unperturbed. Prudy took satisfaction in one small victory in their lives.

The boys were strong and healthy and worked the farm with their father, learning their craft well. They went as far as they could in school, but neither went to high school as it meant living in Mobridge and it was just not feasible because of the distance and expense. Lester saw no need for further education since they could learn all they needed to know from him and he needed them on the farm. The boys didn't mind and were glad to stay on the home place. They could always farm and make money and had not yet learned that circumstances change, that already change was encroaching upon established family farms, creeping insiduously over the coming years to bankrupt many families.

The years passed with little change except for the continued deterioration of the farm buildings on the Deters place. The crops were good, but prices were low and, despite the usual or better than average harvests, there was very little ready money.

It was April 1, 1924, and Prudy was thinking of Alan. It was his twenty-second birthday. He had never been out of her thoughts since he left in the summer of 1918, that awful year when nothing went right, six years before. It seemed like only the day before from the constant ache in her heart, and yet it also seemed like an eternity. A cloudy sky and intermittent drizzle didn't help her spirits. It was dark in the kitchen so she lit the lamp and went about her chores mechanically and without enthusiasm. The men were in the fields, turning over the black earth, getting it ready for spring planting.

Bunting sat by the iron cookstove where it was warm and watched her movements without blinking. Prudy had grown accustomed to her steady stare long ago, but she often wondered what her cat saw or even comprehended. She knew that Bunting loved her and that they shared an exchange of feelings that bound them together in an unexpressed bond, and Bunting did acknowledge Prudy's idle chatter when they were alone. Her ears would stand straight up, she would sit very alert with her tail around her paws, and when Prudy would look at her and pose an implausible question to the cat, Bunting would obligingly blink in agreement. Bunting, too, knew she was loved. She had grown and flourished under Prudy's tender care and was equally at home inside or outside, but preferred to be where it was most comfortable, especially on blustery winter days when she could be found close to the cookstove, venturing outside only to perform her duties hurriedly or to keep the mice in check in the barn. The barn animals watched their step when Bunting was around and a peculiar affinity developed between her and a milk cow, Bessie. It was not uncommon to find Bunting atop her broad back, feet tucked under her, surveying the barn from her safe perch. Prudy wondered how long cats lived, yet she knew that she would make sure that Bunting had many more years left in her.

She took a spice cake from the oven. The fragrant smell filled the house, comforting her. She was stirred from her reverie and her uninspired straightening of the kitchen by a quiet rap on the back door. At the word, "Mother?" she whirled around and was astounded to see Alan enter the kitchen.

"Alan! Oh, Alan!" she exclaimed and ran to meet him as he approached her with outstretched arms.

They clung together and she sobbed her relief at seeing him. Alan cried, too. At last he held her at arm's length and looked at her closely. His joy at seeing her was tempered with sadness to see what the years had done to his mother, but he only said, "Mother, it's wonderful to see you."

"Oh my, I know I look just awful. If I'd known you'd be coming . . ." She patted her hair and smoothed her apron.

"Never mind, you look just wonderful to me."

He had not ever called her Mother, just Mama. How grown up he was, a full-grown man. And he was wearing a black suit with a white collar. Lester wouldn't like that. But Prudy didn't care. Her son was back. He was home. Alan smiled tenderly at her, knowing what was going through her mind, and said, "Don't worry, Mother. Dad can no longer intimidate me. I know who I am and what I believe and I am firm in that belief. No matter what he thinks of me that cannot be diminshed. I love him and I'll tell him so. But, you — are you all right? Has Dad been . . ."

"I'm just fine, Alan, a bit tired, that's all. You know your father's temper. But I've learned how not to rile him so much. We get along, but we're getting older you know. I'm mighty close to fifty."

The look of love and concern on Alan's face melted her reserve and she went to him again, holding him close, tears rolling down her weathered cheeks. He held her to him and stroked her gray hair and grieved for what life had done to her. A moment of doubt stirred in him. Maybe it would have been better if he had not left, if he had stayed and watched over her. He knew the violence his father was capable of. But he also realized that one cannot second guess every decision. Prudy pulled away and smiled happily at him.

"You've grown up so nicely, Alan, and you are quite handsome."

"Now, Mother, I don't think handsome describes me. I have no desire to be handsome. Priests are celibate, as you know. My work is my life."

He had grown from a slightly built, insecure, sensitive young man who was easily wounded, into a tall, good-looking man with neatly groomed brown hair, with brown eyes full of compassion and sensitivity. He had filled out with broad shoulders and a strong bearing that evoked confidence and trust. The worried little-boy look had vanished and a man of purpose in a priest's garb stood before her. She was filled with an immense love and pride in this man who was her son.

"Your grandmother would be so proud of you," she said with intensity. "She grew up in the Catholic faith, you remember, and practiced it to her dying day, even under the worst circumstances. Come, let's sit down; we must talk. Why didn't you write? Where have you been all this time? We've missed you terribly."

She led the way to the front room. As they passed through the kitchen and dining room into the front room, Alan took in the vast downgrading that his home had undergone. He had grown up in this house, yet somehow it seemed smaller than he remembered. It looked so shabby, but he kept his thoughts to himself and concentrated on his mother. They sat on the frayed sofa and he held her rough, red hands in his as he explained.

"It has been a long time I admit. And I apologize for not writing to you, but I was so hurt and felt so rejected by everyone that it took awhile before I could even think of writing. By then I was so caught up in work, in my new life, that I fear everything else ceased to exist for me. I know that sounds selfish, but that's the way it's been. My life now has direction and I have a reason for being. I know that my life belongs to God and to His works. That is most important to me. I knew that I had to come home and tell my family, especially you, Mother, what has happened and to receive your blessing — at least your understanding."

"I'm so proud of you, Alan, and so happy to have you home. But we missed you so and worried so. We gave up ever knowing what had happened to you. We heard rumors of someone who looked like you and being a priest in Mobridge and I wanted to come to see for myself, but — but I wasn't able to search for you, to look for my son. But you can be proud of me, too, because I've learned to drive." She laughed and tilted her head.

Alan chuckled in pleasure and amazement to think of his timid mother behind the wheel of a car.

"Oh yes, I can drive. Lettie — you remember Lettie — sold us their old Model T. Of course, it is your father's and he drives it — actually, it's more like he's riding it. He doesn't know I can drive; he'd frown on that. So please don't say anything. I hope you understand that I just couldn't very well drive off without him knowing about it. That would really rile him, and there were your brothers to think about."

"Where are they? I can't wait to see them."

"They'll be in for dinner soon. They're out in the fields helping your dad plow. They'll be so surprised. Let's see, I'll fix everybody's favorite, ham and sweet potatoes. And you can share a room with one of your brothers. They each have a room to themselves now since you left and John —" She looked at him with wide eyes brimming with tears.

Alan said softly, "I know, Mother. I heard about John's death in the war, but that news didn't reach me until months afterwards and by then the weather was so bad there was nothing I could do. Even telegrams weren't getting through because of downed lines and, besides, I thought a telegram might be too upsetting for all of you. What could I have done? I suppose Dad was in a bad state."

Prudy was crying again. She thought she had cried her heart out years before and that nothing could make her shed a single tear ever again. But seeing Alan and feeling his love and warmth that had been absent for so long released her pent up emotions and she could not stem them. Alarmed, Alan took her in his arms and tried to soothe her.

"I've done you all an injustice, Mother. I should have come."

"Oh, Alan, it's been so awful since you and John left us. Everything's gone wrong and it's all made your father harder to get along with. But, it's all right now. You're home."

"Mother, I'm so sorry. I just didn't know. But I hate to have to tell you that I can't stay but a few hours. I have work to do and was granted only today for some time off to visit my family. I needed to see you all before my duties in the church take up all of my time and energy."

Prudy dried her eyes. "I hoped you'd stay awhile." She wanted to keep him with her forever. How could she let him go again? Who knew when she would see him again? What kind of church would keep a son from his mother? She pulled herself together.

"Well, we'll just have to make the most of it then, won't we? Come on into the kitchen while I put dinner in the oven. The men folks will be really surprised to smell ham and real glad to see you. We'll celebrate," she said as they returned to the kitchen where she busied herself to keep from dwelling on the short time he would be home.

Alan went to the root cellar for one of the cured hams hanging from the rafters. The Deters had never kept pigs, but bought a ham or two for special occasions. Alan noted that his father still kept a plentiful stock of his home brew in barrels set on wood planks in the cool cellar. Prudy accompanied him in a moment and gathered several sweet potatoes and a jar of her home canned green beans and some watermelon pickles and they returned to the house. Alan stoked the fire in the cookstove with corn cobs and went to the back yard to bring in some wood.

"Where's the ax, Mother? It's always been on the stump."

She went to the porch and looked.

"Your father doesn't always leave it there for some reason. I've found it almost anywhere. Sometimes he just gives it a toss if he's out of sorts or flings it into the ground when he's mad. Here it is, under this old chair," and she retrieved the ancient implement from beneath a chair that had been relegated to the back porch after having lived out its usefulness in the kitchen. Alan presently had a stock of chopped wood in the scuttle and soon the ham was baking in the covered roaster with sweet potatoes nestled beside it with a tantalizing aroma dispelling the gloom of the rain clouds.

Bunting had wandered in from the barn to see what all the activity was about and followed them into the kitchen looking for a bite that was sure to follow the delicious smell that had drawn her there. She stopped when she saw Alan, looked him over carefully with her steady gaze, then her crooked tail lifted in greeting and she sauntered over to him and rubbed against his black pantleg.

"Well, what have we here, Mother? I didn't know you liked cats. And what a pretty one this is." He stroked the cat's upraised back and was rewarded with a loud purr.

"I found her at the edge of the clearing a few years ago. You should have seen her, just skin and bones. I named her Bunting and she is mine. Your father has a dog."

Alan sensed from the way she said it that the dog was not a favorite with her. He watched as she augmented the contents of the glowing oven with baking powder biscuits and then poured coffee for him and herself.

"Now tell me what you've been doing all these years and about your church. It's been so lonesome without you. I just died inside with you gone, Alan."

He patted her worn hands. How could he have been so thoughtless? How could he have believed that no one cared? He had convinced himself that he was doing the right thing, that in time it would be all right. He had not comprehended what his leaving and long absence would do to his mother.

"I walked to Spotswood that night, Mother, slept in a livery stable, and caught a ride to Mobridge the next day. I went directly to the Catholic Church and the priest, Father Daniel O'Brian, took me in. He cared for me and counseled me, easing the hurt in my young heart. Later, he made sure that the priesthood was what I really wanted, because once a commitment is made, it is for a lifetime. I didn't give him my real name, fearing he would contact you and Dad, and I think he knew I lied to him, but he was patient with me. Eventually I confessed the truth and by that time I had made up my mind. I would be a priest and serve God and the Church. And I wouldn't come home until I had done what I set out to do so that even Dad could see that I was serious and had made something good of my life.

"I took the training and accompanied Father O'Brian to the Standing Rock Reservation on his regular trips there. He is a fine man and has made tremendous inroads in the miserable lives of the Indians. He established a school in connection with the church and he works with the government as much as possible in trying to direct those people to a productive life. The Indians are wards of the government with little influence over their own lives. Sad to say, liquor — too readily available to them — destroys much of his good work. During the last two years I have spent a lot of time on the reservation, striving to continue Father O'Brian's work. He is getting on in years and has his hands full at the parish in Mobridge. I love it, Mother. I have taken up the challenge and am doing constructive, rewarding work, and the people respect me. The Indians are not the savages they have been portrayed, just an impoverished, misunderstood race of people who have been unjustly used."

Prudy was looking at her son as the words poured from him. His face was aglow with enthusiasm. Respect and admiration welled up in her. She was positive that even Lester would be proud of him. How could he not be?

Alan continued. "When the Spanish Influenza hit, the reservation suffered a great loss of lives. The Indians have little resistance to the white man's diseases. It was shortly after I arrived and I was very young. I was frantic with overwork in what seemed a hopeless task. I fell ill myself, mostly from fatigue, but I recovered after a few weeks in the hospital. I was lucky, because the flu was vicious in killing its victims. So all I could do for John, God rest his soul, was to pray for him. It must have been a terrible time for you, to lose a child, a tragic loss. John was so full of life, a bit over zealous, perhaps — like Dad — but he was my brother and I am sorry to lose him."

"Alan, there were others that the flu took. Dr. Walsh, for one, and — and your Aunt Patience."

He looked as though she had struck him. "Oh no, Mother, not Aunt Patience. I didn't know. She was such a wonderful person. And Millicent — what about her?"

Prudy smiled at him with affection. "Millicent is well. She is stronger than her mother was, despite her sheltered life. She and her husband, Howard, have two children, a boy and a girl. They live in Lars's home in New Ulm. Lars has never gotten over Patience's death and he begged Millicent and Howard to live with him in that big house. As you know, there's plenty of room. And the children provide enough activity to keep his mind off things."

Alan remembered New Ulm and the house and Millicent and, only briefly, did a flicker of an old feeling show in his face. Prudy changed the subject.

"You remember the Crawford sisters, don't you?"

He gave a low chuckle and said, "Oh Mother, we were so mean to those poor old ladies, weren't we?"

"Yes you were. And I discovered that they were really very nice."

"Were?"

"Yes, they're gone, too. Cecelia went first. Poor Penelope found her dead in bed one morning. She just died peacefully in her sleep. Penelope didn't know how to manage after that and got quite dotty in her last years. There weren't any relatives so she was all alone. Mrs. Johnson looked in on her now and then, but she is very old now and laid up with lumbago. Anyway, Penelope got so addled without Cecelia that she finally lost her mind and she just wandered off one day. She was found in an open field curled up in a ball in the tall grass. She died of a broken heart they say. But to my way of thinking it was the elements that helped do her in. Those two funerals were well attended, I tell you. Everybody turned out, out of curiosity, I expect. Those old ladies got a real send-off."

They continued to fill each other in on past events in their lives until noon when they heard the car rattle up to the back door. Lester, Chester and Fred clambered out and stomped up to the porch and into the kitchen.

"What's for dinner, Mama? We're starved," declared Chester.

Prudy stood expectant and fairly bursting, with a broad smile on her face as they came in. The boys were first and stopped stock-still with their mouths dropping open. Lester loomed behind them, his mouth closing in a grim line.

"Well look who's here, the sissy," he growled.

"Lester! Stop it. It's Alan."

Chester and Fred came toward him with their hands outstretched in greeting, grins illuminating their robust faces.

"Is that you, Alan? Holy cow, we thought you disappeared off the face of the earth," said Chester as he pumped Alan's arm.

Alan laughed heartily and put his arms around his brothers. They slapped one another happily on the back, glad to see each other.

"Is that your car out there?" asked Fred. At eighteen his interest in motor vehicles was all consuming.

"Yes; that is, it belongs to the parish in Mobridge, I'm driving it today. It's just an old Chevy, but it runs very well." He looked at his stern, silent father.

"Hello, Dad," he said and walked toward him.

"What're you doin' here, boy? And what kind of clothes are those? Priest's clothes, that's what kind. So you went and did it, didn't ya? I might've known —

just what a sissy would do."

Alan stood tall and confident, letting the unkind words roll off his back. he smiled at his father with a look of peace that totally unsettled Lester.

"I'm here for only a few hours. I wanted to see all of you."

"You took your own damn time in doin' it."

"I'll tell you all about it. How are you, Dad? I see you've grown a beard. And you're still working hard, I gather."

As usual a confrontation confused Lester because he lost the upper hand in failing to intimidate his adversary. Alan's serene demeanor and lack of fear took the steam out of him. His drooping figure turned away, he averted his eyes beneath the bushy brows and muttered, "Put dinner on the table, woman. We're hungry."

"Wow, ham and sweet potatoes. Swell!" said Chester.

"Our favorite," declared Fred.

They ate with relish and ignored their father's grumpiness as Alan told them what had happened while he had been away. Prudy happily fed her men, her family, together again. She topped the meal with her spice cake and basked in the compliments her sons lavished upon her dinner.

The meal ended and Prudy was hoping for a few hours of visiting with Alan, together with Chester and Fred. To relax in the warm, fragrant kitchen reminiscing with her boys around her was what she was looking forward to. They must take advantage of every opportunity to bridge the gap that had developed, a gap that yawned ever wider as time marched relentlessly on. But it was not to be. Lester ordered Chester and Fred to go back to the fields with him. Alan said he couldn't stay longer, much as he would like to; he had to be getting back. They stood awkwardly in the kitchen. Prudy longed to hold Alan to her and to keep him forever, yet she knew that it wouldn't be fair to him. Alan looked fondly at his family, beaming at them with love. He wanted to make the sign of the cross and give them his blessing, but knew that it would only cause an unpleasant scene. He hugged his mother. She wept on his shoulder.

"Don't cry, Mother. I promise to keep in touch."

He shook the hands of his brothers and gave them each a bear hug as they flushed in pleasure and embarrassment. He looked at his father, who feigned disinterest.

"Goodbye, Dad. I love you." He held out his hand.

Lester ignored it, lowered his eyes and said, "Yeah," then turned and left the kitchen, the screen door banging behind him.

Chester and Fred followed him, looking back with happy grins and waving. Prudy followed Alan onto the back porch, her hands touching him, dreading his departure. The drizzle had stopped and the sun was out, shining brightly, contradicting Prudy's sweet sorrow.

"I love you, Mother. You'll hear from me, I promise, and I'll remember all of you in my prayers. May God be with you."

He kissed her and gazed lovingly at her and stepped from the porch. He looked back at her as he got into the black Chevrolet and drove out of the yard.

Prudy watched until he was out of sight and nothing was left but a thin veil of dust hanging in the road. The chickens recovered their senses from all the commotion and resumed pecking in the yard. It was very quiet. The visit had been far too short but it was just what they needed. It was so good for them to be all together again. She could look forward to letters from Alan now. He had promised. At least she knew where he was and what he was doing. The ache in her was not quite so deep now. She didn't need to cry anymore. But she did. Bunting purred and rubbed against her legs. She had forgotten to wish Alan a happy birthday.

CHAPTER FIFTEEN

Chester

Following the brief visit of their brother the adventurous spirits of Chester and Fred were unleashed, Chester's more so since he had always been headstrong. In 1924 Chester was twenty and more than a little restless. He was eager to be out on his own; he wanted to leave the farm and make his own way as Alan had. Who could have foretold that meek, mild Alan would leave while still practically a boy and, all by himself, become a priest with his own church? Chester had always been the daring brother, and the constraints by his domineering father were beginning to chafe, especially since Chester could not see any kind of future for himself in being a farmer, in plodding along year after year doing the same monotonous work for little pay. It took him no time at all to make up his mind.

Chester was almost as tall as his father, who was still a big man despite being stooped by the years. At fifty-nine most of Lester's spirit was gone out of him and in its place it left a sullen, angry man whose life hadn't turned out at all the way he had envisioned, being stuck on a dingy farm all these years and all because of that woman he married. If it hadn't been for her they'd be on a spread in Oklahoma. He conveniently overlooked the fact that it was because of Prudy that he had a farm at all. His rage would periodically erupt and he would strike out at her to Prudy's consternation, as there was no apparent reason for it and she had learned years ago not to get him all riled up. Lester still had abundant energy; he was big and strong and could put in a full day's work and still enjoy a man's right with his woman. To others he appeared to be the same, only older and a bit eccentric, a man who controlled his life and his wife and had money in his pocket. Some wondered why some of that money wasn't spent on upkeep for the farm, but it wasn't their business after all. The boys had grown used to their father's outbursts, they had grown up with them, had taken them for granted even though it bothered them to see him beat their mother. But they were cowed by the sheer strength of him and were afraid that a confrontation would only make matters worse.

Lester chose to look upon Chester as his mainstay, the man in the family. Chester was robust with a stocky build. He was handsome with abundant brown hair and friendly brown eyes. His hands and feet were large and he carried his big frame with confidence and a bit of bravado. Neighbor girls set their caps for him but none caught his fancy. His view of life was much broader than what his father had taught him. Any intolerance he may have had was the result of too little education and an ignorance of the world beyond Spotswood. He knew there was much to see and to learn and that it was up to him to make his life different from what it was. He had to be the one to change it. And that change lay outside South Dakota.

One night after supper he announced that he and Peter Dannenbring were going to California to seek their fortunes. Lester gave a sarcastic snort. When he saw that his son was serious he objected vehemently. He was needed on the farm. How could he do with another lost hand? One day the farm would be his and Fred's. Why did he want to go and give all that up for anyway? But Chester remained unruffled at his outburst and firm in his decision. He finally convinced his father that it would be only temporary, that he could make lots more money in California than on the farm and that he would send money home to help out. He could contribute much more than if he stayed on the farm to work for prices so low that it just didn't pay.

Then, at his suggestion that they all move to California, Lester spat in derision. Nothing doing, he wasn't going anywhere. He was doing just fine right where he was. His contradictory evaluations of his situation had no meaning for Lester — only that he was correct in his expostulations at any given moment.

He asked, "What'll you be doin? Pickin' oranges or workin' in a stinkin' cannery?"

"If I have to," Chester replied. "It pays real good and Pete and I both want to go out there and make some real dough."

"Just how do ya think you're gonna get to California, boy?"

"Pete and I have thought about that. We've decided to hitchhike."

Prudy looked worried. "Isn't that sort of dangerous?" she asked with a frown.

"Naw, and it's easy to get a lift. And it sure beats paying for a train ticket. We've got it all figured out. We'll need some money, naturally, but I've saved a few bucks and so has Pete, so you won't need to give me any." He looked squarely into his father's eyes, destroying any and all objections.

So at the end of May, 1924, after the crops were in, Chester and Peter Dannenbring set out for California after elaborate preparations and admonitions by the mothers. Lettie had anticipated all the objections that could be presented by Lester and she and Meyer delcared they would drive the two boys to Mobridge where they would be more apt to catch a ride west. Their Chevrolet sedan had more room and was a newer, cleaner car, plus it gave them better control of the situation and of their son, much better than handing him over to the dubious care of Lester Deters and his smelly Model T. The mothers had packed an ample store of food to see their sons through several days and both boys had money in their wallets, although none of them had any notion of how much would actually be needed, and the parents were worried about that.

"We'll get jobs along the way if we run out of money, Mama. Stop worrying about it," urged Chester with a good-natured grin, full of self-confidence and anxious to get going.

Lettie sighed. She had had the same talk with Peter before they left their yard minutes before. She tried her best to appear not only resigned to the prospect of her only son hitchhiking to the west coast, but happy about it as well. Peter was a big, strapping blond, an agreeable, likeable young man of twenty, the pride and joy of the Dannenbrings. Peter's two sisters were in tears at seeing their older brother leave on such a perilous journey. They were accompanying the travelers to Mobridge, so Fred was persuaded to go along. He needed no coaxing and crammed himself into the back seat with the girls and Chester. Peter had to content himself to sit between his protective parents in the front.

"Well, I guess we're all ready," shouted Chester happily. He looked at his mother who had previously given him a tearful hug. He had flushed but hugged her back. He had held out his hand to his father, who gave it a hard shake and told him, "Watch yourself, boy. Don't get too friendly with strangers."

"Sure, Dad," he had answered and slapped the suitcases and knapsacks tied to the top of the car. He would miss them.

Lettie leaned out of the front window and said to Prudy. "We'll take good care of your boys. When we get back we'll tell you all about it."

"We'd better be on our way," said Meyer with the patience born of years of living with his take charge wife.

The Chevrolet pulled out of the back yard, scattering chickens in every direction. Dog commenced to bark and Bunting's ears jerked erect, her eyes widened, but she remained where she had been through the entire proceedings, safely perched on the back porch ledge. Meyer honked as they turned onto the road that led to the highway. Prudy stood with her hands in her apron pockets and sighed. Another of her sons gone. Lester swore and stalked to the root cellar.

After the Dannenbrings dropped them off at the edge of Mobridge and turned back for Spotswood and the farm, Peter and Chester waved them off cheerily. When the car was out of sight they headed for the rail yard and hopped a freight that took them as far west as Montana.

They sent postcards from Montana and Oregon and then from California. In July the Deters got a letter from Chester. It bore a postmark from Santa Cruz:

Dear Mama and Dad,

Well we made it. Pete and I didn't have no trouble in hitching rides. Most folks were mighty friendly and helpful. Once in a while we stopped and worked for a few dollars to pay for lodging for a night or two. It sure beats fighting bugs and the rain. We worked our way straight west and then on down the coast.

You'll never guess where we're working. At a lumber yard. On the way south all down the coast we saw millions of trees. I never seen so many trees in all my whole life. And there are lots of jobs for lumberjacks. That's what they call them guys. I didn't even know the names of all the trees we seen, but there are thousands and thousands of acres of all kinds of them. The biggest are the redwoods which are so big around you can't begin to reach around them, and so tall you can't see the tops. And the pine trees smell so nice, some Douglas fir and some hardwoods, all kinds of trees and all shades of green. They make our old cottonwoods look pretty dinky.

Pete and I are rookies in this business, but the boss, Mr. Morgan, is impressed with how strong we are and how good we work. Some guys don't last long because they're just not cut out for this kinda work. The trees are cut close to a railroad or a river because it ain't easy to get the logs out once they're cut down. Then they're pulled out by a long steel cable run by a little engine called a donkey. Ain't that something? They sure have funny names for things out here. The only thing is, the cable jerks the logs so they break the undergrowth. Back home they'd think this is wasteful and real poor farming. But it's the only way to get the logs to the river or the railroad and then on to the mill. We're glad we can work outside and not in the mill. The weather is sure swell here, warm all the time, 'cept today. It's raining, which is how come I got time to write.

I'm sending a few bucks home just like I said. There'll be more later. Don't worry about me. I'm fine and like my job real good.

Your son, Chester

He had enclosed a twenty dollar bill which made Lester grin in satisfaction. He pocketed the bill. He was short a man on the farm and would have to hire someone, not to mention the coming harvest season expenses. Prudy held the letter in her hands, marveling at the odd feeling it gave her to hold the first written communication from one of her sons, an expression of himself. She read it over and over and shared the letter with Lettie, who also had a letter from Peter. They compared notes whenever a letter came and the bond between them was strengthened.

Prudy loved going over to see Lettie, but Lettie had to come and get her because they didn't want Lester to know she could drive. Besides, he usually had the car, driving to and from the fields. It still ran, but needed adjustment from the steady pounding it got from bouncing over the hard ground. On those afternoons spent at Lettie's house Prudy relaxed and enjoyed herself. She was no longer withdrawn, having no need to fear any repression. The women were confidantes, but Prudy often pondered the reason for the friendship she valued so highly.

"Why do you put up with me?" she asked.

Lettie looked at her friend and tried to answer in a stern manner. "I don't put up with you. I like you and always have. Besides, someone has to watch over you. Surely you must know I enjoy your company or I wouldn't bother with you at all."

Prudy was satisfied with that. Lettie had many other lady friends and acquaintants, women Prudy had only a nodding familiarity with at church. It didn't bother Prudy to not be included; rather, she was proud to be Lettie's good friend whether the other women knew she existed or not.

On those afternoons, Prudy would get all cleaned up, put on her best everyday frock, freshly ironed, and look forward to some time without stress, without fear, in a pleasant environment. The Dannenbring house was two miles north of the Deters place and was much the same size. The obvious difference was it had been maintained and improved and looked almost new. The house was painted yellow with white trim around the eaves, windows and doors. The yard was neat with the front planted to grass. The outbuildings were in good condition and painted red with white trim. Prudy always felt as though she were in a chauffeur driven car

120

approaching a fancy house for a fine afternoon when they drove into the yard. Inside, the house was bright and airy, fastidiously clean, with the dining room and living room walls covered with pretty flowered paper. It smelled fresh and the aroma of fresh coffee greeted her as she entered the house. The women cherished those times, sharing confidences, letters from their sons, exchanging recipes, and reminiscing. The time passed all too swiftly and soon she had to go home. Prudy was in good spirits the rest of the day and Lester always knew she had been with Lettie.

"I suppose you frittered away another day," he'd chide her.

"You should be glad I did," she would answer sharply. "It always puts me in a good mood. Besides, my work is done before we get together."

Lester would let it drop at that, but it was an exchange that took place with each of Prudy's visits.

Two years passed with postcards and letters from Chester. The Dannenbrings heard from Peter with the same regularity and enjoyed reading the missives aloud to the Deters the same as Prudy. To everyone's excitement the fortunes of their sons steadily increased and Lester began to boast about his son, Chester, who lived in the state of California and who had a damn good job that paid well. He was a good son, always sending money home. Prudy saw none of the money for herself, but it did ease the financial strain and also Lester's temper. Her pride came from the way Chester was making a good life for himself in a strange land so far from home. She missed him. There was only Fred at home now and he was growing increasingly restless and eager to leave, too. He didn't dare to bring it up to his father, who put great store in his remaining son at home on the farm, a farm that would one day be his.

Then the families were elated to learn that their boys would be coming home for a short visit. Prudy was so excited she could scarcely contain herself. She read the letter to Lettie:

Dear Mama and Dad,

Things are going real good here and Pete and I have a swell chance to go into business for ourselves. But our boss, Mr. Morgan, thinks we should come home first and talk it over with you, get a different slant on it away from work. The deal looks good, but we'd like to talk to you about it. It'll be real swell to come home anyway. Pete feels the same.

I can tell you this much. We want to form a partnership, have our own company. So we'll be home the end of May. Can't be gone from here more than a week and since it takes so long by train to get home and back that means we'll have only about two or three days with you. And I've got a surprise. You'll never guess what. Can you meet us in Mobridge?

Your son, Chester

Lettie had much the same news from Peter, only he made no mention of a surprise.

"Think of it, Lettie; it's been two years. Do you think they've grown any?"

"I imagine they have but I don't see how. They're both big enough now. Prudy, we'll all have to get together at least once while they're here. What do you think about a noon meal here on Wednesday?"

Lettie chattered on happily and was taking charge, as usual. The girls were ecstatic about seeing their brother again and joined in the preparations. Prudy said she'd see what Lester thought, but would love to have a joint celebration. She couldn't see entertaining in her rundown house, no matter how familiar it might be to all concerned.

The Dannenbrings and the Deters each drove their cars to Mobridge on Tuesday morning on a sunny day in late May, 1926. Everyone was eager and expectant. Prudy was especially happy because Lester had consented to her informing Alan of his brother's visit and Alan would be at the railroad station to greet him. Meyer led the way to avoid the dust of the old Model T. Lester loved to ride that automobile like a bucking bronco and it rattled noisily and churned up dust whenever he drove it. The train was on time and they had only just arrived when it puffed into the Milwaukee station. Alan was waiting for them and waved in greeting. The car had barely stopped when Prudy jumped out and ran to embrace Alan.

"Isn't it exciting, Alan? We're all together again. It's wonderful to see you. You look very well."

Alan smiled at his mother's talkativeness. When the others joined them there was time for only a brief acknowledgement from Lettie and Meyer, who shook Alan's hand in friendship, while the girls stood back shyly, never having seen a real live priest, before they turned their attention to the debarking passengers.

"There they are!" exclaimed Lettie.

Peter was ahead of Chester; he spied his parents and sisters and ran to them, looking all of seven feet tall and rugged as Paul Bunyan. He hugged his mother and sisters and gripped his father's hand, finally hugging him, too. Prudy enjoyed the happy reunion, but peered around them, looking for Chester.

"Mama, Dad, Fred — and there's Alan!"

There he was, tall and healthy, ruggedly handsome. Prudy gasped in admiration at her son and felt herself grabbed, hugged and picked up, just as Lester used to do when she was young.

"Holy cow, have you shrunk, Mama? Are you OK?"

"Of course I'm OK. Put me down for heaven's sake." She was blushing furiously.

Chester laughed and put her down, moved to Fred and pounded him on his back, shook Alan's hand in pleasure at his being there to greet him, laughing happily all the while. Then he turned to his father, shook his hand heartily, overlooking any attempt at sarcasm, and then announced, "I have a surprise. I'd like you to meet someone. Polly, come here and meet the folks."

To their surprise a comely young woman stepped forward. She had stayed back until the happy greetings were over. She walked to Chester's side, took his hand, and stood shyly with a nervous smile on her pretty face. She was a small woman with black hair and blue eyes the color of a summer sky and a deprecatory manner.

"Everyone, this is Polly, my wife," he said proudly.

"Your wife!" Prudy exclaimed, not knowing how to react to the unexpected news.

"Yeah, we were married last week."

There were a few seconds of stunned silence; then Prudy stepped forward and touched the young woman's arm.

"Hello, Polly. Welcome. This sure is a surprise. This is Chester's father."

Lester didn't move, but he looked his daughter-in-law over from head to toe, causing her to move closer to Chester. To everyone's relief he remained civil and said, "Yeah, hello. Well, we better be gettin' back."

No one joined Lester as he walked to his car. Chester introduced Polly to Alan, who smiled with pleasure at the addition to the family. Polly was somewhat flustered, but she remained gracious and also puzzled at why he was not coming with the rest of them to the farm. She observed with curiosity the obvious love the three brothers shared, but recognized that there was a family conflict of some kind. Wisely she said nothing, confident that Chester would explain everything. With reluctance they bid farewell to Alan, obeying the impatient horn of the Model T. Alan stayed on the platform until the cars left for Spotswood with their happy passengers. A bittersweet sigh escaped him as he turned from the recent bright reunion which seemed to fade with the sound of the departing vehicles. He envied the good times his family would enjoy without him. He had made his choice and knew his life would always be separate from theirs. Yet he was lonely.

Meyer led the way back to Spotswood with his family in tow. Peter sat in the back between his two adoring sisters. Lettie, in the front, faced her children all the way home, talking non-stop.

"Now, Lettie, let the boy say something. Don't hog the conversation." But he smiled tolerantly as he said it.

Behind them, in the Model T, Lester and Prudy sat in the front with Polly sandwiched between Chester and Fred in the back. Prudy listened as Chester led the conversation and Fred enthusiastically joined in.

"Polly and I met at the lumber camp. I was working my butt off and there she was, nice as you please, working in the office. Turns out her father is the boss, Mr. Morgan. I didn't know that right off, but found out soon enough. I was makin' my move — sorry, honey — and the boss didn't take too kindly to that. 'Course I didn't know what an ass I was makin' of myself, but it must have been OK because he didn't fire me. In fact, he just took me aside and told me real nice and firm like to go away, that she was his only daughter and he wouldn't stand for no nonsense. I can tell you, I got his drift clear enough. Well, one thing led to another and we really took to each other, and Mr. Morgan finally came around, and after a decent time we got married with his blessing."

"Wow," said Fred, impressed.

"But, Chester, why didn't you let us know?" asked Prudy. None of her sons ever told her anything. Lester just stared straight ahead and drove.

"Heck, I figured I'd just surprise you all. I knew you wouldn't be comin' to California to the wedding and it was just a simple ceremony. Pete was best man. Anyway, Polly is a swell gal and I know you're gonna like her." He put his arm around her shoulders and pulled her to him.

"Chester," she murmured with downcast eyes. She sat firmly wedged between the two men, saying little, with a faint curve to her lovely lips. They spoke almost as though she weren't there. But she appeared content and to not mind. Prudy considered this and wondered.

The Dannenbrings honked and waved as they turned from the highway onto the dirt road that led to their farm. When the Deters drove into the farmyard Chester said, "Gee, Dad, you still haven't painted."

"Times are tough, boy. I spend our money on more important things. We've got a roof over our heads and food on the table. That's what counts."

They went into the kitchen. The sun was still shining through the windows, although it would soon be dusk. But the stark nakedness of the poor environment could not be softened. Prudy was embarrassed at what she had to offer her new daughter-in-law and she could sense Polly's disappointment, although the young woman said nothing. Prudy knew what was going through her mind: It will only be for a few days. She showed them up the stairs into the spare room.

Chester teased, "This was my room when I was a kid. Fred and I slept right there on that bed. You must have taken John and Alan's room, huh?" he asked his brother.

"Yeah. As long as I had my pick, I took the biggest one."

Fred flushed thinking of the pretty little woman before him sleeping in what had been his bed. Polly remained impassive and thanked Prudy, who left them to get settled. Soon she heard the three of them coming down, with Fred asking questions about California and available jobs.

After a short visit seated in the front room, Prudy rose and said she must fix supper.

"May I help, Mother Deters?" asked Polly.

"Why yes, if you like." She liked the sound of Mother Deters. "We can get better acquainted that way. There's nothing like working in the kitchen to get to know one another."

Polly proved to be proficient in the kitchen and the women had supper on the table in no time. The pork chops and mashed potatoes and gravy were a big hit with Chester, who had looked forward to one of his mother's meals. Apple pie finished the supper and even Polly was complimenting her. Lester didn't say much, but he polished off his supper in record time, seldom complaining about his wife's cooking. Prudy and her sons regarded Lester's relative politeness as a good omen, because they all knew if he had not taken to Polly he would have said so in no uncertain terms. It was unlike him to be courteous, but they didn't ponder why; they were just relieved.

Only Lester knew why he held his tongue. Polly reminded him strongly of Prudy,

124

a young, pretty, vivacious Prudy the way she used to be, except for the eyes. Polly's blue eyes were large and striking in her pale face with its cloud of black hair. He looked at her often at the table and Polly didn't quite know what to make of it. His glances were flattering, yet unsettling. His weathered face with its unkempt beard and mustache were very unappealing and his dark eyes beneath bushy brows were intimidating. But her love for Chester allowed no disconcerting thoughts, and she dismissed any that came to mind that evening.

Further talk after supper disclosed that Mr. Morgan had been so impressed with Chester that he offered to set him up in business for himself, as a sort of wedding present. He had to invest some money, the sum of $5,000, but that's where Peter came in. He said he could manage to get it from his folks if he could be Chester's partner. What a deal. How could he lose? And he really liked what he was doing, hard work in the fresh, warm air, outdoors where he was his own man, and now he had a great little wife. He'd be a rich man in a year or so. He knew he had told them his stay in California was only temporary. But he couldn't pass up such a good deal and it looked like it would be permanent. He was sitting on the edge of his chair as he spoke earnestly and looked proudly at his father as he finished what he had come to say. Lester leaned back in his chair, his thumbs through his suspenders, looking equally proud.

"Well, now, it looks like that will turn out just fine. You shore are doin' all right, boy. And Fred's still here with me, so don't you fret none. A damn good help he is, too."

He slapped Fred's back, not noticing the look of consternation on the face of his youngest son. Prudy could barely grasp the sense of what was being said. The imminent success of her son overwhelmed her. It made her downright giddy. California had been called the land of opportunity and it looked like that was right. Her dream of her sons rising from a life of hardship and poverty to one of success was beginning to come true and it made her ecstatic. It was exhilarating to have her family, including her nice new daughter-in-law, all together at home. Her cheeks glowed and her face held an animation that was rarely seen. She was happy just listening to the children, all grown up now; she didn't have to say anything. She could see that Fred was excited by Chester's good fortune and that he was eager to be off on his own, and she knew it wouldn't be long before he was gone, too. But he would return, just as Alan and Chester had. Prudy knew hope for the first time in many years.

Lester ventured a few comments about his son being the success he knew he would be all along. A Deters was, by nature, successful. It was clear that Lester had given his blessing. It was on that happy note that they all went to bed.

Lester's good mood extended to Prudy and he made love to her that night, even though she tried to dissuade him. His amorous ways were not unusual, but there was company in the house. It wasn't proper.

"The springs are so noisy. What'll the children think?"

"Children! What's the matter with you woman? What do ya think is goin' on in that bed right now with Chester and that new bride of his? Now come here. I've had lots more experience."

In the morning Prudy awoke to the smell of coffee and thought with a start that she had overslept. She saw that Lester was already up and gone and that she was alone in the bed. As she dressed she heard voices from the kitchen. She checked the other bedrooms and Chester and Fred were still asleep. She washed in the basin and carefully combed and brushed her hair, sighing at her reflection. The gray hair and fine wrinkles around her eyes and mouth were still there. She had hoped her appearance might have improved, since she had felt so rejuvenated the night before. At least she didn't need to try to hide any bruises from Polly. She wanted to make a good impression on her. She liked her and, after having only boys in the house, it was nice to have some feminine companionship that was family. She went downstairs and stopped at the kitchen door. Polly was at the cookstove stirring a big pan of oatmeal. Coffee was cooking at the back of the stove. Lester also stood at the stove, hovering over her. Polly was trying to make casual conversation and to ignore his overfriendly overtures, but she was clearly beginning to panic. Lester slid his arm around her robe clad waist and pulled her close. Prudy pretended not to see that and walked into the room with a brisk, "Good morning. I must have overslept. My, that coffee smells good."

Lester almost sprang back. He gave Prudy a look of guilty anger, which she chose to ignore, puttering around the kitchen, setting the table for breakfast.

"Polly, how nice of you to make breakfast. Chester sure is a lucky young man to have a wife who can cook." She smiled warmly at her.

Polly swept her a grateful glance and received an understanding look from her mother-in-law. There was no need for an explanation. An unspoken comprehension passed between them and a nurturing mutual respect took root.

"Mother Deters, sit down. Let me pour you some coffee. The oatmeal isn't quite done. And I'll fix some toast."

"Ain't you the ambitious one," muttered Lester. He was seated at his place, irritated and sullen at being caught at his old tricks.

"It must be the clear air of the prairie. I slept very soundly. It's very quiet here," she replied, smiling sweetly at him.

Prudy asked, "Where did you learn to cook with such — such simple equipment, dear? I'm surprised you have the know-how coming from such a good background, more well-off, I mean."

Polly's heart warmed to the simple woman who was trying to be tactful and to make conversation under a very difficult situation. She wondered how she managed to live with her disgusting husband and to keep her sanity all alone in a ramshackle farm house making do with primitive belongings.

She replied, "My mother taught me. You see, when Daddy started his lumber business it was on a shoestring when the business was young, but he saw great potential in the vast forests of California. Mother and I worked alongside him, cooking for the crew he managed to get together. There wasn't much to work with at first; there weren't any fancy stoves and we had to drive for miles to a general store. But we managed just fine; we made do just like this."

Realizing how this sounded, Polly quickly said, "Oh, I mean no disrespect, only that I've cooked many a meal on a cookstove and pumped water from a well. My mother died when I was just a child, barely fourteen, so Daddy relied on me a lot. I grew up working hard and cooking for lumberjacks. And it didn't hurt me one bit," she declared. "There, here's a piece of toast to go with your coffee."

"Thank you, Polly. My, I'm not used to being waited on."

They continued talking as though Lester were not there. He finally got up and went to the foot of the stairs and bellowed to the boys to get themselves downstairs for breakfast if they wanted any. Prudy and Polly exchanged a conspiratorial glance, extremely pleased with themselves.

The newlyweds were gone all too soon. Their time was filled, including a hearty noon meal at the Dannenbrings on Wednesday. The following Friday they left from Mobridge to return to California. Prudy hated to see them go. Her sons flitted in and out of her life and she much preferred to have them in it. She didn't cry this time because she agreed with everyone that it had been a good visit, that Chester would make his name in the lumber business, they would return and maybe Alan could spend some time with them next time. Peter had gotten the $5,000 from his parents and was walking tall in the knowledge that he would be in business for himself, in partnership with his good friend, Chester. The Dannenbrings were likewise pleased and confident that they would get their loan back, plus interest, as Lettie's expertise at finances extended to her son, in whom she had the utmost confidence. The future looked bright.

Nothing was said to Chester about the unfortunate incident with his father. Chester promised to continue sending money home. Lester lost no chance in reminding him that it was only right now that he would always be short-handed with him gone to California for good.

When the train departed on its long journey Prudy was convinced there were better times ahead. Meyer and Lettie waved, with Lettie shouting advice until nothing could be heard but the whistle of the train. Prudy's fears had subsided to a subliminal flow. Fred yearned to be on the train with his brother. Lester pondered his son in bed with a young woman eager to have him. They kept their thoughts to themselves on the quiet ride back to the farm.

Helga

CHAPTER SIXTEEN

Fred

In the summer of 1927 Fred was twenty-one. He was restless and discontented. His brothers had left him behind at home and were gone to make their own ways very successfully, and he was at loose ends. He missed Chester. Chester always knew what to do; he was the leader in any given undertaking and Fred had been content to follow his lead. And his parents were beginning to look very old to him. His father was sixty-two, ancient in Fred's eyes. His mother, ten years younger, looked just as old to him. He wasn't getting any younger himself. He wished he knew where his life was headed.

Fred was brown-eyed with brown hair, as were his older brothers, but he was neither as tall and slim as Alan, nor as tall and stocky as Chester, just an average young man with an appealing face and a finely muscled body. Fred's easygoing ways made him a likeable young man, but those ways were also the reason he was still on the farm working for his father, who provided him with any amount of leadership Fred wanted. So far, Lester made his choices for him. He became his father's indispensable right-hand man. He threw himself into farm work and developed a confidence in himself without needing the constant approval of others. He became known as a hard worker who did his job well and for having good common sense. He would never be a leader and needed plenty of time to make up his mind before he decided what course of action to follow. He usually made the correct choice, but not without a cussing out from Lester for taking so long. Nevertheless, Lester was proud of Fred and basked in the praise he heard regarding his son. He was vindicated in keeping the boy with him on the farm where he was needed.

On occasion he even took Fred to town for a beer, over Prudy's protests. But she, too, had been vindicated; Fred didn't like the taste of it. He just nursed his drink all night and then drove his drunken father home in the Model T. Driving was one concession his father had made to Fred's remaining with him and, as far as he knew, was the only other person to drive his prized automobile. Fred enjoyed the freedom the car gave him, but it wasn't enough. He wanted to drive off into the sunset, into the unknown, and make his own way. But he lacked the courage to pull it off and, besides, he would miss his family and the people he knew and grew up with. Some day the time would be right for his leaving. Prudy sensed Fred's longing and worried that he would take out his frustration in drink as Lester had, even though Prohibition had been in effect since January, 1920. The bootleggers extended even into South Dakota and small towns got away with practically business as usual. If nothing was available, customers could always count on home brew and Lester had his secret recipe, which proved to be profitable. The root cellar grew crowded with beer barrels, which Lester periodically loaded into the Model T and drove off into Spotswood to supply the one remaining saloon, Chub's Corner. Any supplier drank for free, so Lester provided plenty of beer and gloried in the notoriety.

It was hot that summer of 1927; it was the summer that made a difference in Fred's life when his dilemma was solved for him. The Dannenbrings' two girls were as different from each other as Prudy and Patience had been. Bridget, at nineteen, was the eldest and very much like her father, Meyer, placid and even-tempered. Both girls were pretty and had strong character in their faces, with Bridget actually being the more attractive with an innate poise, tall and willowy with dark blond hair and steady blue eyes. Her cupid's-bow mouth curved into a half smile which enhanced her bright beauty.

Helga was the younger by two years and full of fire, much like her mother, Lettie. Her blond hair was lighter than her sister's and her eyes were a sparkling azure. She had an ample figure, nicely formed and she was shorter than Bridget. But her size made no difference in the way she faced the world. She faced any obstacle squarely, with spirit and a ready solution. Nothing was impossible. So when Fred asked Bridget to a Saturday dance in Spotswood, Helga did a slow burn. She had set her cap for Fred and he would be hers; not even her sweet sister could stop her. The idea of Fred asking Bridget to the dance when everyone knew she was the better dancer! She moved across the floor with graceful zest. She had the natural style of those women on the ripe side, with smooth, sure movements of purpose. Besides, Bridget was too much like Fred, couldn't make up her mind. Fred needed guidance, guidance which Helga was well equipped to provide. She knew exactly what she wanted and was pretty sure how to get it. It was only a matter of time before Fred became aware of Helga's charms, with an assist from the lady, herself. But Fred didn't know that yet.

He had arrived at the Dannenbring farm to pick up Bridget for another Saturday dance at the Spotswood dance hall, a remodeled saloon, the result of the Prohibition Act. He was seated in the neat front room waiting for Bridget to make an appearance, and admiring the arrangement of the Dannenbring home with its good furniture, fresh smell, and crisp curtains. Bridget was usually late, being naturally slower in preparations than Helga, and assuming that a suitor expected to be kept waiting. As Fred's eyes swept the room they stopped abruptly at the doorway to the hall. He was aghast to see Helga standing there in the setting sun which was streaming from the window on the stairs landing. The beams lit her blond hair with streaks of light, turning it to platinum. Her blue eyes were dark in her oval face, her cheeks flushed. Fred could also see, without a doubt, the outline of Helga's supple figure which was clad in a slip. She was barefoot. His eyes traveled from her blazing hair down to her bare feet and up her nicely curved legs to the straps of her dainty slip. Helga gasped, her hands fluttered to her bosom and her look of embarrassment further confused Fred's sensibilities. He rose quickly from his chair, twirling his cap in his clammy hands.

"Excuse me," he said awkwardly.

Helga remained where she was, allowing him a nice view of her curvaceous figure.

"Excuse you for what, Fred Deters," she demanded. "It is I who should be excused. I didn't know you were here. I'll tell Bridget."

With that she turned, swirling the slip around her hips, causing Fred's mouth to fall even farther, and ran upstairs to inform her sister that Fred was waiting for her. She wiped the smug look off her face before she entered Bridget's bedroom and managed to look flustered as she related what had happened.

"The most embarrassing thing just happened, Bridget. I was downstairs just now and passed the door of the front room and there was Fred, just sitting there. Good night nurse! He saw me in my undies!"

Bridget was shocked. She put down her mirror and asked, "What on earth were you doing downstairs running around like that?"

Helga searched for a plausible answer when their mother's voice was heard. "Bridget, Fred is here."

Bridget got up immediately, threw a look of suspicion at Helga, and left the room. Helga giggled naughtily and went to her own room. That ought to do it. It shouldn't be long now.

Helga was right and brought the situation to a head at the next Saturday night dance. Fred was taking Bridget, as usual, and Meyer always made sure that Fred drove their car. He knew the sorry state of the car that Lester drove into the ground. Meyer was only thinking of his girls. Fred loved driving the smooth running vehicle and was very careful. He was more quiet than usual on the drive into Spotswood, as was Bridget, who realized the threat her sister had become. But, they were both courteous and their spirits rose as they drove up to the dance hall, which was already brightly lit and loud with piano music. The doors were open to allow the free flow of the hot, humid air, which would gradually cool as the night wore on. Helga was at the dance, too, having come with one of the Clanahans over her parents' objections, because the Clanahans were Catholic and they didn't associate with Catholics, because of their strange beliefs and all, plus their strong proclivity for reproduction, causing more than one parent to worry. But Helga was headstrong and for the most part uncontrollable in spite of her seventeen years. She assured her nervous parents that she just wanted to go to the dance and Robbie Clanahan had asked her. She had no real interest in Robbie Clanahan and there was absolutely nothing to worry about. She would not even allow him to kiss her goodnight. She was allowed to go with stern admonitions about being home by 11:00 o'clock. They arrived at the dance before Fred and Bridget and Helga kept one eye on the door, looking for them. Both couples danced around the floor for a few dances, trying to act in a nonchalant manner.

When Helga finagled a dance with Fred, Bridget was furious, because she then had to dance with Robbie, and she didn't want anyone to think she was with a

Clanahan. Helga might not give a hoot what people thought, but Bridget did. Robbie whirled her away with a big grin on his face and Helga nestled close to Fred. One dance was all it took. Fred completely succumbed. The piano player was playing "Jealous" in a slow tempo and Helga was humming into his ear, " 'I get jealous when I think of you —' Isn't that the best song, Fred? I just love it. Have you ever been jealous?"

Fred's neck glowed red under his collar and he fumbled for a reply. Helga's soft white skin smelled very nice.

"You know, I could get jealous of Bridget with her being with you so much." She hummed some more. "Do you like me, Fred?"

"Sure I like you. What a dumb thing to ask."

"I like you, too. You're so big and strong. And you're really a good dancer. Where'd you learn to dance?"

"I've been to town plenty of times. I'm no country bumpkin." Fred felt courage returning to his shaky insides. "My dad and I come to town a lot."

"Oh yes, you come with your father." She left unspoken the inference of his not being able to come to town on his own. Why, he even had to drive her father's car on a date. But she softened it by drawing nearer to him and continuing to hum in his ear. Her breath was sweet and her perfume made Fred's senses reel. He was glad when the dance finally ended.

"It's so hot in here. Let's go outside," she urged, pulling Fred to the side door on the boardwalk and out into the cooling air of the July night. "That's better," she breathed, patting her neck and her rising breasts with her lace hanky.

Fred gulped and looked nervously back at the dancers inside. Perspiration laid on his brow and the dampness was making his hair wavy. He saw that Bridget was dancing stiffly with grinning Robbie Clanahan, but her scowl was not quite so pronounced. He turned to Helga who was right behind him. He bumped into her and she promptly twined her arms around his neck and smiled demurely up into his dark eyes, which were now smouldering with passions he had not acknowledged before. This young woman was wearing him down. He should be inside dancing with Bridget, who came with him, but she seemd to be doing all right and he realized he really didn't care. He bent his head to Helga's parted rosy mouth and they kissed. The electricity that surged through them could not be denied and Fred gave in to his feelings. He pulled her tightly to him and she yielded to him, finally pulling away, wide-eyed and dazed. She hadn't counted on such emotion and it was a distinct surprise to her. They looked in amazement at one another for a long time, not knowing what they should do.

"Hey, Helga, I'm sorry. I don't know what came over me," Fred finally stammered.

"Fred Deters, stop apologizing. Why should you be sorry? You liked that just as much as I did, now didn't you?"

"You know I did."

"Well then, admit it. We were made for each other. What do you think of that?"

"But what about Bridget?"

"Bridget will get over it. She'll have lots of boy friends. She's much prettier than I am. But you are the only one I ever wanted. Did you know that, Fred Deters?"

He smiled in happy confusion and knew that he had found what he had been looking for.

Fred now happily followed Helga's lead, content to let her take charge of his life. They were to be married in the fall, with the mutual consent of their parents. Bridget sulked at first. It was not so much that she was smitten with Fred Deters, but that her younger sister had taken him away from her. After all, she was the eldest and had certain priorities. It was humiliating to be deserted, to be the object of scorn, at least in Bridget's eyes. But, as Helga had predicted, she got over it and finally admitted to herself that she really did not want Fred, that to think of a life with him and his indecisive ways was nothing to look forward to. Helga could have him. Bridget had something else in mind for herself and an early marriage was not one of them. In the fall of 1927 she was enrolled in Northern State College in Aberdeen, ninety miles from Spotswood. She would be a teacher. The job offered security and a certain amount of independence for a woman from a small town. She loved children. Bridget was an idealistic young lady; she would mold young minds and lead them down the path of knowledge and the rewards would be satisfying. The thought exhilarated her and she was filled with the power of the control she would have over her life, as opposed to Helga's, being tied down with a husband and who knew how many babies to come.

Preparations began for an early September wedding in the First Community Church in Spotswood, the church of both families, where the children had attended Sunday School and church, although the Dannenbring girls had a better attendance record than the Deters boys. Bridget would be the maid of honor and, with her newly found positive outlook, she condescended to the honor with style and grace. Helga fretted about all the fuss. She would have settled for a simple ceremony in the parsonage, but her mother insisted upon a church wedding. They compromised on one attendant each for the bride and the groom. Fred wanted Chester to be his bestman, but he and Polly couldn't get away, even though it had been more than a year since their visit. He thought of Alan, but knew he was not permitted to participate in church services in another church. So he settled for a childhood friend, Dick Schmidt. As wedding plans progressed Prudy and Lettie spent hours together, discussing the upcoming event, writing invitations, and taking care of the attendant activities of the exciting nuptials. Lettie and Helga worked well together and were of the same mind in most matters. Prudy envied their closeness and thought of Polly and wished that she and Chester lived closer. California seemed like another country; it was so far away. And there was Millicent; she hadn't seen her niece in years.

As Prudy grew older the need for the companionship of the young people in her life grew. She valued the time spent in getting ready for the wedding uniting the two families. Prudy was always included in every detail because of the long friendship between her and Lettie, even though the bulk of the preparations fell upon the Dannenbrings. Meyer kept in the background, acceding to whatever his womenfolk decided. He and Lester did not share the fellowship their wives enjoyed, so what news Lester had of the festivities he got from Prudy, who happily kept him up to date.

"Seems like a lot of fuss for gettin' married. We done just fine and we plain eloped, remember Prudy?" It wasn't often he called her by name; more often she was designated "woman."

She remembered, but couldn't recapture the feeling. She had trouble recalling the spirit of adventure and the deep love she knew at the time twenty-eight years ago. But she did know that young love would not be denied, that passions ran high, and that Fred was her remaining son and becoming more precious by the day. She had been denied being a part of the lives of the other three and she was not going to let it happen again. She was excited about the wedding, in being a part of the beginning of a new aspect in Fred's life. The marriage would further bind the families and that prospect was deeply satisfying to her. She had something to look forward to. There would be so much more to share. There would be grandchildren. Prudy felt the stirrings of hope. These two would not be moving away. They would not leave their doting parents, would not desert those who loved and cared for them. For it had been decided and agreed to by the couple that they would remain farmers in the area of Spotswood. Anything else would be a waste of their talents. Fred's aptitude for cultivating and working the land and making the prairie bloom and be productive, all the while making a profit, was second nature to him. Helga shared his love of the land, making Fred's love for her all consuming. He knew that he could never move away no matter how he longed for a change, finally realizing that the change he needed did not necessarily entail a departure from the familiar environs of Spotswood. Helga was all he needed. With her by his side he could do anything. They were a part of the land, of the open expanse of prairie where they could stand in the quiet and see for miles, where the sun took hours to sink below the horizon, where the peacefulness could calm an unruly spirit. He would control his destiny as long as he had Helga.

Lettie's skill with the Dannenbrings' purse strings had increased their bank account in Mobridge to an impressive sum. It made little impresison on Lester, but Prudy was in awe of Lettie's ability, of her hold on the lives in her family. She managed to have a tidy, well-kept house and grounds, to have an up-to-date, fine-running automobile, money in the bank, and a profitable farming operation, while just two miles away the Deters lived in poverty. She could never ask Lettie how she did it, really knowing the reason her life was so far removed from Lettie's. It was because of Lester. She faced up to that fact long ago and hated not being able to do anything about it. Prudy's curiosity had never been satisfied concerning Lester's money cache. She knew he had money because there was always some in his pocket. He paid Fred a few dollars each week, bought groceries with cash, and owed money to no one. In their meager surroundings there was little place to hide anything, and she never had discovered a trace of where he kept it. And he was not about to tell her.

The Dannenbrings, as a wedding present, set up Helga and Fred in a place of their own a few miles west of Spotswood, between there and Mobridge. One of their investments had been a vacated farm and forty acres of land surrounding it, a small beginning, not near the spread of either set of parents, but it would be a place to start. Fred was astonished at the gift. A house and land consisted of the basics of a man's life and were not to be taken lightly. He thanked the Dannenbrings profusely.

Meyer just smiled in satisfaction and Lettie said, "We're happy to do it and we're glad you can take it off our hands. You'll have to manage the upkeep and taxes, of course, but you should be able to do that. We only want our daughter to have her own place. Newlyweds need privacy and should be free to live their own lives."

Free. Maybe this was the freedom that Fred had yearned for. He would be on his own, not far from his home and with a competent helpmate for a wife. He was on his way. He straightened to his full height and grinned broadly, shaking hands with the Dannenbrings, promising to not let them down.

When he told his folks of the gift Prudy clapped her hands in delight.

"Well that's just fine, ain't it?" complained Lester. "Just what am I goin' to do for some help around here? Harvest is comin' up and I'll be without my main help."

Fred answered, "I'll be here every day to get the harvest in, Dad. Don't you worry. There's nothing planted at my place yet, and I don't have that many acres to plant next spring."

Lester glared at him. How easily the words "my place" flowed from his lips. How much taller Fred looked to him, how confident. Lester was losing control. Fred was already starting to act like that snippety wife-to-be of his. Lester didn't take too much to Helga because of her free and easy ways, just like her mother. She didn't keep her place in this man's world. She spoke her mind — what there was of it — far too often. Although she was polite to Lester, she was far from cowed by his arrogance, and none of what made up the essence of Helga endeared her to Lester. It was an uneasy truce.

One thing that kept Lester's chronic crossness to a minimum was Prudy's happiness. It gave her a glow, illumined her face, making her look younger. She was better-natured to his way of thinking and he was reminded of a young, pretty Prudy from years gone by when she doted on his every word and obeyed his every command willingly. So when she approached him about a shopping trip to Mobridge with Lettie, Bridget and Helga, he hesitated a moment to let her know he was not an easy mark and then gave in to her eager, smiling face. He played the part of a very generous man and, after toying with her emotions a little, finally agreed. He was surprised by her sudden display of affection when she jumped up and grabbed him around his scraggly neck and kissed him without so much as a grimace at his tobacco stained beard, which is what she usually did when he was feeling amorous, especially when he was full of beer and lust.

135

She said, "The only thing is, Lester, I'll need some money for a new dress — or material to make one — for the wedding."

He made her wait for that and not until she and Lettie and the girls were ready to leave for Mobridge in the Dannenbrings' new Pontiac did he reach into his dirty pants pocket and hand her $11.56.

"But, Lester, I'm sure I'll need more than that," she protested mildly, hoping he wouldn't snatch it back and leave her with nothing. But he merely searched through the pocket once more and gave her an additional $2.00 and some change.

Disappointed, but not daring to ask for more, she whispered, "Thank you, Lester." Then she brightened. She remembered that she had $6.14 of her own money, her egg money, in the old purse she was clutching. Maybe if she was very careful and if there was a good bargain she could find something appropriate. She didn't know yet what Lester was going to wear to the wedding, but she would think about that later. She looked out the back door to where Lettie and her girls were engaged in animated conversation, waiting for her as usual, and she hastily kissed Lester's cheek and hurried from the kitchen. The nagging thought that she needed shoes, too, followed her out the door. She called over her shoulder, "We shouldn't be late, but there is leftover chicken and some potato salad in the ice box. Bye."

Lester watched the happy departure and wondered what his world was coming to after all those years, just standing there and letting his woman go off to Mobridge with his future in-laws, people he was not especially fond of, and giving out his hard earned money in the bargain. He must be getting soft in the head in his old age. He yelled for Fred and they went off to the fields.

The women talked all the way to Mobridge and Lettie managed to pry out of Prudy information on the pittance she had to spend on wedding finery. She was uncertain as to how to deal with it without making her friend uncomfortable and decided to talk it over with her daughters at lunch. They dropped Prudy off at the Catholic rectory for lunch with Alan, something they had told no one about, but as Lettie put it, "How foolish to come this far, to be in the same town as your son, and not see him. In fact, it would be downright criminal." Prudy had agreed without hesitation and had written to Alan, telling him of her impending visit. She waved her friends off merrily and turned to see Alan waiting for her at the door of the rectory, which stood a half block from the church in its imposing majesty.

"Alan, here I am!"

"Mother, what a wonderful surprise. I was so glad to get your letter saying you were coming. Come in. We'll have some lunch."

He led her inside where shades were drawn and it was cool. He showed her around briefly and then led her into a small dining room where a table was laid with a white linen cloth and a silver service.

"You must be hungry, Mother. Anna has prepared a fine lunch for us."

"I think I'm too excited to eat and I'm not used to being waited on. Who's Anna?"

"Every priest has a housekeeper, Mother, and I am fortunate to have an excellent one. She watches over me and cares for my every need. I don't have to worry about a thing. She takes care of Father O'Brian as well. He's getting pretty feeble and no longer performs mass, but he will live out his days right here. We can say hello to him later."

A plump, middle-aged woman appeared with bowls of soup and a plate of bread and crackers. It smelled wondrously delicious and Prudy was surprised at how hungry she was. The soup was followed by a plate of fish and vegetables. Fish was rarely consumed by the people she knew because there was no ready supply available, so it was a delicacy to Prudy's taste. She found it to be light, with a delicate flavor. Alan laughed with pleasure at her relish in the noon repast. A pudding and an iced tea finished the meal and she was satisfied and content. She could stay with Alan all afternoon and forego the shopping, but she knew that Lettie would be back for her very soon.

"Tell me about the wedding. Is there something I can do?"

"I wish you could perform the ceremony, but I know you can't," she replied. "But you are invited, of course. It will be on September 2, so they can be settled before Bridget leaves for college and before the harvest. Fred will help your father with his harvest as he always has, so he'll be traveling back and forth for awhile. He plans to ride one of Meyer's horses until he can afford some sort of car. Helga is very much like Lettie. Maybe you don't remember her so well, being gone for so long. She is the youngest, only just past seventeen, but she graduated high school. It's awfully young to marry, but she and Fred are really in love. I like her very much. Even your father is resigned to it." She paused, aware of a thought that had just occurred to her. "We'll be all alone, your father and me." She gave a nervous little laugh. "We've never been alone, not since before John was born."

That thought worried Alan, too. His conscience still bothered him concerning the abuse his mother had taken over the years, without comment from any of them, and which she was undoubtedly still taking without their knowledge. He looked at her searchingly as she spoke seeing no signs of bruises, but he knew his father was capable of cruel utterances which could hurt just as much as physical pain. And now they would soon be alone in that shabby house. Prudy didn't like to see Alan so upset about her, so she said brightly, "But just think of all the extra time I'll have, time I can use to do all the things I've always wanted to do."

Alan spared her his thought that there was precious little his workworn mother knew how to do except work herself to exhaustion for her family. She continued, "And Lettie and I see each other oftener than we used to. She is such a dear friend. I don't rightly know what I'd do without her. She is very good to me."

"Yes, I want to speak to the ladies when they come for you. But now I want you to meet Father O'Brian, the man who saved my life, my soul, and to whom I owe so much. He is responsible for the direction my life has taken, the reason for my purpose. Come, I think you'll like him."

As they rose from the table Anna came to clear it and Prudy flashed a grateful smile, which was returned. Many people passed through the rectory and she grew to know the problems and joys they brought. She understood at once about Father

Deters' mother. It was all too obvious. She wondered how the good Father's mother had come to such a state, but she kept her silence like the good housekeeper she was. She did appreciate Prudy's manners. More often than not, when other priests were guests in the house, Anna was regarded as part of the furnishing, there to wait on the important menfolk, to be seen and not heard. Thank goodness, Father Deters was not like that.

Alan led his mother up the stairs to the second floor and knocked on the door of one of the bedrooms. A muffled response was heard and he opened the door. Despite the heat Prudy saw a thin blanket covering the legs of a man in an overstuffed chair. He was old and withered and the chair seemed to enfold him in its arms.

"Father, I'd like you to meet my mother, Prudence Deters. Mother, this is Father Daniel O'Brian."

Prudy felt the urge to curtsy, but knew it would be silly, so she walked to him and held out her hand. He took it in both of his and smiled up at her with bright eyes that still held the spark of life and love for humanity.

"Hello, my dear, it is good to meet you at last. Alan holds you in high regard," he said slowly in a wavering voice.

"I'm very proud of him. And I'm glad for the chance to say thank you for what you did for him. You changed his life." She did not add "and ours."

Father O'Brian gave a wheeze, wiped his face with a handkerchief, and smiled at her, his pale eyes twinkling. He understood more than she realized, but he acknowledged her thanks and told her he knew his parish was in good hands. It wouldn't be long; his time was fast approaching.

"God bless you, Mrs. Deters," he said as they left and gently closed the door.

"What a nice man, Alan. I can see why you like him so much."

Alan laid his arm around her shoulders and they went back downstairs. "Tell me, just what are you going to do here in Mobridge with the Dannenbrings, Mother?"

"We're going shopping," she replied pertly.

"And with what, may I ask?" he said just as archly.

"Your father gave me some mony."

They stopped at the foot of the stairs and Alan, after much prodding, managed to find out the measly amount of money she had to spend.

"Mother, I have an idea. I know Dad has no decent clothes to even go to town in; I can give you a suit for him to wear."

Prudy looked curious and didn't understand Alan's certainty.

He continued, "It would be a used suit, but perfectly good. You see, the parish often gets used apparel for both men and women in the event of a death when the family of a loved one has nothing to bury the deceased in, donations from the family of a departed loved one. I'm sure we have some suits in Dad's size that you could look at. This clothing is donated for those in need. Dad won't even know where you got it."

Prudy started to giggle. Alan looked bewildered. When she caught her breath she said, "It's perfect. But so comical. To think of Lester in a used suit of clothes to be used for a dead person. — oh my." And she was convulsed again.

Alan began to see the humor of it and joined her in her merriment. He was relieved that he had not insulted his mother and pleased at her obvious pleasure in her day away from the farm. He led her to the basement and Prudy was amazed at the array of good used clothing hanging on a rack against one wall. The dead were clothed better than some of the living she knew, she thought wryly. They picked out a presentable suit of clothes, barely worn, and Alan found a dark tie to go with it. He wrapped it all in brown paper and tied it with string and it looked like a genuine store purchase.

"I can sew up a shirt. He'll not know the difference. All I have to do is convince him that I got a real bargain and keep a straight face," Prudy said with one last giggle.

They went back upstairs and found that Lettie and her daughters were waiting for them in the living room. They rose when Prudy and Alan entered and Prudy felt an expanse of pride in the reverence inspired by her son, so stately in his black suit and white collar. She did not know how she complimented the picture as she stood so proudly beside him beaming with love. Lettie saw Prudy was in excellent spirits, a match for the others. It would be a good afternoon. Everything would work out just fine. They visited with Alan briefly, affirming the invitation to the wedding. He saw them out and waved them off and wondered about the devious ways mankind was forced to use to survive, especially womankind. But his frail mother was managing quite well and she would survive, he was sure of it. He looked forward to seeing his family in a few weeks.

Lettie drove a few blocks to Main Street, past the Moose Club, Becker Bakery, the Mobridge News, and Larson Brothers Furniture Store and pulled up in front of M. Hellriegel & Co. nestled between the Mobridge House hotel and Peterson's Groceries. An awning covered the front of the store, shielding the windows from the sun. The sign on the display window said "Millinery and Fancywork for Ladies of Fashion." It looked very expensive. Prudy's heart sank. She was positive she would not find a thing with her small sum of money. She would have to ask Lettie to drive her to a more modest establishment. Nevertheless, she was eager to go inside and watch as Lettie and her girls selected what they needed, and they knew exactly what they wanted, of course.

The shop was long and narrow. The walls were hung with plumed and feathered hats and art needlework. Counters contained fancy jewelry and there were shoes of all descriptions on shelves behind them. Along the walls were racks of elegant apparel. Lettie had explained that two sisters owned and operated the shop, a Miss Marie Bogen and a Mrs. Anna Hellriegel. Both ladies were in attendance, regal in appearance and, to Prudy's eyes, imposing. Miss Bogen approached them with a cool smile. She was slender with a thin face and marcelled hair. Wire rimmed spectacles perched on her nose and there was no doubt that she was in full control. Lettie was not in the least intimidated and responded in kind, and soon the two women were assembling the clothing and accessories needed for the wedding. Prudy moved to the rear of the shop to look over a rack which contained a few sale items, but kept her attention on the activities of the happy group and their enthusiastic attendants.

First on the list was the wedding dress and Lettie enjoyed being seated while Helga tried on several selections, finally deciding on a simple white dress which came to her ankles. The puffed sleeves and scoop neck were flattering. The veil hung only to her waist and was secured to her blond hair with glittering beads sewn around a cloche. Prudy was enchanted at the transformation. Helga stood still, admiring the reflection that showed her in a light she had not thought possible. Miss Bogen placed an artificial bouquet in her hands to set it off as she stood before the tall mirror and the picture was complete.

"I want this one, Mom," she declared.

Then a fitting of shoes and the obligatory garter and the bride was attired to everyone's satisfaction. Bridget felt a stirring of something, which she swiftly shoved away, and tried on frocks befitting a maid of honor. Shades of green and yellow were the colors picked by Helga, and Bridget literally shone in a yellow chiffon with a matching head band studded with rhinestones. Next, Lettie selected a proper matron's gown in a light green. She picked out a closely fitted hat with a narrow brim, with matching gloves and shoes.

Prudy had stayed in the background, admiring the clothes and taking delight in the beauty of her friends, all the while haphazardly moving the garments on the sales rack, pretending to search for just the right one. She had more money to spend now that Lester's suit was obtained, but even so she had barely enough to purchase a very plain, very cheap dress. Maybe it would work, could be made to look fancy. And it was new. She had nothing that could be fixed up into a decent gown. This was turning out to be an elaborate wedding and even old Sam, the peddler, and his basket of laces and ribbons wouldn't be able to help her this time. When they had finished and the women were excitedly discussing their purchases that were being carefully wrapped in tissue paper and ensconced in fancy boxes, Prudy was still standing at the rack of pretty dresses she could not afford except for the inexpensive one. Lettie glanced in her direction and sized up the situation at once. With her usual forthrightness she made Prudy's decision for her.

She took the dress from the rack, looked it over carefully and said seriously, without condescension, "This one is nice, Prudy, and it's the right color. The green will look so well on you. Green is definitely your color, you know. With all the sewing I've done over the years for those two girls of mine I have lots of different bits of lace and ruffles that will fancy it up just the way you want it. What do you think? Lucky you're so small. Just look at how I've grown over time," she said with her hearty laugh. She was heavier than she had been when Prudy first met her, her sturdy Dutch figure gradually filling out, but she carried herself with pride and dignity and an inborn confidence. Prudy was relieved and grateful at the solution her good friend had once again provided. Lettie could make things so easy.

"I believe you're right, Lettie. I'll take this one."

She took her small purchase to the counter, along with a plain pair of shoes. They were medium-heeled and tan in color, her first new pair of shoes in years, and they looked very good to her. The total came to $17.68. It gave Prudy great pride to smile into the eyes of Miss Bogen as she gave her the money. Her garment was wrapped in tissue paper and placed into one of the fancy boxes and her shoes in another, and she was treated just as Lettie had been, even with the vast difference in the amount spent. Lettie took pleasure in watching the transaction and in knowing that Prudy could appear at her son's wedding looking just fine and with no need to feel out of place. Prudy blessed Lettie for her tact and perception. She had once more saved the day.

Prudy was so elated that she instructed Lettie to drive them to the corner drugstore where they all had ice cream sodas. With what money she had left Prudy treated all of them, and the women agreed that an ice cream soda had never tasted so good. She even told them about Lester's suit, swearing them to secrecy. They agreed to tell no one, except Meyer, and the four women's stifled laughter necessitated a trip to the ladies' room before they undertook their return to Spotswood.

The cheery mood of the women continued all the way home. Prudy couldn't stop smiling and reveled in her amiable frame of mind. She had something to look forward to, the wedding of her son, with the special event in very capable hands. Her heart was light as they drove into her back yard. She gathered up her packages and thanked Lettie profusely for a grand day.

"We did have fun, didn't we? We'll pick you up if we have to go into town again before the wedding," promised Lettie.

Prudy hummed as she stepped onto the back porch and entered the hot kitchen. Lester and Fred were at the table finishing their cold, but ample supper. Fred grinned and got up to take her packages.

"Hi, Mama, looks like you got what you were looking for."

Lester looked up and continued gnawing on a chicken leg. His beard held a few remnants of his meal. "Did you spend it all?" he asked with his mouth full.

"Yes, Lester, I spent it all," she answered with a bright smile, and she continued to hum as she went up the stairs to the bedroom.

CHAPTER SEVENTEEN

A Beginning, An End

The Dannenbring, Deters engagement was the main topic of conversation in Spotswood. Much of the talk centered on the disparate uniting of the families, but all agreed that Helga and Fred did, indeed, make a very handsome couple. It was a short engagement, full of frantic activities to make ready for the September 2nd wedding date, at the end of summer and before the harvest.

As was the custom, a huge country shower was held for the bride. Mrs. Bernice Schmidt, a widow, and the mother of Dick, the best man, had the shower. She had the largest house and it was not uncommon for such bridal showers to accomodate two or three dozen women of all ages. Some hostesses rented a hall in town or used a church basement. All the women folk were invited with each family contributing part of the refreshment and the entertainment. Exceptions were those of the Catholic faith, of which the Clanahans provided the majority, who were customarily excluded. They, likewise, complied with the custom and excluded all but those of the Catholic faith. There was a tacit understanding about this and no one resented the arrangement. The showers were fun and everyone looked forward to the entertainment. Little girls recited short poems. Older girls sang or acted in skits about married life, and older women ran the gamut from sentimental advice to outright silliness, all with the goal of providing a happy send-off filled with good wishes for the usually nervous bride to be. Helga was not the least bit nervous and enjoyed being the center of attention. At first Bridget envied her younger sister being in the spotlight, but she overcame such unseemly feelings and joined in the fun of the late afternoon festivities.

A country shower was not to be missed. It was a prime social event, guaranteed to please. Womenfolk of a variety of ages enjoyed a sisterhood of togetherness, a sense of a strong bond of understanding, and a congeniality that their men never fully understood. A multitude of gifts wrapped in soft tissue paper and tied with an assortment of pastel bows and ribbons piqued curiosities and with the opening of each one delighted 'ohs'' and "ahs" were elicited. The shower was sure to get a couple off to a flying start, and Helga was regaled with a fine assortment of linens, kitchen utensils, dishes, home canned preserved foods, and other basics to set up housekeeping. Prudy's present of two neatly stitched pillows in fresh, crisp tubing, together with pillow cases with a crocheted edging was acknowledged as being exactly what they needed and she glowed pink from the compliments heaped on her needlework. She was assured that the Deters wedding gift to Fred and Helga, while not nearly so grand as the gift of property from the Dannenbrings, was just as welcome. Two milk cows and some chickens were more than enough, and they would be delivered upon their return from their honeymoon. Prudy spoke in jest of including Dog, but Lester would never part with his pet. Her remark brought laughter, and she secretly wished she could do it, although in reality she wouldn't wish the disgusting hound on anyone. Prudy didn't speak of Lester's baleful comments on such an extravagant gift, at least in his mind, but he had at last consented, not wanting to look cheap in the eyes of the Dannenbrings. After two hours of entertainment and fun and gift opening, with Helga's gracious thanks, the ladies retired to the kitchen where the fragrant aroma of cooked coffee enticed them to the feast that awaited them.

While the women had their fun, Fred's friends took him to Spotswood for a late afternoon of drinking and dancing at Chub's Corner before suppertime. Fathers and sons joined together to send the bridegroom on his way with ribald advice on how to conduct himself on his wedding night and how to keep the little woman in line. Lester went along and was civil enough once the beer took hold, when he became generous and expansive. He had brought a barrel of his home brew which was his contribution to the party, and mighty generous it was he reminded them. A barrel of his special beer took time to make it right and wasn't to be taken lightly. Fred took the good natured jabs like a man and returned them in kind, nursing his drink as long as possible. When the foam fizzled out his mug was refilled, so he couldn't be sure exactly how much he had to drink. But he wasn't drunk and eventually managed to get something to eat into his very inebriated father and himself before he drove them both home as Lester roared bawdy songs at the top of his voice, finally settling into a slurred mumble by the time they drove into the yard. Fred couldn't get him upstairs, so he and Prudy got him settled on the sofa in the front room and hoped he wouldn't get sick all over it before morning.

A few days later Prudy and Lester were finishing their breakfast in the sunny kitchen. Prudy had been happy from being busy with the wedding preparations and in seeing a happy event unfolding so nicely, something she had never been able to manage.

"Aren't weddings fun?" she asked.

"They're OK, I guess. Not bad," he agreed, slurping his coffee. "If I'da known about all the presents and free food we mighta had a wedding proper, too. But it's too late now."

Prudy let his comments slide over her. No matter what she said he managed to find something contrary to say. But she was all ready for the big day and confident that her menfolk would look their parts as groom and father of the groom. And she would not look too shabby herself.

The night before the wedding Prudy was too excited to sleep. So she decided to have her bath. That way she wouldn't be so rushed in the morning to see to Lester and Fred. The wedding was at 2:00 o'clock in the First Community Church and they had to be ready to leave by noon to get there in time and to be ready for any last minute instructions. The men could bathe in the morning, even Lester, whose complaints about an additional scrubbing to augment his weekly bath fell on Prudy's deaf ears. She would prevail for this event. She tried to be as quiet as she could as she got the washtub down, and decided to bathe right there on the back porch. It was practically midnight and silent as an empty church. No one was about except for Bunting, who kept her distance from water. How wicked Prudy felt as she slipped off her nighty and stepped into the tepid water in the old tub on the open porch. She soaped herself and settled back and looked up at the sky filled with stars and let it all soak in. Bunting was perched on the rail, pondering the odd change in routine. Her eyes glowed, but she didn't blink or budge or make a sound, just accepted the actions of her mistress. How peaceful, Prudy thought. I haven't been so at ease and relaxed in years. She remembered her own wedding day and gave a small sigh. How strange life was. It could be wonderful and perfect for some and cruel and harsh for others.

She stared up at the inverted abyss of the dark sky. Stars twinkled and winked at her. She thought of another idyllic time in her life when she had looked up at the sky filled with sunshine and fluffy clouds when Eric appeared, beautiful Eric. A withered seedling that had scarcely sprouted years before took root and expanded in her heart, giving it wings to soar into the timeless space of her mind which melded with the expanse of the universe. The memory of Eric consumed her and she was young again. She reached out for him, yearning for his open arms . . .

"Prudy, where the hell are ya?"

Bunting's ears went up, her eyes widened, and she leapt from the rail, ran across the yard, and disappeared inside the barn.

Her reverie shattered, Prudy quickly rose from the tub and dried herself. She dumped the water over the side of the porch where it slowly seeped into the sere earth. She slipped on her shabby nightgown and went upstairs. Her clean, damp body excited Lester who made violent love to her. She would have to bathe again in the morning.

Fred was the first one up. He cleaned up and dressed in his new suit, one which he had purchased with money he had saved from the wages his father paid him, a pittance, but Fred had no expenses living at home and could save it all. Lester could not see the logic in paying out good money for a brand new suit of clothes which would be worn only once, but Fred informed him that he would be wearing it many times, to church and for dress-up affairs. Lester snorted at the thought of Helga's dress-up affairs.

But nothing dampened their spirits. The day had dawned bright and sunny. Prudy persuaded Lester to let her trim the unkempt hair on his head and face and then to wash carefully in the washtub, including his hair and beard. He did as he was told, not wanting to shame his son, and even Lester was surprised at the difference in his appearance. He looked at himself in the wavy mirror above the kitchen sink and straightened up with a hint of the former arrogance passing across his aging, scowling face. He put on clean underwear and his wedding finery, the shirt that

144

Prudy had sewn for him, the tie that had come with the suit, and the dark suit that Alan had provided. She had told Lester the tie was added as a bonus and he didn't question that. Money spent so foolishly should carry a premium of some kind. He didn't ask where she got the suit, just took it for granted that it was what he had given her money for. She clapped her hands when she saw him all ready, standing straight and tall, his best shoes shined.

'Oh, Lester, you look very fine," she said sincerely. "And have you seen Fred? My, my, the menfolk in this family are certainly good looking."

Prudy's good spirits overflowed and Lester's vanity was touched to civility. He looked at her running around in her slip.

"Are you ever goin' to get dressed, woman? You'd better not make us all late," he grumbled halfheartedly.

"I'm going right now. I won't be but a minute." And she raced up the stairs as fast as she could without slipping on the bare steps in her new leather shoes.

In the bedroom she slipped on her green dress. Lettie had worked wonders. The plainness of the dress had been perked up by a dark green satin border around the neck and short sleeves, with gatherings of ecru lace. The self belt in the fashionable position in the area of the hips was also covered with green satin, fastened in front by an old brooch that Lettie gave her. Lettie had also found a hat she had seldom worn because it wasn't right for her round face, and had affixed the green satin around the crown. The brim was wider than was the fashion, but it suited Prudy's face very well. Her hair had been brushed till it shone with streaks of silver in the formerly dark brown. She was satisfied that she looked as good as anyone else in the wedding party. She went downstairs slowly, savoring the renewal of her self esteem. Lester and Fred turned when they heard her footsteps.

"Mama; You look so pretty," said Fred, his mouth dropping.

"It's about time," Lester remarked, but without any crossness in his voice. Prudy could see what he was thinking as his black eyes smouldered beneath his bushy brows. She was flattered, yet unsettled by his dark look. She blushed and said gaily, "Well now, we'd better be off. It's time."

In the Model T on the way into town Prudy went over the details one more time. She was positive she had not overlooked anything. The invitations had gone out immediately and had been answered. The few on the list from the Deters side was an embarrassment, but it couldn't be helped. Except for her immediate family she knew of no one in Lester's family to add to the short list and he had never told her of his background, just what he had said so long ago and what she had told her mother — that he was an orphan and had been on his own since he was sixteen. He knew nothing of his ancestors except that he was of German descent. Prudy's mother, Molly, had no known relatives. Prudy's father, Patrick, had a brother, Seth, who with his wife, Columbine, reportedly had three children, but no trace of them had ever been found and she was sure they were long gone with Seth's children scattered and unknown, with no way to find them. She wished Chester and Polly could be present, as well as Peter, along with Millicent and her family. She would love to see

Millicent again. But Alan would be at the wedding. That would help. Gifts had come from all of them. She hoped the ceremony would go off all right. Pastor Kaufman would be presiding in spite of his advanced age. He had served the First Community Church for many years and had to be in his late seventies. He had kept his church, for there was nowhere else for him to go. And no other pastor could be enticed to serve the diminishing congregation in the tiny town of Spotswood. However, his mind was alert and weddings and baptisms were what he liked to perform best. He had certainly done his share of funerals. Her musings ended as they turned into the church yard.

They arrived in plenty of time. Lester parked in the rear of the church so no one would bother his prized vehicle. Prudy was grateful for that. She hadn't looked forward to emerging from the dirty conveyance in her wedding togs to the questioning eyes of the guests. They walked to the front and spied Alan standing near the open church door. The sight of him in his black suit and white collar solidified her feeling of joy. Her sustained excitment served as a tonic to her. Years of degredation slipped away. The nearly forgotten feelings of security and the contentment provided by her parents in her childhood returned to her and she eagerly went up the steps to Alan's warm greeting.

"Mother, Dad. It's great to see you and how fine you both look. What a lovely day for a wedding. It's hard to think of you as a bridegroom, Fred," he said as he shook his hand.

"I'm a full grown man, Alan, not just your little brother anymore. You know I wanted you for my best man, but . . .

"I know. Don't think anything of it. I'm just glad I can be here with my family."

Prudy ignored the curious looks of arriving guests, merely smiling and nodding to them. Then she took Lester's arm and they went into the small church. Fred disappeared to the back to await his instructions. He was nervous, yet anticipating the appearance of his bride. He had no idea of what to expect. Alan slipped into a pew and looked around him.

Someone was playing the ancient piano deftly, skipping over the out of tune keys, and soft melodies wafted through the decaying church which had been decorated with marigolds in all three shades of yellow, together with shards of greenery. Yellow and green satin bows adorned each pew on the aisle, which was covered with a worn carpet. Prudy caught her breath at how beautifully the plain old church, which was so familiar to her, had been transformed. Sunlight streamed through the windows adding to its charm.

Soon it was time to begin and Prudy took careful note of the procedure, watching closely as Lettie was escorted down the short aisle, walking with stately dignity, her tall, large figure fairly oozing pride. In a few minutes it was Prudy's turn. Shyly she took the arm proferred her and glanced at Lester for approval. She was dumbfounded to see him frozen in his tracks, panic written over his bearded face. Quickly she apologized to the young usher and took Lester's arm and led him, unprotesting, down the aisle to where they were seated opposite Lettie. The women smiled happily at one another. The suns rays shone in beneficence on the scene through the one small stained glass window above the altar. Then Pastor Kaufman, stooped with age, appeared, followed by Fred and Dick Schmidt, his best man. The piano soared as best it could into the wedding march and the congregation stood in anticipation of the bride's appearance. Bridget led the way in her pale yellow chiffon, carrying a bouquet of baby's breath festooned with yellow and green ribbons. She was followed by Helga, resplendent in her gown, on the arm of her father. Fred's mouth dropped. Helga's serene gaze locked into his admiring look until she reached his side. Prudy felt her eyes brim with tears. Lester stared without moving. Meyer gave his daughter away into the loving care of Fred Deters.

Pastor Kaufman's service was brief, but stirring, his elderly voice still sonorous and emphatic, full of fire, cautioning the young couple to embark on the sea of life to keep the Spirit of the Lord uppermost in their lives. They would be sustained by their pure, unblemished love for each other. Prudy thought it all very inspiring. Lettie didn't stop smiling. Meyer beamed. Fred remained in a stupor. Lester just stared. Prudy hoped he was taking it all in. She had never seen him so muddled. Perhaps the pomp and order of a meaningful occasion was lost on him, or perhaps he was out of his element, or maybe he desperately wanted a mug of beer. She couldn't tell. He had simply retreated. The vows were spoken, music filled the church, and the couple walked swiftly back up the aisle to wait to greet their guests.

Once again Prudy took Lester's arm and led him from the pew and up the aisle, following the Dannenbrings. There was no protest from him, no sound of any kind, just compliance, and Prudy rose to the occasion. For once in her married life she was controlling her husband. It added to her already exhilarated state of mind. They stood in the reception line where Lester endured a hug from his new daughter-in-law and a strong handshake from Fred, and then greetings from the many guests, most of whom he didn't know. Then everyone moved into an adjoining room for the reception.

The room was small but decorated with flowers and ribbons just as the church was. Even the punch was green and Prudy wondered how Lettie had managed that. Lester slowly roused and headed for the punch bowl where he took a long drink to steady himself and elicited a laugh from those in attendance at the look of surprise on his face when he discovered that it was indeed only punch. But he joined in the laughter and even raised his dainty cup to toast the bride and groom. Prudy could not believe her eyes and ears, but decided not to think about it and to just enjoy his uncharacteristic good humor. It called to mind the manners he had exhibited when they were courting and it pleased her.

With the ice broken by Lester's unaccountable behavior people milled about, congratulated the couple and their parents, and the room grew warm with the crush of bodies and the late September afternoon. Spirits rose and Prudy exalted in being accepted as an important player in an auspicious occasion. She responded with many "thank yous" to people who scarcely spoke to her in church on Sunday, receiving compliments with grace. Lettie had time to glance her way now and again to note how well she was handling it all and was satisfied that she had not been wrong in the confidence she had placed in her friend.

The cake was cut and a photographer set up his cumbersome camera and took pictures. Lester consented without any fuss and took instructions on how and where to stand. He stood straight and glared directly into the lens. In his opinion the father of the groom was the most important person present and he played the part to the hilt, a bit rough around the edges, but it was clear to all that he was enjoying himself. The guests forgave him any breach of etiquette and seemed to enjoy the oddity of Lester Deters in an otherwise absolutely perfect wedding. Lester drank his share of punch, to wet his whistle, he would say as guests passed by the reception table. Meyer approached him, having put off talking to him as long as he could. He sipped his punch and the two men stood silently, looking over the crowd, watching the happy couple. Finally, Meyer looked at Lester and, with a straight face, said "Nice suit you've got there, Lester."

Lester stood even straighter, puffed out his chest, and replied, "Right. Prudy done as I told her and got a real good deal. Even threw in the tie."

The tie held bits of frosting, but Meyer duly admired it and agreed that Prudy had done a good job in selecting the outfit.

The affair drew to a close. The sun was sinking low in the west and the couple made ready to leave for their new farm, there to change and to take the Milwaukee train from Mobridge to Aberdeen for a week's honeymoon. With many goodbye hugs and kisses Fred and Helga departed with a group of young people in several cars. They would be driven to the farm and then escorted to Mobridge, but not before a noisy chivaree through Spotswood. Fred and Helga gleefully participated in the wild celebration, in their element with the young folks. Bridget, a vision in her pale yellow dress, waved them goodbye after giving them directions to Northern State College to look around the campus to see where she would soon be furthering her education. She elected to forego the chivaree desite pleas to join the group, thinking the custom quite vulgar. She went home contentedly with her parents.

The ladies aid was clearing away the remnants of the reception table. Pastor Kaufman and his wife had returned to the parsonage. Alan, Lester and Prudy stood alone on the front steps of the church in the waning sunshine. Prudy sighed in satisfaction and peace.

"Wasn't that just wonderful?"

Alan put his arm around his mother's slight shoulders. "Indeed it was. A very nice wedding and such a happy occasion. It was good to be here and to see so many old friends."

"I'm so happy you came," said Prudy as she hugged him hard and then kissed him. "Can't you come out to the farm for awhile?"

"I'm afraid not, Mother. I must get back to Mobridge. I've stayed away too long as it is. But I wouldn't have missed it for the world. I'll write to you, I promise. If you only had a telephone we could keep in touch better." He caught his father's disdainful look at the suggestion and let it lay. "Goodbye Mother. Goodbye Dad.

We'll meet again."

Prudy watched him drive off in the nice looking, quiet black Chevrolet and sighed again. She turned to Lester with a bright smile.

"Wasn't it just wonderful, Lester?"

"Yeah, I suppose so. Come on, let's go."

"And, Lester, I want you to know that I was so very proud of you today. You looked so handsome and you acted so . . . so . . ." she struggled for the right word, her face animated.

"You mean I behaved myself? What's the matter with you, woman? I know how to act." He glared at her.

"I only meant that everything went so well and everyone was so nice to us. It was just perfect. Didn't you think so? Wasn't it just perfect?"

"Come on. Let's go."

Slightly chastened, Prudy followed him to the back of the church to their car. It was the only vehicle left in the yard. The sight of it brought Prudy back to reality. They had the oldest, most decrepit car in the area. She didn't want to think about it. She would think about the wedding. She would hold onto the euphoric feeling of the beautiful day that was fading all too soon. She couldn't just let it slip away. She turned and looked at the setting sun once more, listened to the quiet, broken only by the call of a meadow lark. She felt that she could soar like that lovely songbird, fly into the vastness of the wide, blue sky over the flat endless prairie, swooping in a flight of sheer ecstasy. She would make it last. She heaved one last sigh and turned and got into the car beside Lester. He drove from the church into town instead of taking the road back to the farm.

"Where are you going?"

"Gonna stop at Chub's for a minute. That punch didn't have no kick to it."

"But we should get home. You can have your beer there."

He paid no attention to her and drove to Chub's Corner and got out, slamming the door to secure the latch which had loosened over the years from repeated slamming.

"You comin?"

"No, you go ahead if you have to. I'll wait here. Don't be long, please, Lester."

He ignored her and stepped up on the boardwalk and pushed open the swinging doors. Prudy heard loud shouts of greeting and her heart sank. But he won't be long she kept saying over and over to herself. She had to sustain the happy feeling of the day. He won't be long, he just can't be.

But he was. The sun was down. Only a deep red glow on the horizon was evidence of where it had hung for so long, blessing the land with warm rays that lingered. Finally, Prudy made a decision. She hated what she was about to do, embarrassed and angry, but she had to do something. She would go into the saloon and ask him to come with her, to go home. She climbed from the car and stepped carefully up on the boardwalk. There wasn't anybody around, it being suppertime, so no one saw her in her fancy clothes peering over the swinging doors. She was

149

ready to push them open when she spotted Lester swilling down a mug of beer, his arm around a floozy of a woman in a sleeveless dress that was much too short to be fashionable even in 1927.

She sucked in her breath. Prudy held no illusions about her husband's actions when he went to town. She had just never seen him in the process. The woman was painted like a character in a school play with peroxided hair, and she was permitting familiarities from Lester that shocked Prudy, even after all the years of submitting to him and his violent lovemaking. There were other women in the place and other men drinking and enjoying their company, but all eyes were on Lester, who gloried in the attention and played out his part with gusto. His tie was loose and his suit was rumpled and his shirt was stained with beer. As he drank he ran his hands over the woman's body, pulling her to him and kissing her roughly. The woman laughed and let him buy her drinks and, Prudy thought, let him do what else? And how much money ended up in her hands?

Lester

She didn't go in. No one saw her at the doors. She turned and quietly returned to the car. She slid into the driver's side, transferring the old towel she had placed on the seat when they left for the church. The key was in the car. No one locked their cars or the doors of their houses for that matter. There was no reason to. She had her own key. Lettie and Meyer had seen to that, but she hadn't brought it with her. She knew that Lester would be in town for a long time, maybe even all night. It wouldn't be the first time. She took a deep breath and started the car and drove off with no one the wiser. She drove like an automaton. There were no tears, no anger, just a stoicism and a detachment that formed into a lump and settled, pressing down upon her with its familiar weight. The glow that had clung like an aura around her all day disappeared, with the red glow in the sky.

★

The bride and groom were noisily escorted to Mobridge where they caught the night train to Aberdeen, and it wasn't long before they were blissfully encased in their own private existence in the bridal suite of the newly rebuilt Alonzo Ward Hotel, which replaced the former structure which had been destroyed by fire in 1926. They were oblivious to all but themselves and to learning all there was to know about each other.

The Dannenbrings had been home for a long time. They had their supper and were engaged in recounting the recent proceedings. Bridget was glad she had accompanied her parents home, content to continue her ordered life with them for a few more days until she went off to teacher's college. Any regret she had felt during the day was forgotten and relief predominated, secure in the knowledge that Helga was much more suited to Fred than she ever would have been. Lettie and Meyer were just as pleased to have their remaining child with them for as long as possible. The house would be empty all too soon. They kept on their wedding finery and relived every aspect of the day, with Lettie completely satisfied with how smoothly her arrangements had gone, but she was finally overcome with hilarity at her patient, usually quiet husband.

"Meyer, you rascal! You didn't really say that to Lester, did you?"

"I certainly did. I marched right up to him and I said, 'Lester,' I said, 'Nice suit you got there.' "

Bridget giggled along with her mother and held her stomach.

"You should have seen him puff up at that remark," continued Meyer. "And then he had the gall to say that Prudy did as she was told and got him a 'good deal.' What a guy." Even Meyer began to chuckle. "And then he said they threw in the tie for good measure."

The gaiety at the Dannenbrings rang through the house and it was a contented family that retired that night. As Lettie snuggled up to her husband, she murmured, "Didn't Prudy look nice, though? It's about time that she could really enjoy something without having to worry about that dreadful husband of hers. I'm

151

so glad for her."

At the Deters house, Prudy parked the car in the back yard, went inside without lighting a lamp, took off her nice clothes, carefully hanging up the pretty dress, put on an old house dress and went back outside to milk Bessie. She threw some scraps to Dog who slunk slowly around her, whining, with his tail tucked between his legs. She gave Bunting some milk from the cow and giblets from left over chicken, then returned to the dark house and went up to bed. She didn't sleep for the leaden lump inside her. She laid quietly without moving, staring out the window, and watched the stars come out.

CHAPTER EIGHTEEN

Frailty,
Thy Name is Woman

William Shakespeare

It was May, 1929. Prudy felt very old and she was lonesome. She was alone most of the time now, except when Lester came in from the fields or decided to come back from town where he spent an increasing amount of time. She didn't miss him; in fact, she dreaded his appearance, because he was usually drunk and mean. But she missed her sons desperately. Even Lettie was occupied with Helga and she didn't see her friend as often as she once had.

The day was warm with the promise of new life. But all she felt was the need for the warmth of the sun to loosen her tired joints. Maybe the sun would penetrate the icy tomb of her heart. She walked toward her meadow which was sprouting prairie grasses and wild flowers, the abundant wild roses in pastel colors and the larkspur with its bobbing blue bells. Bunting followed her, her tail held erect and slightly twitching at the tip. Prudy sat on a flat rock at the highest point of the meadow, which was merely a slight mound on the landscape. Nevertheless, it gave her a panoramic view of miles of prairie and a slightly different perspective of her life, a sort of pretense of being above it all, at least temporarily. She breathed deeply of the fragrant spring air, her fingers idly stroking Bunting's fur as she lay curled up close beside her. A sigh escaped from the depths of her troubled being. She was dried up. There was no more reservoir of tears to draw from, just a heavy ache that had grown like a tumor inside her. She would be fifty-four in October, an old woman. She hadn't expected much from her life, but she had hoped for more than she got. How could so much happen to change it so?

It had started out so well. Her John was dead for almost eleven years. His memory had not faded. She could see him clearly. She wondered how he might have turned out had he lived through the war. She wondered how the lives of the others might have been different had he lived. But he had died and no one would ever know. No use crying over spilt milk, her mother used to say. Alan was the priest in charge at the Catholic Church in Mobridge. Old Father O'Brian had gone to his reward and Father Alan Deters had been given the parish. She was so proud of him. She didn't share his faith or even understand it, but she was proud of him just the same. He had made something of himself. Lester could see this, too, if he would only drop his antipathy toward what Alan stood for.

She and Lester were grandparents. Chester and Polly had given them a healthy baby granddaughter named Irene after Polly's mother. Lester had snorted at the first born being a girl, but Prudy could see no logic in that and had placed a photograph of the child on the sideboard in the dining room and gazed at it often. Fred and Helga had a baby within the first year of their marriage, making the birthdates of the two babies very close. Little Frederica was born in the same month of June 1928, causing loud complaints from Lester at two girl babies being his firstborn grandchildren. Prudy reminded him that girl babies were as important as boy babies, as there would be no babies at all without them. It didn't register. Prudy longed to bring the two little girls together, to watch them grow up knowing each other. Family was important. Maybe Chester and Polly could come home soon. It had been so long; they had been home only once and that was three years before. But the lumber business was thriving and Chester and Peter were kept busy. Meyer had been repaid the $5,000 loan, plus interest, and the two young men had built a sound business with a good reputation. Peter had a steady girl friend and there was talk of another wedding.

Helga was expecting again and Lettie was at the farm several times a week, helping her out with her toddler and to ease the strain of housework on the expectant mother. Helga was a strong, healthy young woman and declared that any amount of children would be welcome. Bridget was content to be an aunt and to look forward to teaching any number of children once she had secured a position upon her graduation from Northern State College in Aberdeen. Sometimes Prudy went with Lettie to Fred's place, but she often felt out of place as Lettie and Helga chattered happily away, leaving her out of much of the conversation, not purposely, but because it was the way they got along, almost like sisters.

Prudy envied them their companionship. Even Fred was sometimes excluded, but he was hard at work on the few acres of land he had, as well as helping out his father when he could. He enjoyed the hard work, seeing his efforts come to fruition, plus the challenge of being his own man. Lester took for granted the added burden he placed on Fred. However, Fred didn't complain and got his own work done with an ample amount of time devoted to his father. In 1928 Fred put in wheat and now he was working on his second planting with plans to add a few more acres. Lettie's expertise with money had rubbed off on Helga who turned out to be a very real asset to Fred's newly found confidence in himself and his ambitious plans for their future. Prudy rested easy in the knowledge that the two of them made a successful team in every way. Lester could see that, too, but he didn't like it much. It only brought home to him that it was clear the better Fred managed on his own the less time he would have for him.

Right at that moment sitting in her meadow in the sunshine Prudy really didn't care. The sun lay comfortably on her shoulders. Bunting stretched lazily in the grass and purred against her legs. Butterflies flitted from flower to flower. Her old bones began to loosen up. So much had changed. She couldn't keep up with the changes and found she had ceased to want to try. Her brain refused to take in anymore. Maybe she was stuck in time and nothing could ever be different for her, while all around her everyone else had passed her by, going through their own changes, moving ahead toward a goal. Her goals had long since exceeded her reach.

Now that poor Mrs. Johnson had died mothers with child had to depend on doctors in Mobridge for medical help. As she had aged and could no longer tend to the needs of the folks she had helped all her adult life she retired to her small home in Spotswood and it wasn't long before she died in her sleep. The community said she gave up when she could no longer be useful. Her energetic life had been one of dedicated service, attending to the training of young women in nursing skills, adequate for the times. The spirited young Dr. Michels was one of the beneficiaries of her skills. However, his once lucrative practice with competent nursing help which had flourished for several years had gone steadily downhill as the people deserted the tiny town of Spotswood and the economy declined.

One day he packed up his equipment and medical books, along with the youngest, prettiest nurse, and moved to greener pastures in Aberdeen. It was time to move on. Times grew harder and the town was dwindling. The thought occurred to Prudy that events were inexorably drawing to a complete circle, right back to where they had been decades ago. Soon there might not be a town of Spotswood with no one to know it had ever existed.

She sighed and Bunting stirred, lifted her head and then went back to sleep as Prudy petted her. One thing had not changed and was getting worse, and that was Lester's treatment of her. With few exceptions her life continued as wretchedly as ever. On that lovely sunny wedding day when Prudy's dream of her life changing for the better, of a brighter future for them all had crumbled, any hope she had ever nurtured was forever crushed. Any dwindling hope she may have clung to was squelched after witnessing Lester's lewd behavior that night at Chub's Corner. She dared not hope again, for every time she did it was dashed more quickly and savagely than before.

Lester had come home at dawn after the wedding, dropped off by some of his rowdy buddies. He had stormed into the house and called for her, stomping drunkenly upstairs and pulling her from the bed, raving at her of how she had shamed him by driving off in his car, by not waiting for him. He had beaten her unmercifully, striking her again and again until her face was puffy with welts and bruises and her left arm hung almost useless at her side from the awful wrenching he had given it. He threw her to the floor where she crumpled like a rag doll and collapsed on the bed, leaning over the side, retching the beer that was left in his filthy body.

She shook her head to rid herself of the memory. She didn't want to think about it, but she knew she had to because she also knew she must make a decision. Decision making was not a skill she was proficient in from not having been given much of a chance to make any. But she realized she had to do something, if not for herself, for whom she held no illusions, then for her children and grandchildren. She had to take a stand, to leave if necessary. With the children gone there was no reason for her to put up with Lester's inhumane treatment any longer. She had never understood why he treated her so cruelly. Maybe she deserved it, but she couldn't understand that either.

Her head was beginning to hurt with such troublesome thoughts. Lettie was on her side and always had been and had encouraged her to do something. She had seen what Lester had done when she stopped by the next day to relive the festivities. Alarmed and appalled by what she saw she was vehement in her urging for Prudy to leave if she had to for her own safety. Leave? To what place? Surely not Lettie's. She couldn't impose herself on her good friend despite Lettie's offer of sanctuary. She would talk to Lester first. Something had to be done. Despite his exemplary behavior on Fred and Helga's wedding day he had ruined it, just as he ruined everything of value. She was tired of it, sick of it, and she wouldn't take it anymore. But she wasn't sure she was up to a confrontation with Lester, not unless she caught him at a good time, when he was in a fairly good humor, which was usually after the noon meal when he had gotten over his hangover and had eaten his fill. But a confrontation would surely destroy his good mood. His mood was seldom good those days. He had cut back on his farming operation because, as he told anyone who would listen, he couldn't afford it, not with his last remaining son having deserted him and gone off and gotten married with a place of his own. Fred had no time for his father anymore, he complained.

Most folks understood Lester Deters. They also knew that he was sixty-four years old and not a young man anymore, something Lester never acknowledged. So he leased out most of his land and gladly took the rent money without all the work, giving him more time in town. Prudy never saw any of the money nor did she know how much he was paid as rent. She kept her vegetable garden and still had her chickens and the egg money and she needed very little. Lester told her that often enough. After all, she didn't go anywhere but to church with Lettie and Meyer and hardly went to town at all, and her clothes would last her long enough. She thought of the pretty dress she had worn to the wedding. She never wore it again, but once in awhile she would take it off the rod in the corner closet of the bedroom and look at it, running her fingers over the soft material, taking care not to snag it with her rough hands, remembering.

She made up her mind. She would talk to him the next day after dinner. With that settled she had to figure out just what to say without riling him. She would just ask him to treat her nicer, that's all, or she would have to leave. She lifted her chin to reinforce her decision. But he had always said that he would never let her leave him and put him to shame, that he would kill her first. But he didn't really mean that. Still, it might be a little risky. Maybe she should ask him to leave instead. That way she wouldn't be shaming him. He was gone most of the time anyway. He could take some of his money — most of it if he wanted to — and move to town where he was obviously more at home. She could manage by herself. But could she? Just how would she manage? She would have to ask him for money and he parted with money grudgingly. She sighed. It was hopeless. She'd have to think about it some more, some other time.

She thought about a more pleasant subject, her flower garden. She had decided to plant a flower garden and couldn't imagine why she had waited so long to do it. She smiled thinking how it would look. It wouldn't be a big garden, just a small plot of ground ringed with some rocks from the clearing for protection from the animals and filled with an assortment of posies, as her mother used to call them. She was almost ready to plant them. She had nursed an assortment all winter long in the bay window in the dining room and they were lined up on the back porch in old cans and broken crockery ready to transfer to the newly turned earth.

She would place in the very center of the plot the red geranium given to her by Lettie last year. She had cut it back in the fall when it stopped blooming and it was sprouting again with the beginnings of red buds. She would soon set them all out and enjoy a patch of color all summer. That was a decision she should have made long ago in spite of Lester's remarks. Old Ben, the peddler, was delighted when she finally bought his packets of flower seeds and always inquired how they were coming along on his increasingly rare stops. He, too, was aging and the days of country peddlers was drawing to a close. He told her he would be retiring that year and had given her an extra pack of zinnias as a thank you for her patronage. Prudy didn't know where he lived, just that he had made the rounds of the farms in the area and beyond for as long as she could remember. All the thinking was making her tired; it was too demanding. She would have liked to have lain down in the sweet grass and taken a nap among the wild flowers, but the meadow held too many memories.

To have lain down would only bring them back and make those memories a travesty, especially at her age; yet she cherished those memories as the only really satisfying occurence in her life. Another weary sigh and she pulled her slight frame upright. Her arthritic joints still ached, but the sun had deadened the ache somewhat and the hot summer to come would help even more. Bunting reluctantly roused and followed her back to the house.

Prudy didn't have to act on her decision, at least not in the way she had anticipated. Fate had another plan for working out her problem. On a pleasant morning a few days later in that month of May she awoke to find herself alone in bed again, which was not unusual. It had been happening with regularity. She rose, washed and dressed and went downstairs to fix herself some breakfast. It was Lester's habit to sleep off his drunk anywhere, perhaps in town with that woman, maybe even in the barn, and he would not be in for something to eat before noon. His farm work was down to practically nothing with all his land rented out. He scarcely took the Model T out to the fields or into town anymore. It was parked in the barn next to Bessie's stall most of the time. His trips to Chub's were with his drinking pals who picked him up, along with an occasional barrel of beer, and then delivered him back home in the early morning hours, since they knew he was never in any condition to get behind the wheel of a car.

The sun came through the south kitchen window in long, slanted rays. Bunting was curled up on the floor, absorbing the warmth, but she got up when she saw Prudy, stretched and yawned and, with a lift of her tail spoke to her. Prudy reached down and stroked the cat's back and poured her some milk. Dog was sitting on the other side of the screen door, whining and slobbering, waiting to be fed. Lester didn't take care of his pet and she resented having to feed and water the animal. The mangy hound was an irritant to Prudy. He contributed nothing and barked most of his waking hours, mostly at night. She made coffee and oatmeal and ate her breakfast in peace, facing the sun drenched window and savoring the springtime air. She was glad the winter was over.

It was time to feed the chickens and to milk Old Bessie. She had been a good milk cow, but Prudy didn't know how much longer she would be of any use to them. She opened the screen door and Dog scurried out of the way with a snarl. Bunting followed her, ignoring the dog with a haughty air. Bessie was mooing as she entered the barn and Prudy talked to her as she milked, her head resting on the cow's flank, occasionally squirting a stream of her warm milk into Bunting's open mouth. When she had finished she set the milk pail down by the barn door and called to the chickens as she scattered feed to them. She checked to see if there were any eggs and found five. She carefully cradled them in her apron as she carried the milk to the house, where she poured it into a cream can to be taken to the cellar later. Then she went upstairs to make the bed.

Her movements were unhurried, automatic, a repetition of all the days that had gone before. The hours of each day were no different from any other day. There was plenty of time to do her daily chores. Her eyes followed the steps ahead of her as she climbed the creaky, uncarpeted boards. She reached the top and turned into the bedroom and stopped in surprise. The dresser drawers were pulled open and hung crookedly. She saw with dismay that some of the contents of her drawer were flung to the rough floor. She cried out when she saw Patience's picture torn from its gilt frame, the glass shattered into fragments. She ran to it and snatched up the frame and was relieved to see that the photograph was undamaged.

She hugged it to her; then a thought jarred her into action. She rose hurriedly and looked for her box, the shiny box with the satin ribbon that Patience had given to her long ago. It was her treasure box; it held her identity. Where was it? She rummaged through the drawer with her miserable items of clothing. The shabby garments were in disarray, but the box was there. The thin ribbon had been broken and the box opened and its contents scattered throughout the drawer. Everything was there, the pearl handled hair brush and comb; the nail file with its fancy handle; the nail buffer; the colorful hair ribbons she had never worn; the neatly folded, never used lace handkerchief; and the pretty, empty bottle of hand lotion. Oh no, she thought frantically. Everything was there but Eric's photograph with the intimate inscription on the back. But who would want it? Who would do this? Lester; it had to be him. But why? Why had he been rummaging around in the dresser? He never got into her things, deeming it beneath him, satisfied that his drawers held clothes enough to take care of his needs. And he didn't know about the box. Not until now anyway.

Prudy was chilled with the apprehension that flooded through her. What should she do? If Lester had taken Eric's photograph he would not take kindly to what it said on the back, to put it mildly, to say nothing of a strange man's photograph in her possession. She must get it back. Maybe he hadn't taken it. Maybe it had dropped out unseen and was somewhere in the drawer or on the floor. She took everything out of the dresser, looked beneath the yellowed paper liner, got down on her hands and knees and looked under the bed and all over the floor and under the frayed braided rug. There was no photograph. She stood up slowly, a tinge of fear creeping into her heart. Lester must have come home while she was in the barn. She had no idea why she had not heard him. She had no idea why he had gotten into her things. But she had to know if he had found the photograph. She must have it back. No one could possibly know what it meant to her. She was aware of another emotion, anger. He had no right to do this. No one had any right to go through her things and to take her most valued possession, no right at all. She straightened her shoulders and left the room. She went slowly and carefully down the, stairs and called as calmly as she could, "Lester?"

There was no answer, no sound except for the buzz of an errant bee and the chirp of a robin. She entered the kitchen. It was clear that no one had touched anything. She walked through the dining room, the front room, and down the hall back to the kitchen and called again, "Lester, are you here?"

He must be outside. She walked out onto the porch and looked around. She was about to say his name again when she heard a sound from the root cellar. A stream of profanity followed. He was down there. Without thinking she stepped off the porch and walked the short distance to the cellar which stood wide open. It had been closed only a few minutes before. She stood silhouetted in the bright sunlight, staring into the blackness below, then started down the steep, uneven steps.

"Lester, are you down here?"

Her eyes adjusted to the darkness and to the dim light of the overhead lantern, its dingy glow giving a surreal look to the surroundings, in stark contrast to the warm spring sunshine only a few feet above her. Lester was at the far end of the cellar swaying against a beer barrel that had toppled from the ragged boards on which it had stood. He had evidently fallen against it in his drunkeness and pushed it from its stand. Prudy was stunned to see a quantity of paper money stuffed into a leather pouch beneath the barrel. Lester tried to pull the barrel back up, but was too unsteady in his stupor and couldn't do it. Furious at Prudy's knowledge of where he kept his stash he took a step toward her and could barely keep his balance. Alarmed, Prudy stepped backward. She had never seen him like this, not this drunk, ever. Then her heart gave a lurch, because crumpled in his dirty hands she saw Eric's photograph.

"You goddam bitch," he shouted. "Always knowed couldn't trus' ya. Who the goddam hell's this 'ere Eric? Wha's this fool'sh scribble on back?"

Prudy reached out a hand, pleading, "Lester —"

He grabbed hold of an upright barrel to steady himself. "Goddam bitch, you goddam whore! You shamed me 'gain. Well, you shamed me fer las' time, you no-good goddam slut. How ya like that?"

And he viciously tore the photograph in two, leering at her as she cringed, then tore it again and once more. He spat his tobacco stained spittle at her. Then, his shoulders lowered as if to pounce like some predatory animal and he lunged at her.

"I'll take care a'you," he growled.

She screamed in terror and turned and sped up the steps, upward to the light of day on her hands and feet, scurrying like a scared rabbit. Her heart was pounding like it would burst. She heard his heavy tread behind her, clumsily pursuing her up the steps, panting with the exertion in his sotted state, all the while shouting every profane word he knew at her in his rage. There would be no calming him this time, no reasoning with him. He had never been this bad. She reached the top and ran a few steps into the yard, turned and begged him, "Lester, please. Stop, listen to me."

To no avail. He kept on coming and Prudy fled in fear of her life as gutteral sounds came from him, his face contorted.

"I'm gonna take care a'you for good, you goddam woman, you bitch," he yelled as he emerged from the cellar and wobbled in the brightness of the morning. He stood with his legs spread, trying to keep his balance. He was waving his arms to punctuate his vile words. His eyes were coals in his ravaged face. He really is going to kill me was Prudy's only thought. The reality of her situation was finally sinking in. There would be no more excuses. She began to run to the house and stumbled and fell on the uneven ground. Bunting issued a startled yowl, leaped from the porch and scrambled across the yard and to the top of the chicken coop where she clung, hissing furiously, every hair standing on end. Lester reached Prudy and pulled her roughly upright. He hit her full in the face with his fist and she felt blood gush from her nose. He hit her again and she fell to the ground stunned and groggy. Lester reeled from the exertion but recovered and stood with his legs wide apart, his head raised to the blinding sun, howling obscenities, shaking his grimy fists at the blue sky. Prudy couldn't believe what she was seeing. He was a demented, crazy man. She caught her breath and shook her head. She knew she had to defend herself until she could make it to the house. She looked swiftly around for a stick, a rock, anything, and then she saw the ax on the back porch where he had flung it so many times. While he was diverted, engrossed in his regressed, insane state, she scrambled to her feet as fast as she could, trying to focus her vision on the house. Lester roared and stumbled after her. She could smell him as he closed in on her, his sodden clothes reeking of beer and urine, his breath foul. His hot breath gave impetus to her race to the porch. He would soon be too close for her to defend herself, but she could run fast. She was small and she was terrified and running for her life. She jumped to the porch as he dizzily stomped after her. Swiftly she groped for the ax, felt its handle as her hand closed over it. She spun around, stood on the top step as Lester neared the bottom step. Her tremors ceased as she knew what she had to do. Lester's eyes burned into hers, wild, glaring red in the black abyss of his madness. His mouth was open uttering unintelligible noises, with saliva running into his filthy beard. With one last animal roar he reached for her. She screamed, raised the ax and closed her eyes. With the momentum born of much practice she brought it down.

She felt the ax sink into flesh and bone. The ugly sounds that had been ringing in her ears stopped abruptly and were replaced by a sick gurgle, and then there was a heavy thud and the ax was thrust from her grasp. She opened her eyes and quickly covered them again with both hands. When she opened them she saw what she had done. Lester lay on the ground, arms and legs flung grotesquely. His face held astonishment, his eyes stared lifelessly wide open, and in his thick neck was imbedded the ax. She jumped as the ax fell from its gaping wound which had pushed Lester's head at an awkward angle, and she gasped as blood gushed forth. She stood frozen in terror. She had killed him. She hadn't meant to, but it was as if she had not been in possession of her senses. Nevertheless, she had killed him.

She didn't know what to do. Her shock was dissolved by a low growl from Dog who had slunk from around the barn and was slowly circling the body of his master. He looked at Prudy and growled again in a sinister manner, then commenced to bark. He barked and barked and would not stop. In his frenzy he ran in circles around Lester. The adrenalin had not left Prudy. She stepped from the porch, picked up the ax, turned it around and as Dog crept toward her, his teeth bared, prepared to leap, she swung the blunt end of the ax at him and dropped him on the spot. The barking ceased as abruptly as had Lester's animal sounds. The silence was deafening. She could hear the blood pounding in her ears. Not even the song of a bird penetrated the violent aura that hung over the farm yard. Bunting's hissing had stopped and she had settled into an alert posture on top of the chicken coop, confident that the situation had been taken care of.

Prudy let out a shuddery breath and the ax slipped from her bloodied hands. She stood numbly, her eyes wide at the slaughter she had committed. She had killed. They were dead. But she was forced into it. What now? She began to shake. Uncontrollable shivers ran through her and cold waves ran in tingles up and down her thin body. She sat heavily on the top step of the porch trying to compose herself, trying not to look at the bleeding corpses sprawled on the ground before her. The shaking gradually subsided, but her eyes were drawn irresistibly to her dead husband and his disreputable dog, still and staring at her as their life's blood oozed from them.

Eventually the truth of the matter came to her. She did what she did because she had to. It was either that or be killed herself. What was she supposed to do, stand there and let Lester kill her with his bare hands, then let Dog rip her apart? Not on her life. Besides, it was done. It was finished. They were dead, and dead was dead. With that settled in her mind the next thought was of what to do. Any number of courses of action slipped in and out of her mind, all with the same outcome. There would be questions she couldn't answer. There would be embarrassment. Eventually she would be charged with the murder of her husband.

Something had to be done at once. The sun was high in the sky and what if someone stopped by? It was unlikely, but there was always a chance. Maybe Lettie would come. Maybe Alan. Maybe Fred. What would Fred's reaction be if he were with her at that moment? His complaisance and his easy-going demeanor was vivid in her fevered brain. What she had done would destroy him, to say nothing of the rest of her family and the few friends she had. She made another decision. She got up and walked to the water trough, circling wide around the lifeless forms on the ground. She washed her arms and hands and face, eliminating most of the drying blood from her bruised body.

She stared at the water as it absorbed the pink tinge her own life's blood had put there and soon dissipated. She wiped herself on her apron and then walked purposefully to the barn where she found a shovel. Without looking at what lay sprawled in the dirt she proceeded to the mound of loosely turned earth on the south side of the house between the house and the clearing, the spot she had chosen for her flower garden. It would take time and considerable effort, but she could do it. If no one showed up she could dig a shallow grave and get her garden planted before dark. She outlined the area with the shovel and set to work. She started to dig with methodical grimness. She had never dug a grave and she knew she couldn't go down as far as was customary, but it would work. It was hard, dusty toil and the warm spring day soon turned into one that felt like the middle of July.

She stopped now and then and sat on the tree stump where the ax usually was set firmly, and she scanned the horizon in all directions to keep an eye out for anyone who might come by. But there wasn't even the dust of a passing car on the way to the main road to Mobridge and she breathed a sigh of relief. She had no idea of what she would do if there were a visitor. Her tired mind didn't want to think about it, nor could it have been devious enough to have come up with an explanation, never considering that the truth might be all she would need to tell.

She worked steadily all afternoon and in spite of the fiercely difficult task her spirits started to lift. That puzzled her, too, as well as to make her feel guilty. Hadn't she killed a man? Why the euphoric feeling? She had no answer, decided to dismiss her guilty feelings, and merely enjoy feeling good. Making decisions was coming easier to her.

When the hole was deep enough and with the courage born of the success of her project thus far, she returned to the root cellar and found a gunny sack. She would have to drag Lester's body to the grave, but with his head at that awful angle . . . She surprised and shocked herself with having to suppress a giggle. She musn't giggle. Once she began she knew her energy would be sapped from the effort, as she would not be able to stop. Maybe she was just hysterical. The guilty feeling began to surface. She hurried up the steep steps back into the yard and, willing herself to not think about what she was doing, she bent beside the body of her dead husband. With great care and practicality she slid the gunny sack over his head. She did not look into his glazed open eyes which were beginning to look funny, merely slid the sack down as far as she could, tying it around what was left of his neck. Then she turned him so that his legs were stretched out toward the open hole. She pulled him ever so slowly toward it. He was a big man and it took her a long time, but she was filled with the strength of her determination and she finally had him stretched out beside the open grave. She knelt beside the body and gave it a shove. It fell to the bottom with a muffled thump. She noted with satisfaction that the body had fallen evenly the length of the grave. She began to shovel the dirt back in, then remembered the dog. She returned to the mongrel and dragged him by the tail to rejoin his departed master and tossed him in on top of the partially covered body.

She continued to shovel, then paused and thought again. The ax. It was in bad shape and all covered with blood. It was old, old beyond any further use. Nor could she ever use it again, not after what she had done. She retrieved the ax, gave it a flourish and dropped it in on top of the dirt which outlined the bodies. She continued her shoveling, taking care to jump in and tamp down the ground as it filled. It must be firmly and solidly packed lest it eventually start to cave in. Even at that, her garden plot would have a slightly curved top.

She was hot and tired, but she was almost finished. The hard part was done. The actual planting and watering of her flowers would be easy and would be an actual pleasure after her long, hard day in the sun. Then she'd take a bath to rid herself of any remnant of that beastly day. And when she dumped the bath water it would run down to her garden, washing out the bloody stains which were now thick and black in the dirt in front of the porch. Everything was working out just fine.

She patted the earth with the flat of the shovel. . . . . .

CHAPTER NINETEEN

The Widow

Prudy awoke with the sun shining in her eyes. She lay as she had gone to sleep, on her back, her arms and legs outstretched in exhaustion. Every bone, every muscle cried out in pain. The events of the day before flooded back to her and she groaned. It had not been a bad dream. She had really done it. It could not be undone. She groaned again and shook her head slowly from side to side in an effort to fling it from her, but the memory would not go away.

She had to move, to get up and be about her work as had been her habit for all her married life. She made a half-hearted attempt and sank back onto the lumpy bed. She glanced at Lester's side and tried to imagine him lying there and found she could not. Had she become so callous overnight? All she really could feel was her pain-wracked body crying for relief from the torture she had put it through. She heard old Bessie raising a fuss in the barn. She'd have to decide what to do about her. The milk she gave hardly made it worthwhile to bother to tend her. Prudy was suddenly ravenous and remembered that she had had nothing to eat since the previous morning. Wincing with the effort, she sat on the edge of the bed. Maybe if she moved around some her joints would loosen up. Slowly she pushed herself from the bed and stood up, every sinew in her thin body protesting. She took care of her morning toilet, dressed and went downstairs carefully, one step at a time. She was too old for the strenuous activtiy she had undergone. A new thought entered her rested brain. She had not put herself through anything. Lester had done that. She tried to bring up a pang of regret, a sense of loss, but that would not come either.

She reached the bottom of the stairs and was struck by the appearance of the kitchen, by how nothing had changed. It looked the same. Everything was where it had been. Remnants of her breakfast of the morning before remained on the table like a still life. Bunting sat patiently on the other side of the screen door and she rose and meowed softly when she saw Prudy. Prudy let her in and hurried to close the door to keep out Dog when she remembered she didn't have to do that anymore.

Bunting seemed to have accepted the way things now were better than she had. She talked companionably to the cat as she poured her some milk and put the coffee on the stove to cook. She made the oatmeal and as it bubbled on the back of the stove she cleared away the table, reset it neatly, and sliced bread for toast. Bunting loved buttered toast and the two of them ate their breakfasts in peace, with Prudy now and then asking Bunting some outrageous question with a smile and Bunting blinking her eyes in agreement and smiling back at her. Prudy's aches diminished a little and she settled back to enjoy her meal. Bessie would have to wait.

She poured herself another cup of coffee and stared out the south window, enjoying the sunlight streaming in, as the soft wind stirred the bedraggled curtains. Her brain was clear now and it had been put in motion with a course of action winding itself through its maze. She put the cup down and got up, feeling better. Bunting was licking the sweet butter from her paws, her eyes shut, engrossed in her task, but she stopped and accompanied Prudy as she went outside to the porch. Prudy looked calmly at the ground that only hours ago had contained a scene of carnage. There was no evidence that anything untoward had occured. The ground was dry; in fact, the breeze was already stirring up the dirt. There was no sign of the violence that had taken place. Her eyes traveled the unseen path down the slight incline to the depression between the house and the clearing where her flower garden lay. The plants stood upright and perky in the sun, the red geranium had begun to show its bright color and the rocks outlined a slightly raised mound. The footprints around the garden were hers, designating the activity of planting a flower garden.

She let out her breath, which she had not been conscious of holding, and breathed deeply. Then she muffled a warning to Bunting, which turned into a suppressed giggle as she watched the cat march purposely to the garden and begin to dig. Oh no, she mustn't, raced through Prudy's head, then she laughed aloud as the cat apparently changed her mind, carefully covered the hole she had begun, and ran off into the scraggle of trees. What irony. It would serve them right, but she didn't need Bunting making a habit of that every morning. She wanted her flowers to grow and thrive. It turned out to be the first and the last time Bunting bothered the garden.

Satisfied with what she saw in the back yard, Prudy busied herself with her daily chores. It would be best to keep on schedule. She milked Bessie and gathered a few eggs. She decided that soon she would have the cow turned into some cured meat for the root cellar. She didn't need a milk cow that gave hardly enough milk to satisfy her cat. She'd have room for the meat with the beer barrels out of there. She'd have to think about that, too, about how to handle it. She carried the milk and eggs to the house and found that the milk in the cream can had soured from having sat there too long in the sun from yesterday. Before she dumped it out she would use some of it. Sour milk could be very useful. But, first she'd wash Lester's clothes. She put water in the copper boiler on the cook stove to heat, then gathered up all of Lester's clothes and filled the wash tubs. She still ached, but her occupation with her tasks made her forget about it. She had three heavy loads and used the water as hot as she could stand it, practically cooking Lester's underwear clean, and scrubbing his overalls on her worn scrub board.

His shirts and pants left muddy water, but she rinsed everything twice and hung the clothes on the line to dry in the sun and cool breeze. She was breathing hard from the exertion as she dumped the dirty wash water and then hung the tubs back up on the back porch.

It was noon and she was hungry again, so she had another cup of coffee and chewed on a piece of leftover toast. She would make cookies and her mother's chocolate cake with the sour milk. She could not throw out anything that could be used. Besides, with baked goods in the house she would have something to offer if anyone stopped by. The stove was still hot from heating the wash water, so she threw in extra cobs and some wood and soon had a cake in the oven in her reliable black baking pan. She then mixed up sugar cookies and cut them with the cookie cutter her mother had brought with her from Virginia. She sighed, remembering that it was the boys' favorite cookie and she could never keep enough of them on hand. She wished they were all there with her to taste them again. Times change. Maybe she would be baking them for her grandchildren one day. She sat down to rest as they baked and when she sampled the cookies she declared them to be as good as ever. She had not lost her touch. She had imagined that any task she undertook after what she had done would surely fail and she would never be able to function as before. Her endeavors would surely be tainted. She was driven to find out and was relieved to know that she had passed the test of her baking. Maybe she had even soured the milk in the first place, she thought wryly and with a smile. Old wive's tales were stranger than that, but a persistent one was blaming the souring of milk on women who were in the kitchen while having their periods, and women believed it, until they found out from experience that it just wasn't so.

Next, Prudy brought in the clothes from the lines, carefully folded them, and took them upstairs where she placed the underwear and socks in Lester's drawers on the fresh paper liners she added. She hung the rest in the corner on the rod behind a tattered drape. She was running out of steam.

The day was almost over, the afternoon sun had gone around and was coming in the west window and front door. And she was hungry again. She fixed herself a sandwich and had some milk and a piece of cake. It didn't need frosting, her mother had always said, but Prudy now knew that when she said that it was because she was low on sugar. But she and Patience hadn't minded, because the cake was rich and moist and was delicious without frosting. She was getting weary, but satisfied with her day's work. Furthermore, she had surprised herself with how quickly she had adapted to being in control of her life. The adrenalin gave impetus to her thought processes and she got up and went into the dining room. She stopped at the sideboard and looked with fondness at the photographs lined up on the dingy dresser scarf. All of her sons smiled back at her; John in his uniform looking so young; Alan in a black suit, without the priestly attire to spare his father any undue discomfort; Chester, Polly and little Irene; Fred and Helga with Frederica, and soon there would be more; and even a photograph of Millicent and Howard with their two children, Jeffrey and Jennifer.

She would add the previously hidden portrait of her dead sister, Patience. There were no pictures of Lester and Prudy, except the one taken at Fred's wedding. Lester would never permit his picture to be taken and Prudy was never given the opportunity, nor would she want to have her picture taken. She was far too intimidated by the fine likenesses of others to risk having her picture snapped or ever posing for a formal portrait. She sighed. It didn't matter anymore.

She opened one of the small drawers of the sideboard and searched through its contents. It was a drawer designated for important papers. She had put into it every letter or greeting card the children had given her, loose photographs, tax receipts, rent receipts, and such. Lester had deposited in the drawer the deed which Patrick Malone had given to him and Prudy ages ago. It was his claim to being a man of property and it was still there in the stiff brown file envelope, neatly tied with a thick string. Prudy withdrew it from the drawer, untied the string, and pulled out the deed. It was a green paper, tinged yellow with age. There it was, signed by her father, deeding his claim, his property, to Lester and Prudence Deters, dated and filed in 1899. With satisfaction she returned it to the folder and placed it back into the drawer. Now it was she who was a property owner. The lines on her careworn face relaxed in a smile. Then she pushed herself to complete her work.

She had one more task to perform before she called it a day. She lit a lamp and went to the root cellar. She paused at the top, hesitating. Her recent trauma returned vividly. It had begun as she stood at the top and called Lester's name. But there was no danger now and she had to take care of the matter before it got too dark. She didn't want to do it in the daylight and risk having someone see her, and to do it in the dead of night was something she didn't want to think about. She took a deep breath and descended the steep steps with the lamp held high.

The overhead lamp in the cellar could be lit, but she didn't want that much light, didn't want to draw attention. Her leg muscles twinged with each step, but she reached the bottom and set the lamp down beside the barrels. The money was still there in the leather pouch. The barrel that had hidden it was still tipped against the far wall. She easily retrieved the pouch, stuffed loose bills into it that had fallen out, and drew the drawstrings. There were two more barrels lined up close to the wall. With an effort, she pushed the next one until it, too, tipped against the wall, and she uttered a sound of glee at the sight of another pouch filled with bills. Quickly she removed it and set it beside the first bag. The remaining barrel must have been empty, as it tipped back easily. Beneath it was a rusty metal box. Trembling, she pried it open and shushed it as it creaked. It was filled with coins, all kinds of coins from pennies to silver dollars. There had to be hundreds of dollars and it had been hidden away all that time. Her heart was thumping wildly. She had never seen so much money in her life. She held the lamp high and searched the area for any loose bills or coins, found a few, and stuffed them into her apron pocket. She found a gunny sack and put all the items in it for ease in carrying, and hurried toward the steps, then stopped and thought. She returned and eased the barrels back into an upright position onto the boards. Then she fairly ran up the steps, closed the cellar doors, and hurried to the porch and into the house to count her hoard.

She set the lamp on the kitchen table and dumped out the contents of the gunny sack and clapped her hands in excitement. Somehow it looked like so much more on

167

the bare table. She separated the cash according to denominaitons. Eagerly she counted it and gasped as the total grew. She found a scrap of paper and a stubby pencil and counted it again and added it over and over, positive she had made a mistake, but the amount was always the same, a total of $9,346.00. Then she added up the coins and it came to $159.34.

She was rich. She had never seen so much money and had no idea that Lester had accumulated so much. Of course, they had no debts, he always paid the bills and he paid in cash on time, charging nothing. Still, during the hard times when others around them suffered, the sum was impressive. She could live alone for years on that, collect the rent money on the land, pay the taxes, and live as she pleased. She twirled around and let out a joyful shout, totally unlike herself, causing Bunting to lift her head and widen her eyes in wonder. Now, where to keep it. Surely not in the bank in Mobridge. A deposit of such a sum would surely cause talk and curiosity. And how could she get her hands on money when she needed it if it were so far away? She would keep it with her, but definitely not in the root cellar. In the kitchen somewhere where she could keep her eyes on it. No one would bother her kitchen cupboards. She paused to give some thought as to where it should be kept before she had to exert herself. Her poor body would accept only an absolute minimum of activity that late in the day, and it must be done before she went to bed.

On the top shelf where she kept the few items of good dishes she still had that were her mother's there was a heavy serving dish decorated with painted flowers that had been used for hot dishes. It had been one of her mother's prized possessions that she brought to the prairie. It had a cover and a slot for a spoon and it hadn't been used for years. It would be an ideal hiding place. She took $50 in bills and coins from the stacks of money and put it aside, feeling like a wealthy woman making a withdrawal from her own private bank. Then she put the rest back into the gunny sack and set it on the small counter top. She dragged a chair to the cupboard and climbed onto it, reached up to the high cupboard doors, tugging them open with difficulty. They had warped over the years and gave way grudgingly. Carefully she grasped the handles of the fancy bowl and lifted it to the counter. The cover bore the dust of many years. She was about to wipe it clean with her apron, then decided to leave it as it was. She removed the cover and transferred the money from the sack to the bowl, poking it inside the curves, packing it full of currency. There was more money than there was room and she had to cram a large stack of ones in an old metal tea box in the corner.

She placed the coins in a sugar bowl and creamer that matched the large bowl. The bills made a mound in the dish, but she replaced the dusty cover, making sure no bills protruded beneath it, and eased the bowl, heavier now, back to its place on the top shelf. She hoped it was setting in the same place, but who was to know, who was to look but herself? She set the sugar bowl and creamer beside it, wiped her hands on her apron, and got down stiffly from the chair. She could go to bed now and to sleep. Sleep — what a wonderful word — she would enjoy a beautiful, undisturbed, restful sleep. She vowed not to let the troublesome events intrude into her memory again. It was done. She could not relive it to make it turn out differently, perhaps with herself resting in the flower garden.

She had discovered that she could still function without the sky falling on her. No task had gone badly because of what she had done. A twinge of conscience pricked at her brain, but she swept it away. She would think about it in the morning. She was just too tired and full of pain to think about anything but going to bed. Maybe she'd get that new bed with a soft mattress and fluffy comforter after all. She threw the gunny sack into the coal scuttle, blew out the lamp, and pulled her exhausted body up the stairs and threw herself on the bed where she fell asleep immediately. She was not aware of Bunting as she joined her and curled up at the foot.

Prudy awoke refreshed and found that she had not moved since she had fallen across the bed, still fully clothed. Her apron was wadded into an uncomfortable ball beneath her. She moaned and was surprised to hear a sympathetic meow as Bunting rose, stretched, and padded slowly toward her, her nose tentatively touching her arm.

"Bunting," she croaked in a sleepy voice, "what are you doing up here?"

The cat jumped off the bed at once and Prudy sat up, contrite at having frightened her, and called, "Come, Bunting, kitty, kitty, come on. I didn't mean to scare you. Come here," and she patted the bed. Without hesitation she jumped up, forgiving her mistress her momentary outburst. Prudy petted her soft fur and Bunting's back and tail went up and she obligingly walked back and forth, her tail tickling Prudy's nose, making her laugh hoarsely. It was another thing to get used to, but a pleasant one. Bunting never came upstairs when Lester was around, having been kicked down the steps more than once. Prudy looked toward the window. No sunshine today. It was clouding up. It would rain and that was good, except for what it would do to her aching bones. The prairie needed rain whenever it came. She was glad her garden was in. She wouldn't have to water it today. She changed her clothes and went downstairs for breakfast as it began to sprinkle.

That afternoon Lettie stopped by and yoohooed with familiarity through the kitchen door. She strode into the house and called, "I'm going into town for groceries. Want to go along?"

"Why yes, I guess I could. I — we could use a few things. Just let me change my dress."

Lettie was a bit surprised at the alacrity with which Prudy accepted her invitation, an invitation often given, but not always accepted. Prudy usually hemmed and hawed about asking Lester, or she was anxious about getting back in time to fix supper, but today she accepted readily and with enthusiasm. Well, no matter. It was a nice change and long overdue. Lettie raised her voice as she looked out at the drizzle falling on the flower garden.

"I see you finally got your garden in."

A muffled "Yes" came from Prudy upstairs, but Lettie seemed not to notice.

"That can't be the geranium I gave you, can it? I never thought it would survive the winter. You really have a green thumb, Prudy."

She paid no mind to the absence of an answer.

Prudy's good humor lasted all afternoon and Lettie returned her in plenty of time to fix supper. In fact, Prudy insisted that she try a piece of her chocolate cake before she went home to Meyer. Lettie could never resist Prudy's baking and had her growing figure to attest to her healthy appetite. After an agreeable refreshment, and with a piece of cake to go for Meyer, Lettie took her leave, somewhat puzzled at there being no mention of Lester, but pleased at the change in her friend. Even the rain hadn't dampened the ladies' spirits.

It rained off and on all afternoon with a promise of continuing into the night. As Prudy lit the lamps and was preparing a light repast for herself she heard a noisy car drive into the back yard. She stood behind the kitchen door, out of sight, and watched as three men got out of a delapidated Ford and looked around.

"Hey, Lester," one of the men called.

Lester's drinking pals. Good. They had come for him and his beer. She had it all figured out in her head just how she would handle the situation that she knew was inevitable.

"Lester, ol' pal, come on out, ya ol' bastard."

They looked at one another and at the house and started slowly toward it. Prudy took a deep breath and stepped through the screen door onto the porch.

"Hello, fellas. Lester's not here."

"He ain't? How come? He's supposed to bring the beer."

She managed a frown. "Why, I don't know. That's funny. I thought he was with you."

"Well, he ain't. We come to pick him up. Beggin' your pardon, Missus, but we'd like to talk to Lester. We need the beer."

"Really, he's not here. You sure you're not joshin' me?"

"No Mam."

There was an awkward pause. No one spoke. Prudy was in command of the situation and she knew what to do next.

"I tell you what. If you really mean it, if you're not playin' games with me, you can tell Lester that he missed his supper again. And if you want the beer, you'll have to get it yourself."

The men looked at each other. This had not happened before. Prudy picked up the lamp and led the way to the root cellar. The men stood at the top and did not follow her. She lit the overhead lamp.

"Well now, come on; you don't expect me to move these barrels, do you?"

"No Mam," but --"

"But what?"

"Well, ya see, Missus, ol' Lester never let us down there till he had a barrel at the foot of the steps. Don't know why, but you know ol' Lester. Maybe he was hidin' somethin'." The man gave a toothless grin. Prudy ignored the last remark.

"Well, I can't move those barrels, so you'll have to come on down here and get them yourself."

The men looked at each other once more and then slowly descended the steep steps into the murky cellar. Prudy tried not to think of how the dim overhead lamp made them look. The old saying of how folks are known by the company they keep came to her and she hoped her hands tightly clasped around her arms gave the appearance that she suffered from a slight chill and not that it held back the shudder that was rising inside her. She stood back as the men went to work.

"This one's empty," said the scruffiest man, "an' this one's half full. Ol' Lester better get busy on another batch."

"Here's a full one," said another, as he spat tobacco juice on the dirt floor. The men rolled it to the steps, lifted it easily, and stumbled to the top where they set it on the damp ground and rolled it to the car, leaving odd marks in the mud. They dumped the barrel in the rumble seat of the ancient car and clambered inside. The driver hollared out the broken window, "Thank ya, Missus. If we see ol' Lester, we'll tell him what ya said."

With that they rumbled from the yard and Prudy breathed a sigh of relief. She closed the cellar doors and watched as they disappeared from sight.

She had made it through another day. She wondered what the morrow would bring. Each day was beginning to be a new adventure. She had something to get up for, something to look forward to. The rain began again and she ran through the puddles to the porch and wiped her feet on the ragged braided rug. Her humble home was starting to look good to her, despite its appearance. It was all hers.

CHAPTER TWENTY

The Best Laid Plans

Prudy's life proceeded better than it had in her entire life during that summer of 1929 when she was in control. Then it was the end of October. In later years she would comment, "Good times never stayed around very long in my life." Shortly after Prudy's fifty-fourth birthday the stock market crashed and the country was plunged into the beginning of several years of economic depression. The catastrophic event meant nothing to Prudy. She didn't receive a newspaper, read very little except for her mother's Bible, had no radio, and even if she had kept up with events the ramifications of what happened would have held no meaning for her. She was doing well. She had a house to live in on land that was hers; she had lots of money; she had a car. Life was good. She didn't even have to worry about the future of her sons.

In December little Bernadine, a second daughter, was born to Helga and Fred, making their Christmas a joyous one. Prudy had three granddaughters with another baby on the way in the spring. Polly was expecting again. Prudy had much to be thankful for, much to look forward to. There was nothing to worry about.

The problem of Lester's absence had been solved. The boys had simply accepted it as a disappearance. Prudy had explained to them at first that "he went to town" as she had done so often when they were younger and their father had not come home for supper. As they grew older they understood more than she realized, having seen him in the company of one or more of the women with bad reputations in Spotswood and not mentioning it to her, and refusing to discuss it among themselves. As they had often heard Lettie say, "Ignorance is bliss." They never really understood what she meant by that, but with age comes widsom and they kept their mouths shut. Their mother would never know. At least, they thought she didn't know. Consequently, those who knew of Lester's habits never talked about it, and when Lester's last trip to town stretched into days and weeks and eventually months it became clear that he was not coming back. He had simply disappeared. Mrs. Deters had been deserted.

Lester's drinking pals came again and took with them the remaining barrels in the cellar. They knew someone who had a good recipe and who could keep them filled. Prudy was grateful to not see the men again. On December 5, 1933, prohibition ended after more than a decade, having failed in its purpose. Prudy could never understand why it was called "The Noble Experiment."

Prudy's sons' concern for her was eased somewhat by the change in their mother.

She seemed surprisingly content with her solitary life. She was relaxed, less apprehensive, more prone to laugh, something they had rarely observed in their growing-up years. For the first time they took note of what their mother looked like and how she coped with her life, a life that now seemed much easier. They saw a small, thin woman with steel gray hair, formerly dull brown eyes shining with an unfamiliar light, her wrinkled face made more youthful with a soft smile. The worried furrow between her eyes was still there, but not so deep, and they were shocked and ashamed to discover that they noticed for the first time the absence of black and blue marks on her face and body. Had they become so accustomed over the years to seeing her bruised and battered that they assumed it was the natural state of affairs? Alan had begun a correspondence with his brothers once it became a certainty that their father was out of their lives, and he communicated such observations to Chester in California. He had conflicting emotions about the change in his mother. He was happy to see the abrupt change, yet worried about her living alone. And the guilt that rose to the surface was not easy to deal with, as it brought home to him his former apathy and his unwillingness to do anything about his mother's plight. Now that plight was resolved.

Chester replied to Alan's letters, expressing relief that everything had smoothed out and hoping that he and his family could return for a visit very soon, but with Polly's condition it was hard to say just when they could make it back to South Dakota. It occurred to the three of them that they had all been away for so long and had been so occupied with their own lives that they had neglected their uncomplaining mother. During those years how many times had she been at the mercy of their father, whom they knew was capable of violence?

Fred squirmed at the thought but, being the youngest, he had known little else in his parents' relationship. It was only in his marriage to Helga, whom he adored, that there came a realization of what a woman's role in a marriage could be. They eased their conscience with the knowledge that their mother was finally free of the travail she had known. It was obvious their father was gone for good. There had been no word from him, no trace at all. Such things had been known to happen. Alan also wrote to Millicent and Howard, seeing Millicent's lovely face as he wrote, keeping them abreast of things. Millicent dutifully wrote a letter now and then to her Aunt Prudence, letters which Prudy looked forward to and placed carefully in the drawer in the sideboard in the dining room.

Prudy was ignorant of any worry her family had and enjoyed her newly found life. She tended her flower garden which flourished all summer long, harvested the produce from the vegetable garden and preserved the excess on her hot cookstove in the fall. The shelves in the root cellar filled with the fruits of her labors and, with the disgusting barrels gone, she used the space for storage and shoved boxes filled with Lester's clothing against the far wall. She didn't know why she even bothered, but the clothes were clean and if anybody in need could use them they were available. Perhaps she was keeping up a pretense of their being used again some day. In any event, she was prepared for the coming winter, even to the point of a stack of firewood in the barn provided by Fred who brought it in his new pickup one day. Old Bessie had taken her place in the cellar, too, hanging from the ceiling, nicely cured. Prudy looked forward to an independent life.

And then Meyer died. He was stricken suddenly just before Thanksgiving, 1929. Lettie was prostrate with grief. She had never considered life without Meyer. He was her other self, her helpmate, and had been by her side all of her adult life. Prudy felt totally inadequate to comfort her, as Lettie had comforted her when John had died in the war. But Lettie was always glad to see her and would beg Prudy to stay and hug her to her bosom tightly as she sobbed out her sorrow. What was she to do? How could she go on without her Meyer? It was impossible. The funeral was well attended. It was the largest funeral Spotswood had seen and, although the tiny town was rapidly diminishing in size, The First Community Church was filled with mourners who came to pay their respects to a fine, honest, friendly man.

The children came home and Lettie leaned on them heavily for emotional support. Helga, of course, was her mainstay. Bridget came from Aberdeen, slender and lovely and looking very intellectual in her rimless eye glasses. Peter traveled by train from California to Cheyenne, Wyoming, where he hired a small plane and flew directly to his parents' home, causing a commotion with the landing of the craft in the field across the road. His blond good looks as he strode across the dirt road was a sight to see and was talked about for weeks afterward. He had matured into a fine figure of a man. The family who mourned Meyer Dannenbring gave a dignity to the small church. Though it had seen far better days it was the place of worship where the family grew up in the Christian way, and now it was laying to rest one of its foremost citizens.

Prudy wept openly for all of them, and had no one to comfort her. She was lonely for Chester. Alan wasn't there. She had Fred, but he sat beside Helga. Peter told her that Chester sent his regrets, but he had to remain behind to tend to the business and to be there for Polly, who was expecting their second child. Later, at the lunch after the interment, Peter came to Prudy and handed her an envelope which contained snapshots of Chester and his family and she took comfort in the image of her son, grown into such a straight-figured man, robust and strong, standing with Peter, their arms draped over each other's shoulders in front of the biggest tree that Prudy had ever seen or could imagine. There was a note and she read it through her tears:

Dear Mama,

Sorry I can't be there with you. Please tell the folks I'm real sad about Mr. Dannenbring. He was a swell guy. I thought you'd like to see the latest. The business is really going good and growing, and so is Polly, as you can see. The baby will come in the spring. We're hoping for a boy, but will take what comes. I will try to write more later.

Your son, Chester

Lettie was never the same after Meyer's death. She moped around the house and brooded. Prudy had plenty of time to spare and went to her friend every day. She

174

very capably cranked up the noisy old Model T and drove the two miles down the country road to see her, rattled into the neat yard and walked into the big kitchen where she would find her slumped at the kitchen table, sometimes still in her robe, totally unlike the Lettie she knew, seated with a cold cup of coffee before her.

"Lettie," she would say softly and Lettie would look up at her with sad, dull eyes and grasp Prudy in her ample arms and sob inconsolably. Sometimes they would talk and Prudy would urge her to get dressed while she tidied up the kitchen, a pleasure compared to working in the dingy room in her house. Lettie's kitchen was large and bright with several windows covered with crisp clean curtains. She had running water and electricity, a stove run by propane gas, and a crank telephone on the wall. Prudy enjoyed working there and got a lift from the pleasant, convenient workplace, all the while helping out, being of service. There were other times when even Prudy could not get Lettie to budge from her chair, so she simply worked around her, keeping up a low-key conversation and hoping that Lettie heard her as she stared out the window with tears spilling down her cheeks. During the winter Prudy's visits were fewer because of the cold and snow and by the time spring rolled around in 1930 the situation had gotten worse until one morning she found Lettie still in bed and totally uncommunicative.

Alarmed, she was forced to use the telephone, an activity in which she was not very accomplished. She prayed the other parties on the line would stay off until she got through to Fred. To hear his mother's voice on the other end of the line was enough to alarm Fred and he and Helga were there in no time to take charge. Prudy waited for them at the back door. They arrived in their big Plymouth. Frederica, hardly two, was closely supervising her baby sister, Bernadine, in the back seat. They were bundled up against the sharp spring air. Helga grabbed the baby and Fred picked up the toddler and they came quickly into the house.

"Mama, what is it. What's wrong?" asked Fred, needing to hear her tell him again that his hardy mother-in-law needed assistance.

Helga immediately raced up the stairs to her parents' bedroom and Prudy stayed discreetly in the kitchen, gathering the two little girls in her arms and smiling fondly at Fred. He had grown into a good-looking man of twenty-four, neatly groomed, a sturdy, strong man with muscles finely tuned from years of hard work. His dark eyes were kind, rarely displaying anger or impatience. His rather round face showed contentment and happiness, which Prudy was proud to see. Despite the tenseness of the occasion, she was happy to see him.

"You look fine, Fred," she said. "I'm real sorry to bother you, but she just wouldn't get up today. I've been coming over here every morning since the thaw — to check on her, you know, and I know you're awful busy with spring work and all, but . . ."

"Mama, you did the right thing. We're mighty glad you rang us up. But I still can't get over you driving Dad's beat up old car. You sure surprise me at times. Good thing you learned to drive it, because we weren't planning on coming over till Sunday."

175

Helga came slowly down the stairs and a worried frown was set in her smooth, young face. Her blond hair was pulled back from her face and a braid was coiled at her neck. No time to fuss over appearance she said. Her spotless housekeeping was well known in the community and her two bright, well cared for children were a pleasure to look upon. Her skills made their household run smoothly. But Helga was very troubled. Her ordered life would have to include a further dispersal of her energies. Her father was dead and her mother was sick, and Helga could not manage two households. If only Bridget were home, but she was still in college in Aberdeen and unable to help. Helga soon came up with a solution.

"Fred, dear. We must talk. We have a problem here and something must be done about it."

"Fred obediently sat down at the table with her and gave her his full attention. Prudy occupied her granddaughters, but listened unobstrusively.

"Mother can't go on this way, and your mother can't be expected to watch over her."

She swept aside with a wave of her hand Prudy's preferred protest that she didn't mind, and continued.

"Mother's condition hasn't improved at all and it could get worse. Someone should be with her all the time. I think she should move in with us. We have the room and she might just improve being around the children and the commotion in our house. What do you think; can we manage it?"

"Sure we can, honey," Fred said at once. "That's a swell idea. We'll take her home with us right now. She can have the guest room."

He smiled broadly at his wife. He knew she would come up with a solution to the problem and was glad to do whatever she thought best. Prudy marveled at the way they got along. She couldn't identify with it, but she marveled at it.

However, she was worried. She didn't like to see Lettie carted off, away from her home, and so far away she could not see her very often, even if the old jalopy would hold up. Besides, she had been used to Lettie being the strong one, caring for others. It disturbed Prudy to see her morose and depressed and led away by her daughter to be cared for like some patient in a hospital. But it wasn't her decision to make; she would do what she could to help while she was gone and told Helga that she would take care of the house until Lettie came home.

But Lettie didn't come home. Circumstances contrived to displace those carefully laid plans. Helga was pregnant again and radiant in her condition. Her statement about welcoming as many babies as The Lord would send held true and motherhood agreed with her. Fred was ecstatic. Their house soon became too small and it was clear they would move even further away. The decided to build a house to suit them with their growing family. Prudy's heart sank when they told her they had decided to move south, close to Pierre, the state capitol, located in the center of the state. They would build a big house with plenty of room on a ranch of their own making. They would concentrate on raising cattle; there were acres of grazing land in the vicinity of Pierre and Ft. Pierre across the river. They would raise horses, too, for riding and selling. As Fred excitedly told his mother about their plans in the fall of 1930 she became excited, too. It all sounded like a fairy tale come true, and she could hardly comprehend the scale of living described to her. But where had Fred gotten enough money to do all of those things?

"We'll have to borrow some money if the banks will lend us any. Times are not the best, but I have a good credit rating. And we have a bunch of money in the bank in Mobridge. Helga is a real good money manager, Mama. I've never seen the likes of it," he told her with a grin. "I tell you marrying her was the best thing I ever did, and Mama, I love her so much. How can I be so lucky?" Fred was a happy man.

The house was finished in the middle of April, 1931, just in time for the family to move in and get settled before the impending birth. When they were all moved in with new furniture purchased to fill every room Fred came to fetch his mother to show her the results. Prudy was going to pack a lunch to eat on the way, but Fred assured her that it was not necessary, that they would be there in time for dinner at noon.

"You mustn't drive too fast, Fred," she admonished him when they set off early in the morning.

"Now, Mama, forty miles an hour isn't too fast. The next thing we'll be needing is a bigger car. We've had this one for a couple of years and the doc told us Helga's having twins, so —"

Prudy's mouth fell open and she looked at him in astonishment. "Twins! Fred, how on earth will she manage? Just think of all the extra work."

"Don't you worry none about her, Mama. Helga can do anything."

The drive south was a pleasant one which soothed Prudy in spite of the expectant air of their journey. The warm spring sunshine coaxed the latent green from the earth so recently barren from a severe winter. The landscape rolled into low hills covered with tall prairie grass. The gravel road wound on, seemingly endless, with nothing on either side but the greening hills. It was beautiful, but eerie. It was nice to look at, but desolate. After a ride of several miles with nothing but the smooth running engine to break the silence, Prudy ventured, "Isn't it sort of isolated?"

"Yeah, it is, but we like it by ourselves. We're completely self-sufficient, and if we need to see people we just jump in the car and go. You'll see. We're just about there."

Fred stopped at the crest of a hill and Prudy drew in her breath. At the bottom of the hill on the right side of the road was a stately three-story house painted white with green trim. A long red barn and outbuildings were set back beyond a yard that was sprouting new grass. A tall steel windmill pumped water from a well into the house and provided energy for electricity from a nearby generator. There were no trees, just the low, rolling hills all around, as far as the eye could see, among which the house stood tall and fearless in the elements. Fred glanced at his mother for her reaction.

"Oh, Fred, how grand!"

"Yeah, it is nice, isn't it? Wait till you see inside." He started the car. "We don't

177

have a telephone out here yet, but we will someday. We'll also have neighbors and with them will come the demand for more electricity, including telephones. Right now, the windcharger gives us plenty of power. The wind really blows way out here. You know how the good old South Dakota wind blows, huh, Mama? And we have a battery-powered radio, so we aren't completely shut off from everybody."

"But what if you run out of gas so far away, and where will the children go to school, and —"

"Now, Mama, we've thought that all out. Gas is sorta high. It's over 20 cents a gallon now, but it'll probably go down. I keep a tank of gas in the barn so there's plenty on hand. And the kids'll go to country school just a few miles from here, but that won't be for a few years. I'm gonna make sure they get as much schoolin' as possible, more'n I got. Now don't you fret. There's nothin' to worry about."

They pulled into a gravel driveway that led to a wide yard and Fred honked. They got out of the car and Prudy stood looking at the big house with a porch all around it. She started around to the back.

"No, Mama, we'll go in the front," said Fred, smiling at her tolerantly.

"Oh," she said softly. This modern age had lost some of the polite customs of the past.

"Helga says that front doors were meant to be used and, until we get some neighbors, I guess it don't make any difference anyway."

Helga opened the heavy front door that had a large square window covered with a gathered curtain. She looked ready to deliver at any moment, notwithstanding the fact that the babies were not due for six more weeks. Nevertheless, she was neatly dressed with a wide apron over her expanded middle. She looked tired, but smiled widely and greeted Prudy warmly and led her into the house, then stood back to observe her mother-in-law's reaction.

Prudy didn't disappoint her. The house was even bigger inside that it appeared outside with large rooms and high vaulted ceilings, each with a long, fancy brass light fixture descending from it. The living room walls were covered with pale flowered paper. Mahogany furniture filled the room and the varnished floor boards were covered with a bordered carpet. The dining room contained a shiny table with two leaves in it and an embroidered runner down the middle with a bowl of wax fruit set in the center. Matching chairs with embroidered seats lined the table. A heavy sideboard contained drawers and two doors with ornate handles. On the top was a silver bowl centered on a heavy mirror with crystal candlesticks on each side. The kitchen was several times the size of Prudy's and held a green and ivory gas stove with attached oven, which took up far less room than her woodburning cookstove. There was a porcelain sink with running water, an electric refrigerator, and cupboards painted green and ivory above spotless counters. Off the kitchen was a fully stocked pantry and beyond the kitchen next to the screened-in back porch was the wash room which contained a washing machine, two wash tubs, a wood clothes hanger, ironing board and electric iron. Prudy was truly awed by such extravagant splendor.

Helga laughed and held her side. "I just hope the generator holds out. We need a lot of electricity around here. But the wind never seems to let up, so the windcharger should always do its job. Well, what do you think?" She grasped the back of a chair as she looked inquisitively at her.

"It's just wonderful, Helga. But are you all right? You must be tired. Please sit down and rest yourself. Fred can show me the rest of the house."

"I believe I will. Mother is in her room right now, but she'll be down for dinner soon."

Fred patted his wife's shoulder as he passed her, leading his mother to the hall and the stairway. It was plenty wide, the steps were not too high and each step had rubber padding so her footsteps didn't make a sound as she went up. The second floor held three bedrooms and a bath. Prudy marveled at the bathroom which would make tending to one's toilet an enjoyable experience. The door to one of the rooms was closed. Fred explained.

"Helga's mother is in there. We'll pick her up on our way back down."

He had never been able to call Lettie anything but "Helga's mother." His respect for her caused him to flounder around trying to settle on something appropriate. "Mrs. Dannenbring" sounded too formal, and "Mother" didn't sound right. He didn't call his own mother that. So her called her "Helga's mother." Lettie found it amusing, but made no unfavorable remark, so it remained.

They went up to the third floor which contained three rooms and another bath. They were not completely furnished and the furniture that was there came from their former home. It was tidy and presented many possibilites, either for use as bedrooms, an office or a sitting room.

"Do you like it, Mama?"

Prudy let out a long appreciative sigh of pleasure. "Of course, I do, Fred. I love it. It's so big and so comfortable, with everything a body could need. I am so proud of you and happy for both of you. To think that my grandchildren will grow up here, well, it's just . . ."

Tears glistened and his heart went out to her. He was so filled with pride in his accomplishment that he only just then rememberd that he would be taking her back to the hovel she called home. He assumed she was thinking the same thing and was at once humbled.

"Mama, maybe you could live here, too. Helga's mother is happy here and we've got lots of room."

The earnest look on his face made Prudy realize what he had been thinking. She placed her hands on his arms.

"Oh no, Fred. I couldn't do that. I have no intention of leaving my home. It's the only place I've ever known. I couldn't live anywhere else. I'm just so happy to see things going so well for you. Didn't mean to get all weepy." She wiped her eyes with her torn handkerchief.

Fred's face cleared in relief and he said, "Come on. I think dinner must be ready."

They stopped on the second floor and knocked on the closed door. Fred said, his voice raised a little, "Dinner is ready, and we've got company."

Prudy heard movement, the door opened and Lettie stood before them. She had lost weight and seemed taller, more like she had looked when Prudy first met her. Her hair was much grayer and her face bore fine lines of sorrow that the former fullness never showed. Her eyes lit up when she saw Prudy and she held out her arms and enveloped her friend in a firm grasp.

"Prudy! When they said company was coming they didn't tell me it was you. How wonderful to see you.'

She held her away to get a better look. A smile creased her face, a most welcome smile to Prudy, who had been so worried about her for months. How differently the two women had dealt with the loss of a husband.

Lettie said, "I'm hungry. How about you? After that long trip you must be ready to eat. Aren't we way out in the boondocks, though? Wait till you see how the children have grown." She kept up a steady chatter on the way down to the dining room. Prudy was gratified to see that Lettie had regained much of her former self.

The table was set nicely and the two little girls were seated waiting for their elders, Bernadine in a new high chair and Frederica in the old one that had been remodeled into a youth chair.

Helga said cheerily, "Girls, do you remember your Grandma Deters?"

They just stared at Prudy across the table, looking at their grandmothers, from one to the other, then back again, somewhat perplexed at the differences in the two women called Grandma.

"It's been quite awhile since they've seen me and they were so small then. But my goodness, how they've grown."

Prudy smiled lovingly at her granddaughters often during dinner, admiring their blond beauty, but with brown eyes, which shone from their scrubbed faces. Lettie obviously took great pride in them, too, and it was equally apparent that Helga had been right: to bring Lettie with them to live had been just what she needed to snap her out of the doldrums. Dinner was a happy time and Prudy was impressed with the deference the children showed their father who sat at the head of the table, dishing up everyone's dinners that no one touched until all had been served. Prudy found she had an appetite and cleaned her plate of a pork chop, mashed potatoes and gravy, peas and carrots and home baked bread. Where did Helga get all her energy? As if in answer to her unspoken question, Helga said, "Mother has been such a help to me since she came. I couldn't manage the house and the children without her. We have urged her to make this her home for good."

"I see. I'm real glad you're feeling better, Lettie. I do miss you though," replied Prudy. "I was hoping you'd be coming home soon."

Lettie folded her napkin and placed it beside her plate. "Prudy, dear, I'm afraid I won't be coming home. It just reminds me of Meyer, my sweet Meyer." Tears rolled down her cheeks and she quickly wiped them away. "Sorry, I can't seem to stop that," she said apologetically.

"But what will you do with the house? Aren't you ever coming back?"

"I'm afraid not. As long as Helga and Fred want me I am content to stay. I won't deny it has been good for me to be here, but I won't be a burden. I go to my room when I feel I might be intruding. A young couple needs their privacy, don't you agree?"

Prudy remembered her saying that when they were first married and she and Meyer had given them their first house as a wedding present. But how could Prudy manage without Lettie? She had counted on her coming back. She needed her steadying influence and it was mighty lonesome without her. She knew it was pointless to argue when Lettie informed her she had Meyer dug up and brought to the ranch where he was resting peacefully in a fenced-off area behind the house beneath a small tree with leafy branches. She needed him close to her, she explained. Prudy understood that and her heart felt a pang as she thought of the ones she loved buried in the Spotswood Cemetery.

"There's another reason, Prudy," Lettie continued. "You see, with the stock market crash there is a need for immediate cash. As long as I will be staying here I plan to contribute to the upkeep of this nice house. So I am selling mine."

At last the full meaning of the 1929 crash held meaning for Prudy.

"You're selling your house? But you can't!" she blurted.

Lettie patted her arm. "I'm afraid I have to. It will bring a good price and, unoccupied, it is a liability. It needs someone living in it. The house holds nothing for me without Meyer."

"But how will I see you?" Prudy's eyes were brimming.

Lettie put an arm around her. "I'll come to see you when Fred has occasion to get up that way. Or I can drive myself. I still have our old car. And you can come to see me anytime."

"Of course she can," said Helga amiably. "We've lots of room and you would be such a good companion to Mother after being around the children so much. We can work it out."

"See, Mama, everything's going to work out OK," said Fred, beaming at Helga.

Prudy stayed overnight and Fred took her back to the farm the next day. She was happy for her son and his family and for Lettie, but disconsolate at the turn her own life had taken. She hadn't counted on ever losing Lettie. She would be all alone.

In May, 1931, twin boys were born to Helga and Fred, making their family a unit of six. The boys were named Michael and Mitchell, the first male heirs to the Deters name. Lester would have been proud.

CHAPTER TWENTY ONE

Dust to Dust

Prudy kept in touch with her sons by letter, a leisure time activity she had seldom cultivated. She had time on her hands and she learned to occupy it in various ways. She did needlework and some necessary mending, which she really didn't care for, but she could do some serious thinking while she worked. Her reading material expanded with a gift at Christmas of a subscription to Collier's Magazine from Fred and Helga. She read it from cover to cover and saved every issue. Subscriptions to other publications followed when they found out how much she enjoyed them. It was nice to know she had something in the tattered mail box at the end of the driveway. She grew more proficient in expressing herself in her letters and wrote all the news she could think of, which wasn't much, but they all assured her that they liked to hear what was going on in the old home town and on the farm, no matter how insignificant she thought it might be.

She received another photograph to add to the growing accumulation on top of the sideboard. Polly and Chester had another daughter, little Cora, born in March 1930, right on schedule, and alongside it a picture of Helga's twins, Michael and Mitchell, who were born the following year shortly after Prudy's visit. Prudy looked at the array of photographs every day, seeing the members of her family grow, happy for the healthy grandchildren and lonesome for all of them. As far flung as her sons were, Prudy was the one who was isolated, set apart from the world in her ramshackle house that was rattled by the elements, devoid of paint, with outbuildings falling apart, and only crude comforts that society had long ago passed by on the way to better things.

Times were hard, harder than Prudy could remember. Even the few old timers who were left couldn't recall a worse time. The prairie states were a vast dust bowl. The depression and the dirty thirties lay heavy over them for years. Prudy still had money in the big covered bowl in the kitchen cupboard and in the metal tea box, but it was all she had, except for the land the farm sat on. There was seldom a rent payment because tenant farmers could no longer pay it. Some of them tried to hold on, and when the government bought pigs for $2.00 a head and paid a ridiculously low price for cattle most were forced to sell the animals they had. There was no feed to give them and the government offered ready money, money that was desperately needed, but which soon disappeared.

When farmers were forced from the land because of practically nonexistent grain prices Prudy remained the owner of hundreds of acres of land, but it was unproductive land. Grain grew to six inches and died because there was no rain. Corn ears were mere nubbins and sold for three cents a bushel. And taxes still had to be paid. But Prudy was used to scrimping and saving every salvageable scrap, so she was not worried as long as her money hoard held out. The gravity of her situation never sank in, nor did her sons have any idea of the way things were concerning their mother.

In April, 1931, shortly after she returned from visiting Fred's family on the ranch, a black cloud rolled ominously over the land, blotting out the sun and turning day into night. With the cloud came strong winds which blew topsoil like it was loose sand. A fine dust seeped through every crack and cranny, leaving a gray film on everything. It was a thoroughly frightening experience, completely unexpected, and it proved to be only the first of many such storms. People quickly learned to soak sheets and blankets in water in the bathtub and to cover the windows with them, tucking the wet linens into the corners. The wind rattled windows and flung pellets of dirt against them in its fury. People shoved rugs up tightly against the doors to keep out the dirt that swirled in angry dust devils outside, trying to get in. Their efforts were largely ineffective. The dust seeped in and lay everywhere, on top of every piece of furniture, in the folds of bed covers, plugging window screens. To slam a screen door meant a puddle of dirt on the floor.

Nothing grew because of the drought. No rain of any significance fell for months out of every year. What vegetation there was soon was devoured by droves of grasshoppers. Their arrival in a thick cloud of buzzing wings as they headed for the fields further deepened the gloom and hopelessness of the situation. They ate everything in sight, not only on the farms, but in towns as well. They clung to the sides of buildings, onto screens, and chewed the paint from houses. They remained as long as the yearslong drought lasted and were a familiar, abhorrent sight to the recipients of the devastation. They were squished underfoot and brushed from the clothing of those who had to be outdoors. The odds were great, but most people hung on.

Despite conditions, the Dannenbring farm was sold, as Lettie said it would be. Its many conveniences helped in the sale and it transferred to the new owner before the ready money for bank loans was exhausted. Prudy never got acquainted with the new occupants nor did she have any desire to. The house would always be Lettie's house and she couldn't bring herself to drive over and introduce herself as a neighbor to the strangers living there. The new people, named Gebhart, managed to keep their newly acquired property in spite of the hard times and eventually inquired in town about the Deters place, which always looked deserted. One day Prudy was surprised by a visit from a Mr. Wesley Berg, a banker in Mobridge who said he had a prospective buyer for her place and wanted to know how much she was asking for it. Prudy refused at once, saying it was not for sale. The nicely dressed young man could not change her mind no matter how persuasively he argued and finally left in his shiny blue coupe, shaking his head at the obstinacy of the old woman in the disreputable house who really wanted to stay there. He would try again another time. Surely she couldn't be serious.

Alan had begun the practice of visiting his mother at regular intervals, stopping by every week or ten days, depending on his schedule. She was delighted to see him and would fix him a nourishing meal. He always urged her to leave with him, to come and stay with him in Mobridge.

"Now, Alan, why should I do that? Live with you in the rectory? What a thought. Really, I'm doing just fine right here."

But he continued to worry about her and conveyed that worry to his brothers in his letters. He told them:

I am still concerned about Mother. She is well and looks remarkably content with her life, but I can't see how. I am very sad to say it, but the house is a disgrace, not from her lack of caring for it, but simply because it is past redemption. I have tried several times to get her to leave and come live with me. There is room at the rectory. She could have her own room and I would look after her and take good care of her. My housekeeper would welcome some female companionship. Maybe you could persuade her to leave that awful farm."

Chester and Fred did the best they could, but got nowhere. They had little time to spare on anything but their own lives, being occupied with their immediate growing families and businesses. Helga had another baby, Fred, Jr., born in February, 1933, and declared that this baby was the end of the line, that five children were enough, and that The Lord needn't provide anymore. Prudy was a proud grandmother and grateful that her grandchildren were strong, healthy, and very smart. How could they not be?

But, her complacence was short-lived. As was her lot, fate had other plans for her. No matter how lethargically she plodded through her dreary life or how bleak her future looked, any change caught her by surprise. It was November 11, 1933, and the coolness was welcome after a blistering summer. She was outside, wearing only a light sweater, pulling the dead remainders of her gardens, salvaging what she could of the vegetables and piling the refuse in the old wheelbarrow to dump later. Potatoes seemed to grow no matter what, and they had become a boring staple in her diet to accompany what preserved food was left in the cellar. She was tending to her flower garden, raking it over, when she paused in her labors and tensed with the familiar clouding over of the sun, the sudden eerie quiet, the fearsome lull that everyone had learned to dread. She looked up and dropped the rake. The sky was black, blacker than she had ever seen it during the day, and the horizon was laden with a thick, rumbling cloud moving swiftly from the southwest. Oh no, please God, not again, raced through her mind. Then she ran as fast as she could for shelter, heading for the root cellar, stumbling down the first few steps and pulling the door shut over her head. She sat down to catch her breath; she had made it just in time. She thought of her house, of the open back door, of Bunting. She had forgotten to call her in her panic, but she comforted herself with the knowledge that her pet was very capable of taking care of herself and was probably safe in the barn

184

under a feeding bin. The noise of the storm raging above her was deafening. She might as well have been in the middle of a railroad track with a train bearing down on her. She covered her ears against the racket. It was stronger this time. She could imagine what it was doing to her unprotected house and cringed at the whine of the gale that was coupled with the sounds of objects being thrown about. Real destruction was being waged. Dust sifted through the cellar doors into her hair and onto her shoulders and she moved to get down the steps and to the far wall for protection, but cried out in pain as she stood up. In her hurried descent she had hurt her right ankle. She sat down carefully and inspected the damage. It looked like nothing was broken, but the ankle was starting to swell, and now that she was made aware of it, it really hurt. The cellar doors shuddered from the force of the wind and the dust sifting through became a steady stream. She had to move, but it was pitch dark, and she couldn't stand up to light the overhead lamp that could be heard swinging and creaking. Fear rose in her but she pushed it back. She must move. She had to get away from the cellar doors which had weakened over the years.

Cautiously she inched her way down each step, sat on the clammy dirt floor and pulled herself to the far wall. She leaned against the boxes containing Lester's belongings and took a shaky breath. The boxes and their contents smelled moldy. She was secure for the time being at least. Her ankle throbbed. She reached out to rub it and cried out again. She mustn't touch it. Maybe if she rested until the storm passed over she could crawl up the steps and into the house. If she soaked the sore ankle it would be all right. She leaned her head against the stacked boxes and closed her eyes tightly, lest the tears that were forming should escape. No need to cry. Everything would be all right. The storm would be over soon and if she could just hang on for a little while — but she was so tired. Then for the first time in Prudy's life she fainted.

The black death above her roared over the prairie, picking up what topsoil it could find and depositing it in another state, replenishing itself with more precious life-giving land and scattering it over thousands of miles, raining an arid destruction and despair over God's green earth.

She struggled up to conciousness and moaned in pain. It was morbidly quiet. And it was dark. No light showed through the cracked doors. She tried to focus, to get her bearings. She was in the cellar with the doors closed against the far wall propped against some smelly boxes. The odor of dust and mold was in her nostrils. The storm had passed and she had to rouse herself to get out and into the house. She had no idea what time of day it was or if, in fact, it was still day. She floated in and out of a fitful sleep and was just about to make a valiant effort to pull herself to the stairs when she heard something, a faint "hello," then a louder "Mother! Where are you?" She said as loudly as she could, "Alan," as she attempted to answer him, but it escaped her parched throat as a scratchy utterance. She tried again. "Alan, down here. I'm in the cellar." He must not have heard me, she thought, and her heart sank as his cries diminished and there was silence. Then she heard running footsteps and the cellar doors were thrust open and she saw him silhouetted against a hazy sky. At hearing her relieved sob, he was at her side in a flash. He knelt beside her and gathered her in his arms, but she cried out.

"Mother, what happened. Oh, Mother, you're hurt."

"Alan, I'm so glad to see you. I hurt my ankle getting down the steps when the storm came up. See how swelled up it is. And it hurts me real bad."

"Hush now, take it easy. I'll get you out of here." He looked at her sharply. "You mean to tell me you've been down here all this time?"

He could see that she had no sense of how long a time had passed, and continued, "The storm was a bad one and as soon as it was over and I could get out of the house I came right out here to check on you and it's a good thing I did. I looked for you in the house and you weren't there — and I can tell you right now, Mother, that you are not spending one more minute in this Godforsaken place. God forgive me for that, but it's true. This is no place for you. You are coming home with me right now."

He would not listen to her faint objections, words he had heard so many times he could recite them with her. Tenderly he picked her up and carried her to the foot of the stairs. How light she was. There was nothing to her. He placed his feet squarely on each step as he went up, shoving the packed dirt to the side with his foot, making sure he had a firm grip. It would not do for both of them to fall. Prudy squinted in the queer light. It wasn't yet dusk, but it was past afternoon. The sun in the western sky shone through the haze like a milky veil. Alan carried her to the porch where he set her down on the lone chair that still stood there. It had hooked itself into the railing; otherwise, the wind would have blown it away to join the other one, the wash tubs, the rake, and wheelbarrow that had ended their air-bourne journey in a bank of gray dust, stuck like a montage arranged by a demented artist.

Prudy couldn't believe her eyes. The flat, barren land was rounded out with

186

mounds and drifts of dust. The barn had finally collapsed and lay on its side with banks of dust weaving in and out of its broken frame. The chicken coup and outhouse were flattened. She saw no chickens. The windmill was on its side and the water in the trough was thick with mud. There was no trace of her gardens, only rivulets of windblown dirt, looking for all the world like a dry water landscape.

"This is terrible," she said.

Tears came, but there were no sobs, just a relentless flow of uninhibited tears that failed to relieve the despair in her heart.

"Now you see why you are coming with me, and you are coming right now. I'll listen to no more excuses."

"But, Alan —"

"Don't argue with me, Mother," he said, his features showing genuine anger. He looked squarely at her, unmoved in his resolve. She had never seen him assert himself like that and she meekly ceased her objections.

"All right. Please don't be mad at me. I'll do what you say. But there are some things I have to take. Not many. Just some things that mean an awful lot to me. I can't just leave them here."

"Very well, but never mind your clothes and nonessential things. I'll get what you need. I should have done this long ago, before the situation got so out of hand. What on earth was I thinking of?" He muttered half to himself as he stood before her and stooped to pick her up once again to take her inside. "I warn you, Mother; it's not a pretty sight."

He stopped in the kitchen and she gasped, "Dear Lord."

The house was destroyed. Heaps of dust filled the corners of every room. Windows had blown in and shattered glass littered the uneven floors. Every surface was impregnated with dust, like a thin gray blanket. He carried her into the dining room and set her in one of the few remaining chairs that was in one piece, after brushing it off. Prudy looked around her in disbelief at the strange, unreal appearance of her home.

"Why did this happen? What have we done to deserve this? Why, Alan? Can you tell me that?" She looked at him, staring hard into his face, demanding an answer. He was the priest, wasn't he? The messenger of God? He was supposed to know. But Alan had no answer.

"I don't know, Mother. I just don't know." He shook his head sadly, avoiding his mother's reproachful eyes.

"Well, it's not fair, that's what. It's just not fair. And I'm not going anywhere until I have my things." It was her turn to be angry.

"Just tell me what you want and I'll get them for you."

He looked around and was at a loss as to what there was to be salvaged from the ravaged house.

"Upstairs in my bedroom in the drawer is a pretty box. It's tied with a ribbon. It's a box of things that your poor Aunt Patience gave me years ago and it has all my treasures in it."

"Is that all? Are you sure there's nothing else while I'm up there?"

"My purse. It's in the dresser, too. It has some money in it."

She stretched her throbbing foot and tried to ease it into a comfortable position, but nothing helped, and it was grossly swollen. She heard Alan go carefully up the creaky stairs and he was soon back down with a faded box tied with a frayed ribbon that had once been blue and an ancient black purse with a broken strap. He said, "It's just as bad up there, totally uninhabitable. Part of the ceiling has caved in on top of the bed. Thank God I had sense enough to get out here. I tremble to think of what might have happened if I hadn't." Alan's anger was tempered with relief in his positive approach to a very real danger.

"I'm just fine now that you're here. Don't fret yourself. Now in here I want those things on the sideboard, all those pictures. I'll clean them up later. And in that drawer are some papers I think we'd better take along."

He needed something to put everything in and fetched an apple box from the kitchen and piled all the items in it, including a few pieces of silverware. Then he picked her up and was about to leave the house when she stopped him in the kitchen.

"Wait, there's something else. On the top shelf is Grandma's big covered bowl. I need that."

With some irritation, he replied, "Mother, we have plenty of dishes at the rectory."

"But I really do need it. I want that dish and the creamer and sugar bowl sitting beside it. They match." She was uncharacteristically insistent.

Patiently indulging her, Alan reached up and yanked open the cupboard door. He placed the dish on the counter.

"This is heavy; is there something inside?"

"Yes. Look."

He lifted the cover and made the sign of the cross.

"There was more in it, and there used to be money in the tin behind it, but that's all gone now. I don't know exactly how much is left, but there should be some in the sugar bowl."

"Where did you get all this?" he asked sternly.

"Your father left it. Really, he did. Can't I tell you about it later? My ankle pains me a lot."

He looked at her long and hard, but he picked her up and carried her out to the porch, carefully stepped to the ground and walked to his black car parked in the middle of the yard, leaving footsteps as on a desert devoid of life. He placed her in the front seat, went back for her few belongings, and placed them all on the back seat.

"Is this it, then?" he inquired one last time.

"I guess it is. Doesn't seem like much, does it, when you get it all together? Not a lot for a lifetime."

She looked forlornly toward the house that now appeared completely alien to her, standing at an angle, stark against the darkening sky. The demolished outbuildings gave the whole scene a surreal look. She was leaving her life and everything she had ever known behind. It was all gone. She had nothing except what lay on the back seat. Her vision blurred again and she turned her head so Alan couldn't see. Then her gaze stopped at the edge of the barn. A flash of yellow fur was caught there. Her wail of anguish caught Alan off guard and at first he didn't know what was wrong. When she pointed he walked to the barn, looked down at the remnants of what had been a cat, turned to his mother and shook his head. When he climbed into the car she reached for him. Her upraised face was lined with suffering, tears were wringing the dust from it, and her mouth was twisted in grief, uttering soundless lamentations. He held her and patted her comfortingly, talking to her in soothing tones, until the sobbing subsided into shudders which wracked her frail body.

"It's just not fair," she said, her voice choked with sorrow.

CHAPTER TWENTY TWO

Hills and Valleys

Prudy had a badly sprained ankle which required her to be immobile for awhile, but it healed nicely under the kindly care of Anna, Father Alan Deters' housekeeper. Anna would call her guest nothing but Mrs. Deters and Prudy had to be satisfied with only "Anna" because, she was informed, that is what everyone called her. The women got along famously. They were in the neighborhood of the same age although Prudy, at fifty-eight, was a few years Anna's senior. They were in sharp contrast to each other. Prudy was small and wiry with dark eyes and gray hair. She was slightly stooped from the burdens of her years. Anna was a large, sturdy woman, reminding Prudy of Lettie, with a thatch of graying hair kept in check with a profusion of combs. Her plump face was usually smiling and her energy was boundless, but no matter how busy she was her apron remained spotless.

The women enjoyed each other's company and spent a good part of the day together, with Prudy helping out when she could persuade Anna to let her. Although her ankle was obviously paining her when she arrived she never complained, and pleaded to be of some use, to earn her keep. Anna would not hear of it, nor would Alan.

"Mother, we want you to relax and get well. You've worked hard all your life. You can take it easy now. Please don't fret; let us take care of you."

"But I feel so useless, and I don't want to be a burden."

"Nonsense. You are useful just being here where I can keep an eye on you. I worried so much when you were all alone on that farm, and I prayed for you every night."

But she felt guilty about her easier life. She had never had an easy life and didn't know quite how to deal with it without a nagging feeling that she didn't deserve it. Yet she was loved and cared for in the aging, but functional, clean house, with good plain food that was served to her by a devoted housekeeper. She had decent clothes to wear and felt she was dressed up every day. Who could argure with the turn her life had taken? She would try to accept it all.

Alan's conscience was eased and his news of what had happened was received with dismay, followed by relief, by his brothers and their wives. They were grateful to Alan for taking over the care of their mother. They could more readily get on with their lives. Their lives had also been touched by the drought and depression. Chester's business was still good with the production of timber and wood products continuing, but demand was down until ready money was more plentiful. Fred's ranch was productive, but any expansion of added improvements had halted until times got better. Worry about their mother, who had previously refused to budge from the farm, was lessened considerably. Alan's assumption of the burden had made it turn out well for all of them.

By 1934 close to 40,000 farms, almost half, in South Dakota were foreclosed. The state had the dubious distinction of having the greatest percentage, close to fifty percent, of its population on welfare, a shame that rankled in the hearts of its hard working, upright, proud inhabitants. Thousands of disillusioned farmers made an exodus to the promised land of California, leaving their farms deserted, machinery abandoned and imbedded in drifts of dust impacted with dried out thistles. Among those who left were most of the Clanahans, who found a climate and a culture more suited to them.

The country became deserted; it was no longer filled with closeknit families and good neighbors. Deep cracks in the dry earth opened the land. Skeletons of buildings, ravaged by the harsh weather, stood with empty windows like lifeless eyes staring at the blazing sun. Those who left the state worked as migrant workers in the lush fields of California or in factories or fish canneries and they made money, but it wasn't the same, and many returned to their homeland after a few years when things started to improve in the late thirties. They came home to the great outdoors of the wide open prairies.

There was some good news in 1934. Polly presented Chester with a boy whom they christened Leland, after Polly's father. He, too, proved to be the last child, but Prudy didn't complain. She had eight fine grandchildren, four boys and four girls, and proudly added Leland's picture to the grouping on her dresser. She had Father O'Brian's old room with her own bathroom, sheer luxury to her. She had a closet with a door instead of flimsy curtains in front of a sagging rod, and the closet contained some inexpensive new clothes and two pairs of shoes. Her bed was comfortable and it didn't squeak with every move she made. The dresser drawers held underclothing and hose without holes in them, plus a new purse with money in it. After she explained to Alan about finding all the money under the barrels in the cellar he persuaded her to deposit it in the bank. If she needed money it could be withdrawn at any time. The covered bowl and matching creamer and sugar bowl were donated to the rectory at Prudy's insistence and stood in a place of honor on the sideboard in the dining room. Anna was very partial to the pieces and had cleaned them up and polished them until they shone in their former beauty. How easy and simple her life had become when it had been so complicated.

Many folks she knew didn't have it as good. After the November dust storm Spotswood simply dried up and blew a way. There was very little left of the town anyway. The bank had closed up years before. There was no doctor's office. Pastor Kaufman had died and with him the church died, too. The congregation had dwindled to near nothing and the church could not be maintained for the few families who remained faithful. Prudy hadn't attended church since Lettie had left.

191

The school was a thing of the past. The one remaining general store sold every last bit of its inventory and the owner moved to Aberdeen. By 1935 all that remained of Spotswood was a miserable row of abandoned gray buildings and a few crumpled houses that, one by one, collapsed and were covered by dust and eventually overgrown with weeds. In coming years people would be hard pressed to recall the town of Spotswood. Prudy went back only once. She asked Alan to take her to the cemetery to place flowers on the graves of her parents, John, and little Mary, and was plunged into despair at what they found. Alan held her as she wept and his eyes brimmed, too, at what was once the Spotswood Cemetery. Stones were overturned and grave markers not made of stone were totally demolished. Mounds of dirt covered with straggly weeds covered the graves and markers which had become irreconcilably mixed up.

"May 30th is John's birthday. Today is his birthday," she sobbed.

"I know, Mother. I know."

"His grave is all I had left of him, and of Mary, and of Mama and Papa. Now it's all gone. Is this all there is? Folks shouldn't come to such an end."

She turned her accusing eyes on him. Alan never got used to her accusing eyes when Acts of God got in the way of faith. They left a bouquet of iris stuck in the dirt and went back to Mobridge.

Prudy looked forward to the mail which was delivered twice a day in the hopes of a letter from her sons, and they or their wives were very good about keeping her informed of what was happening in their lives. She wondered if she would recognize Chester. It had been years since she had seen him. She had only snapshots to remind herself that he was her son. She longed to see him. But she knew that whenever it rained in California it wouldn't be long before she got a letter from him. He always took advantage of time off from the inclement weather to write to her. It always amazed her to think of a place where there was winter with no snow.

Dear Mama,

Well, it's raining again. I hear it's really snowing back there. Believe it or not it gets kinda cold out here and we keep a fire going in the fireplace. We have to watch out for the kids though because they like to get close to it. Irene keeps an eye out for Cora and Leland. She's a regular little mother to them and is a big help to Polly.

Pete is getting married next year in case you didn't know. Some gal out here finally caught him. I began to think he wasn't the marrying kind, but he spends a lot of time with us. Seems to like family life and being around the kids. His mother can probably fill you in about wedding plans and all. You'll be getting an invitation. Sure hope you can come. Alan, too.

Business is pretty good. Logging sure has come a long way since I first came out here. We've got trucks and tractors to work with now and gasoline chain saws. It increases daily production a lot and we've got by OK without having to hire extra help. Unions don't like it much, but we pay top wages to our workers and hire only what we need, so with the machines we've got an efficient operation. There's always the danger of forest fires and in dry years like we've been having you never know when lightning might start one. They're hard to put out and afterward they have to be replanted by the Forest Service. It takes a long time to grow a tree.

Polly and the kids say hello. Say hello to Alan for me.

Your son, Chester

Fred left letter writing up to Helga. She was brief and precise, but she left nothing out. Fred would scrawl a greeting at the end of the letters. Prudy kept them all. Her sons' letters represented their lives, an extension of hers. She was building a new life; her old one had died. She carefully tied the letters with a ribbon, one bundle from Chester and one from Fred.

Helga's large, active family gave her plenty to write about. In one letter she was finally able to impart the news of their impending hookup with the Rural Electrification Administration, commonly called the REA. It would assure adequate electricity and access for a telephone. They now had neighbors in the area, as predicted, who took advantage of the comparative low cost of living away from a large town, who were willing to work hard to be independent and self-sufficient. Reliable electric power linked the far flung ranches, and telephones brought the ranchers close enough to be neighbors. In 1935 Fred Deters was one of the first customers to be connected, with the others falling in. This progress made it necessary to cut back on those things they could do without, making do with bare necessities, riding out the rough times together. Subscribers learned to economize. Lights were not turned on until absolutely necessary and they were promptly turned off if they were not being used.

"Juice is expensive," Fred would say.

"But it's so nice," Helga would counter.

The disadvantage of having the comforts that electricity provided, other than the expense, was the proliferation of poles and wires needed to conduct the current, but they soon learned to ignore them. Shelter belts of closely planted trees provided a scenic backdrop, hiding the poles to a degree, plus the added advantage of holding precious topsoil in place, providing shade and shelter from the relentless prairie wind.

It continued beastly hot and dry with little rain. Wells were running dry across the land. People learned to ration food and water. Dish water was poured on gardens. Bath water was shared. The last rinse water on wash day was almost as dirty as the soapy water. 1936 was the worst year. Soaring temperatures made the heat wave intense. People grew weary and listless, desperate for rain, but less than eleven inches fell that year. Temperatures topped $100°$ on more than thirty days. July was the hottest in recorded history. In cities concrete buckled at the seams and asphalt melted. Nothing grew in barren yards but sparse weeds, which the grasshoppers devoured eagerly. People and animals died from the stress.

But that winter lots of snow fell and it was very cold. Then it melted in the spring of 1937 to fill sloughs and lakes and streams. It was the beginning of the end of the dust bowl's descent into its own private hell. Gradually the drought ended, rain and snow fell, temperatures moderated, and people gave thanks.

The country's preoccupation with its economic plight for years blinded some to the very real threat of war. Europe was once again in danger from the Germans and talk was that war was inevitable.

"But there can't be another war, Alan. We had a war and there wasn't supposed to be any more trouble."

"I know, Mother. I don't understand it either. Hard times often lead to unrest and that leads to war to make the situation better and to improve the economy. It doesn't make sense."

Prudy was pensive. "John died in vain then, didn't he?"

Alan didn't know how to answer her. Lately his mother had been unlike herself, often engrossed in thought, or was it moodiness? Anna had noticed it, too, and even her cheerfulness could not always bring Prudy out of the doldrums. Prudy wasn't aware that she was any different and, if the thought came to her, she discounted it as getting old. After all, she was sixty-one.

The economy improved and Alan's parishioners were again able to keep up their tithes with money and not the steady stream of produce and meat products as in past years, although Anna was mighty glad to get them. Necessary repairs were made on the church and rectory, the congregation increased and the church was filled to capacity to hear Father Deters preach. With the years had come wisdom and an ability to speak the Word of the Lord compellingly. Alan was faced with the possibility of building a new church, something he didn't want to think about. The present church had become his home and besides, he wasn't the kind to be forceful and dynamic enough to raise money for such a project. He put off thinking about it and concentrated on his mother.

She enjoyed riding in his car. His old black Chevrolet was outmoded, but it ran like a top and with proper care would last several more years. Sometimes after supper he would take her for a ride around Mobridge and its outskirts and it seemed to please her. She loved to watch the sun set and could sit and gaze at the horizon until it was lined with a red glow that wouuld last longer than Alan cared to remain. Prudy was inaccessible during those times. She didn't speak nor want to answer Alan's tentative questions or observations in his attempt to draw her out of herself. She only wanted to sit quietly and watch the sun go down. When they returned she would go directly to her room and to bed and sleep soundly. Sometimes Anna would pack a picnic lunch and they would go to the Webster City Park located in the very center of town. It was a lovely spot, thickly packed with tall elms and evergreens that had been growing since 1911 when the park was established. Prudy loved to sit on a blanket in the thick grass and gaze around her and imagine she was in a magic forest. She would lean back and look up to the tips of the trees and blink at the sun trickling down through the leaves. The tree trunks cast shadows all around. The verdant park was an oasis and never failed to perk her up.

She went to church with Alan one Sunday shortly after she came to live with him in 1933, but she didn't like it. The ritual and the Latin words meant nothing to her.

It all seemed too mechanical to be sincere. She didn't tell him that, but refused to go again. She was proud to see him before his flock, who responded to him, but it was not the Alan she knew. He would on occasion, invite her to attend church with him again, but didn't urge her when he could see that she really didn't want to.

On one of her particularly moody days in the spring of 1937 he asked her, "Would you like to come with me today, Mother? I have to go over to the Standing Rock Indian Reservation and deliver some boxes of clothing and food my parishioners have given."

Prudy accepted without much enthusiasm, but it would be something to do and she wanted to ease his constant fretting over her. He wouldn't leave her to her brooding and the only way to make him stop was to accede to what he suggested. She needed something to do. She wished she had regular duties like Anna. Then she would feel like she was making her own way. She knew she could contribute to something around the house, but they would have none of it, deeming it to look unseemly for the mother of Father Deters to be doing chores. Prudy couldn't see the sense in that and finally convinced them that helping Anna with the dishes after an unusually large supper for visiting dignitaries was all right. Actually, she and Anna enjoyed the companionship in sharing the work and, as Prudy often said, "You can really get to know a body doing the dishes." But even with that slight exertion Prudy would soon be out of breath and she began to think that maybe they were right and would say to them apologetically, "I don't have much energy lately."

Alan

So she accepted Alan's invitation and they drove out of Mobridge and over the long bridge spanning the Missouri River into the Standing Rock Indian Reservation and into the Village of Wakpala, a community of Sioux Indians. It was like crossing into another country. The land was sprawling and sparsely populated by Indian people. It was primitively scenic with low hills and grazing cattle. Buttes led to a few ridges of mountains a few miles to the west. Square shacks dotted the land, some covered with tar paper, some with peeling paint. Clothes lines held brightly colored clothes that were flapping in the wind. Yards contained scruffy dogs and a few chickens scratching in the dirt. It was quiet. Barefoot children stared as they drove up. Prudy didn't know what to make of it.

Alan took her silence to be sadness at the plight of the Indians. Suddenly Indians of all ages appeared from nowhere, having recognized the car and its driver, and followed the car as it moved slowly to the communal meeting house, a low, unpainted building in the center of the village. Prudy remained in the car when he got out and greeted the men and boys who crowded around him. The women and girls remained in the background, waiting to see what he had brought. He engaged the help of a couple of husky young men who emptied the trunk and back seat, not looking at the tiny woman in the front. Prudy sneaked a quick look at them through the rear view mirror and didn't know whether to say anything or not, but it was not a problem because the men ignored her and never cast a glance her way. She looked at them more intently. She had never seen an Indian. The men were very brown and their hair was black and long and it looked coarse. One of them had his hair in two braids but the other one simply wore his hair long and straight with a twisted bandana around his head to hold it in place. They were dressed as any man would be with threadbare pants and shirts, but they wore no shoes. She could see that the women were clad in long skirts. Some had braided hair and some wound their hair into a bun at the back of their necks. They, too, were barefoot. She would have to ask Alan about that. The car was soon emptied and the boxes taken into the meeting house where it would be distributed. The hubub subsided and Prudy could hear Alan's voice raised in prayer and she imagined him making the sign of the cross. Then a low hum of conversation started and he came out of the building, waved, and got back into the car.

"We can stay for dinner if you'd like." Alan laughed teasingly. "But I didn't think you'd care to, so I declined with thanks. Actually, the cornbread is pretty good." He laughed once more as he looked at her, hoping for a smile.

He drove through the village, turned around, and returned the way they had come. When they came to the bridge he stopped the car.

"Let's get out and look at the water for a minute. It's such a nice day. What a treat to have the warmth without oppressive heat."

They got out and walked to the edge of the bridge and leaned against the railing. The river was long and wide and unruly, and was once again filling up after the drought.

"The Mighty Mo, that's what they call the river, an appropriate name. It runs for

196

miles and miles and connects with the Mississippi and then on to the Gulf of Mexico. Imagine that, Mother, and it cuts the state in half. In fact, Mobridge got its name from the bridge over the river."

"Alan," she said, without looking up, "why weren't those people wearing shoes?"

"For two reasons. One, they don't like to wear them and, two, they can't afford them. In the winter they wear shoes that are donated and they do have moccasins. They are independent people and try to maintain the life their ancestors knew."

"Why do the houses look so rundown?" If anyone could spot a rundown house, Prudy could. Seeing them brought into sharp focus what her previous life had been. She stared down into the water.

He couldn't answer her. His mother could almost always stump him for an answer with her direct questions. He said, "I don't know. The government trys to provide shelter and sustenance for these people, and they want all that, but they can't seem to plan ahead. Maintenance doesn't appear to mean much to them. You remember how Dad was."

She remembered. But she also remembered how her mother had kept the house and how she, herself, had tried to keep it under adverse conditions.

Alan continued, "I do know that the Indians don't want to live like the white man, yet they want what the white man has. The Bureau of Indian Affairs does its best, but I really don't think they have any idea of what the Indian is like, of his culture."

Prudy said almost to herself, "Maybe if they had built the houses in the shapes of tepees it would have worked. Wouldn't that have worked?" She straightened up and looked him straight in the eyes.

"I don't know. I just don't know."

Alan was stumped. His mother's accusing eyes never failed to intimidate him. "We all do the best we can for them, Mother, but it often seems in vain. I, myself, provide them with the food and clothing the parish donates and I endeavor to bring the Word of God for their enlightenment, but they won't even bow their heads when I offer up a prayer for their benefit. It is frustrating."

She stared at him. "Folks just want to live their lives."

They returned to the car and left the barren, unkempt world behind them.

Shortly after that Prudy's mail contained an invitation to Peter Dannenbring's wedding in California. Alan received one, too. To hold in her hands the nicely engraved card gave her goose bumps and she wondered what she could give as a suitable present. She never entertained the thought of actually attending the wedding, even though it would mean seeing Chester and his family. She simply could not think of it. Her lagging energy would not permit it for one thing. She would wait for Chester to come to see her. He should come home. He had been gone far too long. But Alan encouraged her to go. He would be unable to get away, but he knew it would do her a world of good. She was still protesting when she opened a letter that had come in the same mail. It was from Lettie and full of enthusiasm and warmth, just like the old Lettie. She urged Prudy to come to see them on the ranch, that Fred and Helga thought it was a good idea, too. Bridget would be there and it would be just like old times, making wedding plans just as they had done when Helga married her Fred.

"You should go, Mother. It will help you make up your mind. I'll bet with Mrs. Dannenbring talking a blue streak you'll soon change your mind. It won't take long to get to Fred's place. I could drive you to Gettysburg and put you on the train to Pierre, but I think I'll drive you myself. It will be good to see old Fred and his family."

It was settled. Prudy loved to ride in Alan's smooth running car anyway. It was a comfortable drive even on the bumpy gravel.

"One of these days they'll have to fix up this road. Traffic is getting heavier every year," Alan said as they hit a rut and Prudy bounced from her seat, causing her to laugh as she kerplunked down.

Their arrival was greeted with hugs and kisses and the presentation of the children lined up on the front porch. Prudy beamed at them as Helga prompted them to say hello to their Grandma Deters. They obediently recited together, "Hello, Grandma Deters," and stared at her curiously. How unlike their other Grandma she was. Frederica, the oldest, was nine, tall, blond and very mature for her age. She was obviously in charge of her younger sister and brothers. Bernadine, eight, was small and blond, resembling her mother. The twins, Michael and Mitchell, were six and had dark hair like Fred's. They stood close together as though inseparable, and looked identical to Prudy. Fred, Jr. was four and resembled no one, except for his sweet smile, which was definitely his father's. All had brown eyes which looked directly at her. Their solemn demeanor made her want to giggle and reach out for them and clutch each one tightly to her, but she knew she mustn't do that just then, so she smiled and said each child's name as they were presented to her.

They gawked openly at Alan in his priestly garb of dark suit and white collar, but politely said hello to their Uncle Alan. Then they were told to go and play, but not to get dirty, because it was soon time for dinner. Alan took great pride in his brother's family, briefly envious, but mostly happy to see him so content in his life with his beautiful, efficient wife and handsome children. Dinner was a feast with two extra leaves in the table, a fine lace cloth laid out with Helga's good dishes. Helga and Fred sat at opposite ends of the long table, with an adult stationed beside each child to offer aid if needed, Alan, seated between the twins, had fun teasing them, calling them by the other's name, making them laugh. Lettie watched over Fred, Jr., who was content to let her baby him. Frederica sat beside her mother with Bernadine on the other side. Bridget sat tall and lovely beside her mother and Prudy was happy to sit beside Fred.

They were interested in Bridget's account of her life in the big city of Aberdeen, ninety miles east of Mobridge. She described Northern State College in glowing terms, obviously happy there.

"I'm so glad to have been able to attend college there, Mother. And I'm so glad I chose to teach."

"Are you a real teacher?" asked Frederica, her eyes wide with admiration.

"Yes, dear." She smiled fondly at her niece. What splendid children Fred had given Helga and how wise the match had been.

"I want to be a teacher when I grow up," Frederica replied.

"Good for you. Teachers are very important to the future of our country."

Frederica decided she didn't exactly know what her Aunt Bridget meant by that, but agreed wholeheartedly.

"I love the college so much that I decided to stay in Aberdeen and teach in one of the elementary schools. For one thing, I love all the trees, there. You know how precious trees are and how few of them we have."

They all agreed. She went on. "The college is a four story building made of brick with wide steps leading up to a columned entrance. It is surrounded by stately trees and in the fall the brilliant colors are gorgeous. The maples, especially are so colorful. Administrators of the college are fortunate to live in the clapboard houses set on tree lined avenues surrounding it."

"Sounds like you'd still like to be there at the college," said Fred.

She laughed a delicate laugh. "I suppose I do. Right now I'm content to teach the little ones, but perhaps some day I can get my Masters Degree and return to the college as an instructor. I'd really like to be able to do that."

The festive board soon disappeared from the table and Helga flushed from the praise heaped upon her. The children cleaned their plates and sat quietly until the rest were finished. Prudy was amazed at the disciplined manners in children so young, and entranced at how smoothly everything progressed, with the children participating in the conversation but not being allowed to get too rambunctious. Alan regretfully took his leave after dinner.

"You never seem to stay very long," complained Fred as they shook hands. "There's still room if you can stay the night."

"I know, but it's a long drive back and I can't be away too long. Tomorrow is Sunday you know."

They bid him goodbye on the porch, even the children, who shouted, "Bye Uncle Alan." It sounded good to him and he decided to incorporate the blessings of children in his sermon the next day. He would return for his mother in a week.

Lettie was exuberant. "A whole week. Just think what we can do in a week, Prudy. We have so many plans to make. Oh, I know the parents of the bride have the most work to do, but when we get to California I want to do something, too. Imagine, Peter finally married. I'd almost given up on that boy."

That boy was thirty-three years old, but to his mother he would always be her boy. She chattered on as they cleared the table and prepared to do the dishes. Finally, Prudy could be of use to someone.

Lettie talked all the while she washed and scrubbed and wiped off tables and counter tops. Prudy dried each dish carefully.

"I've never been to California, you know, so I have no idea what to expect, except what Peter has written. The weather's pretty good, I understand, but cool at night. Can you beat that, Prudy? He said to be sure to bring a wrap. A wrap in June! And here in South Dakota we pray for a cool breeze when the sun goes down. I think I'll have a little party and treat everybody — Peter's future in-laws, the bridal party, the minister — everybody. You can help me and it will be wonderful. I'm sure we could use your Chester's house for the party. He wouldn't mind, do you think?" And on she went. Prudy relaxed and felt right at home. She was with Lettie.

The days sped by and the weather was balmy and pleasant. One morning while Bridget was occupied with the children playing school, and Helga and Lettie were discussing party plans, Prudy announced she was going for a walk. The morning was bright and it beckoned her outside.

"Be careful, Mother Deters," said Helga. "Don't go too far. It's easy to lose your bearings in these hills. Fred, maybe you should go with her."

"Oh, no, I just want to walk around a little and enjoy the pretty scenery. I'll keep a lookout for the house all the time."

She left by the front door and walked across the road to the shelter belt. Trees held a fascination for her, having been so scarce around Spotswood. She walked the length of the shelter where cottonwoods were planted in straight rows close to each other and decided to move out and do some exploring. She turned, looked through the mass of trees, saw the house and the outbuildings, the REA poles and wires, and made a mental note of her location. She walked down a narrow path where others had gone before her and then up a small hill and looked around. Behind her was the shelter belt, the road, and Fred's ranch, which she calculated wasn't far away. She went down the slight incline and up another one. The hills were covered with short cropped grass where the cattle grazed. It looked more lush up ahead, so she went up the hill before her, breathing in the fresh air, the fresh greenness all around her, the smell of the earth and growing things. A meadow lark circled above her and then settled on an unseen perch and gave her a melodious serenade. She stopped to listen, then went on. She'd go down one more and then turn back. It was turning out to be more strenuous than she had thought. She wasn't as young as she used to be. When she got the bottom she sat down on uncrushed prairie grass and caught her breath.

It really is pretty, she thought, but sort of spooky, and it was so still. there was no beginning, no end, just an endless undulating green earth. She got up, turned and went up a hill. At the top she stopped and looked around. There was another hill before her. She could see better from there. She descended again and climbed the next hill and looked. She was sure this was the one. She should be able to see Fred's place from there. But she couldn't. All she saw was an endless succession of green mounds of prairie. She turned around and around and it was all the same. There was no ranch, no shelter belt, no REA wires, nothing. Panic gripped her throat. She wasn't lost. How could she be lost? Helga had strictly told her to be careful, that it was easy to lose your bearings. How could she have done just that? She'd keep on going. It couldn't be much farther. She must have figured wrong.

200

She went down another hill and her heart was pounding so hard she had to sit down again to rest and catch her breath once more. The hill ahead of her loomed like a mountain, but she was getting closer. She'd be able to see the ranch once she got to the top. Laboriously she clambered upward, pulling herself along, grasping at the tall, sturdy prairie grass until she reached the top and stood up. She began to cry. It wasn't there. Fred's place wasn't there. Where was it? She turned around and around, shading her eyes, searching each horizon, and saw nothing but more green hills and empty valleys. She sat down, hugged her knees, buried her head in her arms and rocked back and forth.

CHAPTER TWENTY THREE

The Discovery

"Mama, Mama! For Pete's sake, wake up!" cried Fred.

Prudy felt herself being shaken.

"Fred, be careful; calm yourself. She's coming around."

That was Lettie's voice. Hands were patting hers. Where was she? Why was Fred so agitated? He never got upset. She opened her eyes, her vision cleared, and she found herself on the living room sofa. Her hand went to her throbbing head where a cool cloth had been placed.

"Oh my," she mumbled.

Fred was on his knees by the sofa, patting her hands. Bridget had a pan of water and was wringing out another cloth for her head. Lettie was hovering over her with a a worried frown on her face. Helga stood back with her arms around the children. The youngsters looked scared. Prudy struggled to sit up.

"Take it easy, Mama. Just lay back," said Fred as he gently eased her down.

"What happened? I don't remember."

Lettie's strong voice intervened. "You must have gone too far and gotten confused. You were quite lost, Prudy, and it's no wonder. Those hills all look the same out there and in the middle of the day there is no sense of direction. I remember it almost happened to me once, but lucky for me I turned around in time. You were gone so long that we wondered what happened to you, and . . ."

"Mother, please," said Bridget softly. "Mrs. Deters has had a shock and she needs rest. I think we ought to call a doctor."

"Yeah, a doctor," Fred hastily agreed.

"Oh no, I'm all right. I'm fine. My head just aches some, that's all. I probably just fainted. Only the second time in my life. I got awfully tired out there. How did you find me?"

"When you didn't come back and were gone so long we figured we'd better go look for you, so I got in the old pickup and Helga took Queenie, her horse, and we went in different directions. We almost didn't see you. You were all curled up on top of one of those hills. You sure you don't need a doctor, Mama?"

"I'm sure. Now help me to sit up." She sat warily on the edge of the sofa and let her reeling senses settle. "I'm truly sorry to cause you all so much trouble. I was positive I had turned back, but guess I didn't, and I just kept wandering around, getting more lost, when all the time I thought I was heading back to the house. I'm so sorry and ashamed."

"Now, Mother Deters, don't you talk like that. There is absolutely no need to feel ashamed. What nonsense. If there is any blame it is on us. We never should have let you go out there by yourself. I'll make some coffee and we'll all calm down."

"Good idea," chimed in Lettie and she went with Helga to help. "Come on kids. Go on and play. Everything's all right."

"Is Grandma Deters going to die?" asked Michael. Mitchell stood close beside him. Both boys had eyes big as saucers.

"No, of course not. Don't be silly. Now go on. You can have a cookie."

Fred stayed beside his mother. Bridget placed another cloth on her forehead and discreetly left the room. Michael's innocent query had made Fred think. How old was his mother anyway? It was hard to tell. She had looked the same ever since he could remember. He had never thought about it. There had always been his mother. She pulled off the cloth, straightened her back, and looked at his worried face.

"Now don't you go gettin' it into your head about me dyin'." She patted his hands. "I'm goin' to be around for a long time yet." She gave him her best smile, hoping to make the frown go away.

When Alan came for her he was disturbed by the news of what had happened. Before he took her back with him, he and Fred took a stroll in the front yard and Alan told him about her recent moodiness and of how he had hoped her visit would bring her out of it and that she might even change her mind and go to California with Lettie for Peter's wedding.

"I'm not sure, Alan. I don't think she's up to it. She doesn't have much strength anymore. Funny how I never noticed it before this. And getting lost bothered her lots more than she let on. It sure scared the hell out of me, I can tell you. If you could have seen her when I found her all curled up in a little ball on top of a hill. She wasn't asleep exactly, more like a — well, a fit, or something. I hate saying that." Fred looked disconsolate.

"I know what you mean. She was probably in shock. Certainly, she was overcome by the vastness of her surrounding and not being able to get her bearings. She has seemed so depressed on many occasions since she came to live with me and sometimes she can't be coaxed out of it. She and my housekeeper get along very well, but there are times when even she can't do anything with her when she gets that way. Sometimes it lasts for days and she scarcely leaves her room. I can't for the life of me figure out what is bothering her. She surely can't miss the home place, not after what she went through for so long. She is really not sick and she is definitely in better health than when she was all alone on that wretched farm."

"Well, she won't be going to California. She's told me that much. She insists that Chester should come to see her. He's been gone long enough to her way of thinking. And she just might be right. Do you think you can handle it? Can you keep on taking care of her, Alan? We have the room here, you know, and Helga's mother likes having her around."

"Oh yes, I can manage just fine. Anna is a tremendous help and there is no difficulty whatsoever in Mother's living with me. I feel better having her where I can watch over her — not that you wouldn't Fred, old boy, but you have plenty of responsibilities of your own, and I welcome having some myself. I was wondering, though, if we shouldn't find a way to sell the farm."

It had never crossed Fred's mind. Mama and the farm were always there. He was surprised. Alan went on.

"It's just acres of idle land. It doesn't generate revenue anymore, but with the economy looking up I think we'd get a pretty good price for it. Some day Mother might need more care than any of us can give her. She's not very strong, as you know, and the money would come in handy. Did she tell you about the money she found in the cellar?"

Fred's mouth dropped. "Hell, no."

Alan filled him in but said that, although it looked like a vast sum of money when she found it, it had dwindled to almost nothing. She seemed to think that the source would never be depleted. He had been thinking about the farm for some time as a way to stop the flow of money going to pay taxes on land that gave nothing in return, and money from the sale would replenish their mother's bank account.

"Mother should enjoy the proceeds while she is alive."

"Sounds good to me. Have you talked to Chester?"

"Not yet. But I'll write to him when we get back. Better yet, I'll call him. Bother the cost. It is something that should be discussed. Even so, I'm not so sure we can sell Mother on it."

"Sure we can. Why would she want to hang on to it? There's nothing left out there."

"You are right, but I've brought up the subject several times and she was almost indignant about it. Her answer was a definite no. She told me about a previous inquiry some years ago by a fellow from the bank in Mobridge. He has been to see me, but Mother doesn't know about that. I didn't want to get her overwrought unnecessarily. I decided to see what you thought before I did anything."

"I didn't know about any of this." Fred looked crestfallen and guilty. Then he brightened. "But we're sure lucky to have you to take hold of all this. You have a head for such things. I think it's a swell idea to sell the farm, and so will Chester. I know he will. Let me know what you find out. You've got my vote." He smiled broadly at his brother in admiration, and slapped him on the back as they shook hands. It was the first really serious conversation they ever had and it was rewarding to both of them.

Prudy sent her regrets to Peter about being unable to attend the wedding, along with a nice gift of embroidered linens, which Lettie took with her. Alan called Chester, who was in full agreement about selling the farm to provide for their mother. To alleviate any fear she might have Alan suggested that Chester and his family make a trip home to South Dakota to talk to her in person. She was lonesome for him and wanted to see the children, and she had much affection for Polly.

Chester readily agreed, especially when Alan reminded him that he had not been home since 1926, eleven years before.

"Holy cow! Has it been that long? Well sure, we'll come, but before the snow flies. I don't think I remember how to navigate through that stuff anymore."

It was arranged that they would all meet at Fred's place in his roomy house, making it convenient for all of them, a central meeting place. In October, 1937, when Prudy turned sixty-two, the best birthday gift she received was a visit from Chester and his family. They flew as far as Billings, Montana, then rented a plane and set down at the Pierre airport. Fred would pick them up. The travelers stepped from the small plane. Chester lifted the children to Polly and they looked around.

"My goodness, it's very flat, isn't it?" said Polly, squinting in the fall sunshine.

"I suppose so, but it's flatter in Spotswood, remember?" chuckled Chester. "We are on the plains of the west."

"Are we gonna see some Indians, Daddy?" inquired Leland, who was only three but knowledgeable about cowboys and Indians.

"Maybe. We'll see."

Irene, the nine year old, took Leland's hand and reached for Cora. Cora was seven and didn't want to be led around and pulled away.

"All right then, but if you get lost it's your own fault," Irene said, pretending not to care.

Chester was amused at her protectiveness. He doubted if anyone could get lost for long on the wide open prairie where you could see for miles in every direction, but then he thought of his mother.

"Cora, stay close to your sister," he admonished.

They had refused the offer of lodging by Fred and Helga because they felt they had a houseful as it was. They rented adjoining rooms at the St. Charles Hotel in Pierre, and Polly was suitably impressed with the accommodations. The five story building had been erected in 1911 by entrepreneur Charles Hyde and he built it in accordance with the ornate tastes of the time. Brass chandeliers hung from tall ceilings. The floor was constructed painstakingly with tiny polished tiles. A grand staircase with elaborate woodwork led to the second floor. The restaurant was spacious and inviting with white linen cloths covering the tables. The food was superb and the menu incorporated local delicacies such as pheasant, prime beef, and fish from the Missouri River. They were greeted warmly when they registered.

"Ah yes, Mr. Chester Deters and family from California. Your rooms are ready. We have a bit more room now that Governor Jensen has moved out."

In answer to their questioning looks the clerk obligingly elaborated. "Yes, you see, the governor's mansion has just been completed. Since the St. Charles was built in 1911 our state's governors have all lived here. Now that a suitable mansion is available that is no longer necessary. We have had other notable guests in our fair city, I can assure you, sir." He was doing his best to impress the man from California and expanded his delivery. "Yes, indeed. President Calvin Coolidge himself once walked right down the street. And in that same year of 1927 Charles

Lindbergh graced the city of Pierre with his presence as well. Yes, that was a very exciting time, an exciting time indeed. We are pleased that you have selected the St. Charles as your home away from home. Just follow the boy and he will show you to your rooms."

The clerk smiled his broadcast smile as he watched them as they followed the bellboy to the fancy elevator, confident he had done a dandy job of pushing the capitol city of the State of South Dakota.

Alan took time off from his duties and planned to stay at Fred's for a few days. Prudy was ecstatic about having her family all together again and hardly slept the night before the trip to the ranch. She was excited about seeing Chester again after so many years. She bought herself a new frock and packed her things carefully, admiring the items she placed in the durable suitcase that Alan had bought her after their first trip to see Fred, when she had stuffed some things in a paper bag. His mother's frugality was a habit she never gave up. Even so, her money was running out and that was the purpose of the family get together, to convince her to sell the farm and invest the proceeds. The rooms on the third floor of the large house were finally completely furnished by that fall of 1937 and there was plenty of room for all the guests. Fred regretted that Chester wouldn't stay with them and couldn't understand why they preferred to settle in at the St. Charles Hotel.

"You're living pretty high on the hog, aren't you?" asked Fred as he gave his brother a playful poke, just as he did when they were kids.

"Well, why not?" Chester replied, poking him back. "The company is doing real well. We have a government contract now which is very profitable, and Pete and I make a comfortable living. With the way things are going I think the country is getting ready to get involved in the fracas in Europe, so the future looks bright — as far as the company goes, I mean. We sure don't need another war."

"Thank God our boys are too young. I couldn't send mine off to some war across the ocean."

"Me neither. Anyway, thanks for the offer, but we'll be staying in Pierre. It's not far from here. And thanks for the use of your car for a few days. Are you sure it won't put you out?"

"Nah. I've got the pickup if we need to get to town for anything. I sure wish you and the family could stay more than a few days. It's really swell to have you here."

"Me, too, but they can't get along without me back there. Now that Pete's up and married, he likes to have his time at home, just like I've had all these years. His wife, Julia, is a real nice gal."

The wedding had been in June and Lettie filled Prudy in when she and Bridget got back with long glowing letters. She continued her recital of the event when Prudy and Alan arrived at the ranch and would talk at length about the train ride, the beautiful weather, the green land filled with crops of all kinds, including fruit.

"You should see the oranges, Prudy. Trees thick with oranges. And bigger and much tastier than what you get at the Red Owl, and you just pick them from the trees."

She and Bridget had their party, as planned, and it went off beautifully. Chester and Polly let them use their house and were impressed and entertained with Lettie's organizational skills. She turned the party into the social event of the season in Santa Cruz, except for the wedding itself. The trip was a tonic for Lettie and she spoke of it for months afterward. Prudy had described Chester's house over and over again, seeing it all in her head.

"It's a nice big house, Prudy, only different from what we're used to. They don't build houses in California like they do out here. They are long and rambling with no basements. No need for them. Just think of that. Why, where would we put our preserves if we didn't have basements? And they have a fireplace made out of big stones. It does get cool at night and the lighted fireplace is a comfort. And they have big, comfy furniture. I tell you, Prudy, I never saw anything like it. Our Peter seems to make himself right at home there. Guess he's done that for all the time Chester's been married. The children love him and call him Uncle Pete. Isn't that something? Uncle Pete. And the minister came to the party and even drank the punch that I just knew had spirits in it. Mind you, I didn't put any in, but it did give a body a lift. And the wedding — Oh, Prudy, the wedding was so beautiful. It was outside, if you can imagine it. Why, in South Dakota, everybody would be blown away in no time."

She laughed heartily at that.

"But it was absolutely beautiful, with flowers on all the aisle seats. Flowers grow like weeds out there, Prudy. All kinds of them. Even some trees sprout flowers. And the minister was in a long white robe; he looked so dignified. It was all very impressive. Julia, Pete's bride, was lovely and our Peter so handsome. My, but he's grown so. He is a big man now, Prudy, and he looks so much like Meyer."

Tears brimmed in her eyes, but she quickly swept them away.

"I wish you could have been there. Bridget was one of the bridesmaids and you know how pretty she is. Chester was so good-looking as the best man, all dolled up in a fancy suit."

Chester had brought some snapshots of the wedding and it was everything that Lettie had said it was, just as she had described it. She looked at the prints many times and wondered at the changes in the lives of the people she knew and loved. Chester had grown into a tall, handsome man. His stocky frame had filled out with muscle and she noted upon his arrival that he moved with a casualness that was very different from South Dakota folks. Polly had matured into a beautiful woman. Her black hair was sleek against her cheek and her blue eyes stood out from her white face, capturing immediate attention.

At meal times the adults used the dining room and included the two youngest, Fred, Jr., and Leland, who were only a few months apart in age. The other six sat around the kitchen table with Frederica bossing them, although Irene soon joined her authority, being of the same age. It wasn't long before the two girl cousins were working together, supervising the younger ones. Their sisters joined in the fun "playing house." Michael and Mitchell sat close together, not saying anything, meekly obeying.

There were few disagreements and the house rang with the sounds of a reunited, happy family. Prudy positively glowed from happiness. A birthday dinner on October 12th climaxed the get together with a fancy cake, decorated with rosettes and eight candles in the center, one for each grandchild. Prudy opened gifts from each family, with the children watching carefully to see how she liked what they had given. They beamed as she exclaimed over the handkerchiefs, stationery, colorful beads, gloves and scarves, and gave each one a gentle hug and kiss.

Alan waited for the right moment when the tables had been cleared and dishes stacked and the children sent out to play. They relaxed around the table with their coffee, and he said, "This is a fine day for us to all be together again, and on your birthday, Mother."

"I thank you all. To have my boys around me and my best friend in the whole world, too, is more than I could ever wish for. And the grandchildren you have given me . . ." She smiled at Helga and Polly. "What a wonderful birthday this has been. I never celebrated my birthday. Today I am sixty-two. Just look at what those years have given me." She looked at them with love.

"Holy cow, Mama. I never heard you talk like that before," said Chester.

"If you'd show up once in awhile you'd know what goes on around here," chided Fred.

"We are fortunate to still be together in spite of years of adversity," said Alan. He cleared his throat. "Mother, we need to discuss something with you."

"Oh my," she said. Alan's formality raised a suspicion in her. She knew it had all been too good to be true.

"Now don't get all upset, Mama," cautioned Fred.

"Upset about what?"

"About what we want to talk to you about," said Chester.

"What is there to talk about? I'm just fine. There's nothing wrong. Alan and I get along and he takes real good care of me. I know I can get a mite moody sometimes, but . . ."

"That's not it at all, Mother," said Alan. "It's about the farm."

"Oh," she said quietly and looked at the napkin beside her cup.

"We've talked it over and . . ." Alan looked away as his mother raised her head and directed her accusing eyes at him. "we've all talked it out and think — that is, we feel you should sell the farm."

He chose not to notice her immediate objection as she opened her mouth to answer him.

"It makes no sense to continue to pay taxes on land that is just lying there. It should be sold. The income would add greatly to your bank account, which is very low right now."

"But I have lots of money," she protested.

"No, Mother, you haven't. There is only a little over $100 left. You should have some ready cash — not that I can't provide for you, but you have the means to augment your income right at the tips of your fingers. The time is right, and we have had an offer to buy the land from a Wesley Berg, a banker in land development."

"I remember him. He came to see me some time back."

"Yes, and he is still interested in that land. He has made a very generous offer."

"How on earth did he know to get in touch with you?" she demanded.

"It's simple enough to find out who owns any land. All anyone has to do is check with the Register of Deeds at the county seat. That's what Mr. Berg did. Then he made some inquiries and discovered that you live with me."

"I own that farm. There is a deed," she said, her eyes dark.

"I know, Mother. You also own other parcels of land. Remember Dad bought up all that land during the time some farmers sold out and moved on? Well, he doubled his holdings and owns a half section."

Alan had said "owns." He continued, "But now, since it appears that Dad — that he's not coming back, you can sell any or all of it. It's been more than seven years. You could declare him legally dead, thereby making you the sole owner of record."

She didn't know that.

"And Mr. Berg has offered $50 an acre for the lot."

She tried to do some fast figuring.

"That amounts to $16,000 Mama."

"Oh my."

"We just want you to have what is rightfully yours, Mama," said Chester. "I think you should take him up on it."

"Me, too," agreed Fred.

"I don't understand your hesitation, Mother," continued Alan. "It can't be that you have some affection for that place."

"And from what Alan told us there's nothing left of the old home place. Everything's gone. In fact, he discouraged me from going to see for myself," said Chester.

"Yeah, Mama, why don't you want to sell?" Fred was just as puzzled as the rest of them.

Prudy's thoughts were not on the same path as that of her sons, and she was growing weary of their badgering. But she could understand what they were saying and she realized that their recollections of growing up there were different from hers. When they left home they left nothing behind them but their youth. When she left, what remained was best forgotten, something she had not been able to do. It was her secret; no one suspected, and it would remain her secret as long as she had possession of the land that had been her home since she was born. Still, it had been eight years since she had planted her garden and it, too, had been eradicated by the dust storms that had swept through year after year. There was nothing to show that there had once been a thriving farm operation. It was an alien, unfamiliar place, covered with mounds of dirt and tumbled buildings. Weeds grew unchecked. There was nothing to mark how it had once looked, except for the filled in well and the old tree stump. They had not interrupted her while she mulled over what they had said. She didn't know how long the deep silence hung over the room. She finally looked up to see them all staring at her, waiting for her decision. She had made one, one of the few arrived at in her troubled life. She took a deep, shaky breath and said, "I guess you're right. I'll sell. What do I have to do?"

They burst into relieved smiles and began talking at once, but Alan shushed them.

"Mr. Berg will prepare a new deed for you to sign, transferring your interest in all of the property in exchange for the money. Do you understand, Mother? We don't want to pressure you into this and not have you understand. We have merely been trying to persuade you that it is the best thing for you to do. It's in your best interest and so much easier to do it now — while we are all here."

Prudy turned her eyes on him and glared, "And before I die."

She regretted it the minute she said it. The pleased faces of those seated at the table were instantly filled with guilt and remorse and her sharp comment had done it. She knew that what they said was right and she shouldn't have snapped at them like that.

"Oh my, I'm sorry. I didn't mean that. I don't know what's gotten into me lately. Must be gettin' crochety in my old age. Please don't all of you look at me like that. I shouldn't have said it. What you say is true. I've had a lot of time to think about things since I went to live with Alan. You know how hard it is for me to make up my mind about things; sometimes I need a push. You're absolutely right. I probably should have done this a long time ago. Sometimes my mind tends to get fuzzy, but today I can see clear as a bell. I know I'm doin' the right thing."

They were surprised at their mother's speech. Seldom had they heard her say much of anything, except to echo another's observation. Maybe it came from being so browbeaten by their father. He intimidated every one of them, even John, and their mother had endured his acts far longer than they had. It was strange to see their mother acting differently, less inhibited, to see her acceptance of the release from her previously difficult life, to know she had an opinion and could express it. They also knew that the process had been a slow one and that if they had urged her to make this decision a few years before they would undoubtedly have failed. But the problem had been solved. The tension was broken.

They all relaxed and Lettie, who had wisely remained quiet during the discussion, got up to go to the kitchen, declaring that this called for another cup of coffee. Helga and Polly had remained by their husband's sides, taking it all in, but saying nothing. Prudy looked around the table and felt herself engulfed by a warm feeling which she hoped they also felt. What fine women her sons had married. What a strong man Alan turned out to be. What a good friend she had in Lettie. How did she deserve it? Her spirits lifted. Now she would have lots of money. She would be rich again. Life constantly surprised her.

Life proceeded through a South Dakota winter. Chester wrote from California that he certainly didn't miss the winters. Polly thought it might be an adventure to tramp through some snow, but he assured her it wasn't all that wonderful. Fred and Helga had the house to themselves again, with Lettie in residence. Alan was no longer anxious about his mother's future. Soon after their return to Mobridge, Wesley Berg came to the rectory with the necessary papers for Prudy to sign. She handed over the original yellowed deed with her father's signature and a few other deeds that Lester had accumulated, signed the new deed to the Consolidated Land Company, a South Dakota corporation, and received a check for $16,000. She stared at the slip of paper which signified the dollar amount of the land that had come into her possession and wondered why she felt so bereft. The land had always been a part of her life; she had depended on it, yet taken it for granted. She knew she didn't need to hang on to it but, nevertheless, the slip of paper didn't inspire the same feeling. It wasn't the same thing. But Alan was thrilled and he soon had it in the bank, drawing interest, and it would always be available to her.

It occured to her to write a will and after a long struggle to say it right she wrote it herself, with Anna as a witness. It was a simple bequest, leaving all her money at the time of her death to her three sons in equal shares. She had nothing to leave to Millicent except the shiny box and its contents that Millicent's mother had given to her ages ago. She knew that her niece would never want for money or material things, and she valued her treasure box more than anything she had ever possessed, so she decided to leave it to Millicent. She added a tender note, tied the box with a new blue satin ribbon and placed it in her dresser drawer. Now she could rest easy. Everything was taken care of.

In the spring of 1938 the Consolidated Land Company sold several parcels of land it had acquired over the years from impoverished land owners. Some of what sold went to the Gebharts who had bought the Dannenbring place. The gravel roads had been upgraded by the Highway Department. Concrete replaced the gravel on Highway 12 from Mobridge to Aberdeen and on Highway 83 from Mobridge to Pierre, and traffic increased considerably, making previously inaccessible points on the map more readily reached. The Gebharts had waited a long time to be able to finally make their dream come true, to become a part of the new pioneer spirit of the traveling public.

The old Deters place was ideal for their plans for the construction of tourist cabins. Nothing would have to be torn down, just cleared away. They would build eight or nine cabins with plenty of parking space, maybe even put in a gas station with one pump and some grocery items. They would plant some trees and shrubs and it would make a nice, restful stopping-off place for folks going to and from Pierre and Mobridge or even farther than that. The spot wasn't far from the highway and would be the only stop for miles. A few appropriate road signs would make it easy to find. It would be a gold mine.

Early in May heavy equipment moved in leveling the earth, pushing debris in piles to be hauled away. It was an arduous job and workers had to drive a few miles to get to it, but no one complained. There was work to be had again. They didn't mind the long hours and their womenfolk didn't mind when their men came home black as coal from stirring up the long dormant dust. Holes for outhouses had been dug in an area to the rear of where a neat row of cabins would stand. A bulldozer leveled and pushed aside a miscellany of rubble, gradually working its way to the dirt road that led to the highway. The burly operator of the machine chewed on a cigar as he worked, aiming to push some odd-shaped rocks ahead of him to a larger pile of rocks near some dead trees beyond a clearing when something caught his eye. He leaned forward and peered ahead closely, then turned off his machine and climbed down. He walked to a faint outline that resembled the shape of a grave and stooped down to get a better look. Yessir, he was right. He wasn't imagining things.

"Son of a gun," he muttered. "Hey, Joe," he yelled. "Come 'ere and see what I found."

CHAPTER TWENTY FOUR

Be Still and Know
That I Am God

Psalms 46:10

Late one afternoon that April in 1938 Anna opened the door to find the sheriff standing there and for a moment was at a loss for words. He removed his hat and asked politely, "Is the Father in, Mam?"

"Yes, he is, but what in the world would you want to be seeing Father Deters for? Oh," she said, slightly flustered, "perhaps you're needing a private visit with him, is that it? Excuse me for being so blunt. It's just that we don't get any policemen here."

"That's all right, Mam, but I'm the sheriff, not a policeman. May I come in?"

"Land sakes, of course. Where are my manners? Come in and you just sit right down for a minute. I'll go and fetch the Father."

She bustled off, scolding herself under her breath for her impropriety. Very soon Father Deters appeared at the door to the front room. The sheriff was still standing, hat in hand. Alan approached him with his hand outstretched.

"Hello. I'm Father Deters. You gave my housekeeper quite a start. She was somewhat befuddled when she came to get me."

"Sheriff Henry Boyle," he said as they shook hands. "Sorry about that. I get that reaction sometimes. Must be the uniform — and the gun."

"Guns do have an unsettling effect. The days are past when everyone wore one, although farmers and ranchers have rifles hung in their pickups, for predators, of course." Alan paused. "I must confess, I am wondering, too, why you are here."

Sheriff Boyle was a stocky, self-assured man. His gun belt was secure around his ample middle, producing a slight paunch in his tan uniform. The star on his chest was brightly polished and his black boots were sturdy and serviceable. His thinning hair was crimped from his hat, which he still held in his hands. He gave a misleading appearance of easygoing calm, an attitude that had tripped up more than a few suspects. He wasn't as much at ease as he looked. Having to come to see a respected priest to whom he would direct some pointed questions was not a mission he enjoyed. He had thought it through how to go about it and had decided that he would get right to the point. It was possible that his visit would be for nothing, and he earnestly hoped that is the way it would turn out, but he wouldn't know that until he had asked his questions. He looked squarely at Father Deters and asked, "Did you at one time live on the old Deters place south of here near the town of

Spotswood?"

"Why yes, I was born there. But I'm afraid there's nothing left and the land has been sold."

"Yes sir, I know that. The owners are right now in the process of clearing the land, going to put up some tourist cabins, I hear."

"That is my understanding. The land belonged to my father, Lester Deters. He's been gone for almost nine years now. Title to the property transferred to my mother and she sold it last fall. I'm sure you'll find everything is in proper order, Sheriff, but if there is a loose end somewhere I'll be glad to do what I can."

"It's not exactly a loose end, Father." He began to look uncomfortable. "What it is," he fumbled for the proper way to say it. This was turning out to be more awkward than he had thought. "What it is appears to be some remains."

"Remains? You mean bones? Surely old bones have been uncovered many times. Animals are disposed of on farms regularly."

"Yes sir, that's a fact. That's what happens all right. But these are not animal remains. In fact, they are not ordinary remains by any means."

Alan frowned. "Sheriff, I think you'd better come right out with whatever you have to say. I can't for the life of me get the drift of what is on your mind."

"OK. Here's how it is. The operator of the bulldozer was working for a couple of days, pushing some old rocks and trash that had been blown all over the place by the winds we had a couple of years back. He was piling it all at the edge of a clearing to where he was going to knock down some dead trees."

"I know where you mean. Please continue."

"Well sir, he was making another pass when he saw something unusual and he stopped his machine just in time. A good thing, too, or the evidence would have been ruined."

"Evidence? What are you talking about? You're not making any sense at all, Sheriff," Alan said impatiently.

"Sorry, Father. You see, it has to be regarded as evidence in view of the fact that the remains are the bones of a man, a real big guy, from the looks of it."

Alan stared at him, an uneasy feeling stirring in the pit of his stomach. He replied, "People are buried on their farms all over the country, Sheriff. You know that. In fact, it was customary in the old days. I have no idea who this poor man was, but our family is buried in the Spotswood Cemetery, what's left of it, that is."

"Yes sir, I know that, too. We checked that. But, these bones aren't that old and the remains are a mite — different."

"What do you mean? How different?" Alan was getting testy.

"It appears that he was decapitated.."

Alan stood stock-still, rigid with foreboding. He was cold.

Sheriff Boyle went on, "Now ordinarily that could happen over the years — the head coming detached from the body, I mean. But I don't think so in this case, because there was an ax, too, in with the bones. And what beats me is that there's the skeleton of a dog with its head all bashed in right in there with the rest of it. How do

214

you figure that, Father?"

"Mother of God," said Alan as he slumped in a chair.

"Are you all right, Father? You look a little peaked. Can I get you a glass of water?"

Alan didn't answer. He just stared ahead of him, comprehension setting in.

Sheriff Boyle moved from where he had been standing all during his recital and went to look for the housekeeper. As he walked through the doorway into the dining room he was startled to find a small, gray-haired woman there, clinging to the sideboard. She was obviously in a great deal of pain and was trying to hold herself to the cabinet to keep from slipping to the floor. She looked at him with wild, crazy eyes. Her mouth was partly open, but no sound came out. He rushed to her.

"Mam! Mam, here, let me help you. Someone give me a hand here," he shouted.

Alan roused himself and Anna swept through the swinging door from the kitchen.

"Lord have mercy! Saints preserve us! Mrs. Deters, what's wrong?"

Prudy collapsed and was carried to the front room and laid on the sofa. A doctor was called at once and a Dr. Jones arrived in a few minutes. He was hurriedly ushered in and given a brief account of what had happened. Dr. Jones examined the frail woman lying limply against a pillow, her skin pallid and moist, and announced that she had suffered a severe heart attack and would need complete bed rest with no upsetting activity.

"Yes, of course, doctor, anything you say. Can we take care of her here?" asked Alan, a worried frown on his troubled face.

"If you think your housekeeper here can handle it, yes. I don't think it would be wise to move her."

"I can watch over her; I'll take real good care of her, doctor. I'll be glad to, and she'll be no trouble at all. I'll have her well in no time at all."

Dr. Jones gave her a glance that made it clear he didn't share her optimism. "She should be put to bed at once and kept there. Now let's see if we can get her to her room without any undue stress. Careful now."

Alan merely picked his mother up and tenderly carried his light burden upstairs to her room. Anna got her into her night clothes and covered her with a quilt. She looked at the doctor with sad eyes.

"She feels so cold."

"Keep her warm and try to get her to take some liquids when she wakes."

Alan knelt beside the bed and took his mother's hand in his, kissed it, then slipped it beneath the quilt. She was so still, so pale, and breathing so shallowly. He bowed his head and said a silent prayer and made the sign of the cross. Anna did the same, stifling her sobs. She remained with Prudy as the doctor motioned for Alan to follow him. When they reached the bottom of the stairs he said in low tones, "I must come right out and say it, Father. You have the right to know that your mother is a very sick woman. She is in bad shape. Her blood pressure is far too high and this heart attack was a bad one. She will not survive another. How old is she?"

"She was sixty-two last October."

"Strange. I'd have thought she was some older."

"The years have been hard on Mother, I'm afraid. Dr. Jones, are you sure she won't recover? I find it hard to realize that she may be facing death. She should have years to live. Her life is easier now and she just has to live to enjoy it. She deserves to have a few more years of a better life than she has known." Tears filled his eyes and he looked at the doctor pleading for hope. "This is very difficult for me to handle."

The doctor returned his look quizzically. Like so many others, he assumed the priest had all the answers to life's problems, to adversities that felled ordinary people. After all, it was to him they came for succor.

"I suggest you call any family you have. Keep her quiet. She needs bed rest and absolute quiet. I'll be by tomorrow."

Alan sighed, bereft of consolation. "Thank you, doctor." He walked him to the door and returned with his head downcast, his heart heavy.

"Sorry your mother is so sick, Father," said Sheriff Boyle. He was sitting patiently in a corner.

Alan looked up quickly, having forgotten all about him. Why was this man here? What did he want? Yet, Alan knew. The sheriff wanted to know the identity of the remains found in the grave and how he had met his death, and he was pretty sure that the sheriff had a good idea that someone in the Deters family had the answers. The reaction to his news must have told him that much. Alan didn't want to believe what he knew to be true, that the remains were those of his father and his mongrel dog. And, worst of all, he dreaded acknowledging that he had been killed and put there by his mother. What had precipitated it? Where had she found the strength to do such a thing? When had it happened? Was it just before his father had supposedly gone to town and never come back? That would have to have been during the time his mother lived all alone and, from what Alan was recalling, the grave must have been the site of her prized flower garden. He shook his head in disbelief. No, it couldn't be. His mother could never kill, not unless she was driven to it. Had she been? The guilt rose up in him again and flooded his body with relentless nagging. He should have done something long ago. All of them should have. There was no excuse for ignoring the travail they knew their mother had endured.

He remembered going to see his mother one day to check on her and to chop some wood before the winter set in and she had said she couldn't find the ax and would he get another one. It all fit. She had kept this awful secret to herself all those years, and now she lay near death from the shock of overhearing what the sheriff had come to say. He straightened. He must protect her and keep her from harm. He wouldn't let this man come near her, to bother her with his pesky questions and cause a turmoil that could easily kill her. He turned resolutely and said in a voice of authority. "Sheriff, this has all been a shock to me. I don't know what to make of it, but I can assure you that I had no knowledge of what you have told me. I'm afraid you will have to leave now. I have some calls to make."

The sheriff didn't budge. "OK, but one more question first. What about Mrs. Deters? She lived on that farm a long time the way I hear it."

"All her life, in fact."

"I'd like to talk to her when she's able. How long has she lived here?"

"Since November of 1933, just after that very bad dust storm."

"I see. That means she was living there when . . ." He frowned, doing some mental calculations.

Alan's patience was at an end. "Sheriff," he said as he opened the door, "I simply cannot think about this anymore at the moment."

Sheriff Boyle stood up and put on his hat. "Sure, Father, I understand. You've had a lot to take in. I'll be in town for a few days. Have to talk to the coroner and see what he found out, but I'll be back to talk to you again. Thanks for your time."

Alan closed the door behind him and walked slowly to the stairs. Anna had just come down and was wringing her hands and crying.

"Father, what will we do? That poor soul lyin' up there so still and white." She wiped her eyes with her apron. "She's sleeping real peaceful now and I'll stay with her tonight. Doctor said he'll stop by in the morning." She looked at him in curiosity. "Did you finish your business with the policeman?"

"No. Anna, I'll be in the study. I have to call my brothers."

Chester and Fred heard the news with deep concern and agreed at once when Alan asked that they come to see their mother. He tried to soften the news of her imminent death, but wasn't successful. They knew her condition was serious. When he hung up he sat for a moment in thought, then picked up the telephone again.

"Hello," said a sweet voice.

"Hello, Millicent, this is Alan."

Fred waited for Chester's arrival and they were in Mobridge two days after Alan's call. They came alone and waited in the rectory front room while Alan drove to the station to pick up their cousin, Millicent. Their arrival had not gone unnoticed by newspapermen, who had gotten wind of a gruesome find on an abandoned farm south of Mobridge. Reporters from Mobridge, Pierre, Aberdeen, and distant Sioux Falls converged to get the scoop on a morbid story that their readers would enjoy. They had already sent accounts to their papers for the past two days, embellishing on what scant news they could learn. Someone in the coroner's department leaked the information that the remains the bulldozer uncovered were indeed those of a big man, that his head had been separated from his body, that the grave also contained a dog with a smashed skull, together with an ancient ax that was being examined for traces of blood. The town was agog over the story, especially shocking since the good Father, Alan Deters, had been born and raised on the farm where the grave had been discovered. Such a nice man, the Father was, and his little mother who lived with him so mild mannered. There was a lot of speculation about what had happened, who had done the grisly deed, and what would be done about it after so

217

many years.

Anna snapped at anyone who asked improper questions of her when she went to the market, telling them that they should mind their own business, that it was sinful to gossip, that Father Deters knew nothing about it. Why, he was just a lad when he came to the church and good old Father O'Brian had taken him in.

Sheriff Boyle was persistent, too. He was not allowed to question Mrs. Deters on the doctor's orders. But he was determined to discover the truth. He would have better luck when the family was assembled. He'd get some answers then.

It started to rain as Alan drove. His spirits matched the dreary spring weather, yet he was filled with anticipation at seeing Millicent again. He had left his brothers behind for two reasons: to keep an eye on the reporters who huddled in their cars, and to be able to get Millicent alone. He didn't want any display of emotion that might surface to be seen. He glanced in the rear view mirror and was angered to observe two cars following him. The reporters had split ranks to cover all angles. He parked the car just as the train pulled into the yard. It began to rain harder. He pulled his umbrella from the back seat and got out, ignoring the men who emerged from their cars and stood back to see who the good Father had come to meet.

Passengers got off the train and were greeted and hurried off to the depot out of the rain. Then he saw her and felt his heart begin to pound. She paused at the train door, tall and slim, wearing a light blue suit that came just below her knees, a small hat, matching gloves and shoes that set off her shapely legs. She was carrying a small suitcase. He knew her at once and hurried toward her, umbrella in hand. She was looking for him and was momentarily startled by the flash of a camera when one of the reporters dared to approach and take her picture. It distressed them both, but Alan reached for her hand and assisted her down the iron steps to the platform.

She was more beautiful and graceful than he remembered. The fact that she was now forty years old, a few years older than he, had long since ceased to matter. And in spite of how he had suppressed any passionate thoughts about her over the long years, they surfaced the minute he saw her. Her silky blond hair was set in soft waves, framing her heart-shaped face. Her blue eyes lit up at the sight of him.

"Alan! Alan dear."

She held out her arms and he went to her. He felt her arms twine around his neck and he found his closing around her. Her perfume was intoxicating; his reeling senses made him weak. He wanted to stay under the privacy of his umbrella. He didn't want to let her go, but she pulled back and kissed him lightly on the cheek. A flash bulb went off, but he wasn't aware of it.

"How good to see you again, Alan. It's been a very long time. My goodness, what a dignified presence you project. I should have called you Father, I presume."

Her smile was dazzling. Alan fervently hoped he looked dignified, as he felt totally undone. He breathed deeply and said, "Millicent, thanks for coming. We all felt you should be here. But let's get away from this place. The sooner, the better."

He picked up her suitcase and led her quickly to his car, covering her with the umbrella and getting her out of the downpour. The rain streamed down the windows, giving them a haven from the reporters, who got into their cars again and waited to follow them to the rectory.

"I apologize for all that. This whole business has gotten way out of hand. Those newspaper people just won't let up." He looked at her. "They were presumptuous taking your picture like that."

He angrily started the car, turned on the windshield wipers, and left the station, his foot heavy on the gas pedal.

She touched his arm, making him tremble. "It's all right. Don't be upset. I suppose they are curious, but I am surprised at all the interest."

She stared at Alan's well defined profile, stiff and stern in his distress. He stared straight ahead and appeared to be flushed, but she noted that he had become a good-looking, confident man which, combined with his sensitive nature as she remembered it, would make for a good combination in a priest. She found it hard to consider him in that way. They rode in silent contemplation until they arrived at the rectory, where she dashed through the downpour into the house with Alan. She was greeted warmly by Chester and Fred. The years fell away as they welcomed her. They were soon showing family snapshots and reminiscing about old times, and the cousins were amazed at how grown Millicent's children were, in their teens.

Anna had turned on the lights in the gloom of the late rainy afternoon. The sound of the storm drummed steadily against the windows. She served the visitors coffee and her good gingersnaps as they talked. They forgot the cars outside with their huddled occupants, waiting with their pads and pencils.

The conversation was lively, but subdued, given the seriousness of the occasion. Anna's refreshments had done the trick. Alan put his cup down, smiled lovingly at all of them and said, "Thank you for coming on such short notice. I think you know that I would not have been so urgent in my request unless it was absolutely necessary. "

"Holy cow, we're glad to be here and want to help," said Chester, shifting his large frame.

"Yeah, and to see Milly again is swell," agreed Fred.

"I've always felt very close to Aunt Prudence," replied Millicent. "She wrote to me many times, giving me the news about everyone. It is truly delightful to see you, and all grown into such splendid specimens of manhood," she teased.

Fred blushed and Chester muttered, "Holy cow." Alan said nothing.

"Now tell us, Alan, how is Aunt Prudence, and what caused this heart attack? She's not that old surely?" Millicent's lovely face showed a genuine concern.

"Yeah, tell us all about it. Shouldn't we go up to see her?" asked Fred. He had seen his mother often, and had never been denied access to her.

"She's been asleep, but should be awake by now." Alan chose his words carefully. "Two days ago Mother was stricken with a severe heart attack. I'm sure it was brought on by something she overheard when the sheriff was here. He had a lot of questions about a grave and some remains that were found on the old home place. They are making preparations to build some tourist cabins there, as you all know, and they came upon this — awful find — quite by accident. The shock of what she heard was too much for her. I didn't want to say much over the telephone, feeling we should talk about it more fully when you got here."

Chester asked, "Do you really think it's Dad?"

"I'm afraid there's no doubt about it. The coroner's report positively identifies him as Dad, all right, and the other factors are conclusive. That has to be his dog, and the ax is definitely his. Actually, it was our grandfather's and we are all familiar with it. I can tell you it was not easy to look at it. I was spared having to look at the other . . ."

"Oh Alan, how dreadful for you," murmured Millicent, her blue eyes filled with compassion.

"I don't get it," said Fred. "Who would want to kill him and then bury him right there?"

No one spoke, but the others, except for Millicent who had remained unaware of Lester's violence, knew who would want to kill him. However, it was totally impossible for them to believe such a thing, that it could happen, and surely not their mother. Alan broke the silence, trying to make his voice encouraging, to rise above the depressing sound of the falling rain. Thunder and lightning were adding to the unhappiness that had pervaded the room. He smiled a smile he didn't feel.

"Surprisingly, Mother is some better today. She is alert and has been asking for you. I explained to her this morning that all of you were coming and that she could see you after her nap. It really perked her up. I don't think she has any inkling of how sick she is and we haven't told her. She mustn't have any undue excitement. Keep your remarks low key. I don't want to alarm you, but the doctor said another attack would be fatal."

Solemnly they rose, bracing themselves for what they knew would be an ordeal. Alan said, "After we see Mother, we have to decide on what to say to those reporters. Maybe they will go away if we give them a statement of some kind. None of us has told them anything and you can see how they behaved. It's totally inexcusable."

Alan showed uncharacteristic resentment, but held it in check.

"Now, if you're ready, let's go up."

He led the way upstairs. Each was deep in thought, not knowing exactly how to deal with what they would find. What would they say to her? Alan opened the door and spoke pleasantly, "Well, Mother, you do look better."

They heard a faint answer, but couldn't make it out.

"Yes, that's right, they're all here. I'm as good as my word. Come in and say hello," he said to those behind him.

Millicent was next in the room, followed by Chester and Fred. They tried to conceal the shock and dismay that consumed them upon seeing the fragile figure on the bed propped against the pillows. It was clear that she was expecting them. Her dark eyes were bright in anticipaiton. Anna had carefully combed the gray hair, trying to fluff it around her pale face. The eagerness with which she greeted her family softened the wrinkles around her mouth and eyes. Dark circles around her eyes were stark in her white face. A soft, pleased "oh my" greeted their entrance . .

Millicent went to her and kissed her forehead.

"Aunt Prudence, it's been too long since I've seen you."

"Millicent, how much you look like your mama. You carry on the beauty in the family." Her voice was low, almost a whisper. "I had a sick spell but I'm fine today." She had moved nothing but her hand. "Tell me about the children."

Millicent stepped back to hide sudden tears and Chester approached the bed, bending down to touch her gently.

"Mama, we don't like to see you sick."

"Where's pretty Polly and the children?"

"They couldn't come. It's just me this time." He was dismayed to find his vision blurred and hastily stood up.

Fred hesitantly approached the bed.

"Mama? Are you going to be all right?"

"Poor Fred. Yes, I'll be all right. I miss Helga and the kids."

"They'll come some other time."

"Lettie, too?"

"Yeah, sure, Mama."

Prudy couldn't get enough of them and gazed from one to another over and over as tears rolled down her weathered cheeks, causing consternation in her visitors. She blinked them away and, with an effort, took a shaky breath and whispered, "God has sent you to me for my redemption. I'm glad. I have something to tell you."

They moved closer to the bed the better to hear her words, and Alan said, "Please, Mother, don't excite yourself. We are here to be with you; we just want to sit with you for awhile."

"I'm not excited," she said slowly. "You must listen." She breathed heavily for a few seconds. "I have to say it while I can."

Her fingers were clasping and unclasping and she was becoming agitated. They filled with alarm. Millicent went to her and sat on the bed, taking the gnarled hands in her soft ones, stroking them gently and making soothing noises.

"Very well, Aunt Prudence. We will listen to what you have to say. Take your time if you feel up to talking a little bit."

Prudy smiled weakly, taking comfort and courage from her beautiful niece, seeing in her her sister, Patience. It was almost like having her back. It gave her strength to go on. She clung to Millicent's hands and looked from one to the other as she began to speak slowly and as clearly as she could. It was vital that they know the truth.

"I heard that man when he came to see you, Alan, and I knew I'd been found out and that you were being blamed for what happened." She paused and breathed shallowly with an ominous rattle in her throat. "I did it. I killed your father. Then I killed the dog and buried both of them in the flower garden, along with the ax. Afterward I planted my flowers. Made a nice looking garden." She stared vacantly into space, reliving the day. She was tired and the quilt was so very heavy on her.

221

"Mother, you don't have to do this," protested Alan, fingering the cross around his neck.

"Yes — I do," she said slowly. "You've got a right to know. I just didn't figure anyone would find out. It was so long ago."

She looked past them, seeing it all, collecting her thoughts, having to say it right. They didn't interrupt her and the sound of the rain beating against the windows reverberated in their ears. A rumble of thunder punctuated the dread that filled the room.

"I had to do it, because he was after me. He'd never been so bad. He could be real mean and I tried not to rile him, but he'd get awful mad at me anyway." She coughed with difficulty. "Then he'd take it out on me."

"We know, Mama," and Chester hung his head.

Millicent's eyes were dark blue and full of surprised anger. She turned to each of them in turn with those lovely eyes suddenly hostile and they could not look at her. She held onto Prudy's hands as she struggled to go on.

"I was used to him, but he was lots bigger and I'd be real careful — but this time he took something of mine and it made him go crazy. He had no right . . ." She stirred the best she could and Millicent patted her hands, shushing her. "I found him in the cellar and he took out after me, hollarin' terrible things, sayin' he was gonna kill me. He was ravin' mad and I ran for my life. He almost caught me once when I fell, but I made it to the porch, picked up the ax and . . ."

Their eyes were riveted on her, their ears hearing what they had hoped not to hear, seeing it happen, not wanting it to be true, and consumed with a guilt that would not be denied. What had they done to their mother by doing nothing? She was tired from talking and her chest felt heavy and constricted. Why didn't someone take the heavy quilt off her?

"Then old Dog took after me so I picked up the ax again and hit him. Don't know where I got the strength. Garden was dug, so I just dug down some more and put them in. Guess it wasn't deep enough." She wheezed and struggled for breath.

"But, Mama," protested Chester, "why didn't you just tell us what happened? You didn't need to go through all that."

She moved her hand feebly and looked at him and managed a faint smile.

"It was a shameful thing I did, killing your father. He always said I shamed him."

"Aunt Prudence, you couldn't shame anyone," said Millicent vehemently.

Prudy patted her soft white hands.

"Mama, it was self-defense, for Pete's sake," said Fred, his voice rising.

"It's a sin to kill, isn't it?" She turned her head and looked at Alan, her dark eyes burning into him. He lowered his eyes lest she see his turmoil. "I sinned against God. Now He's punishing me, but He's given me a chance to save myself by confessing to my sons." She was less agitated and more relieved and lay back, more at ease.

Their voices rose in argument to her last statement and she sighed and closed her eyes. She was so weary and lay pressed against the pillows from an invisible force that assailed her. Yet she was content. She had cleansed her soul. Their voices quieted and they held their breaths. She lay so still. Slowly she opened her eyes, set dark and deep in their sockets, and said, "I have to tell it all."

Thunder and lightning filled the room as she briefly recited the events of the following day, of her hard work, including the baking and washing.

"But, why on earth did you go to all that bother?" asked Millicent.

"No one was s'posed to know he wasn't there anymore. Went to town and didn't come back. He did it a lot; everybody knew that. I kept to my work. His clothes stunk and couldn't stand to smell 'em no more."

She was slumped into the pillows as she looked longingly at them through half-closed lids and a haze that was making seeing them very difficult. Her breathing was labored and the tightness in her chest increased. They look so sad. I want to reach out and touch them. Why won't they come closer so I can touch them? I want to hold them again and I need them to hold me. She had to finish.

"It was because of poor little Mary," she whispered. Her cold hands were limp in Millicent's.

They weren't sure they heard her correctly and didn't understand.

"Aunt Prudence, you mustn't talk anymore."

"My little girl," she murmured and tears flowed freely.

"Mother, you must rest. We'll come back later."

"It was Eric . . ."

"What, Mama?" asked Chester.

Her eyes were closed and she looked very peaceful with a contented smile on her face. They looked at each other, thoroughly confounded. Then they turned their attention back to her still figure, barely making an outline beneath the quilt. She took one last wavering breath, turned her head to look at them, her dark eyes very wide, but seeing beyond them, smiled a beneficent smile, let out her thin breath, and closed her eyes. She lay very still.

"Oh no," wept Millicent.

"Mama," cried Chester and Fred together.

Alan made the sign of the cross and knelt beside the bed.

★

Prudy was released from her desperate, arduous life. Her soul was in the hands of God, whether it was Alan's God whom she didn't understand, or the entity that had concealed itself from her behind a veil that she could not penetrate, thereby denying her a reason to believe with any amount of conviction, only Prudy knew at last. She had done the best she could during her time on earth and left willingly to whatever lay in store for her tormented soul.

The rain let up; thunder rumbled faintly in the distance, and the sky slowly cleared. Prudy's sons and Millicent clung together and cried for her and for what could have been. Then they went downstairs, informed Anna, who wailed her grief, and called Dr. Jones, who arrived and took care of matters.

They did not mention what they had all heard, though faintly. "Eric" meant nothing to them and they dismissed it as being the product of a feverish brain, the murmurings of a woman facing death. It was considered of no consequence and soon forgotten. Prudy's deeds were purged and her children were spared the knowledge that their mother had committed another indiscretion, one they would have had considerable difficulty in accepting.

Then in the front room the grieving survivors came to a decision. The decision was hard come by, but it was necessary to pacify the waiting reporters and the sheriff. They debated all sides of the problem.

They could tell the truth and risk a blemish on the reputations of all of them, to say nothing of their dead mother, who would be labeled a murderer. The truth would accomplish little and could, in fact, prove to be a mistake. The press would have a field day. There would be considerable notoriety at the site of the dastardly deed, perhaps even affecting the sale of the property, maybe even holding up its development indefinitely, thereby causing overwhelming legal problems, to say nothing of the expense involved.

They could declare their innocence of how the body of their father came to be in the grave, and it would be an entirely truthful statement, because they were completely in the dark about what had happened, at least until a few hours before.

Furthermore, it was not up to them to prove or disprove anything. So far, no charges against anyone had been made. Any accusations would be the responsibility of the accusors. Yet, hadn't they all been too impassive and could not that passivity have contributed to the present dilemma?

Alan was especially torn. He was a priest and he had been privy to a confession. Confession was privileged and, by oath, he could not disclose what he had heard. Yet, his family, his own parents were involved, and there had been a murder. Could he in good conscience cover up that fact? His mother had committed a transgression. Should he treat that differently from anyone else just because she was his mother? While the others discussed all sides of what to do, he fingered the cross and bowed his head and prayed more earnestly than he had ever prayed in his life. The words had specific meaning for him; they came from the depths of his soul, and were not mere rote. "Help me, Father; show me the way."

Millicent felt the decision should remain with her cousins, but she expressed her profound regret at not having been able to do something to alleviate her aunt's long suffering, an endurance that had continued, unknown to most, for too long. Unsaid was her deep disappointment in all of them.

In the end, it was decided. They stood up.

"Well then, if we are all agreed, let's get to it," said Alan, his voice choked with emotion.

He opened the door and they stepped outside on the stoop. A rainbow had appeared and remained until the sun went down a few minutes later, bringing a sudden dusk over all. Reporters crowded around, their flashbulbs popping as they fired questions at the sad group clustered before them. Alan raised his hand and they fell silent.

"I have an announcement to make."

EPILOGUE

The writer is compelled to tie up loose ends for readers who may be dissatisfied with the end to the story.

The announcement was made by Millicent, who stepped forward with a brief, concise statement of the events leading up to the discovery of Lester's burial place, and of the complete lack of knowledge on the part of his sons about what had happened. The reporters were satisfied and filed their sensational stories which were read with interest by all who got hold of a newspaper. However, people being what they are, the furor raised soon faded and interest waned. The Deters name became an honorable one. The sheriff was satisfied with the disposition of the matter and the case was closed, there being no one to prosecute.

Prudy was buried in a corner of the Catholic Cemetery in Mobridge and Lester's remains were interred beside her, leaving his sons with a feeling of poetic justice.

Lettie mourned her friend and missed her until the day she died at the age of eighty-seven. She lived out her life with Fred and Helga near the bluffs and rolling hills of Pierre. Fred remained a happy man and his family thrived and prospered. The sprawling ranch soon included Butler storage bins for his surplus grains, oats, barley, and ground feed for his animals. After the war the REA expanded and most farms in the state of South Dakota had electricity and the benefits it provided. Fred was a leader in every new technology, but he gave ample credit to Helga whom he was content to follow as she led him into the good life.

Bridget moved to Sioux Falls to teach and met a serviceman stationed at the air base during World War II. In her mid-thirties she fell in love, having found the man of her dreams. The experience destroyed her when she found he was shipped overseas and killed in action. She eventually got her Masters Degree at the University of South Dakota and returned to Aberdeen to teach at Northern State College, where she lived out her life as a spinster.

Chester went back to California and never returned to South Dakota. He and Peter Dannenbring's lumber business became one of the largest on the west coast, making them millionaires. They were close friends all their lives. In years to come Chester's children and Fred's would meet and the cousins would find that they came from diverse cultures, yet they would also realize a common bond in their shared heritage.

Millicent returned to her family in New Ulm, Minnesota. She and Howard lived in the big brick house caring for her aging father until his death, following which they built a new, rambling house on the outskirts of town to which her children brought their children to see their handsome grandparents and to learn about their relatives on the western plains.

Alan got his new church and his faith back, a faith which had been sorely tested by what he had learned about his parents, a faith that had wavered when Millicent re-entered his life for a brief time, stirring latent feelings. He lived to a ripe old age and was loved and revered by his people. He served his God and his parish well.

Modern highways criss-crossed the state in ribbons of concrete, giving rise to an active tourist business. Mobridge grew and survived drought, blizzards, fire, insects, and a myriad of severe weather conditions. It found its niche as an excellent fishing ground, with anglers coming in droves every season to catch a variety of fish, from walleyes to bass to catfish as long as five feet and weighing over fifty pounds.

And overlooking the Missouri River west of the city on the uppermost bluff is a monument to Sitting Bull with a bust of his likeness carved by the famed sculptor and visionary, Korczak Ziolkowski. Supposedly, Sitting Bull's bones rest beneath the monument. It is a quiet, peaceful spot rising high above the foibles of man, a place suitable for contemplation about the indomitable, indestructible spirit of the people of Dakota.

To purchase copies of
Woman of the Prairie
or
The Bannisters
please contact the author:

Barbara Oaks
4500 East 33rd Street
Apartment 58
Sioux Falls, SD 57103